Sudden

As a child Carol Wyer was always moving, and relied on humour to fit in at new schools. A funny short story won her popularity, planting the seed of becoming a writer. Her career spans dry cleaning, running a language teaching company, and boxercise coaching. Now writing full-time, Carol has several books published and journalism in many magazines.

Carol won The People's Book Prize Award for non-fiction (2015), and can sometimes be found performing her stand-up comedy routine *Laugh While You Still Have Teeth*.

Also by Carol Wyer

What Happens in France

Suddenly Single

CAROL WYER

CANELO

First published in the the United Kingdom in 2019 by Canelo

This edition published in the United Kingdom in 2021 by Canelo

Canelo Digital Publishing Limited
31 Helen Road
Oxford OX2 0DF
United Kingdom

Copyright © Carol Wyer, 2019

The moral right of Carol Wyer to be identified as the creator of this work has been asserted in accordance with the Copyright, Designs and Patents Act, 1988.

All rights reserved. No part of this publication may be reproduced or transmitted in any form or by any means, electronic or mechanical, including photocopy, recording, or any information storage and retrieval system, without permission in writing from the publisher.

A CIP catalogue record for this book is available from the British Library.

Print ISBN 978 1 78863 533 2
Ebook ISBN 978 1 78863 277 5

This book is a work of fiction. Names, characters, businesses, organizations, places and events are either the product of the author's imagination or are used fictitiously. Any resemblance to actual persons, living or dead, events or locales is entirely coincidental.

Look for more great books at www.canelo.co

Printed and bound in Great Britain by Clays Ltd, Elcograf S.p.A.

Chapter One

Snow fell gently; fat wet flakes that at first looked as if they might melt, but soon formed into small white pyramids against the bare branches of the hawthorn hedges that lined the twisting lane. Under other circumstances it would have been a charming scenario and Chloe Piper would have enjoyed observing each deposit of snow grow larger with the hope that soon everywhere would be covered with nature's pure white tablecloth.

Faith scowled as white flurries hurtled towards the windscreen. She turned on the windscreen wipers to clear her vision. 'Perfect, just perfect. They didn't forecast snow today.'

'I quite like it,' replied Chloe, 'especially at this time of the year. It's magical. However, if it doesn't stop soon, we'll have trouble reaching the house. There's a whopper of a slope before you reach the reservoir. Could be slippery.'

'It's certainly rural here,' said Faith, guiding the Audi expertly around sharp bends; the engine growling deeply as if to warn other road users to steer clear. They passed a run-down farmhouse, its windows dark and uninviting, and then a field where woolly sheep huddled together to stay warm, each black face looking expectantly at the

I

sound of the car approaching. In a paddock further on, two chestnut horses clad in warm horse blankets stared as the car rounded the bend, steam emitting from their soft velvet noses.

'Not far to go now,' said Chloe, spotting the sign for the reservoir.

'You are quite convinced about this, aren't you?' Faith had already asked the same question several times during this trip. Chloe was certain. She had never been more certain in her life.

'I mean not many newly single thirty-five-year-olds choose to live on windswept hillsides in the middle of nowhere rather than in a town or city,' commented Faith. 'I really don't know how anyone could survive without coffee shops and bars. Well, anyone other than you,' she added with a warm smile.

Not many people understood her decision. She dragged herself away from thoughts of what had led to it and watched the flakes descending, marvelling at how each one was individual, made up of unique ice crystals. *Like people*, she reflected. People were all different too. They were individuals with different needs, hopes and desires. They were composed of a multitude of different facets, opinions and expectations, and as such, should be allowed to behave uniquely.

'I needed to leave all that village life behind. I couldn't stay hidden there, not after what happened. You know what it's like in that place. You lived next door to me for three years. Everyone pokes their noses into everyone else's business. And if they don't know it, they make it up. It was bearable when I could lay low at home but now... I need to be left alone – completely.'

'Yes, but where will you get the inspiration for your next book? It can be pretty difficult when your new nearest neighbours appear to have four legs and black and white markings. You can't really follow *Spank Me Harder, Vicar* with *Bluebell and Betsy Frolic in the Meadow*.'

Chloe giggled before saying, 'I suppose it was only a matter of time before some of the village folk found out I was actually C J Knight, author of that rather naughty, revealing book. William warned me somebody would work out the book had been written by a villager. He wasn't too happy at the prospect because he didn't want to be associated with the book in any way.'

Her brow creased at the memory of William.

'They only speculated it was you. They had no way of knowing for certain and I assume your identity is still fairly secure.'

'I'd prefer to remain anonymous.'

'I know, hun. Considering William spent three years complaining you were wasting your time writing it, you'd have thought he'd have been blown away by the book's success.'

'Declared it a flash in the pan.'

Faith tutted. 'He has no idea.'

Chloe kept her own counsel. Part of her was beginning to think William had been right. She smiled at her friend.

Chloe and Faith had been thrown together by fate – a cruel fate. Faith's husband, Adrian, a supposedly fit thirty-seven-year-old, suffered sudden cardiac arrest in the back garden and Faith's screams had alerted Chloe, who'd been working in her own garden. She clambered over the fence that separated the two houses and whilst Faith had phoned for an ambulance, Chloe had tried in vain to resuscitate

3

the man. They'd become unlikely friends – Chloe the introvert and Faith the go-getter.

'William wasn't fair to you. I was glad when you outed him for the rat he was. You could do so much better than him.'

'It's unlikely I'll find anyone willing to live with somebody like me.'

'You haven't got a horrible, infectious disease, Chloe. Your condition's debilitating but you were getting on top of it.'

Chloe chewed at her bottom lip. She didn't like discussing the anxiety she suffered in social situations. She'd been trying a new therapy to help her face social situations but William's revelation he was having an affair and his subsequent departure had been a major setback and she'd withdrawn from the programme.

'Anyway, he's completely wrong about your novel. Wait until those royalties come through in March, you'll be able to pay off a huge chunk of the mortgage on this new place and settle all your credit card bills. That'll show him.'

'I have you to thank really for all this, for securing that contract with Upfront Publishing. Without you, I'd have probably been one of many self-published writers scrabbling to make a name for myself, and William would have been crowing about being right. It doesn't matter though, does it? I don't need to prove anything to him. He's already turned his back on me and on what I achieve. He has his new girlfriend – Lilly – now and as far as he's concerned, I don't exist anymore.'

'He's a bastard – a stupid bastard.'

'At least I can follow my dream without criticism and arguments about why I haven't done the washing, or tantrums because I've forgotten to cook dinner because I was carried away with an idea. It'll be nice not to have that tension any more. It'll be a new chapter in my personal book of life.'

She kept her tone light but guessed Faith would know she was bluffing. Chloe's fragile self-confidence had shattered following the discovery of her husband's infidelity.

'As long as this isn't another step in your quest to distance yourself from everyone, then it's okay by me.'

'I'm trying, Faith. I managed to come here alone, meet the vendor, and two of the men who work on the development, and look around the house without bolting.'

Faith patted her knee gently. 'I know and I'm proud of you for doing it, and for tackling all of this head on. It's been a major challenge, but surely it shows you what you're capable of. You don't need William.'

'I know.' Her voice lost its strength. She'd managed to buy a house and visit a lawyer and face up to strangers, but Faith could have no idea of how physically sick she'd been before each of those seemingly normal activities. Or how she'd been awake for nights afterwards, anxious about the impression she'd made. Social anxiety disorder might not be a killer disease but it certainly ruined lives.

The women fell silent as the car reached the top of the steep climb and the reservoir came into view. Faith drew a sharp intake of breath as she gazed over dark still water reflecting the heavy clouds above. It was an impressive sight.

Chloe suddenly realised why she'd fallen for the place. It reminded her of her childhood home on the Isle of Skye. It took her back to a time when she'd been happy before her family was taken from her in a cruel accident and before she developed the debilitating disorder that prevented her from mixing with others. This place was a replacement for that – a faraway haven that transported her back in time.

'It always surprises me too. The water is never the same colour. Some days it's a perfect azure, other days it can be light grey and moody and sometimes, like today, it is dark and brooding just like the sea. It'll be like living next to the seaside without the fish and chips, tacky souvenir shops and sand.'

'It's spectacular. There are woods all around it too.'

Chloe's eyes sparkled. 'I know. It's wonderful. Ronnie and I will be able to go for walks here.' Behind her, a grave-faced dog with large brown eyes, gave her a reproachful look. She admonished it in gentle tones. 'There's no need to look so excited.'

'Ronnie really looks like the saddest dog in the world,' said Faith, giving a little laugh.

'He's pining for the Shih Tzu next door, the current love of his life. She was on heat when we left.' Chloe turned back towards Ronnie. 'And I dragged him away from a pile of steaming cow pats he discovered on our morning walk. Don't worry, there'll be new loves, exciting times, lots of fantastic walks and huge, dopey rabbits for you, Ronnie. Yes, rabbits,' she repeated, causing a stirring in Ronnie's stumpy tail as it thumped against the back seat. His stomach gurgled ominously.

'He isn't going to…?' Faith's manicured eyebrows knitted together in horror.

'Probably. It's the cow pats. They make him flatulent.'

'Don't you dare, Ronnie,' ordered Faith. 'This is an Audi Q7. It cost a fortune. It has leather seats and is not suitable for farting dogs. Pity he couldn't fit in the back with all the boxes.'

Ronnie sunk his head back onto his paws and stared at the floor.

'Don't listen to her. You know she loves you, you smelly old mutt.'

The snow was beginning to ease. They took a left turn, passed a riding school and three identical terraced cottages, joined by twinkling Christmas lights that hung across all three, before reaching a sign marked Sunny Meadow.

They turned into the drive flanked by tall hawthorn hedges that concealed any views and followed it up a steep tarmac drive until the development came into sight. There the drive branched off towards the completed buildings: the first path in the direction of a one-storey barn with an arched porch and large arched windows; the second towards a renovated barn resplendent in size with an impressive timbered conservatory that dominated one side of the building. A massive wooden duck gazed out of the glass-fronted door.

'Looks like I have neighbours,' said Chloe. 'There was no one living in either property when I last visited.'

'When was that?'

'I came up a month ago but I haven't seen the place since then. Thomas Collins, the site developer, took delivery of the furniture I ordered online. He's been so helpful. I don't know how I would have managed without him. He emails me almost every day to let me know how it's getting on.'

'Wow! Who's that?' she added as a slim young man wearing a dark jumper and a beanie hat, balancing a plank of wood on his shoulder, waved in their direction.

'Jack,' replied Chloe, lifting her hand slightly in acknowledgement. 'He's the carpenter.'

'Never seen a carpenter that good-looking.'

'You can forget those thoughts,' said Chloe. She knew her friend's penchant for athletic looking men. 'He's married and has a new baby. His iPhone is stuffed with photos of his wife and kid. He showed them to me when I was here last time.'

Her voice took on the same wistful tone it always did when talking about babies. William had decided his career was more important than children and refused to have them. 'There isn't anything he can't craft from wood. He constructed all the beams for the barns, window frames and doors. He designed and built all my wardrobes. He says wood is a living thing and we should talk to it and look after it for it to look its best.'

'Oh, he's some sort of wood-whisperer, then,' said Faith, making Chloe chuckle.

Jack disappeared into one of the outbuildings. Faith craned her neck to check out the other two builders working on a half-timbered roof of another outbuilding and then whistled under her breath.

'Maybe you *will* have plenty of inspiration for a new bonkbuster novel here,' she mumbled as a lithe figure in fitted jeans and a leather jacket, sporting stubble and a golden suntan turned towards the Audi and gave a white-toothed smile at the two women before leaping into a grey Land Rover and heading off down the hill.

'Okay, who's the Adonis?'

'No idea who he is. He's probably here to deliver some stuff for the builders. There's loads of comings and goings. I don't think it's going to be too quiet for a while, at least until all the development is completed. Here we are. There's Thomas waiting at the door.'

A man in his sixties, ruddy-faced from years of working outside, stood by the front door. His Barbour jacket was open to reveal his frayed sweater and dark, well-worn corduroy trousers. He raised his hand in greeting. Chloe leapt from her seat and darted to the back door where she leant across the back seat to collect Ronnie now struggling to see where he was. She snapped his lead onto the collar and he jumped out, shook himself causing his identity tag to rattle, and relieved himself against the Audi's back tyre.

'Wretched dog,' said Faith with little conviction, patting him on the head. She took three steps forward and stood open-mouthed at the stupendous two-hundred-and-seventy-degree view over fields, woods and into the distance. Ahead of them, the reservoir shimmered like a silver lake.

At last Faith spoke. 'Oh, my goodness! What an incredible house. It's so pretty!'

The building constructed of rich, russet bricks and gleaming, reclaimed slate grey tiles was two-storeys high with skylights set in the roof, allowing space downstairs for the several huge arched windows, fitted where the old barn entrance archways had once stood. They afforded formidable views of the grounds surrounding the house – most of which was yet to be laid to lawn and was currently little more than flattened earth. Below the roof, detailed brickwork added to the character of the house, a reminder of what it had once been: a tractor and grain store.

Thomas strode towards the women, his rough, large hand extended in greeting.

'Congratulations!' he boomed, handing Chloe the keys to her new home. 'You are now the proud owner of Sunny Meadow Barn.'

Faith wrapped her Max Mara black suede coat tightly around her and sighed. 'It's beautiful. I can see why Chloe fell in love with it and wanted to come here.'

Ronnie strained at his lead, eager to check out the new smells, his stubby tail wagging in excitement.

'Nice dog. What breed is it?'

'Pure mongrel,' replied Chloe shyly. Although she'd met Thomas on a few occasions before, she still felt awkward. That was one of the problems of her disorder, together with the fact she had no idea how her body might react. On this occasion it seemed to be holding up. 'It's more a case of what breed isn't in him.' Ronnie's tongue flopped out of his mouth giving the impression he was grinning in agreement. His tail continued to thrash from side to side threatening to send him into a chaotic spin.

'The barn looks superb. You've even managed to slab around the place so I won't be trailing in mud. I wasn't expecting that. You've worked so hard on it.'

'It wasn't me. It was my men. I told them if they didn't finish the place for you on time, I wasn't letting them have any Christmas holiday this year and I was cancelling the boys' night out at the pub. That got them working. They finished all the little fiddly bits on Friday and the cleaner came in and scoured it yesterday to prepare it for your big day. We're working seven days a week up until the Christmas holidays to try and stay on target. The site will shut down then until the new year, so we're finishing what we can now. That's why we're all here today. Normally on a Sunday, I've got my feet up, watching telly. So, are you ready and eager to get into your new home? Hope we put the furniture in the right place for you. We weren't too sure what to do with it but if you need it moving elsewhere, the lads will sort it.' His eyes twinkled with pride as he led the women to the back door and waited for their reaction after he opened the door that led into the kitchen. He wasn't disappointed.

Faith was the first to comment. 'Chloe, it's perfect. So you.'

The kitchen was a blend of contemporary trends of industrial and neutral tones, while holding on to a warm essence. Open shelving created a relaxed atmosphere and the designer Italian stools that stood by a large rustic island would be ideal for casual dining. Mood lighting over the island and task lighting over the kitchen units created a great balance while the natural light that flooded through the huge windows softly illuminated the entire space.

Faith pointed to it. 'I can picture myself sitting there, glass of wine in hand and snacking on some warm, crusty bread. Ah, bliss!'

'You'll definitely come and visit me here in the wilds of Staffordshire, then.'

'You bet. It has a certain appeal,' she added, her eye drawn to the figure tapping on the window attempting to attract Thomas's attention. It was Jack. Thomas stuck up a thumb in acknowledgement and the carpenter departed.

'They're all keen to know if you're happy with it,' said Thomas.

'Very,' replied Chloe, savouring being in her own home.

The island's pale marble top had a hint of pink that was reflected in pink roses that stood in a light pink flower bag. She hastened towards them breathing in their delicate perfume.

'The flowers are beautiful. You shouldn't have bought them.' Her cheeks had turned the same shade of pink as the petals. Thomas merely smiled a response, his attention on Ronnie, who scuttled about the kitchen checking every corner and sniffing the length of every skirting board.

'Is this the lounge?' asked Faith, wandering towards the wooden door at the far end of the kitchen. She opened it and emitted a squeal of delight. 'A whopper of a log burner, and it's alight! It's gorgeous. How toasty! Ooh, lovely huge settees. You have good taste, Chloe. These are much nicer than those leather things you had at the old place. Okay, forget the island and the crusty bread. I'm thinking more of snuggling up in front of this with a glass of mulled wine.'

The smile on Thomas's face broadened. He turned towards Chloe. 'Couldn't have you coming into a chilly house, could we? I got my lad, Alex, to fetch up some wood for you. We stacked it around the back of the house and you should have enough to last you over Christmas.'

'I really don't know what to say. You've been amazing. I'm sure you've done more than you ought to have for me. You've been here to take delivery of my furniture, bought me light shades, sorted out the television aerial man, advised me on materials and design and held my hand during the whole process.'

'We all need a little hand-holding from time to time. The lads and I work on developments all the time. It's our business and it's easier for us to find those little necessary bits and pieces, like toilet roll holders and outside lamps or doorstops, than for you to mess about. We only help out the clients we like though,' he added with a wink. 'Now, can I ask you a favour?' He put his large hand into his coat pocket and extracted a copy of a book.

'My missus would love you to sign this.'

Chloe looked at the cover and gasped. 'How did you find out? I thought I was anonymous here. No one is supposed to know I wrote it. I wanted to keep it quiet.'

Thomas tapped the side of his nose. 'I like to find out as much as possible about the folk who buy my houses and I have a particular fondness for this development. This is going to be my last project ever before I retire and I want it to be special with only the "right" people living here. I've turned down many folks who have put in offers on these properties. I'm only accepting those from people I feel ought to be here. Call me old. Call me stupid, or quirky, but that's what I've decided to do. It's taken four years of planning and arguing with authorities to get it this far. I designed all the houses myself so I want them to be cared for and loved as much as I care about them. Don't worry. I won't spill the beans about you. An old pal in Appletree told me about you. He heard a rumour. You will sign the book, won't you? Patricia loved it. She can't wait for your next one.'

Faith, who had returned from the lounge, pricked up her ears. 'You'd better get that laptop out pretty quickly. You have fans. And they can't get enough of your naughty vicar stories. What a great place to write. It's so peaceful and calm. I expect many more bonkbuster novels from you, Chloe Piper. I'm depending on you to keep me in designer clothes and expensive holidays.'

'This is my agent, PR guru, right-hand woman and best friend, Faith Hopkins,' said Chloe, spotting Thomas's eyebrows lifting in interest. He held out a hand. Faith obliged and shook it.

'You in publishing?'

'I am and Chloe is my star client.'

Chloe took the copy of *Spank Me Harder, Vicar* together with the pen Thomas offered, and wrote a brief message. He read it, smiled, and thanked her.

'Patricia will be stoked and the ladies at her book club are going to be very jealous she has a signed copy. Thank you. By the way, the flowers aren't from me. They're from an anonymous admirer,' he said, tapping the side of his nose with a broad forefinger again. He opened the fridge and pulled out a bottle of champagne which he handed over. 'But this is. From the first time I met you I knew you were the right person to buy Sunny Meadow Barn. I hope you'll be very happy here, Chloe. Now I'm going to leave you and your lovely friend to settle in and if there's anything you need, just come over to the big barn. The lads will be there until four o'clock.'

Chloe thanked the man again and watched as he plodded carefully around the house and onto the gravel drive towards the as yet unfinished outbuildings.

Ronnie's paws pattered on the tiled floors and he plonked down by the door with a sigh and gazed out across the land, watching for movement in the far hedge.

'What a sweet man! Is all the land yours too?' asked Faith, drawn again to the large window.

Chloe nodded. 'Five acres of it surrounded by fields of cows and only four other houses in proximity. There'll only be a handful of human neighbours up here, who, according to Thomas, are also keen to get away from the rat race and other folk. I can do whatever I like, run around the garden naked, hang upside down from the ash tree, turn up the stereo so loudly it makes the walls of the house vibrate. It'll be fine.'

'Come on, show me around the rest of the house and then we'll find some glasses and open up that bottle. You did bring glasses with you, didn't you?'

'I didn't leave everything behind. Besides the glasses were Nanny Olive's, so they really belong to me. I wanted to start afresh. I didn't want to clutter up my new life with too much memorabilia from my past life with William. It's not so much a new chapter for me as a new book.' Nanny Olive had been instrumental in her life. After Chloe's parents and sister had been killed in a light aircraft incident, she'd moved from the quiet island in the Outer Hebrides to live with her grandmother in Birmingham. It hadn't been easy. The trauma of losing her family had changed Chloe – forever.

Ronnie chose that moment to release a gassy emission. He wrinkled his eyebrows in apology. Faith groaned.

'Maybe I should take Ronnie out for a quick walk first.'

Faith fanned her hands across her face. 'Good idea. I'll track down the glasses and you can take that pongy pooch out to see if there's anything out there worth writing about.'

Ronnie gleefully strained in the direction of the muddy field outside the back door, tail wagging. Snowflakes stuck together in clumps like small patches of white flowers against the dark earth and Chloe held fast, dragging the dog down her gravel drive to avoid getting filthy. The wind was picking up. At the gate she stopped to admire the house opposite. Her neighbours had switched on their Christmas lights, reminding her she ought to buy a Christmas tree soon and make some preparations, even if they were only for her and Ronnie. They turned onto the main driveway.

Ronnie snuffled excitedly in the grassy verges, his nose assaulted by an array of interesting scents. She breathed in the fresh air and gazed off into the distance. At that exact same moment, Ronnie's lead slipped from her hand and suddenly he sped off across churned earth littered with bricks and stones in the direction of one of the tumble-down outbuildings on the far side of the site. Aware of the dangers of building sites, Chloe raced after him, yelling at him to return. He ignored her and hurtled onwards, leaving her ever further behind. Her breath came in painful gasps, reminding her she was horribly out of shape. Flagging quickly, she spotted his tail as he leapt onto a pile of debris and disappeared inside the structure. Anxious he'd cut his paws on the rubble she shouted, 'Ronnie Piper, get back here now or there'll be no chicken for dinner.'

Her words were carried away by the wind. She jogged on, fearful he would continue through the open-ended building to the fields beyond, and then onto the main road that ran past the woods. This area was unfamiliar territory to him and he could easily get lost or spooked. Worse still, he could be hell-bent on returning to their old home in Appletree and to the little Shih Tzu on heat. The sky suddenly seemed darker and more threatening. She shivered in spite of the burst of activity. Ronnie meant the world to her. He'd been there for her when she most needed him and now he was all she had left. She couldn't lose him.

Snow began tumbling. This time it seemed less enchanting; cold, wet flurries that blew into her face and stung her eyes, making them water. She ran on, puffing with effort at navigating uneven ground strewn with timber and rubble. By now, she'd covered quite some distance and was entering the area marked 'unsafe'. She clambered over an enormous pile of stones and stumbled into the entrance of a dilapidated building, dropping onto one knee and swearing loudly. Pain ripped through her kneecap but even that couldn't stop the anxiety that continued to rise in her chest. Ronnie was fast on his feet and could be dangerously close to the road by now. With his dark black fur and grey face, he'd be invisible to any motorist blinded by this snow. A large tear escaped and hung on one long dark eyelash as she hauled herself up.

A movement caught her eye. She squinted at an object a few feet ahead in the gloom of the building. It was Ronnie, tail wagging and head down, oblivious to his mistress's arrival. He was wolfing down a delicious titbit he'd discovered.

In spite of the relief she felt, she admonished him in her best schoolmarm voice. 'Ronnie Piper, drop that now.'

Ronnie fell to the floor and squirmed a little way in her direction on his belly, his eyes pleading to forgive him. She marched towards him and grabbed at the object dangling from his mouth. It appeared to be soggy tin foil.

'You disgusting boy, what have you found to scoff now?'

A warm voice responded. 'One large sausage roll, two ham and mustard sandwiches and a bag of cheese and onion crisps.'

She turned to face the speaker, a man in his mid-thirties with dark curly hair, eyes like shining conkers, and a broad mischievous grin on his suntanned rugged face. It was the man she and Faith had spotted when they'd arrived. Heat rose from the base of her throat and warmed her cheeks. It was always the same when she met strangers: her insides went squishy and she had a horrible urge to make a dash for it. Her reactions had intensified since her split from William. She wanted to race back to the house but he continued talking.

'It was supposed to be a late lunch but I left my lunchbox out with the lid off while went to check on some dimensions for this place, and when I returned somebody was tucking into it. On the plus side, he didn't get my apple as I'd already eaten most of that. However, he did manage to wolf down the core and pips.' Ronnie's eyebrows rose and fell in embarrassment at being caught out.

'I am *so* sorry,' she started. The man chuckled. It was a genial laugh.

'It's not a problem. I wasn't very hungry.'

'He's such a scavenger and it's not like I don't feed him or anything. He hoovers up everything and anything he finds. He's a glutton. I'm sure he'll make himself ill one day.' She was babbling to conceal her discomfort.

'He looks healthy enough to me.' Ronnie's stomach gurgled in agreement. 'That, though, looks nasty,' he replied, pointing at her torn jeans. Blood, vivid scarlet in colour, was seeping through the gaping hole.

'It's nothing. A scratch.'

'I've got a medical kit in the car. I'll put some antiseptic cream on that cut.'

Ronnie continued to regard her with abject misery and licked her hand.

'No, it's fine. Really.' The familiar dread was rising in her chest. Soon her body would react and she might lose all strength in her legs or freeze, and the man would think she was crazy or worse. Part of her insisted that the reactions were in her mind, that none of them need happen, that she should be able to have a conversation with the man. But the other half of her mind, the half that couldn't cope with meeting people, screamed she should leave. She was stymied by fear and grateful when Ronnie pressed his damp nose into her hand, giving her the confidence to speak again, albeit weakly. 'I thought he'd run away to find his girlfriend.'

'Dogs, eh? Mine was always going off investigating. She used to come to the sites with me but on Thursday afternoons she always disappeared. It took me over a month to find out what she was up to. She had worked out that the fish and chip van parked up at the village green on Thursdays so she'd go down and beg for food or raid the bins afterwards for leftover chips. I still miss her.' He looked into the distance, a faraway look in his eyes.

Chloe loved dogs and couldn't imagine being without Ronnie. Her lips unfroze and she asked. 'What was she called?'

'Sophie. She was a long-haired German Shepherd. She had a shaggy coat like a wolf's and the most intelligent amber eyes. She was incredibly bright. I swear she understood every word I said. Got her for my thirteenth birthday. We were inseparable right up until I took her to the vet. Hardest thing in the world, saying goodbye to a loyal friend like that, but hey, that's life. You have to enjoy the good times and remember them with fondness. Bet Ronnie has had his moments.' He gave another smile but his eyes hung on to the sad memory. She ought to say something to comfort him but could think of nothing. That was her trouble: she had little or no conversation. William would get cross with her when they used to go out to work-related events for being tongue-tied and awkward...

'Can't you make an effort?'

19

'I am.'

'Try harder. Sometimes it's embarrassing being
with you.'

That was before he stopped taking her along. It had suited
her to be left out. She couldn't face crowds of people, let
alone strangers. She'd become physically ill every time she
was expected to attend a function. Her anxiety would get
out of control and they'd end up rowing about it before
the event which only made matters worse; Chloe would
attend and inevitably end up doing something stupid, drop
a glass, fall over, stare at her feet all evening or say something that made William despair of her. The fact was that
she was simply unable to mix with people. The disorder
had contributed to their marriage breakdown. William's
new love, Lilly, was no doubt gregarious and a delightful
companion – the opposite of Chloe.

She was brought back to the present by Ronnie's
stomach which gurgled again and was followed by an
especially loud outburst of flatulence. The uncontrollable
chattering began again, 'Ronnie! Sorry. We're sorry. He's
sorry. Aren't you, Ronnie? So sorry.'

The man chuckled. 'Poor chap. He's probably nervous
about moving.'

'It's more likely the cowpats he was eating this
morning. I try to keep him away from them. I'll have my
work cut out here. Lots of fields. Lots of cowpats.' She
wished she'd just shut up but as usual, she had no control
over her actions. He didn't seem to mind and kept smiling
at her.

'I haven't introduced myself. I'm Alex Collins,
Thomas's son. I'm the project manager here, so you'll be
seeing me about. I also live here, over there.' He pointed

20

to the first property, the one-storey barn with the arched porch she and Faith had driven past on their arrival.

'I'm Chloe Piper.'

'I know,' he replied. 'Dad told me all about you.'

Chloe groaned inwardly. 'Everything?'

'If you are referring to a certain "naughty" book that caused controversy, then yes, he told me everything. If it is about your fetish for eating noodles with knitting needles or that you wear a yellow neoprene diving suit to bed then no, I must have found out about that on Wikipedia. But don't worry, all your secrets are safe with me.'

She smiled in spite of herself. 'Thomas said he wouldn't tell anyone.'

'I'm the exception. He tells me everything. I have to know who's up here. Don't want any axe murderers moving in, do we?'

'Keep it to yourself, please. I've moved here to protect my privacy. I don't want any more members of the clergy or congregation lobbing sex toys at my windows at night.' Her eyes widened at the memory.

He raised an eyebrow.

'Actually, so far I've only had one other altercation and that was with one of the members of the church choir. Told me I'd go to hell. From what I gather, hell will be much like the orgies they were enjoying each weekend.'

His mouth turned upwards. 'I thought you made it all up.'

'I made a lot of it up but it was inspired by actual events. I base my books on observations and on what I overhear.'

'I'd better watch out then. Can't have you writing about the worm-charming festival, the shin-kicking festival, the nettle-eating contest, or the Horn Dance.'

'You're joking. Surely those don't exist,' she said, mouth opening in surprise.

'Actually, they are real events that take place in villages but not all of them here, although the Horn Dance is famous in these parts, especially at the village nearby. It's performed by six deer-men who wear reindeer horns. The dancers follow a ten-mile course and perform the ritual in twelve different locations in and around the village, whilst the musician plays tunes on a melodeon with accompaniment from a triangle.'

Ronnie's belly grumbled again. He thumped his tail hoping to have been forgiven.

'Sounds… fun.' She suddenly felt awkward again. 'I'd better go back. My friend, Faith, is staying tonight and has already got designs on the bottle of champagne your father gave us. And Ronnie needs… well, Ronnie needs charcoal tablets at the moment.'

'He's always welcome to share my food. I can't say I'd met a sniffer dog before that could track down ham and mustard sandwiches.'

'He can smell ham ten miles away. It's his favourite food apart from cheese and onion crisps.'

The corners of his eyes crinkled at her words. The snow was thickening once more and light was fading. A woman's voice called his name. Neither had noticed the car that had pulled up outside Alex's house or the woman and child who were standing by his front door. The woman shouted again and Chloe saw the child wave in their direction. Alex moved into view and raised a hand in response, then pointed at her leg.

'I think you need to look at that wound.'

She looked down. The patch of red was spreading.

'Yes.'

'Nice to meet you, Chloe and you too, Ronnie. I'd better go. Hope you don't enjoy lie-ins too much. The men will all be on site at about seven.'

'Not a problem. We're early risers.'

She attached Ronnie's lead and picked her way through the site, away from Alex who was striding towards the woman. The snow drove into her face, making progress difficult but soon she arrived back at her new home. Faith was bobbing up and down by the back door.

'Thank goodness. You were longer than I expected and then the snow began to fall heavily. I was beginning to worry you'd lost your way. What happened?' she asked, spotting Chloe's torn blood-covered jeans. Chloe kicked off her boots and wiped Ronnie's feet dry with a towel.

'Slight accident. Ronnie ran away and I tumbled over. I met Thomas's son, Alex. He's moved into one of the other houses. He seems nice. He's got a wife and child.'

'What's he like?'

'Your type – tall, dark and handsome. He's the suntanned Greek god we saw when we arrived.'

'Oh, yes. Wife and child? Shame. First aid kit?'

'Kitchen. In a box marked *Useful stuff.*'

Faith went in search of it. Chloe released Ronnie who bounded past Faith and into the lounge where he dropped down full length on the carpet in front of the log burner with a grunt.

Faith found what she was looking for – a green box with a white cross on it. She lifted the lid and pulled out some antiseptic cream and a roll of plaster. Passing them across to Chloe who'd rolled up the leg of her jeans, she pulled a face.

'Ew! Messy. You better put that on it,' she said, handing over the cream. 'Don't know what germs you've picked up. Maybe you should get a tetanus jab just to be sure.'

'Faith! I knocked it on some rubble. This isn't the middle of a rat-infested swamp.'

'I'd get an injection all the same. You never know what's up here. Anyway, one of your other neighbours came over while you were playing hide-and-seek with Ronnie. Eleanor. She thought I was you. She's erm, how can I put it? Interesting. Yes, interesting. She's calling back tomorrow, so no hiding in your bed. You need to talk to her. You'll be living near her and can't avoid her forever. She left you the wicker basket. She said she used to watch *Desperate Housewives* and the women on the show always brought food over for new neighbours.

Chloe lifted the cloth covering the basket. It was filled from top to bottom with mince pies.

'That's kind of her,' replied Chloe.

'Tell me more about Alex.'

'Nothing to tell,' said Chloe, wincing as she looked at her leg again. It was quite a wide cut. She dabbed some cream on it, peeled back the adhesive on the plaster and smoothed it over the wound.

'He was friendly and likes dogs. That's all I know.'

'Maybe he has some hunky men friends.'

'Faith, I'm not ready to think about men, hunky or otherwise.'

'I know it's been hard for you,' said Faith. 'But you need to draw inspiration from somewhere. A few fit blokes might be just what you need.' She produced a smile when she saw the look of horror on Chloe's face. 'You're lovely, Chloe. Just because that arse William decided to behave badly, you shouldn't give up on all men.'

'I'm not so sure. I can't see what anyone would find attractive about me. I'm not what men want. They want funny, lively, outgoing women who brim with confidence, not women who try and clamber under the nearest settee at the mere thought of going out or having a conversation with a stranger.'

'You managed an entire conversation with delicious Alex.'

'That was different.'

'How?'

'He was being friendly because I'm his neighbour and Ronnie helped break the ice. Now let's drop this conversation. I want to open that champagne and celebrate my new start.'

Faith patted her hand. Chloe was grateful for her friend's presence. Faith had come all the way from London to help her move and make sure she was okay. Although Faith meant well, Chloe doubted she'd find love again. For a start she was unlikely to get over her own crushing self-defeatism. The separation from William had damaged her far more than Faith could ever know. It had taken Chloe years to gain even a little confidence and self-belief, and William had crushed it all.

'You're on. Let's pop the cork and drink to new beginnings.'

Chloe collected the bottle from the fridge. With her head turned away from Faith she could blink back the tears that had formed. Faith had hit a nerve. Hunky or otherwise, it was extremely unlikely Chloe would ever find another man to make her laugh or be happy.

Chapter Two

Sunday, 17th December

Faith drained her glass and released a lengthy contented sigh. The log burner was still glowing orange, and shadows danced across the floor where Ronnie now lay asleep.

'You made the right decision to leave Appletree and start again,' said Faith, holding onto the stem of her glass and eyeing it as if it might magically refill itself. 'This house is much nicer than your old one and William's a complete tosser.'

Chloe didn't respond. She was mellow thanks to the champagne and reality was replacing the excitement of moving. It felt strange being in a house without the memorabilia she'd been used to having around her – the funny animal sculptures she and William had bought together from a local artist, the teapot collection she'd started, the paintings and photographs on their walls she'd looked at every day for the last ten years. It was gone. The smell of the old place, the familiar creaks she'd become accustomed to: the birds that nested every year under their guttering, the crackle of the fire in their large open fireplace and the way she'd sink into the cushions on their old settee were now memories and she had yet to make new ones to replace them. It would take time. William was also memory now – a bittersweet memory.

'It won't last,' Faith continued, referring to William's relationship with Lilly, the Swedish bombshell who was now part of her soon-to-be ex-husband's life. Chloe knew her friend was trying to be supportive but she didn't want to discuss William's latest girlfriend. Whether it lasted or not was irrelevant – the fact was he'd cheated on her and not just the once. Before Lilly, there'd been others and poor dumb Chloe had been too stupid to realise. She threw Faith a smile and pushed herself into a standing position.

'Wine?' she said.

Faith waved her glass in response.

Chloe caught sight of her reflection in the large windows as she walked through to the kitchen. She ought to draw the curtains but there was no one to overlook the house, and by the door, she halted. There was no light pollution at all. The sky was never as inky black as this in Appletree. There'd always been pavements illuminated by street lights or light from people's homes leaking into the manicured front gardens, or car headlights strobing up and down the road. This was darkness like she'd never experienced before and yet it wasn't dark. As her eyes grew accustomed to it, she saw the sky was dotted with thousands... no, millions of pinpricks of lights from stars, and the sudden realisation took her breath away. This was magnificent. Faith shouted out. 'Oy, where's that wine? You haven't gone in search of the sexy carpenter, have you?' She followed her comment with a hearty chuckle.

'Coming.'

She turned from the door, catching again a glimpse of her face – pale, heart-shaped and framed with long dark brown hair – a face that had aged ten years in the last ten months. She'd never been what anyone would call pretty but she'd looked well and now – now she just looked drained. William had sucked all the joy from her, little by little at first and then towards the end, in huge amounts. If it hadn't been for the success of her novel and Faith's friendship, she'd have gone under. She turned away and grabbed the chilled wine from the fridge door, reached for a corkscrew in the top drawer and smiled: she'd gone to the drawer automatically, instinctively, as if she'd lived here far longer than a few hours. She took it as a sign that she'd be fine and yanking the cork from the bottle she raised it victoriously towards the lounge.

'You want a fresh glass?'

'Damn right I do… fetch those ones that look like fish bowls.'

Chloe grinned. Faith was already semi-drunk and would soon be demanding they opened the karaoke app on her mobile and had a sing-along. And why not? The house would probably enjoy it.

–

'What in the name of all things holy, is that racket?' Faith demanded.

'Workmen.'

'It's seven thirty a.m. That's the middle of the night as far as I'm concerned.'

Chloe chucked the crust from the piece of toast she'd been eating into the air. Ronnie, leapt up and caught it.

'It's still dark,' Faith continued. 'How can they see and work in the dark?'

'Looks like they have floodlights. The area around the barn they're working on lit up just after seven a.m.'

'Please tell me you were up writing and not just up for the fun of it… Is that tea?' Faith wondered across to the teapot by the sink, lifted the lid and grimaced. 'Got any Darjeeling?'

'Don't be ridiculous? Where am I going to find that here? That's perfectly good breakfast tea. Want a cup?'

'I suppose so.' Faith slipped onto one of the stools and stared outside into the black abyss of the garden. 'So why were you up at that time?'

'Ronnie needed to go outside and I didn't want him running off.'

Faith's head moved side to side slowly. 'Another reason I don't have animals. I couldn't bear getting up at that ungodly hour.'

Faith was a self-confessed city girl. She liked bistros, bars, the theatre, her exercise classes at the upmarket gym in London and the buzz the city afforded. She hated solitude. Chloe knew the true reason she immersed herself in city life: she had a fear of being alone, one that had worsened following the death of her husband, Adrian. Faith came across as a confident, even arrogant, individual, but Chloe knew it was all a front. She was anything but. Having worked in public relations for a company in town, after Adrian died she took up a position in a publishing house and commuted to London by train on a regular basis. It was all part of surrounding herself with work and distractions, and once her list of clients had grown and her name become well-known, she'd decided to set up her own agency. It had meant leaving Appletree and Chloe, but they'd stayed in touch.

Chloe observed her friend sipping her tea. Faith was showing no signs of a hangover even though it had been two a.m. by the time they'd gone to bed, and the three empty wine bottles now standing by the back door were a sign they'd both had far too much to drink. She recalled singing along to Gloria Gaynor's 1970's classic *I Will Survive* and winced at the memory.

'I have to head back to London this morning.'

Chloe could barely hide her disappointment. She'd hoped Faith would stay a day or two.

'I got a text message from Marty Woodman, the guy who wrote the cookbook *Hot Food for Hot Sex*. He's supposed to be taking part in an interview with Nick Hanson on ITV later today, but he's thrown a complete wobbly and can't face it. I need to go along and hold his hand.'

Chloe had seen the volatile Marty Woodman on television before. He usually ended up walking off the set or hurling abuse at the presenters. It made for entertaining television but kept Faith on her toes and earning her fee trying to smooth over any fallouts from his tantrums.

'You'll be okay, won't you?'

'Of course. I have Ronnie and this beautiful house and there's stacks to do before Christmas.'

'About that: I was thinking maybe you'd like to spend it with me in Barbados. It's only for a week but I don't like the idea of you being alone on your first Christmas after the separation. You don't have to talk to anyone there. You can sit on the balcony and enjoy some sunshine and I'll be right there with you.'

'But Ronnie...'

'Couldn't he take a doggy vacation at the kennels?'

'I can't leave him. He hasn't had a chance to settle here. Thanks for the offer but I'm not leaving him. I won't be alone cos I have him.'

'I guessed that'd be your reaction. I had to ask anyway.'

'You'd be welcome to come here.'

'As much as I love you and think your new house is adorable, I must top up my tan and I need to recharge my batteries. Got a lot of new releases in the coming year and I'll require all my stamina. Sun and cocktails should get me into fighting shape.'

'I'd only fret about Ronnie the entire time.'

Faith gave a small nod. 'I know. You don't mind I have to shoot off earlier than planned?'

'Not at all. The garage is delivering my new car this morning so I'll be sorted. We'll go out and explore and buy some Christmas decorations afterwards.'

'And the writing...' Faith stared at her earnestly. They both knew the effect the marriage break-up had had on her work. Since the day William had confessed his affairs, Chloe hadn't written a word. Upfront Publishing was expecting a manuscript in the next couple of months and she had nothing to offer them. Faith had tried to buy her more time but the publishers were on a tight schedule and a contract was a contract. Chloe would have to deliver soon or risk losing both it and the hefty advance she'd received.

'I'll tackle it. Should be easier now I'm here. Give me another couple of days to get straightened out and I'll start work on it.'

'That's my girl!' Faith finished her tea, stood up and threw her arms around Chloe.

–

With Faith on her way back to London, the house seemed extremely quiet. Chloe almost felt she should be walking on tiptoe as she walked from room to room, nodding in approval at the furniture hastily purchased from websites.

It all worked in harmony. William had never agreed with any of her choices. Whenever they'd needed to redecorate, he'd poo-pooed every one of her suggestions and forcefully decided on colour schemes. She shook her head at the memory of them arguing over a settee. With hindsight she could tell he deliberately blocked her. He'd been obdurate and wanted everything his own way, like a child. A child. The words stirred something deep inside her that she couldn't put a name on. She sighed. How she'd have loved to be a mother. It was yet another choice that had been kept from her...

'I simply don't want children. They've never been part of my life plan.'

William's words are like shards of glass piercing her heart. Why hasn't he spoken to her about this before? The leaflet she's discovered in the pocket of his jacket has left her dumbfounded. He's considering a vasectomy. He's only thirty-eight and yet he wants to ensure he can never father any children. This is something too important to ignore. He continues as if they were discussing their next holiday. 'You know how I feel about my parents. I wasn't close to them and I'd make a shit father. I never said I wanted children.'

It's true. Whenever they'd broached the subject, he'd said, 'Not now. My career is my baby.' She'd taken it to mean he'd want children later, after he'd achieved his goals. He gives her a familiar look, the one that makes her feel she's got it all wrong. She's at fault. She hates it when he stares at her that way: a mixture of sympathy and sorrow. It has the same effect every time. She feels inadequate and stupid and wants to apologise, except this time she can't. He's taking a huge decision that they ought to make together and she speaks out.

'Why do it behind my back?' she asks.

He throws her an incredulous look. 'It wasn't behind your back. I didn't think I needed your permission. Do I tell you what to do with your body? Do I interfere when you get drugs from the doctor or go to therapy sessions to help with your condition?' The last word jars. She can't help the way she is. Her fear of social occasions and mixing with people has come from extenuating circumstances that saw her sent to a town near Birmingham to live with her aged grandmother at the age of thirteen. Her experiences at the new school fashioned her into what she is today. William is only too aware of that past and her fears that she is a lesser person than most. It's cruel to bring it up now. She's about to say more and tell him how she feels and scream at him, when his face changes.

'God, sorry, babe. I'm bang out of order. I shouldn't have said that. I didn't think you'd be so upset. I thought you understood how I felt.'

She's caught off guard and the fight drains from her. She knows all about his abusive childhood and alcoholic parents, and she can comprehend why he'd be nervous about having children, but to consider doing this and to take away the opportunity from her without giving her any thought, that she can't understand. He takes her hands between his and looks into her eyes.

'I'm sorry. I had no idea how important it was to you. I've messed up big time, haven't I? I'm so

33

sorry. But I can't face children. I have you. I don't need anything else.'

His dark eyes are wide and sadness pools in them. She can't fight him. She'll have to accept his decision.

The kitchen had French doors that looked out over woods and fields. She stared over the fields into the distance beyond and watched a small flock of sheep moving slowly up the slope, like small white clouds on legs. The past was the past. This was her future. A movement caught her eye. A blur of red, white and blue had scurried through the side entrance and instead of heading to the front door was making its way to the back. Chloe darted for cover behind the island and squatted there, out of sight. She wasn't up to meeting strangers.

The tapping on the glass was light and persistent, like an inquisitive woodpecker. Chloe cursed. Maybe she'd been spotted before she'd hidden. It would look fairly obvious now if she revealed herself. She'd have to hope the stranger would leave. However, she hadn't banked on Ronnie who suddenly rushed out of the living room to greet the intruder. He barked happily.

'Ronnie, shush,' whispered Chloe. It was a mistake to speak. Delighted at hearing his mistress's voice, he hunted around until he found her on her knees and decided she wanted to play. He crouched on his front legs, nose almost touching her face then pulled away with a joyful bark. It was his version of the game hide-and-seek.

'Go away,' she hissed.

Ronnie pulled playfully at one of her trainer laces and backed away again.

'Get off.' She said. The tapping started again and a muffled shout. 'Chloe!'

'Bad dog,' she grumbled, getting to her feet and feigning surprise.

Dressed in red boots, a white coat and resembling a human version of Sonic the Hedgehog with spiked cobalt blue hair, stood a woman in her early forties. She waved enthusiastically as Chloe emerged. Ronnie trotted beside his mistress and nosed at the door as she unlocked it.

'You must be the wonderful Chloe Piper,' gushed the woman. 'I'm sorry I missed you yesterday, but your friend seemed very nice. I hope you enjoyed the mince pies. I'm not the best cook but it's the thought that counts, isn't it? And who is this?' She bent down and fussed over Ronnie, ruffling the fur on his neck with both hands. His tail wagged faster and faster.

'You must be Eleanor. Come in.' The words almost stuck in her throat. She swallowed and drew a breath. She could do this.

Eleanor didn't need to be asked a second time. Giving Ronnie one final rub, she stood up and pulled Chloe into a honeysuckle and lime scented embrace leaving her glued to the spot as she withdrew.

'I'm so pleased we're going to be neighbours. I hear you've moved from a village not too far away. We're from just outside this area – Derby – but couldn't stand city life any longer and were dying to move. Isn't it perfect here?' She turned sparkling green eyes onto Chloe and smiled. The corners of her eyes creased slightly and her perfectly groomed heavy eyebrows lifted slightly. 'Sorry, I go on, don't I? I'm just so excited to finally meet you.'

As much as Chloe didn't want to chat, she couldn't be rude, especially after such an effusive welcome. Eleanor seemed open and friendly and Ronnie had completely fallen for her. He sat on his haunches, eyes never leaving the woman's face. If Ronnie liked her, she had to be okay. Her voice sounded distant to her ears as she managed to get out perfunctory sentences. 'Nice to meet you. Thank you for the mince pies. They really were delicious. I've got some left. Would you like one and a coffee?'

'That's so sweet of you but I have to get off. I told Fairfax I'd only be a few minutes. We have to check out a new venue!'

'Venue?'

'We run an events company for singletons. We only started it recently and it's taken off like you wouldn't believe. We're constantly on the lookout for more fun activities to offer our clients. Anyway, I wanted to welcome you to Sunny Meadow and say if you need anything at all, just come and bang on our door. We work from home so we're often around when we're not at an event.' She gave Chloe a wide smile.

Chloe shifted from one foot to the other. She had no idea what to say next. She was saved from further conversation as Eleanor dropped down again to stroke Ronnie's head and scratch behind his ear. Ronnie seemed to melt under her hand and threw her a look when she withdrew that made her guffaw. As she turned to leave, she spoke with sincerity.

'I hope you find it.'

'What?'

'Whatever you were looking for on the floor. Was it an earring? I'm always losing mine. The wretched butterfly clips come off.'

Chloe flushed hotly and mumbled something unintelligible. Had she been found out? She hoped not. Eleanor seemed pleasant enough and she didn't want to make a bad first impression.

As she bounded off, Eleanor halted briefly and faced her. 'You must come around for drinks. How about tonight at six? I won't take no for an answer,' she added, wagging a finger.

Chloe nodded with an enthusiasm she didn't feel, and thanked Eleanor who set off once more. She glanced at Ronnie whose nose was forced against the window watching the disappearing tricolour. 'Traitor,' she mumbled.

Chapter Three

Even with a shining new silver Kia parked outside her home, Chloe had still spent the early part of the afternoon feeling cut off. Their home in Appletree had been her refuge and sanctuary for almost five years and to uproot, as brave and necessary a move as it had been, had left her feeling unfixed. The new place was lovely and she would be happy here but she needed time to adjust, make new memories, learn to live with its quirks. The old place was so familiar she could still imagine the creaks that accompanied its night-time settling, or the occasional rumble as the heating system burst into life, or the chirping of sparrows that had regularly nested under the roof's eaves.

A longing to return to that sweet familiarity washed over her like a gigantic wave, so powerful she had to steady herself against the kitchen top. *Be strong*, she told herself. Going back wasn't an option. The house was up for sale and William was living there, no doubt with Lilly. The woman had probably moved in the second Chloe had departed leaving her door keys along with the small elephant keyring William had bought for her on the console table in the hall next to the photograph of her and William on honeymoon.

She ought to go out and buy food but she couldn't face that particular challenge. She'd wait until her phone line had been installed and connected and then order it online as she always did. She had enough stand-by provisions until then.

Chloe picked up the large cardboard box marked 'PERSONAL'. It contained all her precious memories: those of her childhood, parents and life in the Outer Hebrides before her world was shattered into a million fragments and she was left to flounder alone. She extracted a framed picture of Nanny Olive, white hair pulled back in a tight bun and face lined but still the olive-green eyes that had given her name, wide and clear, and hinting at the handsome woman she had once been. Chloe traced a finger over the woman's face and whispered, 'Love you, Nanny.' Nanny Olive, her father's mother, had taken her in after her parents had been killed and brought her up as best she could. It hadn't been easy, given the age-gap and her grandmother's own struggle with health-issues, but they'd managed, cemented by their shared grief.

Moving from the tight community in Scotland to a huge town in the Midlands had been a humongous shock. Life there was completely different from the gentle pace she'd been used to, and her new school was a revelation. A hundred times bigger than her old school in Scotland, she'd immediately wanted to leave. Nanny Olive had understood. Chloe peered inside the box again searching for her most valuable possession and lifted the card bearing a picture of a serene lioness under a tree. She knew its contents by heart. She could close her eyes and picture the spidery writing without looking at it, but she opened it nevertheless and read, hearing Nanny Olive's voice as she did so…

Chloe, poppet, you're going to have to stand on your own two feet now. As hard as that is to deal with, you must face up to it. Life throws us challenges and we have to surmount them whether we want to or not, whether we like it or not. I'll always be here for you but you're going to need to return to school and take your examinations. You have to look to your future. It doesn't feel like it right now, but it will get better for you. One day, you'll have a home and family of your own and this won't hurt as much as it does today. You'll be fine but you need to make some brave steps to reach that goal. I'll hold your hand. I'll hold it while you pick your way through all of this mess and begin to find some peace and even happiness. I may have lost my son, but I still have you, my beautiful granddaughter, and I know you can get through this. You're stronger than you think.

Chloe closed it again and thought of her grandmother who'd written those words to help her through that terrible time immediately after the accident that had stolen her parents and sister from her. She'd clasped both of Chloe's hands between her own gnarled ones twisted by arthritis. Her eyes had burned with passion and love. Nanny Olive was a fighter and Chloe drew from her strength.

–

With hindsight, she'd depended too heavily on Nanny Olive. It had been a terrifying ordeal for the painfully shy Chloe, starting at a new school where everyone seemed unfriendly. She hungered after the solitude of the islands and the home she'd shared with her scientist parents and older sister, Georgia. She was desperate for the misty mornings, staring out over calm waters, listening to the soft bleating of the sheep before joining the few other children from the island at the tiny village school. Most of all, she yearned to be left alone. People frightened her, especially crowds. The schoolchildren who jeered at her soft Scottish accent sent her scurrying back home with tears in her eyes and her heart as heavy as stone, back to her grandmother who stroked her hair and held her tight and repeated it would be alright.

Here she was again, starting out, just like the young Chloe all those years ago. This time she had no grandmother to help her when she was frightened to face people but she had Faith and her novel, and of course, she had Ronnie. Ronnie had been Nanny's dog and after she passed away he had come to live with Chloe, rarely leaving her side. He was more than just a pet.

The writing bothered her. Ever since she'd found out about William's infidelity, she seemed to have lost her writing mojo. Her debut novel had been an incredible success but unless she got her finger out and wrote another like it, she'd soon be a forgotten author, and she'd have to repay the large advance she'd received from the publisher. If she didn't rise to the challenge, she'd have no other form of income. She was due money from the sale of their house into which she'd sunk her small inheritance, but apart from that, she had nothing to live on.

She heaved a sigh and pulled out some more photographs: Chloe as a child with her parents and golden-haired Georgia, outside the stone cottage with a vast sea as a backdrop. She'd long ago stopped wishing she could turn back the clocks. What was done was done. She'd lived through the turmoil and fallout of losing them. She smiled at the photograph. Nanny's words echoed in her mind. *You're stronger than you think.* She placed the picture on a shelf in the living room. She would get through this.

Picking up a spiralled back notebook, entitled *Ideas* and a purple propelling pencil, she flopped onto the settee, hoping for some inspiration. The ideas and indeed all the sexy passages had just flowed for her debut, as if they'd been stored for an eternity deep within her and needed to be freed. Once they'd started, they wouldn't stop like a tap that couldn't be turned, and some days she'd spent hours in front of her laptop, lost in the world of make believe until William came home. Sitting about most of the day had taken its toll on her waistline. With packets of crisps and biscuits to fuel her as she typed, she'd packed on a bit of weight. She'd always been a little on the plump side but now, having eaten more than usual due to stress and heartache, she was comfortable only in elastic-waist jeggings. Although William had professed to loving her regardless of the few extra pounds she'd put on, she now wondered whether her weight gain had helped to send him tumbling into the arms of the svelte goddess that was Lilly.

She tugged at the baggy jumper, pursed her lips and let out a noise that sounded like a tyre deflating. Ronnie, in front of the log burner, lifted his head.

'Not yet. Later,' she said. She relaxed against the padded cushion and shut her eyes. What could she write about? Nothing sprang to mind. She jotted down names and a few woolly ideas but knew it was pointless. The fountain of creativity had dried up.

Outside, the light was beginning to fade and she needed to walk the dog before it was too dark. She wasn't going to have a repeat performance of the night before.

'You ready then?' she asked. Ronnie stretched languidly, then rose and scurried to the door tail wagging.

'Not far,' she said. 'We'll head to the reservoir.'

She'd searched for a suitable walk on her phone and discovered the reservoir was only ten minutes away by foot. If she crossed her land onto the right of way, and then turned left and traversed the field behind it, she'd come out opposite an entrance to the huge reservoir, home to hundreds of birds and covering some 800 acres. With four different routes to choose from along neat pathways, it was ideal for them both.

Ronnie waited obediently as she clipped on his lead, and together they left the warmth of the house and headed outside where the cold air hit the back of her throat and made her cough. She took a second breath and surveyed her land. It was going to be a mammoth task to get it in check. She ought to start contacting landscape gardeners as soon as she had Internet. It was something else to add to her steadily growing list of jobs to tackle and challenges to face. She'd have to combat her nervousness and handle workmen. There'd be no William to do it for her…

'For crying out loud, Chloe. Just for once, can't you deal with the workmen? I have a full-time job. I can't drop everything to hang around the house with you.'

'William, I'm sorry but I can't face it. The last time you called them in, they made me feel so dim. They looked at me as if I was simple and I'm positive they were talking about me behind my back, sniggering and saying stuff.'

43

'They weren't. It's in your head. It's always in
your head. They're too busy to pay any attention
to you. You only have to say hello and offer them
a cup of tea. It's not like you have to stand up
and give a presentation or anything, is it?' His
voice rises in anger and makes her feel even more
helpless. She knows she's being unreasonable yet
she can't help it. The tears begin to fall.

'I hate being like this,' she wails.

'Okay, babe. Okay. I know. Don't get upset.
I'll take a couple of hours off.'

She'd managed certain situations after that one. With encouragement from other sufferers in online groups and thanks to her psychiatrist, she'd learned to deal with day-to-day situations like workmen and delivery drivers coming to her door. One-on-one became easier and if she avoided crowds, she could cope.

As Chloe and Ronnie plodded across the field, she hoped the walk would motivate her muse. She really needed to come up with something before the new year began.

They cleared the stile into the field and made the descent to the road that traversed their side and the reservoir. Ahead of them the lake shimmered enticingly, reflecting the sky with its scudding white clouds. Ronnie began to pant as he always did when excited, pausing every now and then, nose quivering at the scent of rabbits or hares, or any one of a number of wild animals that lived in these parts of the country. The road was quiet although she could hear the sound of an engine rumbling in her direction.

She tugged at Ronnie's lead to make him walk closer to her. There was no way she wanted him wandering ahead of her onto the road and oncoming traffic. The vehicle was approaching and she could make out its green roof. No, it wasn't green. There was a Christmas tree strapped to the roof, hanging over both ends of the car. The car, a Land Rover, drove past, the occupants oblivious to both her and Ronnie. Alex was at the wheel. His passenger, an attractive brunette, was laughing and behind them both, elbows on the headrest and face between the two seats, sat a small boy, face animated. Alex and his family were preparing for Christmas.

'We ought to get ready too.' Ronnie's ears twitched.

It would be her first Christmas alone. Nanny Olive had passed away a few years ago and she had no one else to share the festive season with. Following her grandmother's death, Chloe's condition had worsened again. The fear returned and washed over her, drowning the person she'd tried to become. It was partly due to the realisation that Nanny Olive could no longer be there for her and partly because William squashed the rest out of her. *You're stronger than you think.* She shook herself from her reverie. Tomorrow she'd buy a tree and get Ronnie some doggie treats and wrap them for Christmas Day. She'd be fine.

—

The gravel crunched satisfyingly under her boots, like small pebbles on a beach. She made her way across the courtyard to the far side of the development where Eleanor lived, guided only by the light of her mobile. A wind had got up since her walk with Ronnie and she was glad of the jumper and coat she'd put on. Coloured fairy lights swung from the small tree in the front garden, and

Eleanor had left an outside light on, its warm orange glow lighting up the front door and pathway. Somebody had hung a sign, *No Riff Raff*, on the porch door. She rang the bell. As much as she hadn't wanted to come over for drinks, it was necessary. She was going to be living near these people and ought to be sociable. A drink wouldn't hurt. The walk by the reservoir had taken more time than she'd anticipated and then she'd had a call from an exhausted Faith who'd chatted for almost an hour, leaving her little time to get ready. She'd slicked on some lipstick, a pair of clean jeans and her favourite red jumper. Red always made her feel safe, strong even. She breathed in, long deep breaths and focused on a special place in her mind to calm her heartbeat – her parental home.

Muffled chimes rang out in the house. The wind gusted around her ankles and chilled her legs; however, it was anxiety not cold that made her shiver. A lifetime ago she'd been brought up in rough winters on the island of Skye. The cold didn't usually have much of an effect on her. All of a sudden, a light came on in the hall and a face, a round cheerful face with sandy hair and matching eyebrows and brown button eyes, appeared.

'Come in,' he boomed. 'I'm Fairfax. Great to meet you.'

The voice was sonorous and pleasant and, accompanied by the broad smile, put her at ease.

She shuffled into the entrance and offered up the bottle of wine.

'You shouldn't have,' he said, taking it from her and waving his other arm like an enthusiastic conductor. 'Come in. Don't stay in the cold.'

'Seriously, you shouldn't have,' chorused Eleanor, appearing from nowhere and sweeping Chloe into her arms like a long-lost friend. She'd put her hair up in a high ponytail so it now seemed as if she had an exploding firework or a bright blue sparkler on her head. Chloe decided it suited her effervescent personality. 'Fairfax went to Costco and has bought enough booze to open his own pub.'

He grinned amiably, revealing a slight gap in his front teeth. 'It's the festive season. I had to ensure we had enough for entertaining the troops.'

'We do have quite a lot of guests coming over Christmas and the New Year,' she agreed, ushering Chloe into a living room that was not dissimilar in size to her own but resembled a room in a small chateau or palace, furnished as it was with antique furniture, striped chairs with wooden armrests and claw feet, glass-fronted ornate cabinets housing porcelain vases and dishes, dark wooden tables bearing knick-knacks, and on the walls a mixture of paintings, some large and in heavy gilt frames, others in oval frames made of black onyx – a collection of portraits and of men and women.

'Fairfax used to be an antiques dealer,' said Eleanor, seeing Chloe's eyes open wide at the sight of a bronze sculptured boar on a round table. 'That's an Italian sculpture.'

'An Uffizi boar or "Il Porcellino",' said Fairfax. 'Can I take your coat?'

'See, to me that's just a scruffy bronze sculpture of a pig, but to Fairfax it's an Ufizz-y.'

'Uffizi,' he repeated with an Italian accent, making it sound as if there was a 't' before the 'z'. 'It's the famous art gallery in Florence and Mr Porky is certainly not scruffy. But I shan't *bore* you about it.' He waited for the pun to sink in. Eleanor rolled her eyes. Chloe smiled politely and he bowed taking her coat with him.

'He's always doing that. Cracks me up,' said Eleanor. 'Where's your handsome mutt?'

'I didn't think it appropriate to bring him over.'

'He's always welcome. I love dogs. Bring him with you next time.'

Chloe warmed to the woman with her crazy hair and open face. She took a chair near the roaring fire. 'You didn't opt for a log burner?'

'It didn't fit in with all the furniture. The open fire works better. It's a bugger to clean out each day, though. I've delegated that job to Fairfax. Now, what do you want to drink. We literally have everything.'

'Wine's lovely. White if you have any?'

'Oh, we have.'

Fairfax reappeared and Eleanor left them to chat. 'So, where've you come from?' he asked.

'Appletree. It's a tiny village the other side of Lichfield.'

'But that's not where you're from. I detect an accent. A slight Scottish one, if I'm not mistaken.'

Chloe was surprised. 'You can? I've lived around the Midlands for over twenty years. I thought I'd lost it.'

'It's still there.' He sat back. 'I have an ear for accents. I used to practise mimicking them when I was a kid. It was my party piece.'

'He's always been a joker,' said Eleanor, coming back into the room with two glasses of wine in her hands. She passed one to Chloe, the other to Fairfax, before departing again.

Fairfax explained. 'I was the smallest, ugliest kid in school. I had to come up with something to fit in, so I took to impersonations. I could do passable ones of most

48

of our teachers. My mates loved them. I was so good at impersonating our English teacher, a Canadian, the headmaster overheard me one day and actually thought I was him.'

'You still do them?'

He grinned wickedly. 'I most certainly do, Miss Moneypenny,' he replied, emulating Sean Connery and raising his glass. He changed to Humphrey Bogart. 'Here's looking at you kid.'

'Oh, not already,' said Eleanor. 'He's only known you ten seconds and he's launched into his voices.'

'I literally have no idea what you are saying to me,' he replied, Donald Trump to a tee. 'I have tremendous respect for women though. I want to tell you.'

Both women laughed.

'Here's to us all and happy days here at Sunny Meadow,' said Eleanor.

'Amen to that,' Fairfax replied, still in Trump's voice.

'We lived close to the centre of Derby before coming here. Great for work but we needed some space. We both craved green fields and countryside and to get away from town life. We heard about this development, came up to see it and *kaboom!* we fell in love with it,' said Fairfax.

'That's pretty much the same for me. I wanted a place away from it all and as soon as I drove over the reservoir, I knew I had to move here,' said Chloe.

'Didn't fancy returning to Scotland?'

Chloe shook her head. It held too many memories of her family. It wasn't a place she wanted to revisit. She was best moving forward. 'I'm settled in this area. I just need a change. I've recently split from my husband.' The words spilled out of her mouth at speed. Best to get it over with. People would be curious as to why she was living alone.

There was no shame in admitting to the failure of her marriage, although saying it made it seem even more real.

'Oh, I'm sorry to hear that,' said Eleanor. 'Honestly. We both understand how it feels. We've been through divorces too.'

Fairfax nodded. 'It's a tough gig but you'll pull through. Give yourself a chance to breathe, take it all in and then allow yourself to move on.'

His words were sincere, as were his eyes fully focused on her. For a crazy moment she felt as if she'd known this couple for a long time. The wine was smooth and cool and the light flavour of peaches burst on her tongue as she took a small sip.

'Thank you,' she said, not knowing what else to offer. She was saved by the phone and Fairfax beetled off to answer it. He was only a few minutes, during which Eleanor spoke animatedly about the new house. Fairfax returned, a smile on his face.

'It was your dad, something about picking up a costume for a fancy-dress party next weekend.'

'Oh yes, it's a Seventies-pop-star-themed party. They're going as members of ABBA. Dad wants to go as Agnetha. I said I'd collect their costumes for them.'

Fairfax laughed. 'That sounds just like him. You know, Chloe, he's just turned seventy and recently bought a Harley Davidson. He plans on taking Eleanor's mum on Route 66.'

'Really?' Chloe was astounded.

'He's always been adventurous,' said Eleanor proudly.

'I think you inherited your wild streak from Tug.' He looked across at Chloe. 'Ask her how we met?'

Chloe was intrigued. 'Go on.'

Eleanor took a sip of her wine, swallowed then giggled. 'I was his skydiving instructor. He was doing a skydive for charity and bricking it. It was a tandem dive so he was strapped to me. I almost had to chuck him out of the plane he was that scared, but it was a great dive and as soon as we landed, he was so elated to have done it and stayed alive, he asked me out.'

Fairfax gave another smile that lit his eyes. 'True story,' he said, amused by Chloe's open-mouthed expression.

The fire popped and snapped gleefully in the grate, tiny explosions as flames, a kaleidoscope of magenta, yellow ochre and paprika, rose and shimmied like exotic dancers with arms outstretched upwards. The room was filled with the scents of a pine forest warmed by the sun, and as she relaxed into the chair Chloe felt something she hadn't experienced in a long while – a feeling of belonging.

Chapter Four

'Don't say a word.' Chloe addressed her words to Ronnie who stared dolefully at her. The pounding of a hundred hammers beating out a crazy xylophone tune on the stretched nerves in her head made her want to throw up. She reached for the aspirin and swallowed two, chugging an entire glass of water. She'd only been in the house two days and both mornings she'd woken with a thick head and nausea. Today's was the mother of all hangovers and embarrassingly, she couldn't quite remember what had happened towards the end of the evening at Eleanor's.

Having eaten nothing before drinks with Eleanor and Fairfax, it hadn't taken much alcohol for her to feel less inhibited. Her hosts had ensured her glass was topped up and had insisted she have another and another. She remembered telling them about her parents and Georgia, and later playing charades but it was all too foggy after that. She hoped she hadn't said or done anything stupid. Surely she wouldn't have blurted out the fact she was a writer, let alone she was C J Knight, author of *Spank Me Harder, Vicar.* She held her head in her hands, cool fingers massaging her temples and groaned. She'd have to move again if she had let it slip. The whole point of this process had been to hide away and remain anonymous, yet within forty-eight hours of moving in she'd possibly told her new neighbours all about her life.

She shuffled into the room she'd designated as her office, slumping onto the ergonomic chair she'd bought to fit under the simple solid oak table. The room was a small work space but the Japanese desk had caught her eye, having not only a discreet integrated drawer but an innovative storage system nestled between the frame's legs where she could store paper or notepads. The glass top gave it a pleasing aesthetic appearance which she hoped would help encourage her to sit down and reach a daily word count of 3,000 words. She pushed away the notepad and, with elbows on the table, stared at the small black and white sketch of Ronnie she'd had commissioned after she'd received her first royalty cheque. Would she get over this writer's block? She needed to or she'd have to find a job again. The last one had been in a bookshop but that had been over five years ago. She wasn't sure she could be that person again. It had taken so much effort and confidence-building to get the job. Nanny Olive had been instrumental in helping her overcome her difficulties to face the public and take up the position. William had eroded what confidence she'd gained, little by little, stealthily, and she hadn't realised until it was too late.

Ronnie, who'd followed her into the room, pushed his nose into her heel and snuffled.

'I know. You want a walk.' A steady thump of his tail against the wall was all the response she needed. It lifted her spirits. She could always count on Ronnie for that. There was no way she was going to be able to write this morning. It was already nine-thirty. She may as well get some fresh air and let it work some magic on her head, along with the pills she'd just taken.

The knock on the door gave her a start. Ronnie dashed off to see who the visitor might be. She followed him, wishing she'd changed out of her pyjamas before coming downstairs. She ran a hand through her unruly hair and opened the door.

'Morning. You not dressed yet?' Fairfax was in a coat, gloves and a ski hat with bright red pompoms hanging down beside his ears.

Her bewildered look gave him the information he needed. 'You've forgotten, haven't you?'

She nodded. There was no point in pretending otherwise.

'The tree. We talked about it last night. We've got an open-backed Nissan truck so we said we'd help you chose a tree from the Christmas tree farm and bring it back for you. And we're going to visit the reindeer. You do remember the reindeer, don't you? Once we told you about them, you seemed very keen to visit them.'

A vision of her wearing a felt reindeer headband, complete with large antlers, waving a wine glass about and excitedly declaring she'd love to see the reindeer flashed before her. Then another of her and Fairfax singing *Rudolph, the Red-nosed Reindeer* loudly. 'Oh Lord, I was truly drunk, wasn't I?'

'Not at all. A little merry,' he replied. 'You were great fun. We both thought so. Eleanor's almost ready. I thought I'd come and see if you were still up for it. Thought we'd go ahead of the crowds. It's always quieter there before lunchtime. If we're lucky we'll be the first there.'

She couldn't back down now. Besides, if she went along she'd find out just how much she had revealed the night before. She gave a nod. 'I won't be long.'

'No hurry.'

'I ought to just take Ronnie out for a quick walk.'

'Oh, it's okay. Bring him with you. He can run around with us. Plenty of room in the car.'

'Thank you. We'll be over in ten minutes.'

She charged upstairs and grabbing clothes from the floor and the wardrobe dressed as quickly as possible. There was little time to dwell on what she was doing. Hopefully, there wouldn't be many people at the farm. She had to do this. 'You are stronger than you think.' She repeated the mantra aloud twice more. At least she'd be able to prepare the house for Christmas. It would look cosier with a tree up in the corner of the sitting room.

Picking up the lead from the kitchen top, she called Ronnie. 'Come on. You're going to see lots of trees. Lots and lots of them. Don't try and pee up them all though, or we'll both be in disgrace.'

As she dashed out of the house, she caught sight of Alex in his work clothes, carrying a large hammer. He waved and walked across to them. Stooping to pat Ronnie, he gave her a smile. 'So, you've met the neighbours.'

'How did you know?'

'The carol-singing outside my door at one a.m. kind of gave it away,' he said with a grin.

Her mouth dropped open.

'You mean you don't remember?' He stood up and she had to lift her head to look into his eyes. She shook her head. 'Oh dear, the demon drink. Did Fairfax ply you with his famous raspberry liquor?'

Another blurry vision of them downing shots and Fairfax explaining how he brewed his fruit alcohol, of the back of her throat burning and then a feeling of euphoria and lightness.

'I'm terribly sorry. What must you think of me?' She shook her head in dismay.

He let out a soft laugh. 'I'm only winding you up. I've fallen foul of Fairfax and Eleanor's hospitality myself. You didn't come carol-singing at my door. I spotted Eleanor and Fairfax walking you home at about midnight. You all seemed a little worse for wear, but no singing. Just a lot of weaving about and giggling.'

'Oh, thank goodness.' Her relief was swiftly followed by irritation. How dare he tease her like that and how stupid she was to have believed him.

'You headed over to them now?'

'We're going to buy a tree.' She didn't know why she was telling him anything. Maybe it was because he was looking at her intently and she didn't know how to end the conversation without appearing to be rude. Heaven knows what impression he'd already formed of her.

'Is Ronnie behaving? You haven't been feeding him cow pats again.'

A light had crept into his eyes. She was sure he was mocking her now.

'No, but he did steal and scoff four leftover mince pies, so I'm expecting trouble later.' She immediately regretted saying anything. Once again her cheeks heated up and she shifted uncomfortably on the spot. She'd made a complete fool of herself. She glanced away and spotted Fairfax waving at her. She made her excuses, keen to get away. 'Sorry. I think they're waiting for us.'

'Sure. Have a good time.'

She raced off, heart pounding. Alex would think she was an utter idiot, saying dumb stuff and getting drunk. She'd avoid him in the future. He made her feel uncomfortable and she couldn't face any more knocks to her confidence. It was more fragile than she thought.

'Morning,' said Eleanor. She was wearing sunglasses. She lowered them in a conspiratorial manner to reveal bloodshot eyes. 'Hell of a night, eh? You feeling as rough as I do?'

'Not too good,' Chloe confessed.

'You'll both survive,' said Fairfax, leaping into the driver's seat. 'Come on, Chloe. You okay in the back with Ronnie?'

'Thanks. You sure you're happy about him coming along?'

'Of course we are. Hop in.'

She opened the back door and waited for Ronnie to jump in and settle down on the back seat and then joined him. The car was more spacious inside than she'd imagined.

'Off we go.' Fairfax put the car into gear and they drew away. Chloe caught sight of Alex talking to one of the workmen but lowered her gaze. She didn't want to be seen staring out at him.

–

Christmas Tree Farm was an actual working farm that had turned the festive season into a lucrative sideline to its agriculture business. A large wooden sign with a friendly cartoon face of a reindeer welcomed them to the place, and the outside of the farmhouse was lit up with fairy lights trailing down the sides of the worn brickwork. Hand-crafted wooden signposts directed customers to the trees, a Christmas gift shop, a grotto and the reindeer stables.

The Nissan was one of only three cars in the car park. 'You have to see the reindeer first. Then we'll get Ronnie and take him for a walk around the trees,' said Fairfax, leading the way to the stable block where each reindeer was housed.

The smell of warm hay rose to greet her as she entered the covered building. Her headache was waning and she was able to focus on her surroundings. Christmassy harnesses hung on the wall of *Santa's Tack Room* under names of Santa's famous reindeer. In the distance, rustling and the odd grunt indicated the animals were up and about. Someone was there ahead of them – a woman with two small children who clasped pots of reindeer food eager to hand them out. Chloe smiled at the children's faces shining with pure joy. While people bothered her, she never felt ill at ease with young children. Chloe closed in on the pen where a gentle brown face, wearing a harness, pushed away from the other reindeer to nuzzle against her hand, hoping for feed. She had none but moved out of the way so the youngster beside her might hand out his offering.

The place had been cleverly decorated with Santa's chair covered with a furry blanket adjacent to a mock log fire in one corner. Large stockings hung over a mantel-piece and next to the chair, an extremely long scroll – a list of names of children who'd been good. Eleanor gave her a nudge. 'Is your name on there?' she asked with a grin.

Chloe returned it. Memories floated through her mind: of her parents and Georgia singing along to Christmas music on the radio as they extracted baubles and decorations from the cardboard box they kept in the attic, attaching each object – a snowflake Chloe had made at school, a hand-painted red and silver ball purchased on holiday at a German Christmas market and many other objects, each representing a precious memory – to the branches of a pine tree. Christmas did that to you, she mused. It made you think of the past, your childhood and of a time when things seemed perfect. Christmases after her parent's death never felt the same, and William had hated the whole commercial aspect. He'd gone along with whatever she'd wanted to do, and while Nanny Olive was still alive, they'd had her over for Christmas lunch, but it was rarely a truly joyful time. For all her preparations, William would inevitably turn up late for lunch, having been down the pub beforehand, and usually fell asleep before the Queen's speech. It stemmed back to his child-hood, one spent hiding from a stepfather who hated him and a mother who wasn't strong enough to stand up for him. Chloe had understood. Christmas was synonymous with families and neither of them had one to share it with. They only had each other and that had always been enough for her. It hadn't for William.

'Okay, stand over there,' said Fairfax, lifting his mobile and waving it at her. He was pointing at a white-faced reindeer with large brown eyes and long eyelashes, leaning over the barrier.

'You'll need this,' said Eleanor, fishing in her bag and dragging out the headband with the felt antlers Chloe recalled wearing the night before. She was about to ask why when it hit her. She'd agreed to something. What was it? She shuffled over to the animal, antler headband in hand. The nametag around the creature's neck gave her mind the jolt it needed…

'And one of them's called Piper,' says Fairfax,
swaying as he pours the clear liquid into her glass.

59

*It smells wonderfully fruity, of raspberries, but
when she takes a sip, flames shoot down the back
of her throat, making her gasp. Eleanor laughs.*

*'No. You have to knock it back. Like this.'
She chinks her glass against Chloe's and chugs the
liquid in one. Chloe joins her. This time it doesn't
burn.*

*Eleanor holds up her glass towards Fairfax.
'More!'*

*He refills both glasses. Chloe is feeling comfort-
ably numb. Her limbs are heavy and her lips
plumped as if swollen by bee stings that no longer
hurt. For the first time in weeks she feels properly
relaxed and that she could stay in that armchair for
the rest of her life. She accepts the drink and they
all down their glasses. Eleanor speaks again. Her
voice is distant, like she's on a boat or a mountain
far away. Chloe tries to focus on her words but
only catches snippets as they bob away carried on
an invisible breeze.*

*'Event… you'd love it… this week… photo-
graph for profile…perfect with reindeer… please
say yes.'*

*Chloe beams at her new friends. 'Yes,' she says
and they both cheer.*

She stood next to the reindeer called Piper who seemed
content to have a woman wearing a headband by her side.
Fairfax had told her that all the reindeer with antlers are
most likely to be either females or young males as the
older males lose theirs in December. Judging by the size,
this one was female. Piper snorted gently, like a horse, and
Chloe rubbed the animal's snout.

'Say, "I'm a cheery singleton",' called Fairfax and Eleanor encouraged her by mouthing the words.

Chloe's stomach dropped as it dawned on her what she'd actually let herself in for. She'd agreed to join their singleton club and attend their events. One was happening soon. She couldn't for the life of her think what it was. The reindeer pushed at her hand for food. Oh goodness! She'd have to think of a way to pull out of it. She tried to calm her frantic heartbeat. It would be okay. She'd think of something. She'd throw a sickie or say she was too busy. Eleanor was still encouraging her to smile.

'Come on. Don't be shy.'

Chloe forced her lips into a semblance of a smile then said, 'I ought to buy Piper some feed,' and hastened to the kiosk to purchase a small tub. As grateful as she was for Fairfax and Eleanor's kindness, she really couldn't face a room full of people. *Why, oh why had she agreed to this?* She turned back as the young man filled the tub, and spotted her neighbours chatting animatedly to a family. They really were terribly nice people. She couldn't let them down. The young man at the kiosk gave her a wide smile that unnerved her, his eyes trained on her face. She wasn't accustomed to friendliness: Appletree was filled with people who'd lived there all their lives and didn't take to strangers, even if those so-called strangers had lived in the same village for five years. Chloe's only friend had been Faith, while William had managed to muddle along with a group of pub frequenters. If it hadn't been for the book, nobody would have even noticed Chloe as she went about her business.

She was thinking of answering with a smile of her own when he pointed at her head. 'The food for you or the others?' he asked. She lifted her hand, her fingers brushing against the soft felt of the artificial antlers. Instantly tongue-tied, she had no retort. Her voice deserted her. She backed away, wishing the young man would look elsewhere. Heat flooded her veins and turned her face crimson. This was exactly why she didn't go out to such places. Her knees began to buckle slightly and her stomach somersaulted. Thankfully the family who'd been chatting to Eleanor and Fairfax were approaching the kiosk for reindeer food and distracted the man. She stumbled away, ripped the headband off and hastened to the pen to join the peaceful Piper.

—

'It's a beaut!' said Fairfax in an Australian accent.

'Not too big and it even has roots so you can plant it in your garden afterwards to remind you of your first Christmas at Sunny Meadow,' Eleanor said.

Ronnie had run himself ragged and was now panting by Fairfax's feet. The tree trussed up in netting was in the back of the Nissan truck, strapped down with bungee clips, its top overhanging the tailgate. Chloe was feeling more clear-headed, and trudging through woods to the cabin where they selected the tree had been the tonic she needed. They'd walked a man-made track from the wooden shack through dense forestation and out into an opening with far-reaching views over fields and hills, before returning to the car park where the tree was wrapped and waiting beside the car for them. While Fairfax and Ronnie had played with a well-chewed tennis ball, one of his favourite toys, Eleanor had accompanied Chloe into the almost empty gift shop and helped her select all manner of decorations, including a sweet porcelain reindeer with a nametag – Piper.

Chloe climbed back into the truck with a satisfied smile on her face. *You* are *stronger than you think*. She placed an arm around Ronnie and joined in with the others as they sang along to a CD of Christmas music in loud, cheerful voices.

—

'Would you like a coffee or anything?' Chloe offered as they stood beside the erected tree, now in a sensible-sized festive pot she'd obtained from the gift shop.

'Love to but we have to get ready for tomorrow. I bet you're excited about it, aren't you?'

Chloe flushed and mumbled, 'I would be if I could recall what it was I'm supposed to have signed up for.'

Eleanor's lips parted in a wide 'O'. Fairfax clapped his hands together in delight.

'You don't remember at all? Oh, that's priceless! Okay. We'll leave it as a surprise then. Just dress in loose-fitting clothes tomorrow afternoon, come around at four o'clock, and we'll do the rest.'

'Don't leave me guessing,' Chloe pleaded. 'I hate surprises.'

'You'll love this one,' Eleanor said, giving Chloe a hug. 'Trust us.'

As the door banged shut, Chloe turned to her dog. 'What on earth have I let myself in for?'

Ronnie didn't lift his head from his paws but his tail thumped the once.

Chapter Five

After an afternoon spent adorning the tree with new shiny globes and attaching pinecone garlands on the sitting rooms beams, Chloe was feeling an even greater sense of belonging. She collected her mobile phone and Ronnie's lead, intending to walk around the reservoir and then settle down to some writing. A vague idea, like a transparent-winged butterfly, kept flitting across her mind but departed before settling. A walk might be the catalyst she needed to anchor it. Four months had passed since she'd signed the contract with Upfront Publishing and she hadn't come up with anything concrete for the new book. The original plan had been to base it around village gossip supplied by William, much like she had her first book. The local pub was a mine of information but without William in her life, it couldn't happen.

The repetitive hammering coming from the building where she'd first met Alex indicated the men were hard at work. A collection of vehicles scattered haphazardly on the terrain outside the building confirmed there were at least eight men on site. Squinting, she made out two figures stretched out at frightening angles across a bare-timbered roof, and decided they must have either a head for heights or no fear. Chloe wasn't keen on going up stepladders, let alone hanging off a wooden platform attaching slate tiles seventy or eighty feet up. The house was beginning to take shape quickly. Only two days had passed since it had seemed to be little more than a tumble-down cowshed, yet now it was closer to resembling the final result, another smart addition to the development. She wondered who might move in, and hoped they'd be as easy to get along with as Eleanor and Fairfax.

Her phone rang. It was Faith.

'I'm making sure you haven't been eaten by wolves.' Judging by the clinking of glass and modern music in the background Faith was in a trendy bar.

Chloe laughed. 'There aren't any wolves up here.'

'You know what I mean. How's it going?'

'I spent last evening with Eleanor and her husband, Fairfax. They got me blind drunk, and I mean completely plastered.'

Faith released a light chuckle. 'You're really funny when you're drunk. What did you get up to? Did you play hopscotch in their kitchen, using a bar of soap to mark out the numbers on the tiled floor?'

'That was years ago,' Chloe protested, wincing at the memory. She and Faith had had a girl's night in while William was away and it had ended with them playing the ridiculous game.

'Only three.'

'Seems like a lifetime ago. It was mad, wasn't it?'

'Yes, but enjoyable. I hadn't seen you like that before. You should let your hair down more often.'

The comment stung even though Chloe knew her friend was right. She could be too intense for some people. It wasn't deliberate. She merely had trouble loos-ening up unless she had a few drinks.

'When's your bloody internet going to be connected, by the way? I hate this old-fashioned way of communicating. You know I prefer to chat face-to-face, and I wouldn't mind you getting that dishy carpenter over to say hello either.'

'The engineer's due Friday. He has to connect a line from a cable somewhere in the development into the house.'

'Not a minute too soon. That development is like the land time forgot. Beautiful and wild but I could barely get a signal on my mobile let alone any 4G when I was there.'

'It's a dead zone,' Chloe explained.

'Trust you to move to a flipping dead zone. Are you deliberately trying to stay out of contact with everyone?'

'Not at all. I'll be online again soon and we'll chat properly.'

'Good because I miss you.' Faith's words touched Chloe. Without being able to talk online, she'd have felt even lonelier over the last few months. Faith had insisted on regular Skype video calls and helped her through the dreadful period after she'd first found out about William when she was unable to even saunter out for a walk with Ronnie; she'd let him run loose in the garden instead, shutting the door as soon as he returned. Faith had been by her side, albeit virtually through the internet, and had prevented her losing her way completely. She'd be grateful to be connected to the online world and talk to Faith again while actually seeing her face. She preferred the cyber world to the real world at times. Besides, she needed to get some ideas for her book and as Faith had commented, the 4G signal was next to useless on the hill. She'd been so absorbed talking to Faith, she hadn't heard the faint crunching of gravel behind her or the sound of a running engine. She jumped when a voice called out her name. It was Alex leaning out of his Land Rover window, one arm on the steering wheel.

'Chloe, I'm in a hurry. Have to get to the suppliers before they shut.'

She tugged Ronnie out of the path of the vehicle immediately, cheeks on fire. Alex didn't look best pleased at her holding him up and she'd no idea how long he'd been waiting for her to finish talking.

'Sorry,' she mumbled. He didn't wait for her apology and instead wound up the window before racing off down the track, leaving her with the impression she'd annoyed him.

'What's going on? You lost your signal.'

'No. Alex is cheesed off with me for blocking the road,' said Chloe.

'The good-looking one who you fell for – literally!' Faith stifled a snigger.

'Ha! I won't be falling for him again. He has a way of making me feel...'

'What? Sexy?'

Chloe sputtered. 'No. Not at all. In truth I feel awkward and inferior.'

'For crying out loud. You barely know him.'

'It's only a feeling.'

'Well, bury it. Give the guy a chance. His wife chatted to you yet?'

'Not yet.'

'Shame he's married. He's gorgeous.'

'He's not my type.'

'What is your type? Remind me again? The stuck-up-their-own-arse type?'

'Faith, you know what I mean.'

'Yes, and you know what I think about all of this. I know you're not divorced yet, but you *are* separated and you need to have a little fun. You've been behaving like a hermit for far too long. I understand you have issues meeting people but as your number one cheerleader it's my duty to encourage you to make the effort.' She burst into a nonsensical cheerleader chant that ended with the words, 'Go Chloe...Go Chloe... Go!'

'Very good. It's worked. I'm going out tomorrow with a group of single people.' There, she'd said it and committed herself further to the event. There'd be no pulling out now. Faith would want to know every single detail of it.

'Shut the front door!'

Chloe had no idea where her friend had picked up such an expression or what it actually meant. 'I don't know where we're going.'

'This is major. How did Eleanor convince you? Torture you until you agreed?'

'I was drunk.'

'Ah. And now you regret it and will back out. I know you, Chloe Piper. You will find some excuse.'

'No, I'll go.' The clawing in her stomach said otherwise.

Faith's voice became softer. 'Try, hun. I know how hard it is for you but Eleanor will be there, and you don't have to stay if you don't like it. But it might be just what you need right now.'

They chatted for a few minutes longer and Chloe filled in Faith with her news as best she could.

'Maybe this is even the spark you need for the new book,' said Faith. 'Not that I'm pushing you to get it written. I've got your back on this but sometimes, distraction can help clear your mind and with all the crap you've been through the last few weeks, you need that.'

Chloe pulled a face. The problem was unlikely to be fixed by hanging out with a bunch of people she didn't know but she understood Faith was only looking out for her and wanted her to be happy. She was going to explain she had truly hit a writing block that might never be lifted when Faith suddenly said, 'Shit, I have to go. Client's just walked in. Love you.'

Chloe shoved the mobile back in her pocket, thoughts turning to the irritated look on Alex's face.

'Well, if ever I find my muse,' she said to Ronnie, 'I won't be modelling any of my male characters on Alex.'

–

The marshmallows were at the perfect point of melting, half-submerged like mini fluffy icebergs on top of a large mug of hot chocolate. Chloe, dressed in her comfortable baggy writing jumper teamed only with over-the-knee woollen socks, spooned out two white ones and popped them into her mouth where they continued to melt on her tongue. She wriggled her toes in delight. The walk had been exhilarating and with cheeks, lips and chin stinging from the cold air, she'd raced up the hill with Ronnie and now she felt in better spirits. There was nothing to beat an uninterrupted walk on crisp leaves among trees where only light, musical sounds from winter birds could be heard.

She'd smash this novel. All she needed to do was conjure up similar emotions and feelings that had fuelled her thoughts the first time around. She needed to feel her characters and so far, she hadn't been able to summon them up. She had a vague idea about her heroine, who she was tempted to model slightly on her sister, Georgia. Georgia had always been the more adventurous of the two of them – the hyperactive, curious teenager who'd not only been a proficient skier and snowboarder at a very young age, but had obtained her pilot's licence as soon as she hit seventeen. She'd planned to travel, work abroad as a bush pilot or go to Alaska and work with the ice pilots. Nothing fazed Georgia who took after their father, a marine biologist who was also an accomplished pilot and scuba diver.

Georgia had been a shining star – a bright ball of energy. Chloe hadn't tried to compete with her sister; they were chalk and cheese and Chloe had never felt envious of her. Georgia was big-hearted and game for anything, a sister to be proud of. Georgia shouldn't have been on board the plane that tragic day. She should have been with Chloe. She never should have begged to go along with their parents, until finally they caved in and agreed she could be a passenger on the trip. Georgia ought to be alive. If she had been, she'd have been doing amazing things with her life, not hiding away like Chloe. But Chloe was not Georgia. She thought back to the Chloe who made it through school and began working at the book store – a place she loved and where she'd felt comfortable. There'd been a spark of something in that Chloe and she might have managed to become stronger still if she hadn't become so dependent on William. She thought of Nanny Olive's card. Chloe could transform back into that person. She had to reach that point again, and writing this book would help her get there. That's what made beginning the book all the more important.

When she'd written her debut novel, William had provided much of the fodder with stories regaled by his almost nightly trips to the local pub, and she'd drawn on her own passion, unleashed by the man she loved, to develop some of the raunchier scenes. However, with William no longer in her life, she felt unplugged. As if all the ardour inside her had drained away. She couldn't imagine creating such wickedly suggestive scenes for the new book, but try she must.

She aimed the remote control at the television and stared at two naked bodies making out on a wide bed, each groaning with desire. It seemed fake to her ears but research was research, and if this could ignite a flicker inside her she might be able to start writing. The male was dark-haired and broad-shouldered with smouldering eyes that never left his lover's face. He bore a slight resemblance to Alex. She snorted at the thought and lifted the mug of chocolate to her lips, oblivious to the chocolate foam moustache above her lips.

The couple on screen became more physical, their desire more ardent. Chloe shut her eyes and tried to picture her new male protagonist. Would he perform like this? Would he be strong and dominant? Would he have passionate depths or be a cad, a rogue even, who broke hearts? Ronnie suddenly leapt to his feet and began barking. Somebody was at the door. She placed the hot chocolate next to the opened bag of marshmallows on the table and pressed the pause button.

Alex stood on the doorstep, a black handle in one hand. He held it out to her as a peace-offering. She noticed telltale purplish eye bags and his stubble seemed thicker today.

'Hi again. Sorry about earlier. I was in a terrible rush. Stuff had gone wrong on site and I didn't have much time to get it sorted out. I might have sounded a bit brusque. Didn't mean to.'

She gave him a nod.

'I need to change your log burner handle. They're faulty. One fell to pieces on us over at number four. I thought I'd change yours before that happens here. I wouldn't want you to burn yourself. Is it okay if I come in?'

'Sure.' She waved him through, glad that he wasn't annoyed with her for blocking his route. He'd been in a rush, that was all. Overseeing the development must be stressful. She trailed after him into the sitting room and caught sight of her face in the glass reflection of a picture. *What the hell?* She paused to check her face. A creamy brown stain lined her top lip. *Shit!* She licked her finger, rubbed at the foamy mess and peered again at the painting, hoping she'd removed the worst of it. She looked up. *Double shit!* Alex was standing stock still in front of her television set. The image frozen on the screen was of a full-fronted naked man who undoubtedly resembled Alex. She choked an apology and launched for the control to shut off the television set, knocking the marshmallows onto the floor.

'It's not what it seems,' she said, words sticking in her throat as she flicked the off button and tried to shoo Ronnie away from the sweet treats now on the floor to no avail. 'I was looking for inspiration.' She flapped at Ronnie who was snaffling the small marshmallows at speed.

'Well, that bloke certainly isn't leaving anything to the imagination,' Alex said. She tried not to groan. Bending down he deftly unscrewed the handle and replaced it with the new one. Ronnie had hoovered all the marshmallows up and was wagging his tail. Chloe stared at the now empty bag and the huge mug of chocolate and tugged at the baggy jumper which reached mid-thigh. She must look ridiculous in her socks and jumper, face covered in hot chocolate. *She was a complete twonkarina. Why was it that every time he saw her she made such a bad impression, and why hadn't she turned the damn television set off?*

He stood again. 'There you go. That one shouldn't break.' He gave her a grin. 'I'll leave you to your research.'

'It really is,' she offered.

'Sure it is,' he replied with a wink. As he left, whistling, she was torn between the urge to race after him and insist she was only watching the film to help her thought process or hurl a bag of marshmallows at his head. Once again, he'd succeeded in making her feel utterly ridiculous.

Chapter Six

'Reckon I look okay?' Ronnie didn't move. He was sulking in his basket in the kitchen.

'You say all the right things, don't you? She crouched on her haunches. The seams on her jeans stretched tight against her thighs, threatening to pull apart. She hoped they'd hold and whatever was planned for them wouldn't involve too much physical activity. She ruffled the fur on his neck. 'I won't be long. You can have a nice nap and enjoy guarding the house.'

For the umpteenth time she tried to think of some way to pull out of the outing. People who didn't suffer from her condition had no idea of how terrifying it was to meet groups of people. She wiped sweaty palms on her jeans. She had to face up to her fears. She'd be with Eleanor, she reasoned. She could always say she felt ill and leave if it really became impossible *or, here's an idea*, her inner self said, *explain to Eleanor that you have social anxiety disorder that got completely out of hand following the death of your sister and parents, and that meeting more than one or two people at any time sends you into meltdown.* She shook her head. She'd had the chance to do that when they'd first proposed joining the club. It was too late.

The internal turmoil continued. She closed her eyes and thought of Dr Melanie Turnpike, the gentle mild-mannered physician who'd understood her dread in certain situations and tried to help her control what was more than mere shyness…

Dr Turnpike rubs the lenses of her round glasses with a large white cloth. Nanny Olive is in the chair next to Chloe, one cool hand on top of hers. Dr Turnpike smiles warmly at them both. Chloe can't meet her eyes even though she's friendly, and looks down at her school uniform skirt. She hates the way it fans out around her thighs. She hates everything about her uniform and the school she has to attend. Nanny Olive doesn't know the half of what's been happening. All she knows is Chloe cries a lot because of the pain in her stomach. Her forehead is wrinkled and lined with anxiety.

'Chloe is exhibiting the classic symptoms of what we call social anxiety disorder. She blushes easily, feels embarrassed and breaks out in a sweat, or has a panic attack at the thought of mixing with others in a social situation. Is that right, Chloe?'

She nods. She answered all the doctor's questions honestly but now she wonders if that was the right thing to do. Nanny doesn't seem too pleased with the doctor.

'People who have this disorder often suffer physical symptoms too: stomach problems, maybe diarrhoea and muscle tension and I believe Chloe's digestive issues and muscular pain are arising from her anxieties.'

Nanny squeezes her hand.

'There's no one thing that causes social anxiety disorder. Sometimes genetics is likely to have something to do with it, maybe there's another family member with social phobia?'

Nanny wets her lips before answering in a stiff tone. 'There's no one in our family with it.'

The doctor continues. 'Well then, it could also be linked to having an overactive amygdala which is the part of the brain that controls the fear response, or it could be something else.' She pauses for an instant and Chloe knows instinctively what she's going to tell Nanny Olive. 'If we consider what has happened over the last year — the loss of her parents and sister and then having to attend a new, unfamiliar school — it is unsurprising that this has occurred, Mrs Piper.'

It seems strange hearing Nanny Olive addressed as Mrs Piper. Chloe thinks of another Mrs Piper — her mother — now gone forever and swallows hard. Maybe she ought to have told the doctor about what's been happening at school: the name-calling, pupils stealing her lunch money and pens and ridiculing her for her accent.

'Social anxiety disorder can be linked to a history of bullying, teasing or abuse.' Her words are serious and heavy but Nanny Olive shakes her head.

'She's not been abused. What are you saying? I hurt her? Her parents hit her?'

'I'm not suggesting any of that for one minute. I'm merely explaining what can trigger such a condition and in Chloe's case there are several factors: the loss of her parents and sister and then moving from a very familiar environment to another quite different one. Chloe is struggling with it all, Mrs Piper.'

Nanny has two fire-red spots on her cheeks. 'Are you saying I can't look after my granddaughter properly?'

The doctor holds up both her hands. 'Not at all, Mrs Piper. I think the change of school has been a real issue for her.'

'I'm sure it has, but she has to go to school, hasn't she? What else am I to do? Home educate her?'

'Please, there's no reason to get defensive, Mrs Piper. I'm sure you're doing an admirable job.'

'Don't you patronise me. You've no idea what we've been through. Both of us. Come on, Chloe love. There's nothing more to be gained from sitting here.'

'Please, don't go. We haven't discussed how best to treat Chloe.'

'What do you suggest? Drugs?' Nanny's voice has changed and become hostile, her eyes narrow slits.

'Well, there's some antidepressant medication available that might help but I was going to suggest cognitive behavioural therapy with a therapist.'

'Antidepressants? A therapist? She's not crazy, you know. She's a lonely, sad little girl who's lost her family. She doesn't need behavioural therapy. She needs time. She needs to adjust. That's all.'

'With the greatest of respect...' the doctor began.

Nanny pushes back her chair and tugs at Chloe's hand. Her eyes have filled with tears. 'With the greatest of respect, I shall look after my granddaughter. Good day.'

Nanny had never entirely grasped what was happening to Chloe until it had taken full hold, and at sixteen Chloe had finally been put on a treatment programme. Poor Nanny had never forgiven herself for not acting sooner. Up until recently, Chloe had had it under a certain amount of control. She could cope with a few people at a time and as long as she didn't have to face crowds or new people alone, she could get by. William's deception had sent her spiralling backwards. His actions had brought back the insecurity and self-doubts that had plagued her in her youth. This time it was harder to fight them off. She knew what was happening to her but powerless to bat away the phobias. Her daily meditation wasn't working and without internet she couldn't contact the online support groups upon whom she had come to rely. Her stomach lurched. She had to try and battle against the panic that threaten to flood her body with an uncomfortable warmth and make her heart beat uncontrollably quickly until she thought she'd pass out. She had to fight it and go out and meet new people.

In spite of the pep talk she'd given herself, she couldn't face the day trip out to meet the other singletons. The fear had beaten her again. She picked up her mobile to ring Eleanor.

'I'll say you're ill,' she told Ronnie who ignored her. 'Okay, maybe that's bad karma. I don't want you to be ill. I'll say I have to go out to an appointment.'

The phone was slippery with sweat. She released a lengthy sigh. How she hated being like this. She dialled

Eleanor's number and cursed. There was no signal in the room. She made her way into the kitchen, studying her phone, waiting for a bar to appear. She waved it high and low but there was no signal until she reached the front door where she breathed in deeply, ready to make her excuse and tried dialling again. Pharrell William's *Happy* was suddenly audible, followed quickly by Eleanor's voice.

'You're keen, aren't you? Don't panic. We're right outside your front door.'

She looked through the small square of glass and sure enough, Eleanor was there, phone pressed to her ear and wide smile on her face. There was no getting out of it.

–

Fairfax and Eleanor weren't giving anything away and it wasn't until they turned into the car park at the snowdome that Chloe had an idea of the activity planned.

'I'm really no good on skis,' she said. 'Terrible sense of balance.' She blushed at the memory of the ski school in Aviemore, Scotland, where they'd headed for a long weekend, of hands scrabbling for William's jacket sleeve as she slid downhill backwards on the nursery slopes, screeching for help before falling on her backside in front of a small group of children who were no older than three and who had skied around her with a skill she'd never possess. It had been the only time they'd been on a skiing trip.

'You're not skiing,' said Eleanor. 'Now. Let's see who's here.'

Chloe chewed at a nail. Her heart was beating so loudly she was sure Eleanor could hear it. Her neighbour picked up on her sudden nerves. 'They're just as worried about meeting up as you are. It's always strange the first time you come to these events but we make them easy so you don't feel awkward. I'd really like you to meet Sean Campbell first. He owns a bookshop, *A New Chapter*, in Uttoxeter. It's only a small establishment but it's charming and I happen to know he's on the lookout for some assistance there. After what you told us about your previous job, it might suit you.'

Chloe nodded dumbly. She'd told them about working in a bookshop. She clearly hadn't said anything about being a writer. At least that was something.

'And there he is,' said Eleanor waving furiously at a man in a black beanie hat and a black wax jacket.

Sean responded with a small nod and came towards them. At about six foot, he towered a good half a foot over Chloe.

'Sean, meet Chloe,' said Eleanor.

'Recognised you from your photo on the website,' he responded, large hand extended. His voice was melodic and with a transatlantic twang.

Chloe shook it. It was a firm, warm handshake. She flushed. 'I'm the one with fake antlers,' she said and immediately wished she hadn't. Why did she always come out with such dumb statements? Sean smiled politely, heightening her discomfort further as she felt he was only humouring her.

'I think that's Jacqueline's,' said Eleanor, pointing out a red Ducati motorbike near the entrance. 'Let's go and check. We're due to meet at reception.'

They crossed the short distance from the car park to the main entrance. Chloe cringed at her rubbish comment about the antlers and wished she could turn around and go home.

'Chloe's heavily into books,' said Eleanor.

'Are you?' His large blue eyes crinkled behind his steel-rimmed glasses. 'What genre are you into?'

'Most really: classics, romance, historical fiction, thrillers. You hand me a book and I'll read it cover to cover.'

'Favourite author?'

'Enid Blyton. As a child, she offered me the best escapism possible.'

He nodded approvingly. They'd entered the snow-dome. Talking about books had briefly interrupted her concerns, but once again Chloe was aware of a drumming in her ears as she spotted the small gathering of people. She fought back the sudden urge to flee. Sean and Fairfax now flanked her and to run would be impossible. A rush of air cooled her as a woman in a bright red woollen coat and red gloves that matched her hair arrived in a rush. 'Sorry everyone. Traffic was bad and I was so nervous I needed to go to the loo first,' she panted. Chloe concentrated on her breathing. Eleanor greeted everyone warmly and fell into hostess mode with ease.

'Looks like we've all made it,' said Eleanor. 'Thank you all for coming and I hope you all have a terrific time. As most of you know, it's called *Speedy Speed Skating Date* but as with all our events, there's a difference. You'll see how it works once you come through to the ice rink. It's ours for the next couple of hours. If you'd like to collect your skates from the lodge over there we'll get started.'

Sean picked up the conversation about authors, distracting her from the warm bodies around her, and before she knew it, Chloe found herself in the queue. She'd never skated before but if past performance on skis was anything to go by, she'd be on her backside within a few seconds of getting on the ice. She clenched her teeth tightly together to stop them from chattering. Sean was talking in an easy slow manner about classics he enjoyed and how as a child he'd read extensively. He attended a local book club and this month they were reading the Golden Man Booker Prize winner, *The English Patient* by Michael Ondaatje. He also ran a book review blog and posted about latest releases from many new authors who were on virtual book tours. It was soon her turn to collect her footwear for the rink.

'Size six,' she said and received a pair of ice skates. She stared at them miserably. Sean caught her expression.

'Never skated before, huh?'

She shook her head.

'Half of the secret to skating is to lace the boots up properly,' he whispered. 'Don't tell anyone here but I'm a pro at this. Ice hockey is Canada's national winter sport. I grew up wearing blades.'

They made their way into the cool ice rink area, a domed arena with maroon stepped seating for spectators. The others were talking in low voices as if in church, frightened their voices would echo around the large space. Three women aged somewhere between thirty and fifty were grouped together on the front benches, hunched forward pulling on boots. The woman with bright red hair had removed her coat to reveal a red jumpsuit and was chatting effortlessly to a bear of a man with neck-length black hair and bushy eyebrows. Other members were scattered, some experimenting standing on their skates for the first time whilst clinging to the handrail. Chloe and Sean took a vacant bench.

'First thing is to position yourself correctly when you put the boot on,' Sean said in a lazy, low drawl. 'Loosen the laces and press your foot firmly into the skate, then take hold of both laces, one in each hand, extend your leg enough so you can rest your weight on the heel of the boot with your toes pointed slightly upward.' He demonstrated with his own skate. Chloe stared at the bright pink socks he was wearing. 'My daughter's' he said. 'Mine all had holes in them.'

'How old is she?'

'Suzy's thirteen. Well, thirteen going on twenty.' he replied.

Chloe felt herself ease in his company. He didn't mind if somebody saw he was wearing pink socks. She liked that and the fact he was clearly proud of his daughter. His eyes lit up when he spoke about her.

'Now tighten the laced part and loop your first two fingers through the lace here and grabbing the laces firmly, push down with the ball of your foot while still pulling up on the laces.'

He continued to demonstrate and showed her how to take up the slack afterwards and how to deal with the excess lace.

'Don't want to trip up on those,' he commented.

The boots felt comfortable. He grinned. 'Now you won't fall over.'

Fairfax addressed them all.

'Welcome again. I knew this would be the first time you'd all meet each other so we thought we'd provide an event to help *break the ice*.' He waited for the groans and they came. He held up his hands. 'I'm also sure some of you have never been on skates before so we're going to make this an easy event, as easy as possible. Travis!'

A young man emerged from a side entrance to the ice. He was pushing a large plastic polar bear with a comical face.

'These are adult skating aids and today you'll be using them to make your way around the ice, unless of course you suddenly feel all Torvill and Dean about it and decide to perform the *Bolero*.' Catching the look on a couple of blank faces he added, 'You need to be of a certain age to appreciate that reference.'

Eleanor joined in. 'We're going to start with a speed skate date. You'll all find a partner and together, using the skating aid, skate around the arena once. During that time, you should try and find out as much as you can about each other. When you get back to the start, you'll swap partners. Those on the left will move to the bear behind.' She paused for effect and was pleased to see a few smiles. 'Everyone will get the chance to skate with everyone else, men and women. This is the opportunity to learn something about each other and to help each other around the ice, of course.'

The young man had brought out three more polar bears that now stood in front of the group. He added another one and moved to the side of the rink.

'Grab a partner – any partner,' said Eleanor. 'Let's start with boy-girl couples.'

Sean looked at Chloe. 'Be my partner?'

'Thanks. I'd like that.'

They drifted onto the ice, Chloe taking tentative baby steps. Sean gave her his hand to hold onto and guided her to the nearest polar bear. She clung onto the handle behind it, legs wobbling slightly.

'Just fixate on staying upright,' he said with a smile. 'I'll glide us around. The best thing is not to be stiff. Just try to relax and enjoy.'

They set off ahead of the others, Sean talking all the while. 'So, I own a bookshop in Uttoxeter called *A New Chapter*.'

'Eleanor told me. She knew I worked in a bookstore for a while.'

'That figures. Hence you're a reader.'

'I've always been a big reader. Started young,' she said, trying hard not to think about dark nights on Skye, curled up on the settee with the old table lamp throwing a warm yellow glow onto the pages of her latest adventure, and Georgia in the faded leather chair opposite, flipping through a magazine.

'Once a reader...' he grinned. She looked up at him and then wobbled, feet trying to skid from under her. Behind them came laughter. Sean continued, oblivious to it. 'You know about me. I'm originally from Canada – Toronto – been divorced for three years and my daughter stays with me once a week. I joined the events company because my daughter said I needed to get out more and meet people. Apparently, it's not cool to spend all the time at home reading or writing blog posts. What about you? Your turn.'

She'd been listening so intently to Sean, she'd not stumbled once but now the focus was on her, she felt her feet give way and she slid to the floor.

'Up you get,' he said, putting strong hands under her arms and lifting her effortlessly until she was upright once more. 'Hang on tightly. I probably pushed a little too fast.'

'No. It was me. I'm still finding it hard to get about.'

'Doing great for a first-timer,' he said. 'So, come on.'

'Not much to say. You already know I like reading. I've recently separated from my husband and live on the same development as Eleanor and Fairfax, who convinced me to join up after I got rather drunk on their homemade raspberry liqueur. I don't have a job but I do have a dog.' She kept her eyes downcast. She could feel Sean's gaze burning into her. He glided effortlessly at her side, slightly turned to face her. She focused on moving her feet, little by little. Holding onto the skating aid gave her more confidence and with Sean pushing it ahead of them, she wasn't finding the skating too difficult.

'You'd be very welcome at the bookshop. It's conveniently placed in the pedestrian high street right in the centre of town. I like to think of it as a haven for people to enjoy quiet time browsing and reading. There's a special reading area. It's open every weekday with the exception of Wednesday afternoons. That's when I collect Suzy from school in Birmingham and she stays over. I'd rather keep it open, especially as there's a toddlers club who want to use it to read to the little ones, but what can you do? I really could do with an assistant.'

She knew he was hoping she'd volunteer. She'd enjoyed working at the book store near Birmingham. It had been an antiquated shop: a labyrinth of rows of dark wooden bookcases and a spiral staircase to the second floor where all the non-fiction was housed. The people who'd frequented the place had all been regulars and Chloe had been content to work there. There was something about bookshops that put her at ease.

'Tell you what, why don't you drop by sometime and see if you like the place?'

She thanked him although part of her knew she'd not manage the challenge of going through a busy town to reach it. By now, they'd completed a circuit of the ice rink and it was time to change partners. She'd enjoyed talking to Sean and was reluctant to move on, but the rules dictated they did so. Her next companion, the huge man with dark hair and unkempt eyebrows, soon shuffled into place next to her. She took hold of the handle, preparing to skate. He spoke as he joined her.

'Hi, I'm Robert. Call me Rob though.'

'Chloe.'

'Nice name.'

'Thanks.'

'I think the best way to get to know each other is to ask a load of questions.'

'Sure. Go ahead.' They pushed off, each easing forward gingerly.

'Mars bars or jelly babies?'

'What?'

'Which do you prefer?'

'Jelly babies.'

The man grunted approvingly. 'Me too. Football or tennis?'

'Neither. I'm not a sports fan.'

'I love American football or soccer as they call it. Big Chicago Bears fan. You play any sports?'

'No.'

He shook his head. 'Okay. Not sports then. Classical music or rock?'

'I quite like pop although I'm pretty easy about most musical genres.'

'I'm definitely into rock: The Rolling Stones, Def Leppard, Guns N' Roses. Usually try to get to their concerts when they're performing in the UK. Love a bit of rock. I play air guitar too. I came twenty-fifth in the air guitar championships.'

Chloe went for a small smile. He was at least trying to engage her in conversation even if they didn't have much in common. His next question threw her.

'Cabbage Patch dolls or Barbie?'

She glanced up to see if he was joking but his face was serious.

'I'm not into dolls.'

'I meant when you were younger,' he said with a sudden smile that revealed very even, slightly yellowed teeth.

'Oh, erm. I wasn't really into dolls then either. I had a collection of Pound Puppies and My Little Ponies.'

'No dolls?' he said.

'No. You had a doll?' she asked, expecting him to say he owned an Action Man.

'Oh yes. I had Barbie and all the Rock Star dolls. My mother didn't believe in stereotyping through toys and encouraged me to play with dolls, plastic ovens, makeup sets, anything really. She didn't want to foster a sexist attitude.'

'Commendable.'

'And healthier for a child,' he replied. 'Okay, here's an easy one, dogs or cats?'

'Definitely dogs. I have one.'

'I've got two cats – Smokey and Tigger. They're my cute little fur babies,' he said in an icky voice, completely at odds with his looks. Chloe couldn't think of an appropriate response. His face had taken on the look of a proud parent.

'Got some gorgeous outfits for them too. Last Halloween, I dressed Smokey up as a little bat and Tigger as a pumpkin and took them trick-or-treating. They were so adorable and we got a bucketload of sweets.'

Chloe shut her mouth that had fallen open. Rob continued talking about his cats and all the things they got up to.

'Sometimes, I hold them up to the mirror, just so they see how pretty they are. You ever do that with your dog?'

'He's a bit big for that and I expect he'd just bark at himself, thinking it was another dog in the mirror.'

'See, that's the difference between cats and dogs. Dogs are less intelligent, aren't they?'

They'd reached the end of the circuit and Chloe was glad to change partners. Rob had been intense. She took a deep breath. *So far so good* she told herself. She was meeting new people and the urge to flee wasn't as strong, what with concentrating on not falling over and listening to cordial people chat about themselves. She looked up briefly as the woman wearing the red jumpsuit skated into place. Her face creased into a smile as she took hold of the handle and spoke.

'Only fallen on my arse three times. Pretty good, eh? Hi. I'm Jacqueline,' she said.

'Chloe Piper.'

Jacqueline nodded. 'Tigers or elephants?' She grinned widely at Chloe's startled face. 'I met Robert, call me Rob the Rocker, first. I think he's trying to frighten off everyone with his chat up lines. Did he tell you about his cats?'

Chloe nodded.

'I thought so. Poor man. I reckon he's lonely. So, what about you?'

Chloe told her the same thing she'd told Sean.

'That's shitty. It's really tough when you come out of a relationship. It feels raw for a while.'

Chloe thought that was an appropriate word.

'I left my husband five years ago. He wasn't cheating or anything. He was a good man. I just got bored. Dreadful thing to admit, isn't it? We got hitched when we were eighteen – way too young. By the time I got to almost thirty, I figured our relationship had run its course. I packed my bags and went travelling. Took my bike over to Mexico and got on the road north to south. Got it all out of my system. I'm ready to settle down again now, but of course, it's not so easy to find somebody when you're a bit older and out of the dating game, so this seemed like a good thing to do – sign up, make friends, and see what develops. You got your eye on anyone here today?'

'No. I'm not ready for that yet.'

'Yeah. Give it time. You need to find yourself first. I know that sounds a bit new-age, but it's true. When you share somebody's life for years, you can't help but grow into one fused person. It's tough to break apart again. You have to take some time to remember who *you* are.'

Chloe thought that sounded sensible. In some ways, Jacqueline reminded her of Faith. She warmed to her.

'Oh-oh, I think that guy likes you.' Jacqueline nodded at Sean who'd sailed past with a new partner, a pretty girl with dark curls and a fresh face.

'How do you know that?'

'The way he beamed over here as he went past. I'm pretty certain he wasn't grinning at me. Shame. He's hot. I'd let him ride pillion with me any day.'

'That's Sean. He was my first ice partner. He's very nice. He's Canadian but lives over here.'

They moved away. Jacqueline had an easy manner and Chloe soon found herself chuckling at her stories about her crazy trip through Mexico. As they drew to a halt, Jacqueline looked across at Rob now accompanying a woman called Neats, who he completely dwarfed. She chuckled deeply. 'You know who he reminds me of?' she waited for Chloe to shake her head. 'A Bond villain. I can picture him sitting at home behind a desk, stroking a white fluffy cat.'

Chloe couldn't help but laugh at the image and as she and Jacqueline parted, she realised she wasn't feeling so nervous about talking to these people any more.

Chapter Seven

Thursday, 21st December

'And then we played a game called *Four Corners* where each corner of the ice-skating rink was numbered and by each corner there was an ice skate containing numbers. We had to skate around to music and when the music stopped make our way to one of the corners. Eleanor chose a corner at random and a person there pulled out a piece of paper from the skate, call it out and everyone standing at the corner that had been called was out of the game. The person would replace the paper and we'd go around again. Sean won. He's such a good skater, he got to the corners faster than the rest of us.'

'Sounds bonkers,' said Faith. 'However, you've managed to mention the name Sean at least six times during this conversation, so that bodes well. Tell me more about this mysterious, handsome Canadian.'

'I've already told you everything and don't sound so animated about it. He's just a nice guy.'

'Ye-es,' said Faith in a knowing tone.

'That's all.'

'Come on, Chloe, didn't you fancy him a little bit?'

'Like I said. He was really nice. A proper gentleman. I didn't fancy him. He – well – he just didn't excite me in that way.'

'Okay. I'll wait to hear what manifests when you visit him at his bookshop. You're not going to take him up on his sort of job offer, are you? I need you behind your laptop, grafting on the new novel, not sitting behind a desk reading Jilly Cooper.'

'Jilly Cooper?'

'Well, if you are going to be stuck in a bookshop, read something that'll give you some inspiration for your own book. *Barnaby Rudge* or *The Pickwick Papers* are hardly likely to get your pulse racing and ignite any sparks in your imagination, are they?'

'Dickens? You mentioned two novels by Dickens. I thought you hated classics.'

'They just happened to be first two books that sprung to mind. I was listening to a radio presenter interview Celia Wainwright last night and Dickens came up in the conversation.'

'Oh, right.'

Celia was an up-and-coming writer of women's fiction whose debut novel had gained notoriety. Faith sounded vaguely apologetic that Celia had been interviewed on a radio show and not Chloe. It wasn't Faith's fault. Chloe hadn't made herself available for interviews, and there was no doubt that hiding away on the hill wasn't going to do her career any good. It had been fine up until recently. The identity of the author of *Spank Me Harder, Vicar* had been kept under wraps. No one had been able to uncover any facts about C J Knight, which worked in Chloe's favour. There was no way she wanted to face book clubs and interviewers or turn up for book signings or anything that involved engaging with others. It's not that she wasn't grateful to her readers. She truly was, but the prospect of going to such gatherings and mixing and worst of all, talking about herself, was one step too far for Chloe.

Faith had actively encouraged her anonymity, not merely so the villagers of Appletree wouldn't storm her house, but it was a terrific marketing tool. It had added a layer of intrigue to the whole process and Faith had remained coyly tight-lipped whenever she was asked to reveal the true identity of the author behind the book. Faith had handled all the interviews herself, talking about the talented C J Knight and even suggesting the author might be male. However, with Chloe's cover now partially blown and a few people – largely those in the village of Appletree – in the know as to who had written it, Chloe had less reason to keep a low profile, yet that was what she wanted to do.

'Was it any good? The interview?'

Faith paused. 'Yes. Celia was very enigmatic. There was a significant spike in sales of her book immediately after the broadcast.'

Chloe waited in case she was pressed further to appear on a show herself, but Faith sidestepped the issue, leaving Chloe wondering if her friend was losing confidence in her. Agents worked for their authors, trying to get them good publicity as well as deals with publishing houses, and Faith had done her bit for Chloe. She had other writers who needed her attention far more than a hopeless one who was not only reluctant to face her readers but couldn't drum up a second novel.

'I'd better get on with some writing then,' said Chloe.

Faith perked up. 'You started?'

'Yes.' The lie stuck in her throat.

'That's great.'

'I'll chat again soon.'

'Skype me as soon as you're online. You can run the plot past me.'

Chloe ended the call with a promise she would. After she hung up the phone she heaved a sigh. She couldn't put it off any longer. She'd have to get some ideas down and start working on a new manuscript, even if what she wrote was rubbish. She couldn't fib again to her friend, especially if it was face-to-face online. Faith would immediately see through her.

She settled down in front of her desk and began…

Laila MacDonald blinked hard but still stars exploded in front of her eyes.

'You okay?' The voice was low and filled with concern.

'I think so.' Her voice seemed to come from far away as if it wasn't her own. Was she dreaming? With a sudden clarity she recalled what had happened. She'd been skating, floating across the pure ice-blue frozen lake, like a gliding bird, faster and faster, revelling in the sense of freedom that the activity always brought. She'd been coming to the lake every winter, ever since she was a teenager. She'd ingested the cold air, right into her lungs and lifted her head to the clear skies. In her opinion, Canada was at its most beautiful during winter. As usual, she'd laced up her skates tightly and cautiously stepped out onto the ice where she'd twirled and danced and glided until… until she'd collided with something or someone.

'I called out. You didn't hear me.' Her eyes began to focus on his wide mouth – lips plump and reddened by the cold air and then onto his

eyes, the colour of honeycomb, and onto his dark
curled hair. Her heart jumped.

'I'm fine,' she said.

He held out a large hand to help her up. 'I
think you should get that looked at. It looks deep.'

She glanced at her knee, now crimson...

Chloe groaned loudly as she read through the chapter. It was utter crap. Saving the document so she wouldn't be lying to Faith, she turned off the laptop and went into the kitchen where she grabbed a bag of honeycomb dipped chocolates and munched on a few. Ronnie looked up hopefully.

'Not a chance, matey. Chocolate's bad for dogs,' she said. 'Don't suppose you fancy a new outfit for Christmas, instead? I could dress you up as an elf or a Christmas tree or a yuletide log.'

She put the bag out of Ronnie's way. She ought to take her dog out. The skies were darkening and if they didn't go soon, she'd get soaked. *Anything to get out of writing.* With coat and wellington boots on and the dog on his lead, she strode out over the fields. The chill wind stung her face and lips but Ronnie didn't seem to notice as he snuffled under bushes and spun around to get the scent of animals who'd trailed the same path before him. Chloe had to keep stopping to untangle the lead from his legs. She decided to follow the right of way path leading towards a small hamlet rather than trudge around the reservoir. After a quarter of an hour she stopped and looked back at her home, a tiny doll's house of a place with large welcoming windows lit by the lamps she'd left on. It was charming. She really couldn't have chosen a better place or location. From her vantage point here, she could see Eleanor and Fairfax's house with drapes at the French windows and a tall Christmas tree lit up in the window. Beyond that was the long barn where she'd stumbled and met Alex, and further away still the roof of his house.

As she pulled her woollen hat further down over her ears she wondered if she would ever feel as comfortable there as she had done in her old home, if William and Lilly had put up a tree in the same spot it had always stood, and if they'd adorned it with the silver and red baubles she and William had bought together.

She sighed. Christmas was a lousy time to be suddenly single. She looked again at her own property with its neat roof and arched windows and was struck by how inviting it appeared to be. Smoke curled from the chimney, the grey wisps thinning into strands until they disappeared into the atmosphere. It would be toasty inside, and when she got back she'd plug in the lights on her own tree, stick on some Christmas music and treat herself to some mulled wine. A gust of wind shook the empty branches of the oak tree and three crows flew overhead. Ronnie strained at his lead, eager to cover more distance. She yanked on it.

'Come on, boy. Time to go home.'

–

'Oh, I like this one,' she said to a disinterested Ronnie as she turned up the radio to listen to Brenda Lee's *Rockin' around the Christmas Tree*. After a large glass of mulled wine, she was feeling more enthusiastic about the festive season and had wrapped Ronnie's presents ready for the actual day when she and Ronnie would unwrap their gifts – hers from Faith – and tuck into a turkey breast roll she'd order once the internet was up and running.

She increased the volume and began twirling about the kitchen. She and William had danced a lot in their house when they were first married. After dinner, he'd often sweep her into his arms and smooch with her to a love song. The early days had been the best. She shut her eyes and thought back to the time when her arms would have been around the nape of his neck, fingers caressing his hair and her head on his shoulder, while his own arms would have been around her, pulling her closer to him until she could feel their hearts beating rhythmically as one. That had been before the misery. She shook herself free of the memory. Soon she'd be picturing Lilly and William swaying together and she wasn't going to allow herself to tumble into gloom. She snatched up the reindeer antler headband she'd worn at the Christmas Tree Farm and put it on, singing along to the song as she did so. 'Come on, Ronnie. Join me,' she shouted and patted her thighs to encourage him. Sure enough, he picked up on her enthusiasm and scurried over, where he weaved in between her legs.

Dancing left and then right, she raised her arms and moved them in time to the music, skilfully avoiding his paws. 'You're a good dancer.' They continued until the end of the song, when she stopped and curtseyed for him. 'Thank you for the dance.' She laughed at his face, tongue now hanging from his mouth and patted him, then turned away and caught sight of two amused faces at the window. One was a gaunt-faced man in a khaki-green jacket, holding an enormous metal case. The other was Alex.

Face beetroot red, she opened the kitchen door. She could barely look Alex in the eye. The man next to him was struggling to keep the grin from his face.

'Hi. I was – um – well…'

Alex intervened quickly and saved her from an awkward explanation. 'Sorry to interrupt your training for *Britain's Got Talent*, but the telephone engineer is here. He came to my door by mistake.'

'Oh, I wasn't expecting you until tomorrow.'

'Weather looks bad for tomorrow and I was in the area so I thought I'd get you online today. Not inconvenient is it?'

'Gosh. No.'

'I love *Britain's Got Talent*. You really going on it?' The man was goggle-eyed at the revelation.

'Oh yes, she is. Ronnie can perform a few dances. Which routine was that, Chloe? Rock 'n' Roll?'

'Yes, that was it,' she mumbled.

'Get on! Well, I'll be blowed.' He studied Ronnie who wagged his tail. 'When are you on the show?'

'She's not allowed to say, are you, Chloe? She signed a disclaimer.'

'That's right,' Chloe said slowly. Alex winked at her. He'd been helping her save face.

'I'll be glued to it and cheering you on when you perform. What's his name?'

'Ronnie.'

'Ronnie, eh? What a clever dog, you are, Ronnie.'

Ronnie barked once.

'He understands me. Brilliant. Okay. I'll start out here. Just got to fit a cable through your window frame. Where do you want your modem?'

'In the utility room. It's behind the kitchen. If you walk around the house, you'll see a small window. That's it.'

The man wandered off.

'I'll leave him with you,' he said. 'Hope you've got some provisions in. It looks like we might be cut off if the forecasters are right.'

'No, I haven't. I was going to shop online.'

'You'll get no deliveries up that slope once it starts. You've probably got time to nip out to the supermarket in town before the snow settles.'

'Er, well. Yes. Thank you.' She couldn't divulge her condition. He wouldn't understand why she hated supermarkets and besides, he'd already helped her look less of a twit than she felt. 'Thanks for... you know,' she added.

'It was nothing. You do realise he'll be telling everyone he knows about the woman on the hill whose dog is appearing on that talent show?'

She giggled.

'He's going to be disappointed when you don't appear. Unless you enter last minute. I reckon Ronnie could pull off a mean Salsa.'

'He'd stand more of a chance of winning if he could twerk,' she replied.

The smile broadened. 'I'd pay money to see that! Best get off. We're shutting down the site for the time being and the lads are leaving. I want to make sure everything's secure before they go. Oh, one last thing, you might want to remove the antlers before you talk to the telephone engineer again,' he whispered.

'Oh no!' She tugged at the headband.

'Don't forget to give him Ronnie's autograph before he goes.' He left with an airy wave.

Chapter Eight

Chloe stared out of the window at the completely white scene. Snow covered every inch of her land, turning it from a muddy mess to a magical wonderland. The wind had howled all night and brought with it copious amounts of fluffy white flakes that had now drifted into piles against the hedgerows and tree trunks. Alex had been right when he said they'd be cut off. There was no way she'd get off the hill. She ought to have taken his advice and gone to the shops, but after the engineer had left she hadn't been able to make herself go to the supermarket.

'Looks like we'll both be sharing your dog biscuits,' she said as she pulled out a box of Bonios. 'I suppose it won't hurt me to go on a diet.' She ran a hand over her round stomach and sighed. She'd piled on weight. She really ought to sort herself out and shed a few pounds. This might be the opportunity she needed. A Christmas detox.

She checked her supplies: two apples, an orange, four bags of honeycomb chocolate dips, four bottles of wine, two leftover mince pies and a box of cereal. She'd survive. She'd foolishly pinned her hopes on getting a food delivery in spite of Alex's advice, and had spent an enjoyable hour shopping online, choosing all manner of exciting edibles for the festive season. She thought about the ham joint and specially prepared turkey breast she'd ordered for their Christmas lunch, and the extra fruity plum pudding and custard she'd planned on eating as dessert. Looking at the build-up of snow outside, she'd be lucky if it turned up by the new year.

Grabbing a bag of chocolate dips, she headed for the office. She had to write something more before Faith Skyped her. She popped a large piece of honeycomb into her mouth and let it melt until it oozed onto her teeth and stuck them together, then she chewed. At the same time her fingers flew over the keyboard.

> *Laila MacDonald breathed in deeply. There was something about libraries that dragged her to far distant lands and venues she'd never visited but had read about. Books had a special smell: it was the scent of escapism. She lifted the tome from the nearest shelf and squinted at the title, Alice's Adventures in Wonderland. She turned the page and read 'Illustrated by Salvador Dali'.*
>
> *'It's a 1969 Maecenas Press/Random House edition, signed by the artist. There are only 2,500 copies in circulation. Unfortunately, I don't have the leather Solander box it originally came in, or it would be worth far more. One sold recently for over twenty thousand dollars.' He rested casually against the library door frame, a smile on his face.*
>
> *Laila stared at the volume. 'Twenty thousand dollars?'*
>
> *'There are books here worth more than that, first editions I've accumulated over the years, but the one you're holding is one of my favourites.*

It contains twelve illustrations from the painter himself, and next to books, art is my love.'

Her eyes opened ever wider. Dorian was a man full of surprises, from his mansion high on the hill with its vast collection of books housed in a library she could have happily lived in, to his handsome face with its amber eyes that glittered hungrily as he approached her. Her insides squirmed at the intensity of his gaze which fell to her shoulders and dropped lower, little by little, until she felt her body stroked by one longing regard.

'Do you dance?' he asked.

She laughed openly. 'Why?'

He produced a small remote control from behind his back, aimed it at a shelf, and from speakers hidden somewhere within the walls, came the sound of an orchestra playing one of her favourite songs, Lady in Red. 'Dance with me,' he whispered as he swept her into his arms. A warm hand found the small of her back and pushed her closer to his muscled chest and they sashayed gently in front of the shelves, in time to the music.

Faith's flashing avatar accompanied by the familiar Skype ringtone announcing the video call broke Chloe's train of thought. She saved the manuscript and turned on the camera icon.

'Yay! You're back in the land of the living! And a day sooner than expected. I was so happy to get your email this morning. So, what's happening?' Faith sat back in her leather chair. Her hair was scooped up from her elfin face and huge red and purple earrings that complemented the red blouse she was wearing, dangled from her neat lobes.

'Nice earrings,' said Chloe.

'These are as festive as I intend to get; I flatly refused to wear Christmas baubles like Maisie,' she replied with a grin. Maisie was her assistant, a comely woman in her fifties who worked mornings only and who was renowned for her outrageous dress sense. 'She's also wearing a Christmas jumper – of a snowman, no less, with red leather shorts and black knee-high boots!' Faith whispered.

Chloe smiled at the thought. Maisie didn't care what stares she attracted. She was her own woman and if she felt like coming to work in a see-through negligee and Doc Martens, she probably would.

'Still got her buzz cut?'

'No, she's growing it out so she can have it cut into a Mohawk. Apparently they're very fashionable at the moment. Now, tell me, what's going on there?'

'Not much at the moment. We're snowed in.'

'What, properly snowed in? Like several feet of white stuff, or half an inch and you're making excuses for not leaving the house?'

'Proper snow. Proper deep and crisp and even snow. Look.' Chloe lifted her laptop and carried it to the window so Faith could see the outside wintery landscape.

'Oh my! That's a lot of snow. You'd better trade Ronnie in for some huskies and a sledge, or at least train him to cart you about on a makeshift one. You okay up there, alone?'

'I love it. I have Ronnie so I'm not alone and I would never trade him.'

'I know. Only kidding. Hi, Ronnie. I can see you snoozing on the mat.'

Chloe returned to the office and sat down again. Faith was in serious mood now. 'This new book. Tell me about it.'

Chloe took a deep breath. To be honest, she hadn't got a clear idea of where she was going with it. 'I have a character called Laila, a young innocent woman, who meets a sexy, mysterious man, Dorian, at an ice-skating rink. They both share a love of books and she discovers he not only owns a bookshop but invites her to be his assistant. It soon transpires he isn't the man she believes him to be. He's not only wealthy and extremely passionate but somewhat kinky. She falls for him and allows him to involve her in his sex games but then it gets complicated.' She read out what she'd written so far.

Faith listened intently, giving nothing away and nodding periodically as Chloe stumbled over words and finally came to an end. Then she steepled her fingertips together and eased further back in her chair. 'Okay, I'm going to wear two hats now. The first is my agent hat. Please, don't be upset but you know I prefer honesty. That idea stinks: it not only sounds like a rewrite of *Fifty Shades of Grey*, it's not you. This isn't C J Knight. *Spank Me Harder, Vicar* was genius and it was genius because it felt true-to-life and it was funny. God, it was funny. You drew inspiration from real life and brought your characters to life so much we all felt we lived next door to them. I'm sure Laila and whoever Dormat, Doreen, pervy boy is would be well developed, but this whole idea sounds too woolly and is certainly not gripping enough. Now, before you say anything, I'm changing hats and talking to you as a friend. You've been through hell. William's actions have hit you deeper than you realise and you need some time to get over it. I accept you are confused and unhappy and those

105

emotions – no matter how many times you tell me you're okay – are clouding your ability to turn out the sort of book I know you are capable of.'

Chloe gulped back tears. Faith was right. Her book was crap. She'd struggled with every word, sentence and thought and all the while, when she wrote the sex or love scenes, all she could see was William's face. 'I can't do it, Faith. I've lost it. I lost William, my life and my ability to write.'

'That's utter crap. Your ability's always been there, hidden inside you. You ignored it all those years you lived with William because you didn't believe in yourself enough, and then when you finally did his actions crushed your spirit. You are gifted and you have oodles of talent in every bone of your body. I don't take on just anyone at this agency. I didn't ask to represent you because you were a friend. I chose to represent you because I believed in you and I still do. Now *you* have to believe in yourself again. You're also partly experiencing what we call Second Book Syndrome, which is quite natural among authors. I have other writers who are panicking because they don't think they can produce a book as good as their first. You have to relax. The ideas are inside you. Let them escape and don't force them.'

'I don't have any ideas,' sobbed Chloe. 'I got all my inspiration for *Spank Me Harder, Vicar* from conversations and gossip William shared with me after his night in the local pub. It was going to be the same for this book. I have nothing now. I have no one to share silly stories with me or give me a kernel of an idea.' She pulled out a tissue from a box on her desk and blew her nose.

'Oh, hun, that's utter rubbish. William may have given you a seed of an idea but you grew it and turned it into something magnificent. You wrote most of that novel from imagination. You have a powerful ability to get inside people's heads, write about what is happening in people's lives even if you don't physically socialise with them. You can do it again. Now, we'd settled on a title, didn't we, before all this shit with William happened.'

Chloe nodded. '*Oh, Ambassador!*'

'And where was the inspiration for that going to come from?'

'William knew an ambassador who had outrageous parties and told me a couple of stories about him.'

'Can you remember them?'

Chloe nodded.

'Then start with those and make the rest up. Easy.'

'Not really. I feel... dried up. I can't come up with anything funny or light-hearted, Faith.'

'Hun, that's why you need to chill out, have some fun and stop fighting your inner self. Why don't you go along to another singleton event? It wasn't as bad as you feared and now you know a couple of the people who attend so it won't feel so threatening.'

Chloe blew her nose again and shrugged.

'My offer's still there. You can come with me to Barbados tomorrow. I can book you on my flight and we'll go drink cocktails together in the sun.'

'I can't leave Ronnie and besides, I don't think I can get off the hill.'

'Oh shit. I forgot about the snow. So, you'll be stuck there for Christmas Day?'

'Probably. Unless we get a sudden heatwave and it all melts. I wasn't planning on doing much anyway.' She offered a small smile that was reciprocated.

'I know all about being lonely at Christmas, hence my trip away, but don't let it eat you up. This time next year, you'll be a new person; one that's full of confidence and one who's written another best-seller. Don't let this time of year get to you. I understand how daunting it can seem to spend Christmas alone.'

'I won't. I have plans. Ronnie and I are going for a long walk to bark at ducks on the reservoir and then we'll build a snowman in the garden.'

Faith laughed. 'I can actually imagine that happening. Do it and send me a photo of you both with the snowman. I'll Skype you first thing on Christmas Day. Nine o'clock your time.'

'That'd be really nice.'

'Feel better?'

'Sort of. I still have no idea how to begin the book but I'll get there.'

'That's my girl. Don't put too much pressure on yourself. I'll try and wheedle some more time out of the publisher. It's office party season so I'll try and get them when they've been at the wine and are feeling more generous. Maybe you could come up with something for when I return, so I can keep them off your back a little longer.'

'Thanks.'

'I have to go. Must pack my bikini. I'm taking my Christmas pressie from you with me. It looks very exciting. Can't wait to open it.'

'I've got yours under my tree. We'll open them together on Christmas Day when we Skype.'

'I'll speak to you in two days. Bye, babes.' Faith blew her a kiss.

'Bye, Faith. Have a good flight.'

'First Class comfort, endless champagne, an eye mask, noise cancelling headphones and then seven hours of sleep. I think it'll be good enough.' She smiled.

Faith disappeared and Chloe deleted the document on her laptop. Faith was spot on. The book wasn't right for her. She recalled the first time William had mentioned the ambassador he'd met on the golf course and shut her eyes. She'd start with that story as Faith had suggested.

She thought briefly of William, head back, his white teeth on display, laughing like mad...

'So, nobody knows anything about this mysterious woman who's moved to the massive house at the end of the village and won't answer the door to anyone. The villagers all come up with wild assumptions about who she is and what she does and someone says they saw a man – her partner – go into the house a few days earlier, but he hasn't been seen since. And then, late Friday night, one of the local farmers spots her, dressed completely in black, tugging a large bag out into her garden and depositing it into a ready-prepared hole. He bounds down to the pub and tells everyone there and somebody decides she's murdered and buried her partner, and they want to call the police. Well, you can imagine the discussion. Another local says they can't do that without evidence and he and his mate creep back up to the house and retrieve the rubbish bag from the hole. It's really heavy and they drag it out and discover it's filled with rubbish. Nothing more than that. It's just rubbish.' He laughs again. Chloe can smell the alcohol on his breath but doesn't move from his side as they sit

on the settee. She likes it when he's in a good mood like this. She isn't bothered about not going to the pub. It's mostly full of men and William enjoys some time out on his own. She waits to hear what else he has to tell her. Some of the stories are so far-fetched she wonders if they are fabricated, but William seems to think they're true. He wipes his eyes, damp from laughing, and continues.

'And then they find out who she is. It's only Helena Marshall-Thomas.'

'The socialite?' She asks. Helena Marshall-Thomas is well known for her parties and looks amazing for fifty-three. She looks younger than Chloe.

'That's her and she's been laying low because she's had extensive plastic surgery and doesn't want anyone to see her until she's fully recovered. Apparently, she has it done regularly!'

'No! I saw her interviewed on television and she denied having any surgical intervention.'

'Well, that's a big fat fib, I can tell you. She and her husband Richard, who's an ex-ambassador, threw a massive party for all the villagers in return for their discretion. There was no expense spared and they opened up their house to everyone, including the indoor pool, and even had an unlimited champagne fountain set up in the entrance. There's also a rumour she paid off the guy who found out about the surgery and he's now bought a cottage in Wales.'

'It can't be true,' says Chloe.

'It is. Every single word of it and I've been sworn to secrecy. Anyway, Richard and Helena *have stopped going out in their village and started using the pub in Appletree as their regular haunt, so I should bump into them. I wonder if I should hint that I know about the surgery. I'm itching to get an invite to their next party.' He yawns suddenly. 'I'm pooped. Might head off to bed.'*

'It's not ten o'clock yet.'

'Busy day tomorrow. I need some beauty sleep.' He stands suddenly and heads off. Chloe is disappointed. She's changed into her best dress and done her hair especially and had hoped he'd notice her efforts, but once again he isn't interested in her. It's been happening more and more often. She makes every effort to look her best, prepare a tasty meal and wait for him to share it with her, but he heads straight down the pub from work and when he returns, he only wants to go to bed. She heads to the fridge and pours a glass of wine then wanders into her small office where she fires up the laptop and starts on the edits of her debut novel, Spank Me Harder, Vicar. At least within its pages she can lead the fantasy life she craves.

'Okay, Ronnie, let's write down something Faith will like. I can do this. I'll start with what I know and work with it.' Chloe opened up a new document, named it *Oh, Ambassador!* and began typing.

Chapter Nine

Sunday, 24th December

Chloe lifted the box of cereal and rattled it. Ronnie's ears pricked up at the sound. 'Shit! Christmas Eve and we're already down to the last of our food. And there's no milk to go with it. I hate dry cereal. Oh well, there's no choice but to improvise,' She ripped open the packet of granola and dried berries into a bowl, throwing a piece high in the air for Ronnie to catch. 'Ha! You just ate one of your five-a-day without realising it.' She bent to kiss his nose. He smelt of strawberries. She pulled out a half-opened bottle of wine from the fridge and poured it over the cereal and spooned it into her mouth, wrinkling her nose, before nodding approvingly. It tasted rather nice.

She carried both the bowl and wine bottle to the table and sat down to look at the view. Snow had built up along the window ledges and frosted against the glass. Outside the landscape was pure white. There was no doubt she was living in a winter wonderland. She took another mouthful and chewed thoughtfully. She could possibly make her supplies last a further two days. At least she had plenty of blubber to live off and Ronnie had enough biscuits to see him through as long as the snow melted soon. She wondered if she could walk to the nearest village and buy some basic provisions. It'd be heavy going in this weather.

A rap on the back door set Ronnie off and barking he loped to greet the visitor.

Eleanor wearing jeggings, furry ski boots and a parka with a large furry hood that covered most of her head, stood on the doorstep. Chloe could only see a nose and painted blue lips.

'Hey! Came to see how you were getting on and to ask you a favour.'

'Come in,' said Chloe, not wishing to leave the woman outside in the cold. Eleanor pulled off her boots and fussed over Ronnie, then followed Chloe into the kitchen. 'Brr! Cold or what? Thank goodness we have log fires.' Ronnie dropped his favourite ball at her feet, eyes trained on his new friend.

'Ronnie, don't drool on Eleanor. Take your ball away.'

'Oh, bless him. He's lovely.' She fussed over the animal some more.

Chloe watched her pet roll over to have his stomach rubbed. He didn't do that for many people, only those he truly liked. 'What can I help you with?'

'We were expecting fourteen guests for Christmas lunch and now nobody can reach us. The snow's disrupted all travel arrangements so we're stuffed... well, actually the goose is stuffed and nobody to eat it but Fairfax and I. Honestly, we have a mountain of food. I know you will have too but I wondered if you'd come over tomorrow for Christmas Day and help us out. You can bring Ronnie.'

Chloe shifted from one foot to the other. She liked Eleanor and Fairfax but she'd genuinely been looking forward to having time alone with Ronnie and to chatting to Faith to run through some of the ideas she'd been having for *Oh, Ambassador!*

Eleanor caught the look on her face and said dismissively, 'I know it's a crazy idea. I don't know what I was thinking of. You'll be just like us and everyone else at this time of year with stacks of food that'll go off if you don't eat it. I wish I hadn't gone so overboard. Why do we do it? A goose, a duck, a chicken, sausages, gammon joints, enough cheese to feed the entire population of France and booze galore!'

Ronnie's stomach growled ominously, and as Eleanor turned towards him to comment her eyes lighted on the wine bottle and cereal bowl on the table. Chloe squirmed in embarrassment. 'I ran out of milk,' she said before Eleanor could speak.

'You should have asked us for some. We've plenty of milk. Mind you, I think that looks a far more appealing combination. What does it taste like?' Eleanor edged towards the table with a smile.

'Pretty good. Want to try it?'

'Go on. Why not?'

Chloe shook some granola into a fresh bowl and passed it together with a spoon to Eleanor, who sat down, added her own wine and tasted the combination. 'Yummy! It would make a fab dessert. Although, I've already got mince pies, chocolate logs and a monstrously large organic plum pudding with enough brandy butter and cream to last for several weeks.'

'Yes, please. We'd like to come to Christmas lunch,' said Chloe in a rush, the thought of eating properly overcoming her shyness. 'I'm not just out of milk. I actually don't have any provisions at all unless you count Ronnie's dog biscuits and half a bag of chocolates. I ordered everything for Christmas online, and then the snow arrived and my delivery couldn't get through.'

'You must have been starving for a few days! That's nuts. You ought to have come around to us.'

'I didn't think of it.'

'We're neighbours. It's only natural to ask us if you need anything. That decides it. Can't have you living on this, as tasty as it is. Come back with me and help yourself to some goodies to see you through until the snow melts sufficiently for us to be able to drive again, and then tomorrow you're both officially invited for Buck's Fizz and canapés at eleven. How does that suit you?'

'Perfect.'

Eleanor threw her a warm smile and then, finishing the last of her cereal asked, 'I don't suppose I could have another bowl of that, could I?'

–

'Merry Christmas!' said Chloe, shoving into Fairfax's hands her last bottle of wine, which she'd wrapped especially.

'You shouldn't have,' he replied.

'My mother always told my father it was impolite to turn up at a house empty-handed.'

'A wise woman. Come in.'

He opened the door wider, standing back to allow them both to enter. 'Come in. Our other guest is here, Eleanor,' he called out.

'Take her through. I'll be there in a minute,' shouted Eleanor.

Chloe followed Fairfax into the sitting room, where a fire roared through the grate, fairy lights twinkled on the large pine tree and Alex stood with a flute of orange juice in his hand.

'Hi,' he said, an easy smile on his face. Ronnie strained to reach him. 'Happy Christmas.'

'Happy Christmas,' she replied. 'What are you doing here?'

'Same as you. Accepting Eleanor and Fairfax's hospitality.' He raised his glass.

'Would you like a Buck's Fizz, Chloe?'

'Yes, please,' she replied.

'You can release Ronnie. I'm sure he won't be any trouble.'

She detached his lead and he headed immediately over to Alex to be stroked, sitting beside him without any prompting.

'He knows you're a dog person,' she said as he rubbed the animal's head with his free hand.

'He's a lovely dog. Got a nice temperament.'

'Don't praise him too much, he'll get big headed. Are you alone?'

'Yes. I was supposed to go around to Dad's today and join him, my sister and her son, but obviously we can't get out and even if we could, I doubt I'd manage to climb the reservoir road to his farm.'

'I didn't know you had a sister,' she said absent-mindedly as she accepted the chilled glass of orange juice and champagne from Fairfax. Tiny bubbles rose gently to the top of the glass as she lifted it and toasted everyone. She took a sip. The cool orange mixed with the fizz of the champagne was a perfect combination. Alex picked up the conversation again.

'Yeah, Ashleigh. You saw her the day you moved in. She was here with her lad, Charlie. She normally lives in Bristol but she's up here for Christmas.'

'That was your sister?'

'She was the last time I checked.'

'I thought…' A familiar heat warmed her cheeks. 'Nothing.'

His eyes twinkled merrily. 'You thought she was my wife or partner, didn't you? No. She's definitely my sister. She's staying with Mum and Dad at the moment. I'm not married or engaged or anything.'

'Good, then you can join our group of singletons,' said Eleanor, appearing from nowhere and looking resplendent in an embroidered kaftan and headband. 'Chloe's signed up, haven't you? It's in its infancy and we only have a few members at the moment, but interest in it is growing at a fast rate and we'll soon be offering events all over the country. It's a monthly fee and for it you can go to all the events, so it's excellent value. There, that's the spiel over. Chloe came ice skating with us on our last outing and as I recall, she almost won our little contest. She'd never even been skating before that day.'

'Did you?' Once more his eyes sparkled. Chloe mumbled an incomprehensible reply. She hadn't exactly planned on going to any more events.

'So, will you come along to the next event, Alex? To be honest, we're short of men. Not that I'm trying to play matchmaker. The whole event would be better if we had equal numbers of men and women. I can't say any more for the moment but you'll be bowled over.'

Alex looked across at Chloe. 'You're going, are you?'

Put on the spot like that, she didn't know what to say.

'Of course she is. Right. That's it. You're both in. Now, who would like some pigs in blankets. Ronnie. You would, wouldn't you?'

The meal and afternoon drifted into the evening as the quartet ate, drank and spent the afternoon playing Monopoly. Fairfax looked over his stack of playing cards and twirled an imaginary moustache and in a voice that reminded Chloe of Fagin from *Oliver Twist* said, 'Now then, m'dear. You've landed on Mayfair, a magnificent area with not one but three five-star hotels. I believe you owe me some rental income or I shall have to throw you and your furry chum out onto the streets.' He gave a villainous cackle. Chloe snorted. She couldn't keep the happy grin off her face: her stomach was full and content, and she felt light-headed. The fire crackled and roared. Ronnie had fallen asleep full-length in front of it and Chloe was the most relaxed she'd been in months. She waved a twenty-pound note at Fairfax.

'Oh please, landlord, don't throw me out. I'll be forced to shelter on the streets under cardboard boxes and my faithful hound will catch pneumonia. Take everything I have and my savings too.' She lifted her three property cards and held them out. 'I'll even throw in the family jewels.' She removed the plastic ring she'd won from one of the crackers pulled earlier and placed it on the board. 'This is a family heirloom and priceless. Take it to pay my dues. Spare me the snow-filled streets and alleyways. My poor doggie will perish from the cold.'

Eleanor chuckled merrily at the exchange and Alex shook his head in mock dismay, grinning all the while. Ronnie released a loud sigh that set them all laughing.

'Give up, Chloe. He's beaten us all. Frightful man,' said Eleanor, dropping a kiss on Fairfax's head.

'I'm just extremely entrepreneurial,' Fairfax replied. 'Ought to have been a property mogul.'

'And determined. He almost always wins at Monopoly. That's why he chose to play it, rather than Trivial Pursuits,' Eleanor said. 'He's no good at that. Can only answer the pink card questions.'

'True,' said Fairfax, shuffling the Chance cards back into a neat stack and replacing them in the set.

'Anyone want a top-up?' said Eleanor, attempting to get to her feet.

'No, thank you. I have to take the canine-shaped floor mat over there for a walk and then get on with some work…' Chloe bit her tongue.

'Work?' Too late. Eleanor had picked up on it. 'What sort of work?'

'Housework,' she replied quickly, knowing she was flushing pink again.

'On Christmas Day? Are you mad? Have another glass of wine.'

'I'd love to but I really do have to take you-know-who out for a while, and if I drink any more, I'll probably fall over in a snowdrift and you'll find me frozen solid in two days' time.'

'I'm sure Ronnie would save you,' said Alex. He stretched his arms above his head. 'Actually, I ought to move too. It's been wonderful. Thank you for inviting me over.'

'You're welcome to stay longer,' urged Eleanor.

'That's very kind but I must get going. I said I'd ring my parents to let them know I was okay. They still treat me like I'm a teenager at times.' He shrugged and got to his feet. Ronnie looked up hopefully and seeing Chloe make a move, bounded up in one.

'Okay. Well, we'll see you again soon. The next adventure for the singletons is in five days, on the thirtieth. We should have lost the snow by then. At least I hope we have by then or we might run out of food and start eating one another.' She burst out laughing, then put a finger to her lips. 'Oops. Maybe I'm a tiddly bit drunk. We'll pick you both up at ten.'

'What are we going to be doing?' Alex asked.

'I'm not so drunk I'm going to spoil the surprise. You wait and see. It'll be a huge laugh. I'll guarantee that.' She staggered into Fairfax, who put an arm around her waist.

They said their goodbyes and Alex started walking away from the house alongside Chloe. Ronnie bounced on ahead.

'That was a really nice day. I feel quite mellow now,' he said.

'It was a much better day than I expected.'

'I know what you mean. I don't much care for Christmas. It's a long holiday and unproductive. I usually try and get away, somewhere warm,' he replied.

'My friend Faith's in Barbados, soaking up sunrays and cocktails,' Chloe said.

'Sensible idea. Still, there's something romantic about a white Christmas. You can't beat cold air, snow-covered branches and a magical setting like this. What had you planned on doing today?'

'Building a snowman with Ronnie.' She'd said it before she'd thought about it. He would think she was quite crazy. Instead he laughed.

'What a tremendous idea. Why don't we?'

'It's getting too dark to see.'

'My house has outside floodlights that will illuminate the back garden. Come on. We'll make one.'

The child in her shrieked yes and watching Ronnie leaping about snapping at stray snowflakes, her heart lifted. 'Why not, indeed?'

Chapter Ten

'All aboard,' shouted Fairfax, head out of the window.

Chloe and Alex sprinted towards the car. Heavy rain tumbled from dark clouds, soaking them as they ran from opposite directions, pulled open the rear doors and jumped onto the back seat at exactly the same time.

'Phew! What a monsoon!' said Alex.

'I know. What a shame. I preferred the snow. Now everything looks all muddy and dreary. A river of mucky water raced past the wheels and into the drain on the driveway.'

'Let's go,' said Fairfax, putting the car into gear and pulling away. Rain hammered on the metal roof drowning his words, even though they were shouting. That and the slushing noises coming from under the car as they drove through vast puddles made any conversation almost impossible.

Chloe was glad they couldn't talk without yelling at each other. She couldn't have joined in anyway. She was fighting back the usual fear now bubbling inside and watched as rain splattered across the screen, all the while mindful of Alex next to her. They'd not bumped into each other again or chatted since they'd rolled snow together and made a snowman on Christmas Day. It had been a hilarious hour, fuelled by alcohol and a feeling of wellbeing, and after finishing an enormous snowman complete with large black stones for eyes and a stick for a nose and Alex's beanie hat, they'd thrown snowballs for Ronnie to chase until they were all tired and it was too dark and cold to continue. Back home, she'd written a chapter of the new book before settling down to watch a film with her dog by her side and reflecting on the fact she'd had a much better time than she could have ever imagined and moreover, she hadn't thought about William and Lilly once.

The rain eased slightly and Alex spoke up.

'I was getting used to seeing Mr Snowman outside my window. It was sad to watch him morph into Mr Puddle.'

She half-smiled at the remark. 'Did you rescue your beanie hat before it started pouring down?'

'I certainly did. I'll need it as soon as we start working again on the site. The wind doesn't half blow up at Sunny Meadow.'

'Goody. Snow, torrential rain and wind. Remind me again why I moved?' she said.

'Because of the phenomenal views,' he replied.

'And the superb neighbours,' said Eleanor from the passenger seat. 'Ah, here we are.'

They pulled off onto a track leading to a football training ground.

Chloe's heart began thudding alarmingly and her neck became damp with perspiration. No matter that she knew some of the others who'd be there, or that Alex, Fairfax and Eleanor were with her; she really wasn't looking forward to socialising again. She reprimanded her inner self who was now quaking deep within. This was crazy. She'd met these people before. She'd spoken to them all and got to know a little about them, so she shouldn't be feeling so anxious. She reminded herself of the new book Faith was expecting. She had to go through with this for its sake. She had to speak to and listen to people, extract snippets of knowledge, and use what she uncovered. That's what writers did. She attempted to calm her breathing now coming in short gasps. Alex threw her a look of concern. 'You okay? You've gone a funny colour.'

'We're not playing football, are we?' Chloe asked. 'I'm rubbish at it.' She hoped he'd think that was the reason for her apparent concern.

'No, but there is an indoor football court that we're using,' came the response.

Alex pulled a face at Chloe and shrugged. He had no more idea than she did of what they were going to do. Another heavy downpour bashed against the roof. Fairfax drew up outside the main door. 'It's lashing it down. Make a run for it. I'll park up and meet you inside.'

Doors flew open simultaneously and Eleanor, Chloe and Alex raced for the entrance. Alex opened the door and herded the women in. Several people looked up at their entry. Chloe recognised most of them from the skating event. Sean was one of the first she spotted. He lifted a hand and made a beeline for her. She was pleased to see him.

'We were speculating as to whether or not you'd make it. Somebody said you'd been snowed in and we weren't sure if the event would be held. Hi, I'm Sean,' he said to Alex and held out a beefy hand which Alex shook.

'Alex. Chloe, Eleanor and Fairfax's neighbour.'

'Good to meet you. Fairfax not with you?'

'Parking the car. He'll be here in a sec,' Alex replied.

'We were snowed in for a few days,' said Chloe aware she hadn't taken Sean up on his offer to visit the bookshop. 'How was Christmas? Did you spend it with Suzy?'

'Christmas was quiet. Weather was too bad to go out but I managed to drive over to her mother's and collect her on Boxing Day. We watched movies and ate too much junk food and played on the Nintendo I bought her. She's a brilliant gamer so she beat her old man, hands down. You?'

'We all had lunch at Eleanor and Fairfax's house and afterwards Alex and I built a snowman.'

A slow grin spread across Sean's face. 'You made any snow angels?'

'It was too dark by the time we finished. We chucked a few snowballs about and drove Chloe's dog crazy,' said Alex.

Eleanor clapped her hands together. 'Okay everyone, listen up. Thanks for making it today in this lousy weather. I know you're all keen to know what we've planned for you and I really hope you enjoy yourselves. If you'd like to go through the double doors over there, you'll find out just exactly what today's activity is. I thought we'd end the year on a high. Before we go, this is Alex. He's another of our neighbours. Don't think we're signing up everyone who lives within a five-mile radius of our house, because we're not. It just so happens that Alex was free today.'

'Hi Alex,' called Jacqueline, looking very fetching in tight black trousers and a loose red jumper. A few others joined in with greetings. Eleanor ran through everyone's names for him. Alex lifted up a hand by way of a hello at each mention. Introductions over, the group headed across to the large orange doors that opened onto a full-sized indoor pitch. Instead of a goal post at the far end of the room, there were two sets of ten enormous inflatable skittles, larger than a person, and two massive plastic inflatable balls. Four people all dressed in tracksuit bottoms and yellow T-shirts bearing the logo *Extreme Bowling*, were waiting for them, hands behind backs, smiles plastered across their faces.

'Welcome to human bowling!' Eleanor shouted. 'Where you take on the role of the ball and knock down the skittles, or should I say pins?'

Chloe's nerves had no chance to get the better of her; Eleanor gave no one any opportunity to speak as she dived straight into the rules of the game, which involved each member of the team climbing into the human hamster ball, one at a time, and by running forwards inside it, direct and aim it at the inflatable pins supported by their team members. It was up to the person inside the ball to knock down as many skittles as possible in one strike.

'Both teams will consist of six players. Team A; that's Alex, Sean, Rob Jacqueline, Kaisha and Chloe, you'll be up against Team B: Neats, Danielle, Ed, Tim, Fairfax and me.' Fairfax burst through the door, water dripping from his coat and hair. He was greeted with a cheer from his teammates.

'Winners receive a Jeroboam of champagne which works out at about twenty-four glasses, and the losers will get a couple of litres of lemonade. Right, sort yourselves out and decide which order you want to play in, tactics and so on, and then let's get this game underway. I'd better warn you team A, I'm very competitive.'

Sean took charge of Chloe's team, and huddled together like a rugby or football squad they discussed how best to play the game. 'I bet Fairfax and Eleanor have done this or something similar before too. Anyone here ever been in a zorb ball?' he asked.

Kaisha Lewis, a young woman in her twenties, with a pretty face and a sprinkle of freckles across her nose whispered. 'I went water zorbing on holiday. You just run inside the ball and it propels forward. You'll lose your balance though and you'll fall over and turn upside down, especially as the ball rolls, so the best tactic is momentum. Keep running steadily, like a hamster, to give yourselves the best chance. If you fall over, you'll have to go with it until the ball stops. It's fun. I loved it.'

'Great. You will probably be more accurate at hitting the pins than the rest of us. I spoke to Neats Kelly at the last event and found out she runs marathons. I reckon they'll leave her until last as their secret weapon. You mind going last too?'

'I'm happy with that.'

Sean spoke again. 'Okay. Anyone else? Anybody else good at running?' He was met with shrugs. 'Looks like we'll have to give it our best shot and hope. Who wants to go first? Rob?'

Rob, who towered above everyone, including Sean, looked down briefly. 'I'm not too quick on my feet. I tend to fall over them. I might even be a hindrance to the team.'

'None of us know how we'll perform. I doubt you'll be any worse than the rest of us. Only Kaisha's done it before,' said Sean, kindly.

The others agreed.

'How about I start us off?' said Alex. 'Someone has to and it's always better if someone's gone before you. Don't hate me if I miss the pins though. I'm not a great shot.'

'We won't,' said Jacqueline quickly and flashed him a bright smile. Alex returned it. Chloe couldn't ignore the spark between them. Jacqueline hadn't taken her eyes off Alex since they'd arrived. No doubt she'd be soon introducing him to her motorbike and offering to take him home on the back of it. She pushed away such sour thoughts. It wasn't as if she and Alex were even dating each other. They were no more than neighbours and besides, Chloe wasn't looking for romance. Good luck to them, she thought, her attention now on the ball. She was going to make a complete mess of it. She had absolutely zero coordination. Soon after she and William had got married, when she'd felt able to handle going out with small groups of people, she'd gone bowling with her husband, one of his work colleagues, Henry, and Henry's wife. They'd had the large rubber bumpers that beginners and children used put in play because her ball kept heading off down the channel. Henry had made several wise cracks about it, but the more he joked, the worse she played, and the worse she played, the more annoyed William became. Afterwards, when she'd apologised, William had said it didn't matter but she knew she'd let him down. It was evident in his demeanour and he hadn't taken her bowling ever again.

That occasion had been the catalyst for her condition worsening. She'd deteriorated quickly afterwards. William had a way of looking at her that drained her confidence and in spite of his words or apparent concern, she'd flounder and within weeks of marrying him she had turned back into the frightened Chloe who couldn't cope. Nanny Olive had noticed the decline. She had warned Chloe that William was sucking the life from her and tried to get her to see reason, but by then it was too late and

Chloe, who loved William with every molecule in her body, couldn't have left him or stood up to him.

She knew she was going to be dreadful at this activity but she couldn't back down. With the first human ball and pusher chosen, the other members of each team were dispatched to watch over the inflatable black pins, arranged as they would be in a bowling alley and balanced on inflatable rings, to ensure they were replaced after each knock-down attempt.

The Human Bowling staff members had moved the giant see-through balls onto the starting line and were holding them in place. Team B had selected Danielle Ryan, a single mother to three teenagers. When Chloe had talked to her last time she'd been wearing a bobble hat and a huge knitted sweater that reached her knees, and she'd been quietly spoken and shy, almost as afraid as Chloe of meeting new people. Today she was in another baggy jumper that swamped her slender frame, eyes large as she took up position. Tim, a plump man with jet-black thick hair, who could have been any age between twenty-five and thirty-five, rolled up the sleeves on his fleece top. He was going to push her away from the start line.

Alex removed his shoes, then squeezed through the entrance flap in the side of the ball, held apart by a staff member. He dropped into the ball and landed on his back-side. He pushed up with difficulty, the staff holding the ball in situ, and once erect, stood with arms outstretched waiting for the game to start. Sean was going to give him the initial push to the second line marked out on the floor where they had to release the ball, allowing the person inside to guide it towards the pins. They'd decided he wouldn't push too hard in case Alex lost his balance, but sufficient to get momentum and for Alex to propel it forward.

Team B had won the coin toss and went first. Tim let loose a roar as he ran up to the ball and heaved with all his might. Danielle fell onto her knees almost immediately. She scrambled up only to tumble again, and the ball veered to the left. Her team mates yelled excitedly at her and she tried to roll around to make it change direction, but her antics only caused the ball to bounce up and down gently until it finally collided with one outside pin, which knocked into another behind it, and she scored two points.

'Mistake,' said Kaisha to Chloe. 'He should have pushed it more gently.'

Chloe heard her mumble something about kinetic energy but her attention became focused on Sean who rolled their team's ball forward with curved hand movements, like she and Alex had when rolling the body for their snowman. Alex began scrabbling as if climbing up a mountain quickly. The ball picked up speed but retained a straight line. Alex ran even faster, arms and legs a blur, and as the giant ball bounced and rolled, he maintained his upright position until the second he struck the front pin full on and as he toppled over, so did all the other pins. Jacqueline yelled, 'Strike!'

Next up were Rob and Jacqueline. She'd opted to go inside the ball and Rob, having watched Sean's method intently, tried to copy it but under the guidance of his meaty paws, the ball spun off the planned route, and in spite of Jacqueline dropping on her backside and rolling in every direction possible to prevent it from missing the targets, it did just that and ended up in the far corner of the room. Neats, on the other team, fared much better and cries of jubilation came when she scored a strike.

Alex and Chloe were up next. No sooner had she yanked off her shoes than her knees weakened like somebody had snipped the ligaments with a pair of scissors. It took a mountain of effort to clamber into the zorb. The interior was ridiculously bouncy and as she wobbled to her feet, breathing in damp plastic and perspiration, she wondered how on earth she was going to hit the pins: vague, black objects that could barely be seen from the interior of the ball now cloudy with breathy exhalations. She was aware of Fairfax and Eleanor shooting off to her right and of people cheering, but the majority of her attention was on her hammering heart and her unsteady legs. She'd be lucky if she could manage three steps forward. For a second, she thought of her sister, Georgia, who'd have loved this activity. Sorrow replaced the panic to be replaced again by thoughts of her character, Laila, in *Oh, Ambassador!* When Chloe wrote, she tried to get into the character's head and even act like that character. She could pretend to be the character here, now. She conjured up Laila – ambitious, daring and fearless. Her body toppled forwards as the ball began to move. She was off. With arms outstretched, she emulated Alex's climbing technique, all the while imagining she was the carefree, bold young woman who was dealing with a randy guest at one of the handsome ambassador's parties in an unusual manner, and before she knew it, Chloe collided with a pin. The ball then bounced high and off to the left and Chloe was thrown first onto her knees, then her back and was spun upside down several times, as if inside a tumble dryer on low spin. At last, disorientated and breathless she collapsed on her back, legs akimbo in the air as the ball drew to a final halt. The staff members had caught it. She emerged from the plastic sauna, hair awry and sweat on her brow.

'Did I hit many pins?' she asked.

Sean high-fived her. 'Hit many? You smashed them all to smithereens. We couldn't believe how fast you were going. We all had to jump out of the way. You were like a human cannonball.'

'Really?'

'Really. Strike.'

She wiped her forehead. It was a good result. Chloe had gone through with it and had scored a strike. Nanny Olive would be proud of her. Chloe had to admit though, it wasn't her doing. Alex had pushed her and set the ball off on a straight line. He had helped her yet again. Her pulse raced a little at the thought and she flushed at the realisation that she really liked Alex.

–

'Not a bad result, eh?' said Alex as they sat once again in the back seat of Fairfax's Nissan truck. The rain had stopped at last and the group were tired but content.

Chloe agreed. They'd shared the champagne with the losing team and it had been a hugely fun event. She'd spoken to everyone and there was no doubt she was more relaxed around these people, so when Eleanor asked if they were up for the next event the following week, she found herself agreeing to it immediately.

'You around tomorrow?' asked Eleanor as they drew up outside their house.

'I'm going to see Sean at his bookshop in Uttoxeter,' said Chloe. Sean had asked her to drop in and she couldn't refuse him.

'I'm going to a motorbike event in Wales,' said Alex. 'Jacqueline assures me I'll become a convert afterwards and will trade my Land Rover for a Ducati.'

'I was thinking about tomorrow evening,' Eleanor replied. 'It's New Year's Eve. We're having a few friends over and my parents are coming. Why don't you both join us?'

'Not sure what time I'll be back,' said Alex with a small shrug of his shoulders.

'I'm going out too,' said Chloe quickly. She hoped nobody noticed the tell-tale red spots in her cheeks that always appeared when she didn't tell the truth. It was only a white lie. She would go out – with Ronnie for a walk, and then watch the celebrations on television. She liked to be with him in case anyone let off fireworks at midnight, as they had done in Appletree. She didn't want him frightened and alone.

'Shame. Oh well, another time.'

–

Chloe was surprised at how flat she felt when she opened her door. Even Ronnie who threw himself at her, shaking a sock he'd found in one of the bedrooms, and who lavished her with massive amounts of love, couldn't detract from the disappointment she felt that Alex was going out for the day with Jacqueline. She'd been hopeful for a moment that there'd been something between her and Alex but clearly it was one-sided. She should have known he'd prefer being with exciting Jacqueline rather than dull Chloe. She shook her head to dispel the gloomy thought. She would look forward to visiting *A New Chapter* instead. Sean had given her directions of how to reach it that would enable her to avoid shoppers and other people. Moreover, she had Ronnie who never let her down. She hugged him fiercely and whispered. 'You want to go for a walk?'

Chapter Eleven

Sunday, 31st December

'It's seven forty-five in the morning and already twenty-five degrees, and I'm melting,' Faith complained. She was dressed in a white swimsuit and crocheted top that set off her golden skin perfectly.

'You look fabulous,' said Chloe and meant it.

'You say the nicest things. You look good too. In fact, you look like you've lost some weight. I thought everyone ballooned over Christmas. What's going on? I don't speak to you for five days and you shed pounds? You on a miracle diet?'

Chloe laughed. 'You're imagining it although I think all the walking and exercise is doing me good. I suppose I lost about five pounds in that wretched zorb ball.'

'Sounds hilarious,' said Faith. Chloe had already filled her in with the events of the day before. 'You seeing in the new year?'

'I was invited to a party but I'm going to stay home and guard Ronnie. I don't want him scared by random fireworks going off.'

'Where is the mutt?'

'Asleep.'

'Why does that not surprise me? He's always asleep when I call you.'

'He's worn out from walking.'

'Has he lost weight too?'

Chloe grinned. 'You partying?'

'There's a big bash in the hotel. I'm getting a full facial, manicure, pedicure, haircare package and then I shall be the belle of the ball until the clock strikes midnight, at which point, I shall beetle back to my room before I turn into a pumpkin.'

'That's not likely, is it? You never look anything other than a princess. Is there nobody you fancy at the hotel?'

'Everyone's coupled up this year although there are a couple of handsome waiters, and the yoga instructor is very tasty... or maybe I'll wait for a single multi-millionaire to drop by later.' She gave a wry smile before changing the subject. 'Tell me more about Canadian Sean.'

'Nothing to tell. I'm going to visit him this afternoon like I said.'

'Good, good. Anything else you want to share with me, your best friend?'

'No.'

'Your face says otherwise.'

'Well, I had a really good Christmas Day with Alex and we got on ever so well and I think I hoped... oh... I don't know. He's going out with one of the women from the singleton club.' She blurted it out quickly.

'A-ha. I see.'

'See what?'

'You fancy Alex.'

'No. I only want to be friends with him. I like him.'

'Well, why do you look so dejected then?'

'I don't.'

'Okay.'

'Okay what?'

'Nothing.' Faith shook her head innocently. 'I'd better zip off to my yoga class. I have to perfect my Warrior poses. Happy New Year for tomorrow and I'll text you tomorrow.'

'You too and behave yourself tonight.'

'I always behave myself,' said Faith. 'Except when I don't.'

They ended the call and Chloe checked her reflection in the mirror for the umpteenth time. Sean had given her instructions on how to reach the private car park at the back of the shop, so she wouldn't have to walk through town. She could access the shop through the staff entrance which meant she felt a great deal happier about visiting him. It was almost one p.m. and time to go.

As she drove away from her home, she passed Alex's Land Rover parked on his driveway and was reminded he was out with Jacqueline. No doubt they'd be getting along really well. Jacqueline was bright, outgoing and dazzling. She released a heavy sigh. Faith had been close to the mark. She'd come to like and rely on Alex very quickly – too quickly as it happened.

—

There was a buzzer on the back door marked *A New Chapter*. She pressed it and within seconds, Sean was beaming at her.

'Come in. Glad you could make it. You picked a good time.'

She navigated the corridor into the back of the shop. She let out a gasp of delight. The bookshop was one of the prettiest she'd ever seen, with white shelving set against pale duck-egg blue walls. The place was uncluttered, with ample browsing space between sections marked with copperplate written signs indicating romance, thrillers, horror, science-fiction or non-fiction sections. The ceiling, complete with wooden beams was whitewashed, giving an impression of a pretty country cottage sitting room. An open fireplace was at one end of the shop, decorative dried flowers in a milk churn standing in the grate, and beside it, two wooden swing seats with indigo cushions, attached by hefty ropes to the beams. Arched windows with white frames added to the allure of the place, and imaginatively designed white wooden tables stacked with fetching book displays completed the picture.

'It's lovely,' she said.

'Thank you. I had a local designer work on it. I wanted old-world charm meets modern chic – an escape for readers or customers. If they want, there's a smaller reading room through here,' he said, taking her through an archway into another brightly lit room, with a window and another swinging seat.

'The seats are really comfortable. When there's no one about, I always have a quick swing on them.' He grinned.

The shop smelt of a mixture of lavender and books. Chloe inhaled deeply. Paper had a special scent of its own and she was transported to a time in the past when she'd spend lunch breaks upstairs in the quiet history and science section of the shop where she worked, huddled in a huge leather chair in the corner of the room, reading a book she'd purchased.

'It's been a labour of love,' Sean said, guiding her around the place. She could see shoppers walking down the cobbled pedestrian street that passed his shop. She'd seen photographs online of the shop's exterior, with its inviting azure façade and the black iron railings either side of the four steps leading to the front door. The name of the shop was handwritten in large black letters over the door. A colourful mixture of winter pansies in wrought-iron planters under each window added the final welcoming touches. The shop promised escapism and delivered it in spades.

'Honestly, it's the nicest bookshop I've seen.'

'That makes me very happy. If you fancy doing a few hours here on Wednesday, I'd love to have you work here.' When she didn't reply he changed the subject. 'So, what books do you most enjoy? I know I asked you when we were ice-skating, but if you had to choose a book today to read, what would you choose?'

'That's hard. I pretty much enjoy anything that's well written.'

'What are you reading at the moment?'

She'd been caught out. She hadn't read a thing since her break-up with William and her attempts to write a second book. She was unable to digest other writers works when she was focused on her own but she couldn't tell Sean that.

'I've got out of the habit what with the break-up and moving.'

'Sure. That happens. You get out of sync.' He removed his glasses and checked for smears on the lenses and wiped at one with the corner of his sweatshirt.

Chloe couldn't help but notice his eyes. The glasses detracted from the intensity of colour, a deep forget-me-not blue. 'What would you recommend?'

'Depends on what you fancy.' He held the glasses up to the windows again and satisfied they were clean, put them back on.

'Something light-hearted. I can't handle anything too serious at the moment.'

'You like romantic comedy?'

'I'm not really a chick-lit sort of person. I like happy endings but life isn't like that, is it?'

He shook his head. 'Nah, generally it sucks. Oh, I have just the thing for you. I read it a few weeks ago. It's hilarious – a bit naughty if you don't mind that sort of thing, but so funny. I was in hysterics. Suzy kept asking me what I was laughing at but it's too grown-up for her.' He strode over to the rear of the shop, reached to a shelf and returned with a paperback. 'By far the best read this year.' He held out a book Chloe recognised immediately. She took the copy of *Spank Me Harder, Vicar* from him unsure if he knew or guessed she'd written it and was winding her up, or if he was testing her. Her cheeks burned as she pretended to study the retail description. What should she say? Should she admit the truth or take the book and pretend to read it? She couldn't do that. There was no way she could keep up the pretence like that.

Sean misunderstood her silence.

'Oh, sorry. I didn't mean to offend you. It's saucy in parts but it's really well written and I thought it would make you chuckle. It really is comedy gold. I didn't mean to embarrass you. Oh shit! Sorry, Chloe. What must you think of me?'

She couldn't bear his dismay. He was only being kind.

'You haven't offended me,' she said, giving a small cough. 'Not at all. Can you keep a secret?'

–

'No. You're kidding me.' Sean shook his head again. 'You?'

140

'C J Knight. I know. I don't come across at all as witty or funny. I still don't quite know how I managed to write it. It went through quite a few editing stages…'

'It's not that. It's the sex scenes. They were so raunchy and you're so…'

'Prim?'

'Not prim exactly but some of the stuff in there…'

She lifted her hands, palms up. 'What can I say other than I have a vivid imagination.'

'You sure do! Well, I shall be looking at you through very different eyes now.'

'Please don't. It's only a book. Don't judge me by its contents.'

'You got me wrong. I mean I shall be in awe now. You're really great at writing. I loved every one of the characters and the entire book. I've been recommending it to everyone who comes into the shop. You writing anything else at the moment?'

'I'm supposed to be but I've got a case of writer's block and need to shake myself out of it. I've made a start on the sequel, but I'm lacking inspiration. My agent thinks I need to relax and have fun. Blames it all on my marriage break-up.'

'So you became a member of the singleton club for some fresh ideas?'

'Far from it. That was Eleanor's fault. She got me drunk and had me signed up before I knew it.'

'Why wouldn't you want to join? I know I was hesitant at first but I'm quite shy and awkward and you, you're the opposite.'

It was her turn for her mouth to drop open in surprise. 'What?'

'Well, you are. I was drawn to you instantly. You have such a wonderful smile and I felt at ease immediately. I don't normally find it easy to chat to women but somehow it was different with you.'

'It was the other way around. You put me at ease.'

'Get out of here. I did not. Most women are bored rigid by me. All I do is blether on about books and my daughter.'

'That's definitely not true.'

'It is. That's why I've been single since my divorce. Suzy's my life. Not many women are interested in a guy who already has a love, even if she is his daughter.'

'That you care about her so much shows who you truly are. Besides, women like you. Jacqueline thinks you're hot.'

He blushed then laughed. 'Okay, let's stop the mutual appreciation fest. Are you trying to convince me that C J Knight, author of the hilarious and sexy *Spank Me Harder, Vicar*, is timid? I don't believe it. What about your profile photo with the fake antlers. That doesn't scream shy at me. That says, *I enjoy a laugh and don't take myself too seriously.* Look at how you performed at the bowling. You were on a mission, lady. You slammed those pins to the outer universe and everyone likes you. After you left, everyone said how engaging and natural you are and Rob the rocker is smitten by you.'

His incredulity was genuine and etched across his face. That, coupled with the fact he'd just revealed several facts that couldn't possibly be true, led her to blurt out the truth about her social anxiety and the fact she had a disorder that was as debilitating as it was embarrassing to own up to. Her hands began to shake and she wrung them together to prevent him from noticing.

'I hate meeting people. Really hate it. Especially crowds of strangers. I come out in spots and hot sweats and I feel as if my heart is going to burst out of my chest, and sometimes I get so panicked I'm physically sick. It's honestly a nightmare to live with. I had it under control to an extent when I lived with William but it got worse after I found out about his affairs. I went to pieces and became even worse. If it hadn't been for my friend Faith, I don't know what I'd have done. Probably shut myself away in that house forever and let him carry on with his philandering, but she took charge, coaxed me out, and convinced me to buy a new place and start again. Sunny Meadow Barn is perfect for me because I can retreat from it all. I don't have to go out or see anybody.'

His brows knitted together at her words. She continued, unable to stop. She wanted him to under-stand. 'That's why I didn't come and visit you when you first invited me; I was terrified of walking through town. When you told me that I could drive around to the staff car park and come through the back door, that made it all easier. I've been scared all the way here that the shop would have too many customers and I wouldn't be able to stay. I don't even think I could take up your offer to work here because I might not be able to face coming in and meeting new customers. It was different before... before my marriage broke down. I had more confidence but now...' Her face crumpled. It had been a risk to tell him but he ought to know the truth. She was a hopeless case and the fact she'd managed to attend a couple of events didn't change who she was. The panic could rise at any time and prevent her from living a normal life. He was going to be so disappointed in her. She'd not be able to face any more events and see that disappointment on his face.

'I know about this disorder,' he said, quietly.

She sniffed back the tears that were forming. 'You do?'

'My mother suffered from social anxiety disorder. It became so bad she wouldn't leave the house and she didn't for twenty years until the day she passed away.' His face became even more serious. 'You have to keep fighting it, Chloe. My mom didn't and in the end, I think it helped kill her.'

He walked over to the front door and turned the open sign to closed. 'I've got tea and coffee upstairs in the flat. You want a cup?'

She drew a breath. He understood. Her hands stopped shaking and she gave him a grateful smile. 'Thank you. I'd like that.'

—

Eleanor knocked at her door ten minutes after she got home from town.

'Hi. Just nipped over to see if you'd changed your mind,' she said.

'Oh, Eleanor, I'm sorry but I'm not really in the mood for partying,' she said.

'Rubbish. It's New Year's Eve. We have champagne. My dad's brought his karaoke set. Why not come over? You can't spend the night alone. I won't hear of it. It's my duty as your favourite neighbour to keep an eye on you and not let you procrastinate instead of writing, especially tonight.' Her eyes sparkled merrily. Chloe was touched. Eleanor had rapidly become a good friend, but no matter how much she pleaded Chloe wasn't going to a social gathering.

'I know it sounds odd but I'd really like to be alone tonight. So much has happened over the last few months and although I'm grateful to you for inviting me over, I honestly won't be good company. I'd rather have some quiet time with Ronnie. I need to get my head around a few things and mentally prepare myself for the new year.' She'd been as honest as she dared to be. She did truly want time to reflect on recent events, plan her new book and be with Ronnie. She enjoyed her own company. She wanted some private time to think about her family who could no longer share celebrations with her and Nanny Olive who'd also gone. She wanted to think back to life on Skye and try and recall who she'd been before William had come along. She hadn't been quite so scared of everyone then, had she? She'd had difficulties but she hadn't felt so afraid. Talking to Sean had helped her appreciate she needed to get a grip of her situation and talk to her online support groups again and start living. *You're stronger than you think.* She would spend the evening making resolutions she wouldn't break, that would see a new Chloe emerge – more like the woman she was before she met William.

'Okay. If you're positive. I just didn't want you to be alone or unhappy.' Eleanor's sincerity was touching. She patted Chloe's hand. 'If you change your mind, come over. You'll be very welcome and none of our friends bite! I've been over to see Alex in case he wanted to come but he's still out with Jacqueline. I don't know if anything will come of their date but if it does, it can't last. Shame really.'

'Why not?'

'Oh, didn't you know? Alex is only living here until the development's completed. Thomas told me. As soon as they finish the last house, he's selling up, no doubt making a healthy profit in the process, and moving to Spain. He only came back to help his father out.' Seeing Chloe's face, she added. 'I know. Shame, isn't it? He's so nice and easy to get along with. I really hope all our other neighbours are going to be as friendly as him… and you,' she added. She gave Chloe a hug and raced off. Chloe looked at Ronnie who looked as crestfallen as she felt.

'Oh no. There'll be no more ham and mustard sandwiches or cheese and onion crisps for you to steal from his lunchbox. What a pity!'

Chapter Twelve

'Happy New Year, Ronnie!' Chloe raised her glass of champagne in his direction. She sipped the contents allowing the bubbles to burst on her tongue releasing a light citrus flavour. Her phone which was sitting on the table lit up, and she read the message from Sean wishing her an adventurous, happy and writer's-block-free new year. He'd completely understood her. Even William hadn't completely comprehended what it was like to live with social anxiety disorder but Sean did, and to know somebody not only grasped the difficulty of her situation but still liked her was the best start to the new year. She'd taken the first step on the ladder. The second had come during her conversation with Sean. She'd stayed well into the afternoon and early evening, chatting about all sorts of subjects...

> *'Talking of keeping secrets, I have one to share with you.'*
>
> *'If it's a secret, you ought to keep it,' she says.*
>
> *'It's fine to share this one, especially as he wants to invite you to the pantomime. He's building up the courage to ask you.'*
>
> *'What are you talking about?'*

'Rob. He's got a front-row ticket for the pantomime *Cinderella* being performed in Lichfield, just for you.'

'That's weird. A pantomime? Why hasn't he asked me, then?'

'Hasn't found the right moment, I suppose, but he will. So, on that basis it's fine to tell you the secret.' He gives her a broad smile and his eyes light up. Chloe likes his gentle, easy manner.

'Tell me what?'

'Rob is a pantomime dame.'

'Rob? Never?'

'I swear he is. He's playing one of the ugly sisters. He plays dames every year in panto.'

'Rob?' she repeats. 'The same man who likes rock music and looks like a bouncer for a nightclub.'

'The very same. Neat, eh? He's the last person I would imagine dressed in a hooped skirt and make-up.'

'You're fabricating this, aren't you?'

'Cross my heart,' he replies making the sign of a cross on his broad chest. 'You want me to take you so you can see for yourself?'

'I couldn't.'

'Chloe, you can't hide away on the hill. It's not good for you. You heard what I told you about Mom. You have to try to get out and what better way? It's not going to be so bad. It'll be dark in the theatre and you'll be with me. Rob would be so pleased you went.'

'I don't want to encourage him and give him the wrong idea. I'm not ready for another relationship.'

His stood with eyes downcast. 'Sure. I don't want to sound pushy either. I get you. Just promise me you won't shut yourself off from the world. It'd be the worst thing you could do. I'm at the end of a phone and always happy to chat. I'll even drive out to you if you want.'

'Thanks.'

He pauses and then lifts his cup to his lips. 'Poor Rob. He'll be crushed. He'll have to pass on his free ticket to another unsuspecting lady.'

Chloe wondered what the year would bring. Could there be any romance between her and Sean? She searched her heart and found the answer simple – no. They got on really well, but he already felt like an older brother, and as hard as she tried she simply couldn't fancy him. She fancied Alex but Jacqueline had designs on him and how could she compete with such a vibrant woman? And besides, he was leaving the development and the UK altogether. Rob? No way. Tim, the boy-man? No. And Ed, a fifty-something-year-old with a grey pony tail and so quietly spoken she had to strain to hear him. No chance. The fact was, she didn't need romance in her life. She'd had it once and it had been followed by heartache. She couldn't face any more of that.

She snuggled under the fleece blanket on the settee with Ronnie and watched fireworks light up the Houses of Parliament in London. She'd turned down the volume and stroked her dog whose eyes reflected the bright flashes on the television set.

'We're fine just as we are,' she said. Ronnie licked her nose.

A rustling made his ears suddenly prick up and he shifted stealthily from the settee to the curtains in front of the French window where he snuffled eagerly.

'What is it?' She stood up; the blanket fell to the floor. It might be burglars. Without thinking she picked up the nearest object to her and followed Ronnie who moved quietly towards the back door. She followed him. She'd read about robbers targeting houses on New Year's Eve, knowing the occupants would be out partying. With her curtains drawn, the house was in complete darkness and somebody was prowling about. She held her breath and listened for sounds of breaking glass. She ought to ring the police but it was unlikely she'd get a rapid response at two minutes past midnight on New Year's Day. Ronnie gave a low growl. She steeled herself. She couldn't cower inside and wait for somebody to strike. She had to be brave, like Laila. Ronnie growled again, a low warning. She had Ronnie. He'd protect her and she'd scream and shout and make so much noise it would set him off into a frenzy and together they'd frighten off whoever it was that was lurking about.

She left the kitchen light off and padded to the back door in darkness where Ronnie now stood, nose to it, eager to get outside. She placed a restraining hand on his collar. She'd surprise whoever was there. They'd not bargained on her being home. With one hand still on his collar she turned the latch as quietly as possible holding onto it for a second, then yanked the door wide open in one swift movement. A dark figure froze on the path. Releasing Ronnie and wielding a luminous green chew-toy dumbbell high above her head, she yelled, 'Get him, Ronnie!' Ronnie hurtled outside legs flying, and jumped up at the intruder.

'Down, Ronnie!'

She identified the voice in an instant.

'Alex?'

'Help! I'm being licked to death by your dog. I'm drowning in saliva.'

She marched outside. 'Ronnie. Sit.'

Ronnie raced around his quarry before leaping on him again, paws on his chest, enjoying the game.

'Ronnie, down!'

He dropped to his feet and backed off, tail wagging. Alex lifted his head from his crooked arms and stared up at her. 'Hi.'

'What are you doing here? I thought you were with Jacqueline?'

'We returned over an hour ago and I came to do some first footing.'

'First footing?'

'It's a Scottish tradition and good luck for the house if a stranger, well, technically a dark male, is the first to cross the threshold on New Year's Day and for him to bring you coal, salt, shortbread, a black bun or a wee dram of whisky on New Years' Day. I've not got any shortbread, salt or a black bun but I have brought you a piece of coal and this.' He held up a whisky miniature. 'Got it from a hotel room free bar. I was saving it for a special occasion.'

She couldn't wipe the smile from her face. 'I know what first footing is. I was brought up on Skye. You'd better come in before Ronnie thinks you've got a black edible ball for him.'

Alex stumbled inside, removed his shoes and presented the piece of coal to her with a sweeping bow. 'Happy New Year.'

'And to you too. How did you know I was in?'

'I didn't but your car is in the drive and there's smoke coming out of your chimney so I took a wild guess.'

'You could have gone to Eleanor's.'

'Ah, but I didn't want to go to Eleanor's. I heard Eleanor's dad, Ted, belting out *My Way* at the top of his voice earlier and decided it was wise to give that particular party a wide berth. Besides, I wanted to come here.' He gave a lopsided smile. 'You want to share my very expensive bottle of whisky with me?'

'Only if you think it's a worthy occasion.'

'Oh, it's worthy enough. What did you plan on doing with that?'

He pointed at the green, plastic dumbbell in her hand. She gave it a squeak. Ronnie barked at the sound. 'Batter you to death with it after my dog had chewed off your leg.'

'Geez, you're scary,' he replied. 'Especially in that outfit.'

She stroked the sleeve of the polka dot fluffy onesie. The Laila in her vanished in a flash. 'True. I wouldn't have scared off an actual robber.'

'You might have. Seriously though, you shouldn't have confronted me. If I had been a burglar or if I'd had a weapon, you could have been hurt.' His face had taken on an expression of concern.

'I had Ronnie. He really would have savaged you if you'd tried to harm me. He has a nose for bad people.' She threw Ronnie the dumbbell which he happily caught and took off to one corner to chew noisily.

They moved into the sitting room where she pulled out two whisky tumblers from a cupboard. He poured equal measures of whisky into them. 'To the new year,' he said as they clinked glasses.

'To the new year.'

They sipped and he let out an appreciative sigh. 'Not bad.'

She nodded.

'I didn't mean to frighten you,' he said. 'I think you're pretty secure up here. Especially with Ronnie.'

'Funnily enough, the house makes me feel safe, like it's watching over me. Oh dear. I sound wacky.'

'No. I get it. Some houses have a friendly feel and this one definitely does. I don't think mine's the same. Yours is warmer, cosier and happier.'

She assumed it was because his home was only to be temporary. No one spent time making a place homely if they planned on moving. It was a blow he wouldn't be staying the long term. She changed the subject. 'How did your date go?'

'Date? Oh, you mean Jacqueline? She scared the life out of me on that bike of hers. I thought we were going to come off on a few occasions. She's a really interesting woman, and the bike event was cool, but I don't think I'll swap my Land Rover for a motorbike, ever.'

'So, you seeing her again?' She cursed herself for asking. Why did she want to know?

One eyebrow lifted in response. 'Would it bother you if I did?'

She stared intently at her glass, wishing she hadn't said anything.

'Of course not. Just idle conversation.' She finally replied. Ronnie chose that moment to squeak his toy endlessly, making any further conversation difficult. She didn't reprimand or stop him. It gave her time to recover her composure.

'That was no date. If it had been, it'd have been the only one I went on with her. She's not my type,' he said quietly once Ronnie had ceased chewing and the noise had abated.

'Oh.' Chloe couldn't think of anything else to add.

'She's very independent and forthright. Don't get me wrong, I enjoy her company too, but I prefer quieter types.' He stared at her for a moment.

She wasn't sure if it was the combination of champagne and then the whisky, or the warmth of the log burner and the general feeling of well-being that rushed through her veins, but she looked him in the eye as he continued speaking.

'This is probably the whisky talking or the several bottles of beer I drank before I came over to see if you were in, but do you fancy going out with my sister, Ashleigh, and her boy, and me tomorrow… I mean today? Ash is really easy to get along with and Charlie's a nice kid. I know a really nice pub in the Peak District that has a superb lunch menu, and then we could visit Dovedale. It's seriously impressive there. Good walks, great scenery. Ronnie would love it. You can even cross the river at one point on stepping stones. I doubt it'll be too busy because it's out of season and the first of January. I expect most folk will be nursing hangovers. What do you say?'

She swallowed hard. Her head was screaming at her to say no and stay at home out of the way of everyone, but she allowed the confident character, Laila, to take over. Her mouth opened, her lips parted and she said, 'That would be lovely. Thank you.'

-

'I don't have anything to wear,' she wailed, standing in her underwear. Every item of clothing she owned was piled on the bed, a jumble of black stretchy leggings, mishmash of jumpers and far too much denim. It was almost eleven o'clock and having faffed about putting on her makeup for far too long, she had left it too late to choose something to wear.

She snatched a pair of navy jeans from the top of the pile. They were a fraction too tight but she'd finally decided to wear them. She stretched them over her feet and calves and shimmied and jumped about, pogoing them over her hips until they were on, as tight as if they'd been sprayed onto her legs. She groaned. They were too tight. What had she been thinking of? And there was no way she was going to be able to get them back off without her face turning beetroot red through exertion. She sucked in her stomach and tugged at the button forcing it through the buttonhole. It would have to do. She'd take a safety pin in case it broke. She threw on a baby blue jumper that not only covered her belly but her bum, and then checked her reflection. The colour was more spring-like than mid-winter, but at least it didn't make her look so sallow. Her wardrobe was sadly lacking in informal, smart clothes. Her usual uniform for writing consisted of either pyjamas, a onesie, or comfortable trousers with an elasticated waist. William had often been critical of her attire and it hadn't taken long for her to come to the conclusion she looked dreadful in everything she owned. Once the weight had started piling on, she hid her frame in baggy jumpers and so the downward spiral had begun. She thought back to the beginning when William had loved her for who she was and had never commented on what she wore. What had happened to them? She'd allowed him to trample her feelings and crush what little confidence she had. It was her own fault the relationship had broken down. She ought to have made a stand. Georgia wouldn't have let anyone dominate her. Talking to Sean at the bookshop and then to Alex had changed her. There'd been a subtle yet noticeable difference between the Chloe who spent every day shut away in her house in Appletree and the one who now lived at Sunny Meadow Barn. There was, as Jacqueline had suggested, another Chloe buried deep within her, who'd always been there but who hadn't found a way to make herself heard. She was beginning to have a voice. Two men had expressed an interest in her, three if she counted Rob. William had made her believe nobody could ever want her. William had been wrong. It was heartening, or it would be, if only she could find an outfit that made her look more attractive and less dumpy.

She huffed in annoyance and decided there was nothing more she could do. Alex would be waiting for her. She picked up her Christmas present from Faith – a pair of earrings, soft blue feathers fashioned into the shape of butterfly wings, and put them on. The effect was instantaneous. Suddenly, she was coordinated and the earrings that dangled from her lobes caressed her cheeks and softened her face. She blew a kiss to Faith who'd be asleep in Barbados now. The text Chloe had received overnight indicated Faith's night had gone as well as her own. She read it again:

My year is going out with a bang!

Happy New Year, Lovely. Hope it's pure magic and you sell gazillions of books. Love you. X

A knock at the door sent Ronnie haring off. She crossed her fingers and hoped the day would go okay, although did it really matter? Alex wasn't going to stay at Sunny Meadow once the development was completed. It hardly seemed worthwhile to get to know him only for him to up sticks and leave. A second rap at the door galvanised her into action. Whatever would be, would be. The fact was, she was going out for the day with a good-looking guy and that in itself was progress. Faith would be ecstatic and William would be horrified by her outfit and amazed any male would want to take her out. That was enough for her to shout, 'Coming!' as she bounded down the stairs.

–

'Ashleigh's missed a treat,' said Alex as he popped a new potato, dripping in butter and topped with fresh parsley, into his mouth. 'She loves salmon and this is some of the best I've had in ages.'

Chloe didn't mind that it was just the two of them. In fact, she was relieved and even more pleased to discover there were no other visitors in the pub where they were eating. She pushed her knife and fork to one side. Alex was right about the salmon – succulent and perfectly cooked, it had been delicious. She sipped the crisp white house wine and gazed into the fire burning brightly. She imagined the room hadn't changed in decades: low beamed ceilings on which hung rows of polished horse brasses, round wooden tables and chairs that bore the scars of time, faded cushions on wooden benches under large windows that looked out over hills and fields, and the enormous fireplace complete with a basket currently stacked with thick logs waiting to be burned. It was stuck in a time warp, and Chloe could imagine local farmers stopping off for a drink after working in the fields or eating a ploughman's lunch or playing dominoes with friends, such was the feel of the place.

The woody aroma was heady and comforting and she didn't want to move from her seat. Ronnie, asleep in front of the blazing fire, seemed equally content.

'Skye,' said Alex suddenly, wiping his mouth and sitting back with his own glass of wine. 'Tell me about it.'

'It was such a long time ago. I left when I was thirteen.'

'But you remember it.'

Chloe could recall everything clearly: the tiny village school in grey stone, more like a cottage than a place for twenty children to learn about the world; Miss Hebdon, the class teacher, in a plaid skirt, white blouse and cardigan, no matter the weather; the windy days when she and her father would go exploring the cliff tops, hand-in-hand or make their way down to a beach to search for shells; her mother, hair under a scarf, baking cakes for afternoon tea and Georgia, hands in the air, pedalling her bike over the pathways and singing, not afraid of coming off. There were hundreds of memories she could have shared but she stuck to descriptions of the houses and families and scant details about her scientist parents.

'Sounds spectacular. I'd like to go there one day,' he said, rolling his fingers around the stem of the glass. 'It must have been quite a shock to move from somewhere so wild and beautiful to a city.'

'A huge shock. I was lucky I had Nanny Olive though. I can't imagine what it would have been like if I hadn't had her to look after me.'

'What was your grandmother like?'

'A trooper. She tried her best even though she was in pain too. She'd lost her son, daughter-in-law and one granddaughter. It wasn't easy for her.'

He shook his head. 'I'm sure that's true. Too much sorrow to bear. We take everything for granted until it's gone, don't we?' His gaze dropped to the back of his hands and Chloe was sure he wanted to say more. His words had hinted that he'd suffered too. She should say something that would allow him to talk about it but as she opened her mouth he suddenly straightened up and said, 'Now, what about this book of yours. How did you come up with that idea?'

She was grateful for the change of direction in the conversation. She could talk about the villagers of Appletree and the book more easily. She didn't want to forget her family but sometimes it was better to put such sorrow behind.

Chapter Thirteen

Saturday, 13th January

The next two weeks flew by and before she knew it she was once again in the back of Fairfax's truck, next to Alex, on their way to the singleton meet-up.

'What's this event called?' Alex asked.

'Hold on tight!' Eleanor said.

'It's not ziplining or circus acrobatics or something crazy like that, is it?' Alex asked.

Eleanor pretended to zip her lips.

Chloe shifted uncomfortably. Even though she knew the singletons, there was still an element of concern. She hadn't said anything to Alex about her condition. She'd avoided discussing William, her marriage and the reason she preferred to hide away from people. Not everyone understood what it was like to suffer from the disorder and the last thing she'd wanted to do was put him off. Their outing on New Year's Day had gone very well: they'd followed lunch with a brisk walk alongside a meandering river where they'd chastised Ronnie for getting into the water and laughed when he'd ignored them and submersed himself with evident glee in pursuit of a moorhen who was much faster than him. There'd been no need to taint it with talks of ex-husband or social anxiety. Unfortunately, they'd not seen each other since.

He'd taken his father's urgent phone call as they were about to drive home. A tree had collapsed during a storm and broken through an elderly aunt's farmhouse roof in Norfolk, causing serious damage. Other buildings were also in need of urgent attention and Alex was duly despatched to see to the work. He'd only returned to the development that morning. New Year's Day now seemed an age ago and for Chloe it had passed by quickly – too quickly – and she'd been left wanting more. How Alex felt was another story.

Chloe hadn't been lonely. She'd spent considerable time trying to work out how best to plan and set out her garden. It was a challenge. She was good at looking after plants and had always tended their garden at Appletree but setting one up from scratch and knowing what to plant was beyond her capabilities. She was wary of employing a landscape gardening firm, her fear of strangers overriding the necessity to find somebody with whom she could entrust the project. She'd found out as much as she could about the sort of trees and vegetation she should plant, but it was a mammoth task. Meanwhile, Eleanor had dropped around to invite her over for coffee and Sean had rung her a couple of times to check on how she was doing and Faith, finally back home in London, had Skyped her. She'd also managed to write a few more chapters of the new book. There was no denying who she pictured when she described the sensual, masculine ambassador in her novel – the scenes had flowed from her fingertips as she'd imagined exactly what it would be like to be in Alex's arms and in his bed. The wall that had been her writer's block was gradually tumbling down brick by brick. Life was beginning to take shape for Chloe. Almost two weeks into the new year and she was making progress in many ways.

The truck trundled down country lanes and over a single arched bridge into the village of Weston. Chloe's eyes were drawn to the church with its bell tower and the sign near it marked 'VILLAGE DUCK POND'. They passed characterful houses and proceeded along the road for about a mile, past sloped fields dotted with grazing sheep. They rounded a bend and a magnificent building came into view – Weston Hall – and as the car's indicator began to click repeatedly, Chloe became glued to her seat: it was one thing hanging out with ten people with whom she was acquainted and quite another going into a hotel where many others might be.

'Here we are,' said Eleanor. 'Beautiful or what? It's a Grade II listed building that was once a grand house. It's used a lot as a wedding venue but today we're using one of their function rooms for our event. Ah, there's Rob, Sean and Danielle.' She waved at the group. Rob, surrounded by a halo of smoke, shoved a vape pen in his coat pocket and strode purposefully towards the car.

He opened Chloe's door for her with a shy hello. Her mouth opened and closed. He was going to invite her to the pantomime and she didn't know how to handle it. She didn't want to go or indeed give the man any false hope that there could be something between them.

'Hi,' she replied eventually. 'Thanks very much.'

'You didn't open my door.' Eleanor tugged her jacket into place.

Rob smiled. 'Ah, but you have Fairfax to open your door.'

'See, Fairfax. That's what a gentleman does: opens doors.'

Fairfax shrugged good-naturedly.

Chloe couldn't get her legs to work and summoned up every ounce of courage to descend from the vehicle and accompany Rob to the entrance. Alex had spotted Jacqueline's bike growling into the car park and gone over to greet her, leaving Chloe and Rob alone. Rob gave a small cough and displayed his yellow teeth. *Like a wolf's.* She knew what was coming next.

'I wanted to catch you on your own before we went inside,' said Rob, hand in his pocket. 'I've got a front row ticket for *Cinderella* at the Garrick Theatre in Lichfield. I'm appearing in it and I'd really like you to come along. We could have dinner afterwards. You do enjoy pantomimes, don't you?'

The huge man in front of her resembled a hopeful child, with eyes wide and a smile on his face, and as much as she didn't want to disappoint him, she couldn't lead him on. It had taken courage to approach her and it wouldn't be fair to him. Honesty was once again the only policy. 'I've never been to a pantomime,' she began. He visibly brightened and opened his mouth but she continued speaking in hushed tones, 'I can't accept your offer.'

'I don't understand. Why not?'

'I have a problem going out – anywhere. Even to these events. It's difficult to explain but I get overwhelmed in company and I can't face crowds or people I don't know. I'm trying hard to reign it in but it's an issue I've had for many years and going to a theatre might be one step too far for me.'

His heavy brows furrowed instantly. 'I see. You're giving me the brush off.'

'No. Not at all. It's absolutely true. I have social anxiety disorder. It's a miracle I've managed to come along today. If it weren't for Eleanor's insistence and the fact I've come to know you all and you're such nice people, I don't think I'd go out much at all.'

'I see.' He shoved his hands deeper into his pockets. 'Okay. Well, I hope you get better.'

'Please don't tell the others. I don't want them to know. I hope you find someone else to take the ticket.'

'I'm sure I will.' The silence between them had become awkward and with a final nod, he moved off. Chloe inhaled deeply. It hadn't gone well. Now Rob had taken umbrage and it was her fault. She felt terrible. This was why she didn't tell people about the disorder. They never fully grasped what it was. She wished she'd come up with some other excuse. There were hundreds she could have made up. Why had she settled on telling him something so personal?

'What did Rob want? He looked very intense,' said Alex, ambling over with Jacqueline by his side.

'Oh, not much. He always looks intense, doesn't he?'

'He didn't invite you to his pantomime, did he?' Jacqueline asked, running a hand through her short hair, flattened by her helmet. 'Oh, he did, didn't he? He asked me and then Danielle at the skating event, and after that, he asked Kaisha at the bowling event. We all said we were all washing our hair that night. What was your excuse?'

'I don't much like pantomimes,' said Chloe, relieved she hadn't been the only one to reject him.

'He'll be running out of potential dates soon, unless he moves onto the guys,' she added with a tinkling laugh. 'He's playing one of the ugly sisters. Maybe we should all go together en masse to cheer him on.'

'Oh no, we shouldn't,' said Alex.

'Oh yes, we should,' replied Jacqueline.

They all chuckled. 'I felt sorry for him,' said Chloe.

'I wouldn't. He has the hide of a rhinoceros. According to Danielle, he's a serial dater. He went out with one of her friends but was put off when he found out she owned a python. At least that's what she told him. He kept going on about his cats and she'd had enough of him. This group isn't about finding a soulmate; it's about enjoying life with like-minded people.'

Sean meandered over with Danielle. 'We can't guess what we're doing,' he said.

'Alex suggested ziplining or circus acrobatics but I don't think that'd be possible given where we are.'

'I'd love to try acrobatics. I did a fire-eating course once,' said Danielle who seemed to have got over her initial bout of shyness and was now smiling confidently.

Alex let out a low whistle.

'It's not hard. You have to be careful though. I set fire to my moustache. At least it saved me from getting it waxed that week.' She choked back a laugh at Alex's face.

'You ready?' shouted Eleanor from the top steps.

Chloe made her way with the others, keeping her head lowered. Jacqueline had given her an idea. Her character, Laila, could own a python. As she walked towards the building, feet crunching on the gravel, she conjured up a scenario that would have her readers guffawing and squirming in delight. She was so absorbed by her thoughts, she didn't register they'd all arrived inside the function room, stripped bare of furniture, with a large circular mat in the middle of the floor until Jacqueline drew to a halt and giggled. Tim next to her, laughed raucously, head tipped back at the sight in front of him.

Chloe followed his gaze, her eyes alighting upon Fairfax, a massive naked, baby-like Fairfax, wearing only a red thong. Laughter rose like bubbles, popping and echoing around the room. Fairfax was wearing a flesh-coloured padded sumo wrestler suit.

With glances at each other and sniggers, the group calmed down bit by bit. Eleanor once again began proceedings.

'Delighted today to introduce you to Japanese Sumo wrestling, where each of you will take on the role of a *rikishi* – that means wrestler in case you were wondering – and attempt to push your opponent out of the *doyho*, which is Japanese for the ring, which you can see on the floor. You are not allowed to touch the ground with anything other than the soles of your feet. Fairfax will now demonstrate.'

Fairfax waddled into the middle of the circular mat, his seemingly tiny arms dangling from massive padded sleeves and he half bowed in the direction of a blond-haired man in a similar suit with a pink thong. They then rushed at each other, attempting to grab each other by any part of the suit, pushing and grunting as they did so. Fairfax lasted about thirty seconds before he landed on his back just outside the mat and had to be hauled up by his opponent.

Eleanor smiled at the sight. 'See. Easy, isn't it? We have padded suits for all of you and we've drawn up a knock-out challenge board, resulting in a semi-final and a final. You'll be fighting for this wonderful trophy.' She held up a crystal trophy bearing a plaque. 'Okay, get ready and we'll begin the tournament.'

The members made their way across to Fairfax and his companion who were now handing out the ridiculous-looking suits. Chloe slipped off her shoes and pulled hers

166

over her head. She laughed at the irony of it. She'd been hoping to lose weight but this made her look like she was at least thirty stones. She strapped on the helmet that came with it. Jacqueline waddled across to her.

'Bloody hell! It's warm in this thing. How are we supposed to push anyone over? It'll be like thrusting at a giant marshmallow?' The atmosphere had turned convivial with everyone joking about how ridiculous they looked. Chloe caught glances from the other others and knew they all felt as ridiculous as she did. There was nothing more levelling than all looking like giant babies in thongs. Her earlier apprehension dissipated to be replaced by a sense of belonging. Sean pulled a face and pretended to pat his huge stomach.

'Want me to take a photo of you for Suzy?' Chloe asked, lifting her mobile from her bag on the seat next to her.

'Would you? She's going to love seeing her dad in this outfit.'

Chloe snapped a picture and also took one of Alex who was engaged in a belly fight with Tim.

'I'll text it across to your phone,' she told Sean.

'Thanks. You want one of you?'

'No thanks. I remember being almost this size without a suit,' she joked. She put her phone back and turned to see Rob half-walking and half-bouncing in her direction. She gave him a smile. 'About earlier,' he started.

She opened her mouth to apologise but he continued in a whisper. 'I'm sorry about putting you on the spot. I didn't mean to make you feel bad. I find it hard to mix too. I try hard but I say the wrong thing sometimes. I've been diagnosed with slight autism and sometimes it makes me blurt out stuff that scares people off, so I understand what it's like to feel left out or to be different. I put people off.'

'You didn't put me off.'

'I know. I appreciated your honesty. The others made up excuses about washing hair and stuff, but you told me the truth and I'm grateful for that. I've just invited Neats and she really wants to come along. She loves pantos. Thought you'd like to know.'

'I'm really pleased for you.'

'Yeah. I think it'll be good. I hope you get over... you know...'

As Rob bobbed away, she caught sight of Sean looking at her. 'He asked me to go to the panto as you suspected and I refused, but Neats is going instead,' she said.

'That's great. I quite like Rob. He's an interesting guy. Not what you'd expect. You know he runs drama classes for troubled adolescents?'

'Really?'

'Yeah. He volunteers once a week. Funny what you learn about people. Ed nursed his wife for two long years through cancer. His granddaughter who's at university signed him up to the site. She paid for a two-months' subscription out of her part-time earnings as his Christmas present. Thought it would brighten his life.'

'Oh. That's really sweet.'

'Sure is.'

Ed, the last person to get into his suit, was now ready and Eleanor, not wearing a Sumo wrestler outfit, stood at the front of the room.

'We're going to draw the first pair of contestants out of the hat.' She lifted up a wrestling helmet, dipped her hand in and extracted a folded piece of paper. 'Alex. You'll be going up against...' She pulled out a second piece of paper

168

and unfolded it. 'Jacqueline! The winner of this bout goes through to the next round. Let's wrestle!'

Jacqueline pulled a mock angry face and dialled up the comedy by stomping around the room and grunting before getting into the circle.

Alex emulated her and marched around in turn. The others applauded.

'You're toast, chubby baby,' said Jacqueline.

'Come on if you think you're big enough,' Alex replied. There were hoots of laughter.

Jacqueline dropped her head and charged at Alex, her helmet sinking into his padded stomach. Alex placed hands on her shoulders and forced her away.

'A-lex… A-lex…' shouted Tim then added, 'Jac-que-line… Jac-que-line!' as the two remained locked in combat. Alex's grunts became genuine as he fought to keep Jacqueline from toppling him. His brow creased and his face turned red with exertion but she kept pressing forwards until he took a step backwards. Neats cheered.

'Come on, Jacqueline! He's giving way.'

Jacqueline drove him back another step and then another. Grunts came from both contestants. Alex was dangerously close to the edge of the mat. He released a loud roar and pushed even harder, the tendons in his forearms straining but it was to no avail. Jacqueline kept walking forward with determination and with a loud release of air, Alex took one final step outside the mat.

'The winner is… Jacqueline!' shouted Eleanor. Jacqueline gave a wide smile and shook hands with Alex who returned to stand next to Chloe.

'Phew! She is so competitive. I reckon she'll go all the way. Tougher than she looks. I'm exhausted now.'

Chloe had to admit he looked hot and bothered. 'Never mind. You put up a good show.'

'Sean, you'll be facing Tim.'

Sean's huge padded belly bounced up and down as he moved to the far side of the mat. Tim gave a wicked smile as he bowed. Both men decided to ham it up as well and went into a ridiculous bowing routine that lasted several minutes before Tim suddenly barged at Sean who was ready for him, and with his long arms outstretched he held Tim, the shorter of the two, at bay, whistling nonchalantly as Tim thrashed at him with arms that made no contact.

'Let him go!' Danielle called. 'Boo! It's a foul, ref!'

'No chance. He'll knock me over,' said Sean. 'I'm trying to tire him out.' His comment earned more laughter which increased when Tim wriggled free, raced behind Sean at speed and grabbing his knees, which were just visible under his outfit, felled him so he toppled over on the mat. He rolled over and congratulated Tim and both went into a silly bowing routine again. Faces were animated and a loud cheer went up when Eleanor announced the winner of that round who jogged a victory circuit of the room, hand-in-hand with Sean.

–

With everyone having taken a turn, the room was filled with high spirits. The event was proving to be a huge success. They'd lost their inhibitions and were rooting for each other vociferously. Chloe had made it through to the final round and was up against Neats who had been hilarious in the first bout when she'd beaten Rob, and in her semi-final against Jacqueline. Rob was staring at Neats starry-eyed as she and Chloe squared up.

Sean shouted words of encouragement. 'Come on, Chloe. Show her what you're made of.'

'Padded foam,' called Tim, earning groans.

Neats stepped up to the mat and placing her tiny hands on her enormous hips walked heavily like an overweight penguin around to the far side of the mat, her bobbed hair swaying rhythmically.

Chloe heard her name being chanted and caught sight of Alex clapping for her. She stamped up and down and earned some more cheers.

A knock on the function room door and a member of staff, a man in a porter's outfit, poked his head around the door. Eleanor rushed over and nodded.

Neats released a blood-curdling growl and launched at Chloe who side-stepped gracefully before facing her again. She bared her teeth in a mock defiance. She was actually enjoying the silliness of the event and Neats was making her laugh with her exaggerated eyebrow move-ments and pretend snarls. She imitated them and as they grappled to grab hold of each other's costume, hands slipping over the smooth padded suits, the door opened again. Chloe stopped in her tracks and released her hold on Neats's foam bottom, staring at the man in fitted chinos and a dark shirt that set off his glossy black hair who'd just come in. Neats, with her back to the door, was oblivious to the man's entrance and having slipped away from her opponent's clutches, now hurled herself at Chloe with all her might, and meeting no resistance whatsoever caught her adversary off-guard. Chloe's helmet dislodged and she toppled backwards before landing with a hefty thump. Her head connected with the floor and as she blinked back stars, the room began to fade to grey. Somebody rushed over to her but she couldn't move or speak. All she could do was wonder what on earth William was doing at the singleton club.

Chapter Fourteen

'Honestly, I'm fine.' Chloe wanted Eleanor to stop drawing even more attention to her with her fussing. The room felt claustrophobic and she needed to get away from everyone including William, especially William whose mocking smile, the last thing she'd seen before she tumbled, had cut into her heart.

'I'll take her outside for some air,' said Sean, putting his arm around her shoulder. She didn't shrug it off. It was comforting to have him there.

'I'm really fine. I'll be back in a moment for the award ceremony,' she said.

'You sure?' asked Alex. His face, the first she'd seen as she came to, had been pure concern.

'Absolutely. It's nothing. The suit saved me and the floor isn't made of stone,' Chloe insisted.

They left by the same door William had come through. He hadn't spoken to Chloe but as she walked out with Sean, suit now discarded, he offered a small smile which she didn't return.

'Bad luck, Chloe,' William said.

Sean waited until they were outside before he said anything.

'He knows you.'

The urge to unburden was too great. 'He's my ex-husband or rather soon-to-be ex.'

'What on earth's he doing here?'

'Beats me but it caught me unawares and once again I've showed myself up in front of him.'

Sean took her hands in between his and breathed in. His bedside manner reminded her of Dr Turnpike's, his eyes as serious and well-meaning. 'Chloe, you didn't show anyone up. You have to get that into your head. All he'll have seen was a crazy Sumo wrestling bout. We were all having a blast. It got a bit boisterous and if he hadn't turned up, you'd have probably beaten Neats.'

Tears burned her eyes. 'It's not even about winning. I was actually enjoying myself. I was feeling better than I have for so very long. I don't want William to be involved in my life in any way. He'll spoil it.'

'Then, honey, don't let him. You have friends here. He can't change that. You're your own woman – a successful writer with an incredible house on the hill and another book underway. He can go and take a swing.' He tapped the end of her nose gently, like he might his daughter's.

'You're so kind to me.'

'That's because I like you. I'm certainly not kind to everyone. Ask Suzy's mom.'

'Bet that's not true.'

He shook his head sadly. 'It's true. I fucked up things between us because I was a self-centred arsehole. Now, I'm trying not to be, and just be the father my daughter deserves. Okay. How are you feeling? Dizzy? Got a headache?'

'No.'

'How many fingers am I holding up?' he asked, putting his hands behind his back.

'None.'

'Good. I don't think you're concussed. Come on, let's go back. Ignore William.'

They trundled back inside in time to watch Neats collect her award. She gave a cough and addressed everyone.

'Thank you to all my supporters, my trainer who got me into shape for this big match, and to my opponent, Chloe. She was a very tough cookie – well, actually not tough at all... pretty soft really... as indeed we all were. Thank you, Eleanor and Fairfax. It's been a knockout!' She smiled across at Chloe who applauded.

Eleanor stepped up. 'Thank you, Neats, and to everyone for coming along. Can I remind you our next event will take place on the twentieth of January at the Arts Centre in Uttoxeter. It's called "Lighten up". Now, the bar here is available to us, so if you fancy staying on, the drinks are on the house.' Everyone clapped and she moved away to join William. Alex found Chloe. 'You want to hang on for a while or shall I get a taxi for us both? I'm not staying. I'm absolutely done in. Two hectic weeks working on the farmhouse and then grappling with giant sumo wrestlers. I need to crash.'

'I'll join you. Do you mind, Sean?'

'Not at all,' he replied.

'I'll tell Fairfax we're off,' said Alex and moved off again.

'You fancy coming into the bookshop this week? I can guarantee you a quiet corner with a swing chair all to yourself.'

'I'd like that. Which day suits you best?'

'Wednesday. If you come at two, I'll have locked up. Suzy's being dropped off this week, after school. You could meet her.'

She gave him a warm smile. 'Thanks.'

'My pleasure. I'd enjoy the company. I get a little bored when I'm on my own, and I could do with some advice.'

'From me?'

'Yes. I want to run something past you.'

'Okay.'

Alex returned. 'Taxi's on its way. Want to wait here?' People were moving from the room, towards the bar. Eleanor however was still in the corner, talking animatedly to William. Chloe avoided looking in their direction as she and Alex slipped away.

'No. Let's go.'

Outside once more she took a deep breath of fresh air. It was like ingesting clean medicine. The sky had begun to cloud and fresher winds were strengthening. She pulled her coat around her.

'You didn't half give me a shock when you hit your head,' said Alex, looking at a sheep on the other side of the fence, who had raised its black face to check them out.

'No damage done. I think it's made of concrete,' she replied jokingly. She didn't want to be reminded of the incident. It only made her feel foolish. It was the first time she'd seen William since he'd left her to be with Lilly, and she'd been wearing a ridiculous costume and made an arse of herself. It ought not to have mattered but it did. Her pride was damaged, yet again.

'You blacked out for a minute,' he said.

'I did?'

'Only briefly. I patted your hands to wake you up. You called me William.'

'Oh shit… shit… shit. I'm sorry.'

He studied her carefully, his eyes searching her face. 'You were desperate to get out of the room. I understand you felt embarrassed but you were among friends who were only concerned. We all looked as stupid as each other and you had no reason to feel ashamed. And when you came back in with Sean, you couldn't look at the bloke talking to Eleanor, even though he kept looking across at you. You know him?'

For the second time in the last half an hour she explained who he was. Alex nodded. 'Bummer. I take it you weren't expecting to see him?'

She shook her head. A people carrier bearing a phone number on the side panels arrived. It was their taxi. Once they were inside, Alex fell quiet and she didn't know what to say to him. He seemed distant, probably annoyed she'd called him William. She kept her focus on the road and tried not to think about her husband or why he'd turned up at the hotel and how he knew Eleanor. She was so fixated on the fields flashing past, she almost didn't hear him when he finally spoke.

'You miss him?'

She faced him. 'Honestly?'

'Yes.'

'No. Seeing him today only served to prove one thing – we've grown apart. I couldn't look at him because he makes me feel awkward and stupid and ugly.'

Alex stared into the distance and a silence fell again. She wondered if she ought to continue but it seemed wiser to remain quiet. The sky was becoming ever darker and she wondered if it was going to snow again. She wanted to take Ronnie out before it became too cold or rained. They were now turning into the track that lead to Sunny Meadow and her heart lifted at the sight of the development on the hill. She was home – her sanctuary. Alex was looking at her earnestly. 'I understand how you feel and it hurts like hell. I've been in a similar situation myself. People can mess with your emotions and head big time.'

The taxi pulled into the first driveway – Alex's house and they both got out. Alex insisted on paying and as the taxi drove away, she turned to thank him. His eyes had dark circles under them she hadn't noticed earlier that day.

'For what it's worth, you are far from awkward, stupid or ugly. Don't let him get to you, Chloe. Now, are you sure you haven't got a headache or dizziness?'

She tapped her skull with a balled fist. 'Solid wood. I'm fine.'

The corners of his mouth tugged into a smile. 'You definitely are,' he said. 'Fancy checking out the pub in the village tomorrow? I hear they have craft ales and some decent wines. It'll be full-on once the site's back up and running on Monday, so I ought to make the most of my last day off.'

She wanted to so very much. She wanted to be able to walk into the pub, and have a night out with him. Her heart thudded dramatically. She wanted nothing more than to take him up on his offer but the village pub brought back memories of William and gossips. She couldn't go. 'I'm a bit nervous about villagers and pubs. Don't want anyone to find out who I really am. Appletree is only twenty miles away and you know how news can travel.'

He nodded. 'Sure.'

He was about to turn away. Chloe stayed rooted to the spot. If he walked off, she might not be given a second chance. He wouldn't invite her anywhere again. If she didn't act, he'd think she was rejecting him. She ought to tell him the true reason. She couldn't go to the pub but she couldn't face his reaction. She opened her mouth. 'How about you come over and I'll cook you lunch, instead?'

'That'd be great.'

'Don't expect anything gourmet, will you?'

'Don't go overboard – no Sunday roast and all the trimmings. Anything hot will do.'

'Okay. Toasted sandwiches it is,' she said with a smile. 'See you then.'

As she walked towards the house, she heard a familiar voice whisper in her head, *You* are *stronger than you think.* Nanny Olive would have loved this stronger, happier Chloe, more like the woman she'd been before William.

–

Back in her office, once again dressed in her onesie, she thought about the day. She might have made a fool of herself in front of William but Alex, Sean and Rob hadn't thought badly of her. As she opened the document entitled, *Oh, Ambassador,* she wondered once again what reason William had for meeting Eleanor and visiting the singleton club. She shoved thoughts of her soon-to-be ex out of her mind. She had more important things to get on with and the ambassador in her novel was going to host an unusual party, one that involved bare-chested women, wrestling and thongs.

Chapter Fifteen

Sunday, 14th January

'Ronnie, no!' A puddle of drool had formed on the kitchen tiles in front of the oven. She flapped her tea towel at him although she couldn't blame him. Not only did the meat smell delicious, but he could see the actual chicken through the glass-fronted door. He urged closer. 'Ronnie, you'll burn your nose. Scoot! Bed.'

He moved away as instructed and Chloe checked she had everything she needed. Goodness knew why she'd ordered the chicken online. It would have been far too large for her and Ronnie to manage, but it had proved to be a wise choice. If she hadn't bought it, Alex might have had to eat toasted sandwiches after all. She had roast potatoes, part-cooked and waiting to go in to be turned golden brown and carrots which she'd mashed with butter and would reheat nearer the time. It wasn't a feast but it would do and there was a rather sumptuous apple pie and custard for dessert.

The knock at the door came ten minutes earlier than expected. Gentle-winged butterflies took off in her stomach and she tugged at the strings of her apron with one hand and cast an eye over the kitchen to make sure it looked clean and tidy. She told herself it was only lunch but her pulse quickened at the thought of spending time with Alex.

She smoothed away a stray hair, plastered a smile on her face and threw open the door. Alex lifted both hands up, a submissive gesture.

'I'm so sorry. I've just received a call from the police station. Somebody's broken into the warehouse near Dad's farm, where we store all the building supplies and equipment, and made off with some of it. I've got to go over there, make a statement, work out what's missing, and then deal with the insurance and source replacement tools and machines which we'll need tomorrow. Bastards have definitely taken the cement mixer and goodness knows what else.'

Her heart dropped like a stone. 'Oh no!' Her reaction wasn't only at the awful news of him losing expensive building materials but at the thought of the afternoon being ruined. She'd had hopes, albeit distant ones, that they would have become closer over lunch and wine and an afternoon together. His eyes were stony with anger at the theft but his expression was one of sorrow at letting her down.

'I'm truly sorry—' he began.

She stopped him with a headshake. 'No. I understand. It was only a spot of lunch. We can do it another time.'

'Yes. Thanks. I'd better go. I thought I'd let you know first. I hope you didn't go to too much trouble.'

'Not at all. You get off. I hope you haven't had too much stolen.'

'Me too. It's devilishly expensive kit. See you soon.' He turned on his heel. Ronnie gazed forlornly after him, a present of a chewed sock in his mouth. Chloe looked down at her dog.

'Don't suppose you fancy a nice chicken dinner, do you?'

–

She'd wasted the afternoon away in a lethargic stupor, watching a drama series that hadn't really held her attention whilst consuming the entire contents of the bottle of wine she'd hoped to share with Alex and simultaneously digging out and scoffing the centre of her apple pie with a tablespoon, before filling it with custard and finishing it all. Ronnie had polished off more than half the chicken and by four p.m. she decided she'd wallowed long enough in self-pity and taken him for a walk.

There was no sign of Alex's Land Rover on his drive. He'd been out all afternoon – a full six hours. As Chloe walked past his house, she wondered for a brief moment if he'd made up the burglary, then immediately berated herself for even thinking such a thing. He wouldn't have let her down with some ludicrous excuse. The robbery had happened and poor Alex was still dealing with the aftermath. She needed to get a grip on her emotions and feelings of self-doubt.

Her phone buzzed in her pocket. Eleanor was on the line.

'Mum and Dad have gone home and Fairfax wants to play Bananagrams. I wondered if you fancied joining us. He's a total cheat unless a third party is keeping an eye on him. Bring Ronnie too.'

Chloe had little idea what the game entailed, but given she had nothing to look forward to back home she agreed to wander across.

Eleanor greeted her as soon as she rang their bell, as if she'd been lying in wait by the front door. She didn't seem her usual self, with her blue hair tied back rather than styled and her face drawn. She rushed them both into the sitting room where Fairfax, sat on a chair next to a low table, was shaking a yellow banana-shaped bag.

'How are you?'

'I'm fine.'

'I was so concerned when you got knocked out.'

'As you can see, nothing to worry about.' She was about to ask about William but Eleanor spoke first.

'Can I get you a drink? Wine, gin, tea, juice, or if you want to be on a health kick like us, sparkling water.'

'Water's fine. I need to rehydrate. We've been on a long walk.'

Eleanor nipped off to fetch it and Chloe dropped onto the floor next to the table where Fairfax was placing small square tiles face down.

'Take a seat.'

'I'm okay on the floor, thanks.'

'Sure?' He leaned in in a conspiratorial fashion. 'We aren't really on any health kick. Eleanor got sloshed at lunchtime and woke up from her nap with a dry mouth and a blinding headache. I'm just keeping her company. Glad you came over. She's a bit down today.'

'Everything okay?' Chloe asked.

'She's been working too hard and worrying too much. Thought a game would cheer her up. Ronnie, don't eat the letter tiles.' He rubbed Ronnie's snout, affectionately. 'Don't want you leaving little messages around the house tomorrow.'

'That's an old joke,' said Eleanor, returning with Chloe's drink.

'Old but still funny,' Fairfax replied. 'Like me.'

She gave a wan smile that accentuated lines around her eyes. She definitely had been overdoing it. She patted Chloe on the shoulder lightly. 'Really glad nothing serious happened.'

'I took my eye off Neats, that's all,' said Chloe and once again opened her mouth to ask about William, but this time was prevented from speaking by Fairfax whose face had become serious.

'Enough about yesterday. All's well and everyone had a great time. You did, didn't you, Chloe?'

'Yes. It was hilarious.'

'See, Eleanor. You can stop worrying about it all now and concentrate instead on beating your old man at Bananagrams.' Fairfax placed the last tile on the table, rubbed his hands together and looked directly at Chloe. 'Ready?'

'Actually, I've never played this game before,' she confessed.

'Oh goody. A newbie. You've missed out. It's brilliant,' said Fairfax. He lifted a tile to reveal the letter A.

'Looks like Scrabble.'

'You have to make word grids but that's where the similarity ends. The rules are simple.' He explained the procedure and demonstrated how to make a grid, what to do if she needed new tiles and how to change an unwanted letter.

Eleanor took up her position on the floor, opposite Chloe. 'Thanks for coming over. It's okay with two but better with more people playing. I rang Alex but he's not in.'

'His dad's premises got burgled and he had to go and sort out missing stuff. The cement mixer was stolen.'

Fairfax pulled a face. 'I bet he had some valuable gear stored there. If he's lost all his equipment, it'll put them behind schedule. They're due to return to work tomorrow, aren't they?'

'That's the plan.'

Fairfax shook his head. 'Bloody shame. Hope it hasn't messed up things too badly for him. He's a nice bloke and he works really hard. I like living near him. Dead handy too if anything goes wrong or there's a snagging issue. He can sort it. I'll miss him when he leaves. Right. Have you got the hang of this game then, Chloe?'

Chloe blinked. She'd been thinking how much nicer it would be if Alex stayed too. She brushed away such thoughts. 'I think so.'

Fairfax put the tiles out afresh and they each took the same number of tiles. Eleanor called, 'Split!' and the game began.

—

After Fairfax trounced both women three times, Eleanor put an end to proceedings. She pressed hard on her temples. 'I'm sorry, but I can't shift this headache. I'm going to have to call it an evening.'

Chloe stood up. 'I ought to go. It's been lovely. Thanks for showing me how to play it.'

'I voted for a Bananagrams contest for the singletons but Eleanor shot that idea down. She said it's not interesting enough. People want to do things they haven't experienced before and not games they could play at home with friends. See that's why she's the brains behind the business and I sort out the website and ride shotgun.' He pretended to draw and fire a pistol then chuckled.

There'd been no opportunity for her to bring up William's name and ask what he'd been doing at Weston Hall. The game had been fast and furious and required all her concentration. It was little wonder it had worsened Eleanor's headache. There'd be other opportunities when Eleanor wasn't feeling ill. Besides, Chloe didn't want to admit William had been the reason for her losing concentration and being felled during the bout. Eleanor had obviously taken Chloe's tumble badly enough and for her to know that she had unwittingly been responsible for the distraction that had caused it wouldn't be helpful. At least now Chloe didn't feel so down-in-the-dumps. One thing was for certain, Fairfax was superb at keeping people entertained.

She wished them goodnight and stumbled out into the dark once more. Ronnie snuffled on ahead, leaving her trailing behind using the torch app on her phone to guide her. It was almost eight p.m. and looking across at Alex's place, she couldn't make out any sign of life. He couldn't possibly be at the police station or sorting out stolen goods at this hour, could he? She swung her light in the direction of the house, allowing it to sweep across the driveway and pick up his Land Rover. She paused and screwed up her eyes. There was something parked on his driveway. Her mouth dropped open in disbelief. It wasn't his vehicle. It was a motorbike. Had he lied to get out of lunch with her? She ran the beam as far as it would stretch. It was definitely a bike. Alex was at home with Jacqueline.

She turned away and blinked back a salty tear. She didn't mind so much that he was with another woman; what hurt her most was the deception. William had lied to her, and on almost every occasion she had believed him because she'd wanted to believe him. Her faith in him hadn't been justified and she was never going to go through a similar scenario again. If there was no trust in a relationship then it stood no chance. There would never be one for her and Alex.

Chapter Sixteen

Tuesday, 16th January

Monday had been a productive work day. Chloe's fingers had clattered over keys and she'd written 5,000 words. The book was taking shape although she needed to work on the humorous angle a little more. She read out what she'd written to a disinterested Ronnie, making sure it sounded okay to her ears. She'd incorporated her experience of the Sumo wrestling day into the newest chapters and fleshed it out adding some riskier sections that were little more than pure fantasy. Laila now drove a Ducati bike – a shining red example – and was a siren that no man could resist.

There'd been no point in brooding over Alex. She wasn't going to waste time on a man who was not only going to be leaving in a few months but who was willing to lie to her face. If anything, she felt disappointed. Her choice in men was proving to be poor.

'Looks like I'm destined to live like a celibate forever more,' she declared as she saved her manuscript with a click of a button and headed off to the kitchen to make herself a cup of tea. In spite of the setback with Alex, all was going well. The writer's block had cleared and the singleton events were not only providing material for her book but had helped her surmount the feelings of anxiety she permanently carried.

Outside a weak sun was trying to pierce through a veiled sky. Days like this gave her hope. Spring would soon be upon them and she'd try and do something with the wilderness that was her garden. She picked up the sheet of A4 on which she'd been sketching at breakfast. Garden design wasn't her forte. So far, she'd envisaged an avenue of cherry trees leading to a wild flower meadow that would attract all manner of bees, butterflies and insects during the warm months, but as for borders and planting she was at a loss. The garden would soon need attention and in reality she needed assistance. She pushed the paper to one side. She clearly hadn't thought that side of things through when she had purchased the house. She'd somehow convinced herself Thomas would lay the garden to lawn, but of course, he hadn't.

Turf would cost a fortune and grass seed would take far too long to germinate. Her cheeks puffed out. She'd clearly overlooked this fact in her haste to get away from Appletree and its memories.

'Catch!' She tossed Ronnie a biscuit and drank her tea. In the background, machines chugged and a lorry beeped noisily as it reversed up the main drive. She hadn't been across to see Alex and ask how much of his machinery had been taken in the robbery. Judging by the sounds, not much. Earlier, deep drilling had shaken her house and made Ronnie bark. The site was a hive of activity and she'd taken to the fields away from the development to avoid passing the workmen.

She wandered back to the sitting room with her mug of tea in her hand and halted in her tracks. A massive spider was crawling across the floor. As much as she didn't like the look of it, she'd never harm a spider and she certainly didn't want Ronnie to spy it and attack it. The creature paused as if it had spotted her and hunkered down on the wooden floor. With its huge hairy legs and fat body, it was by far one of the largest she'd ever seen, and although she wasn't terrified as such, she was wary of it and didn't want to chase it only to lose it and then imagine it to be hiding somewhere in her home. She shivered at the thought of it suddenly dropping on her head. She couldn't bear that scenario. She backed away slowly. The arachnid remained in position. She hastened to the kitchen, shut Ronnie in the utility room, tossed the contents of her mug down the sink and grabbed the A4 sketch of the garden. The spider was still in position. Chloe was convinced it was waiting to scarper off as soon as she approached it. With mug upturned in her hand she pounced on the spider, covering it with the now empty mug and simultaneously sliding the piece of A4 paper under the mug. It was a trick Nanny Olive had taught her. Her grandmother had brought her up to harm no living creature.

She cringed at the thought of the monster spider in her mug, and sliding her fingers carefully one by one under the paper so she could press the paper gently against the lip of the mug to seal the spider inside, she scurried to the back door. Once there she had a conundrum. She couldn't let go of the paper or the spider would drop out and she couldn't open the door because she was holding the mug with her other hand. Mild panic set in. If the spider escaped, heaven knew where it would end up. She hopped from one foot to the other, wanting the spider out of her house and life.

There was only one thing to do: release her hold of the mug and hope it remained balanced on the paper. She did so and tugged at the door which had swollen slightly and stuck in the frame.

'Shit! Open up.'

She tugged again and the door flew open, causing her to step back and the mug to slide from the top of the A4 and crash to the floor with a clatter. Ronnie barked furiously. The spider, now free, raced for Chloe's slipper. She screamed and raced outside, jumping up and down, fearing the spider was somewhere on her person.

'You okay?' Alex said.

'Spider!'

'Where?'

'I don't know. It was on my slipper – eek!' Her arms flapped wildly as she spotted the spider racing up her sleeve towards her shoulder. 'Alex!'

'It's okay. Stand still.'

Everything was a blur. Chloe did as she was told, eyes shut, face contorted. She couldn't bear it if it got into her hair. She felt gentle brushing and then heard the words, 'It's gone.'

She opened her eyes. 'Where is it?'

He held cupped hands out. 'You want to see it?'

'Please get rid of it. Don't kill it.'

'I'll put it down over there. You want to make sure it's gone?'

She followed him to the main driveway and observed him place the spider on the tarmac. It raced off in the opposite direction.

'Oh, thank goodness.'

'It was a whopper. A wolf spider, I'd guess. They usually try and hide indoors when it's cold.'

Chloe squirmed in embarrassment. 'I thought I had it but I dropped the mug and...'

'It's cool. Plenty of people don't like spiders. Lucky I was here.'

'Yes, thank you. I'm not too bad around them but I don't like them on me.'

Now the spider had gone, she felt self-conscious. She didn't want to ask about the break-in and cause him to lie again. 'How come you're here?' she asked.

'Came to apologise again for messing up Sunday lunch.'

She cursed. Now she would have to ask about the burglary. 'Was it as bad as you thought?'

'Worse. I spent hours trying to organise replacement equipment so we could get back on the job yesterday. Had to drive to Stoke and convince a mate to loan us some machinery until we could buy some more. I spoke to the insurance company too and it's all covered, but what a ball ache. I was out until late Sunday night. Didn't even get any food in the end unless crisps and chocolate buttons count.' He smiled.

She couldn't return it. She'd seen Jacqueline's motor-bike that evening. He had returned and he'd probably eaten as well.

'Ronnie scoffed your lunch.' She hadn't meant it to come out so coolly but it had.

He cocked his head. 'You're annoyed with me, aren't you? I couldn't help it. I didn't want to mess you about.'

'I'm not annoyed. I have to go. I'm really busy. Thanks for helping me with the spider.'

She spun on her heel. He reached out for her arm. 'Chloe, what's wrong?'

'Nothing. I don't know what you mean.'

His eyes searched her face for a clue. She wanted him to go away and leave her alone. She didn't want to challenge him and she didn't want to be told any more untruths.

'Chloe, something's up. Are you angry with me because I let you down last minute? Tell me.'

'No.'

'Then why are you freezing me out.'

'I have work to do.'

He blocked her path. 'Please explain what I am supposed to have done wrong.'

The look on his face persuaded her. He looked panicked. 'You said you didn't come home until night time but you did. You *were* at home at eight.'

'I wasn't.'

'I saw a motorbike outside your house. Jacqueline's bike.'

A furrow appeared between his eyes. 'Jacqueline wasn't there.'

'Bye, Alex.' She tried to walk to her house. His expression had changed. The eyes were shining again.

'It wasn't Jacqueline's motorbike you saw. It was Jack the carpenter's bike.'

'He drives a blue van not a motorbike.' She wasn't going to back down. William always had an answer ready when she had challenged him – some convoluted response that she'd been gullible enough to believe. Not this time. She'd seen a red bike like Jacqueline's. He wasn't going to pull the wool over her eyes.

'Jack owns a motorbike as well as his van. He rides it at weekends. He used to ride motocross before he got married. It's a sports bike, similar in design to Jacqueline's Ducati but not the same make. It's a Honda SP1, I think.'

'Maybe he does but that doesn't explain what he was doing here while you were out.'

'He was with me. After I finished with the police, I met up with him at my house and we travelled to Stoke together. He knows the guy who lent us the equipment much better than I do. He left his bike on my driveway. If you don't believe me, go and ask him… now.'

She looked at her slippers. Her anger had faded. She mumbled, 'I'm sorry. I thought—'

'I'd ditched you for Jacqueline.'

'I thought you'd made up some excuse and not told me the truth. William did that a lot to me. I can't stand being lied to. I really can't. I jumped to conclusions, didn't I?'

'Given the circumstances, I'll let you off. I was worried you thought badly of me for letting you down last minute. Turns out I had reason to. Still friends?'

'You saved me from the killer spider. Still friends.'

'Good.'

Jack shouted from the end of her driveway and waved at them both.

'Sounds like I'm needed. You want to check with him to see if I'm telling the truth?'

She shook her head.

'I hope Ronnie enjoyed my share of lunch.' He gave her a warm smile.

'I didn't mean to tell you that. It just came out. Although he did. He gobbled it all up. Sorry.'

'Hopefully another time,' he said. Jack called him again.

'Yes. Another time.'

Chapter Seventeen

For the third day in a row the workmen arrived at seven a.m. on the dot and Chloe had woken to steady reverberations. Ronnie added his voice by barking loudly to be let out, and a sleepy Chloe had stood outside the back door with him, to ensure he didn't run off to greet everyone.

She watched as a red globe rose on the horizon turning the sky a deep pink. She'd never seen a fuchsia-pink sunrise before and it held her spellbound. Once Ronnie was back inside, she rushed to her office to make note of what she'd observed. She could use it somewhere in the script. She'd been up until the small hours writing and was beginning to feel she might have at last cracked the backbone of her book. She'd made some notes of plot to keep her on track and character summaries so she could refer back to them, should she need to.

She hummed to herself as she waited for the kettle to boil, the only other sound was Ronnie lapping up his water. She was going to visit Sean later today and was curious to know why he would want her advice. Maybe he was going to sell the bookshop. She hoped not. She'd become used to his frequent phone calls that didn't last long but were full of funny details about who'd been into the shop and what they'd bought, or the latest thriller

Harlan Coben he'd picked up. He was such a bookworm and got through several books a week. He'd come up with some great recommendations. She'd been on his book blogging site and been astonished to read the review he'd written for *Spank Me Harder, Vicar*. He'd genuinely liked it as much as he'd claimed and judging by all the comments below his post, so had many others. Maybe he wanted some advice about his blog. She wasn't into blogging at all. She had nothing to write about that would interest folk and besides, it was difficult enough to write a novel, let alone regular updates or posts. Many authors wrote blogs to stay in touch with their fans and readers but given she hid under the guise of the mysterious C J Knight, she didn't have to do that.

She poured the water into her mug and reflected on how much better her life was becoming. She actually had friends. Following the fiasco with the spider, Jacqueline had rung to see how she was after the fall at the wrestling event and to tell her about a disastrous date she'd had with a fellow biker…

> *'Oh Chloe, it was pigging awful. The fact he was at least twenty years older than his profile picture was only the start. It was the hair that did it, the curly grey hairs sticking out of his ears. I couldn't tear my eyes away from them. I wanted to pull them out with my tweezers and every time he said "pardon?" I wanted to respond with, "Clean your ears out." And the slurping! Have you ever been out with anyone who slurps their soup? I thought it was a Chinese thing. It's in their culture to slurp noodles noisily – a sign of politeness or something – but this guy, he slurped everything: soup, beer and even the custard on the apple pie. Nightmare!'*

'I take it you won't be seeing him again?'

Jacqueline makes a noise akin to blowing a raspberry.

'What about Alex?' The words are out before she knows it. She makes a face at her reflection in the window. Why did she ask the question?

'He's gorgeous but we aren't suited. Besides, he bears a striking resemblance to my kid brother. It would be too weird if we got together. I only took him to the motorbike event because he showed an interest in my Ducati. I reckon I put him off by having a bike. He looked like a ghost when he dismounted and he threw up in a bush.'

'He didn't?'

'Sure he did. As soon as we arrived at the venue. Don't tease him about it, will you? He's too nice a bloke to tease. Still, you know that. You must see him all the time.'

'Now and again. The houses are spread out so I only go past his if I use the driveway. I tend to stick to my patch.'

'What do you do all day?'

'I'm still busy getting the place sorted. I've been trying to decide how best to tackle the garden.'

'Rather you than me. I hate gardening. That's why I have a flat. Are you looking for a job because I think there's a position going at the factory where I work. It's not bad hours and the money's good. You only have to shove chocolates in boxes and try not to eat any.'

'You work in a chocolate factory?'

'Been there for a year. I'm a qualified dive instructor but there's not much call for that in these parts.' She laughs. 'Actually, I'm training part-time to become a life coach.'

'I think you'd make a terrific life coach.'

'Really?'

'Absolutely. You were made for that job. You're full of energy and life and I reckon you could easily enthuse people into sorting out their lives.'

'Aw, thanks. That's made me feel even more positive about it. Normally people roll their eyes at me when I tell them about it like it's mumbo-jumbo. I really enjoy it. Makes me feel I have some purpose. Beats stuffing milk chocolates in a cardboard box. Well, if ever you feel like teaming up for a girls' night out, ring me.'

Chloe says she will and for a moment believes it. There is a faint possibility she'll go out with Jacqueline. She certainly enjoys the woman's company and if they meet up, Jacqueline can test out her new skills as a life coach on her.

A New Chapter bookshop was empty. From the partly open window the clanging of metal posts as traders dismantled the mid-week market stalls rang out, along with calls as they cleared away and shouted directions to van drivers. One lone market stall owner was still trying his luck with any remaining passing trade. 'Four for a pound, cauliflowers. Lovely caulis. Four for a pound.'

'I reckon he'll be taking those vegetables home with him,' Sean commented. 'He's been trying to shift them for the last half an hour. The price keeps dropping. They were one pound fifty each at the start of the day.' A shining gold ribbon of sunlight had entered the room and shimmered against the wall briefly before disappearing again. Chloe swung idly on the seat. It was therapeutic being with Sean.

He cleared his throat. 'Here's what I wanted to run past you. I've been giving it some thought and to be honest I'm afraid of making an idiot of myself. I want to know what you think of Jacqueline?'

'She's bubbly, bright and fun.'

'Yes. Are she and Alex an item? I know they went to a biker's event together.'

'Funnily enough, I asked her about Alex only this morning when she rang me. No. He reminds her of her brother. They're not an item.' She waited for more. Sean swallowed hard. 'Do you think she'd say yes if I asked her out?'

'I think she would. I know she likes you. She said you were hot at the skating rink. You can only ask.'

'Ah, there's the problem. I haven't been on a date since high school. Rachel, that's Suzy's mom, was my first proper girlfriend and I've not been out with anyone since we divorced three years ago. I have no idea how to handle it. I'm also worried about Suzy. I don't want her to feel left out.'

'Have you mentioned it to her?'

He shook his head.

'You ought to. From what I gather, you're really close and she suggested you join the club. She must have been hoping you'd meet somebody. I bet she'd be really happy to know you even fancy anyone.'

'You reckon?'

'Definitely. I'd talk to her, see how she really feels about the possibility of you going out with a woman and then ask Jacqueline.'

'Okay. I'll try that. Second question. Where do you think I should take Jacqueline? She's so vibrant and up for everything and I can't think of anywhere that would appeal to her. She has a wild side. I don't want to be Mr Dull and Boring.'

His words resonated with her. She often felt she was dull and boring too. She considered what Laila might enjoy. 'What about a karaoke night?'

'What if she can't sing?'

'I think she'd still try.'

'What about me? I can't sing a note. I'm as flat as the proverbial fart.'

'That could be a problem. An amusement park?'

'They're all shut for winter.'

'Take a dance class together – tango or something sexy like salsa.'

'Okay. That's a possible.'

'A comedy show. Laughter's a great way to break the ice and you could go out for drinks afterwards.' Chloe was on a roll. All the things she'd have liked to have been able to enjoy but couldn't, came thick and fast. 'Take a cookery class together. You can go to ones where you make chocolates and then eat them, or a pottery class like in the film *Ghost*, except you won't be dead… go rock climbing… take a helicopter tour. Oh, that last one might be too expensive.'

'Whoa. You're going way too quickly for me. I'm gonna have to make notes. Geez, I can see why you're a writer. You do have an imagination.'

'I live out life and fantasies in my head,' she said undeterred. 'Go to the zoo or, my favourite idea… take a life drawing class together, although you both get to keep your clothes on,' she said triumphantly. She'd written a scene in which Laila took one such class, that morning.

'You know, I reckon she'd love all of these. How about I write them all down and she gets to choose one. Maybe put all the ideas in a glass jar and she pulls one out, and if it goes well she can choose another date?'

'I love that idea.' Chloe clapped her hands together in delight. 'She is definitely going to want to say yes to you.'

He beamed at her. 'I hope so. You've given me the balls to at least ask her. I'll run it past Suzy first. Make sure she's cool with it and then ask Jacqueline at the next event. I've got over three weeks to prepare for it.'

'Why don't you ring her and ask her out, instead?'

'I really need the time to build up my confidence.'

'I can't wait to find out if it comes off.'

'Well, if it doesn't, maybe you could come to a life drawing class with me just to make sure I keep focused on my pencil and not the naked model, you understand?'

'I have a feeling that won't happen. She'll probably jump at the chance to go out with you.'

The corners of his mouth lifted. 'Cheers. I feel a little easier about it. Just got to hang on to my courage. The events have helped. Not that we've been to many but they sure help you bond in a way, don't they? How are you enjoying them? Not too onerous for you?'

She considered his question, swinging backwards and forwards in a gentle rhythm. 'Not any more. It's beginning to feel more normal to be part of the group, although I won't lie: I still get terrible stomach pains before the day. I went online yesterday and talked to fellow sufferers. Some are very helpful and come up with ideas to help combat it. I know what I have to do to beat it. I have a list of things I'm supposed to go through regularly, like affirmations, and various tests I can perform online to show the progress I'm making. I've even started performing Qigong in the mornings. It's good for meditation and self-healing. I've practised yoga for years, but I fancied a change so I'm using a DVD I bought online.'

'You know that makes me so happy to hear it. My mom wouldn't listen to any advice or take any medication. On my father's insistence she visited a therapist but she just couldn't or wouldn't help herself. Some days she wouldn't get out of bed or even talk to us.'

'It must have been hard for you to watch her decline.'

'I blamed myself for years. Thought I was the reason she wouldn't go out. I wasn't an easy child. I got into trouble a couple of times with the law. Nothing major but I was driven home in a police car once and I got a severe warning. It took some time for me to understand why she was the way she was. I wasn't in a good place for a few years after her death. My black period. I took drugs and hated the world for quite a while. I came to the UK to escape, trained to be a social worker, met Rachel. Things got better but then I found that job too difficult. There was too much heartache involved and I felt I wasn't making a big enough difference. Things became tense at home. I took out my frustrations on Rachel. You understand how these things escalate; they start off as dumb arguments that get out of hand and before you know it, you're both saying a bunch of stuff you don't really mean, and then the rot sets in.' He shrugged. 'It wasn't great and in the end Rachel decided we'd be better off apart.'

'You didn't try couple's therapy?'

He shook his head. 'I knew she was right. I'd started drinking and, well, it was better for both of them to have me out of their lives. After we broke up, I spiralled out of control. Night after night, I'd hit the bottle until I fell unconscious. I had no job, no family and no home. I was renting a crappy place in a ghastly area and I didn't care. I was happy to let myself end my days like that, not that different from my mom in some ways. I think at that point I understood how she felt – she simply didn't care any more. Then one day, I was sorting through my wallet looking for some money to pay for a beer, and pulled out a photo of Suzy. I saw my reflection in the bar mirror and I didn't like what I'd become. I was almost as bad as my mother. I was hiding from reality and the truth, and I realised I was the only person who had the power to change things. I gave up the alcohol, sorted myself out, found a job in a bookshop. It's been slow progress but Suzy's back in my life again, and Rachel and I can actually talk like two grown-ups. She's in a steady relationship and I think it'll go to the next level soon, from what Suzy says. It's time I made more effort in that department too. I don't want to be alone.'

Chloe had listened intently. It was difficult to imagine Sean being anything other than the gentle soul he appeared to be. He had the ability to empathise with others and his soft accent was soothing. It was strange to realise he'd had such a traumatic time reaching this point in his life, and it served to prove one person could never tell what lay behind another's exterior. Chloe imagined people, like onions, were protected of hidden by several layers. She was swathed in many thick covers too.

'You definitely should talk to Suzy and then to Jacqueline.'

'A new chapter,' he said, pointing around at the shop. 'Appropriately named, eh? So, how about we make a pact? I ask Jacqueline out and you come to the shop again next week only on Wednesday morning. You don't need to stay if it fills up with customers. You can hide upstairs until I've dealt with them.'

'I think I could handle a visit and maybe a few customers.'

'Excellent. You've made another big step. You've said yes again.'

Chloe cocked her head. He was right. She'd agreed without hesitation. She was making strides at last. Nanny Olive would definitely be proud of her.

The doorbell rang. 'Suzy,' he said, jumping to his feet.

Chloe waited, aware of murmured voices then clumping as both father and daughter mounted the stairs. A young girl, hair in a long pigtail and still in school uniform breezed in filling the room with an energy of her own.

'Hi, I'm Suzy,' she said.

'Hi, Suzy. I'm Chloe. Nice to meet you. Heard a lot about you from your dad.'

'Dad's told me about you too. You flattened the skittles at the zorb event. Those zorb balls look really cool. My friend went in one and was sick.' She dropped her backpack on the table.

'Want a drink, sweetheart?'

'Got any cola, Dad?'

'Always. For you my fridge is full to busting point.' He opened the door to reveal a shelf filled with red cans. He lifted one and tossed it across to her. She caught it deftly and popped the lid.

'Nice catch, baby girl.'

'Good teacher,' she replied, slurping her drink.

There was no escaping the rapport between father and daughter. Nothing was forced between them and Suzy, who had the same piercing eyes as Sean, was as easy and comfortable to chat to as her father. After half an hour, Chloe left them to it, and driving back home, windscreen wipers swishing at the light rain falling against her wind-screen, she couldn't help but wonder what sort of child she might have had, had William only been willing.

Chapter Eighteen

Saturday, 20th January

'Sorry we can't drive you and Alex to the Arts Centre on Saturday but we've headed to Scotland to check out some new ideas for the singleton club and we won't be back until Saturday. We'll stop off at the centre on our way back. It's going to be a hoot, so make sure you're both there.'

Eleanor's cheery message left Chloe perplexed. She'd spent two days building herself up to visit the couple again and subtly ask why William had appeared at the wrestling and now she'd have to wait to find out. She'd told Faith about the incident at Weston Hall and she'd been outraged.

> *'What the fuck was he up to?' Faith says.*
>
> *'I don't know but he was alone. Lilly wasn't with him and somebody told me Weston Hall is used as a wedding venue. Maybe they're planning on getting hitched,' Chloe replies.*
>
> *'Nah. Your decree nisi isn't through yet and the decree absolute will take a few months after that. Besides, it doesn't explain why he was talking to Eleanor. Maybe he's hoping to offer some experience for you all to go on.'*

'If he is, it'll be one I'll avoid,' Chloe replied.

'Wise decision, hun. Time to end this call. I must prepare for a book fair and talk to an unhappy author who wants to jump ship from their current agent and come and join me. I'll be needing more full-time staff at this rate. Love the new ideas for Oh, Ambassador and can't wait to read the finished result.'

'I'm a hell of long way off finishing,' says Chloe. 'I'm only on the first draft.'

'Ah, you'll belt through it. You've got your writing mojo back and a sound plot.'

Chloe is pleased. It matters greatly what Faith thinks about her work and she trusts Faith's instinct implicitly. She's enjoying writing the book: the characters are now taking on a life of their own and the subplots are shaping up nicely.

'If I were you, I'd ask Eleanor what William was doing there and explain your relationship – or lack of it. At least you'll be in the know and it won't distract you any more.'

'I'm not distracted,' Chloe protests.

'You are. You've popped at least twenty-two Maltesers in your mouth, one after another, since we started this conversation, and I bet you've almost finished the bag. You always scoff chocolate when you're bothered by something.'

Chloe picks up the family-sized bag and peers inside. Only three remain. 'Crap. That means I can't have an extra glass of wine with dinner.'

'You dieting?'

'Calorie counting and trying not to go over fifteen hundred a day. Wearing that awful Sumo

*suit reminded me how much weight I had started
to put on.'*

*'You look lovely. Don't go mad. I don't want
a skeletal friend. There's only room for one under-
nourished skinny in this relationship.'*

Chloe beeped her horn and waited for Alex to appear. It
took only seconds for him to lock up his house and join
her. He leapt into the Kia with ease.

'This seems odd – just the two of us going to an event.'

'At least it's not far away so we won't get lost. I'm not
great at navigation,' she answered.

'That's why Sat-Navs were invented. I'd get lost all
the time if it weren't for mine. I'd hoped to catch you
before now for a chat but it's been mental at the site. Well,
you've probably noticed with all the row we're making,
and I've been up to my eyeballs in meetings with planning
committees. You'd think we were attempting to build the
Shard, not develop a site.'

'Is it difficult then?'

'Nightmarish. Trying to get applications accepted and
relevant permissions and then get the electricity board
and gas to agree as well – complete headache. I don't know
how dad stuck it for so long.'

'How is Thomas? I've not seen him for ages.'

'That's because he's cleared off to Tenerife with my
mum for a few weeks. He doesn't like the cold weather.
Plays havoc with his arthritis. They're renting a villa there.'

'Nice.'

'Alright for some, isn't it? Still, if he can't take time off
for a while at his age, who can? Ashleigh's gone back to
Bristol so there's only me in charge.'

'Lots of responsibility.'

'I have wide shoulders. I'll cope,' he replied, eyes crinkling. 'What about you? How's it all going?'

'Oh fine. Writing, dog walking, planning on what to do with the garden when the weather gets better, searching for more furniture for the place. It takes forever to purchase everything you want – new towels, sheets for the spare bed, matching duvets. I get absorbed for hours tracking down the exact colour yellow throw to harmonise with the cushions for the bed.'

He barked a laugh. 'If only. I've got a load of stuff from my mum and sister so none of it matches. It'd be nice to be coordinated. I'm not very good at all at that sort of thing. Dad is. I've got an eye for architecture and interior design but not for those final touches that make a place stylish.'

'What about your last place?'

'Caravan on a site in Spain. No need for anything other than basics.'

'And before that?'

He suddenly steered the conversation to a new supermarket being built. 'That's going to be a monster of a place. Glad I'm not in charge of that construction.'

They'd arrived on the outskirts of Uttoxeter and found the Arts Centre without any difficulty. There were only two other vehicles in the car park, one of them Fairfax's Nissan.

'Looks like we're the first to arrive,' said Alex.

'Sean could be here. He was walking. His bookshop isn't too far away.'

'I've not visited it. What's it like?'

'Lovely. So charming.'

'I can't remember when I last read a book. Oh hang on. It was one my mother got signed by the author recently.'

'No. You read it?'

'Had to know what the fuss was all about. No wonder you wanted to get away from Appletree. What a bunch!' he gave a wide grin.

'I made up most of it,' she protested.

'Made up or not, it was very entertaining.'

'Good. I'm pleased. You haven't said anything, have you?'

'No. I still haven't told anyone.'

'I told Sean. He tried to give it to me to read.'

Alex burst out laughing. 'That's priceless! I'd love to have seen his face when he found out he was giving it to the actual author.'

'He was a little embarrassed, but I was too, so that helped.'

'I won't say a word.'

'Good. I'm working hard to maintain anonymity.'

Jacqueline's bike arrived with its usual roar. She pulled up close to the building, some distance from Chloe's car, and dismounted. As she removed her helmet, Sean jogged up to her. Alex unbuckled his seatbelt and had one hand on the passenger door handle when she stopped him.

'No. Don't go yet. Stay here. Pretend we're engaged in deep conversation.'

'Ok-ay.' Alex glanced at her, a furrow appearing between his brows. 'Any special reason why?'

'I suspect Sean might be inviting Jacqueline out on a date. He asked me if I thought she'd accept. I think he might be doing it now before everyone turns up.'

Alex peered across.

'No. Don't stare at them. Be subtle.'

He grinned. 'Like you, you mean? Your neck is craned so much, you look like a meerkat on sentry duty.'

She shrank back down in her seat. 'Funny!'

'You can use that line in your next book if you want. You're welcome,' he added.

She shook her head with a smile. His boyish grin put her at ease.

'Ah! Judging by the head-nodding and smiles, I'd say she's said yes. Can we get out now or shall we continue our deep conversation?'

Jacqueline and Sean disappeared through the glass doors.

'Okay. We'll go now.'

—

Jacqueline, now standing next to Kaisha and Danielle, waved enthusiastically at them both as they entered the room, a large empty space consisting of little more than a wooden floor that reminded Chloe of her school gymnasium. A notice board to the left contained posters and announcements of future events, largely coffee mornings, exercise classes and choir rehearsals. Chloe broke away from Alex who went to join Sean and Tim, and headed towards the women, pleased she didn't feel the dreaded panic that usually accompanied such moments. She greeted the women and politely asked about their families.

'I've got the weekend off,' said Danielle. 'No kids. No housework, no meals and no breaking up arguments. All three are at friends' houses. First time ever. I don't want to waste the opportunity. I was just asking if the girls fancied going out somewhere later. Pub maybe. Do you fancy joining us?' Chloe was taken aback. These women wanted to spend time with her. She nodded, all the while wondering how to get out of it.

'That would be lovely.'

'Great. We'll sort it out after this event. Here come the others.'

As Danielle left to say hello to Neats and Rob, Jacqueline grabbed Chloe gently by the arm and whispered, 'Sean's invited me out. I'm going back to his bookshop after this event to find out where we're going. It's a surprise. How exciting! I love men who can surprise me.' Her face suddenly changed. 'Oh! I think I know what we're going to be doing today.' Chloe followed her gaze. Two authentic-looking tribesmen wearing traditional Maori costume and make-up had walked into the centre, followed by Eleanor and Fairfax.

'Hi, everyone. This is Nico and Tane, tribesmen from New Zealand. They've obtained special permission from their tribal elders to teach the Haka to groups at team-building events and have come here today to pass on their knowledge. Fairfax is going to be joining in on this one to make up equal numbers and we have two new members of our club coming along too, so it'll be a great way for you all to break the ice. Nico, over to you.'

She stepped away leaving the floor open for the tribesmen. Nico, squat, wide and ferocious-looking with his war paint gave a warm smile that transformed his face. 'Hello. You've probably all seen the Haka performed on television. Traditionally it was used as a war dance for the indigenous Maori people of New Zealand, and then more recently for the New Zealand All Blacks rugby team. It's become increasingly well-known thanks to prestigious events such as the Invictus Games. It is our privilege to tell you about it and teach you about this powerful dance. Let's demonstrate what we mean.'

He and Tane suddenly launched into the war dance with such energy, the floor of the building trembled with each footfall. Chloe watched, mesmerised by their coordination and passion. As they came to the end of their dance and acknowledged the applause, she turned to Alex whose eyebrows had lifted in approval.

'Impressive,' he whispered.

'This'll be a laugh. I can't wait to see Sean and Rob perform this,' said Jacqueline, on the other side of Chloe.

'First, we're going to teach you the words and learn the dance then, we'll show you how to apply the traditional war paint we call "moko", and then it'll be your turn.'

Eleanor spoke up 'And, we're going to record your performance for our website!'

'We'll divide the group into two so both Nico and I can go through the words and movements with you and you'll meet up at the end to perform together. Have you any questions?'

Nobody spoke. Nico had stunned them all into silence. Then with a sudden movement, he slapped his meaty thighs gave another ear-splitting grin and said, 'How about we go straight down the middle? I'll take everyone standing on the left and Tane, you take everyone on the right and the two people, hovering by the door. Too late guys. You can't escape now.'

Eleanor turned around quickly. 'Hello! Welcome. Everyone, meet our two new members. There's Michelle on the left and William on the right.'

Michelle, a short, dumpy woman in her fifties waved furiously. 'Hi.' The man beside her gave a smile and lifted his hand in greeting. Chloe's insides turned liquid. *How could he? Why was he doing this? And where was Lilly?* She had no time to actually ask him the questions. Nico was rounding up his group: Chloe, Alex, Jacqueline, Sean, Rob and Neats, and directing them to the far side of the room.

Alex took in her concerned look. 'Don't give him a second thought.'

She swallowed hard. Her voice was unsteady and weak. 'But why is he here?'

'It doesn't matter. What matters is that you're here and we're going to do this dance together. Besides, I can't do this on my own.'

'Neither can I. Forget him for now. You're part of our team, Chloe,' said Sean.

His words echoed in her head. She couldn't up and leave. It would draw far too much attention to herself and besides, she liked being with these people. Nico looking ferocious, took up his position in front of them. 'We're going to learn the war dance with which you might be familiar, often performed at rugby matches, called Ka Mate Ka Mate. You're going to perform it like proper warriors.' He gave a stern nod. His entire aura commanded respect, and Chloe didn't feel as she usually did when meeting strangers. She would draw from his strength and become a warrior. She wasn't going to let William ruin this for her.

–

'Oh, my goodness! Who'd have thought it would be this much fun?' said Jacqueline.

Neats agreed. 'I think I've strained my tongue.' She stuck it out. 'Yes, definitely feel strained.'

Jacqueline continued. 'I was convinced the words were "cuppa tea, cuppa tea Nora". That's what they always sounded like to me. Now I know differently.'

Rob had been getting his make-up applied and suddenly looked quite the part with magnificent black swirled markings on his face. Neats checked him out. 'You look great,' she told him. He stuck out his tongue and snarled.

'Wow! And scary!'

'It's much like getting made up for panto,' he replied, peering at the finished result in her compact mirror. 'Although it makes a change from looking like Widow Twanky or an ugly sister.'

Sean and Alex were going through the words and moves together, slowly, ensuring they were in synchrony. Chloe was the last in the group to be made up. An hour of chanting, thigh slapping, face pulling and dance movements that made them laugh at each other had eased any tension they might have felt at first. Nico had been an incredible instructor, patient and fun at the same time. She'd not had any opportunity to look at the other group to see how they were progressing, although judging by their loud chants, they were enjoying it just as much. Now she had time to, however, she resisted the urge to seek out William.

Nico daubed gently on her cheeks. 'I won't do it heavily,' he said. 'It should come off with ordinary wipes. We provide packets for use after the performance, so you don't have to go home looking like this.' His voice was calming.

'Do you miss New Zealand?' she asked.

'Very much. I miss my family. Tane and I are both returning to New Zealand in March. We've been here six months and that's too long to be apart from friends and family, and I have a five-year-old son. I want to return to him, be his father again.'

He continued with light touches, his eyes like dark conkers checking her over, ensuring he did his job perfectly. Like the war dance, it was important to him. Chloe picked up on it.

'This war dance, it's very special to the Maori people, isn't it?'

'Yes. It is not a joke to us. We take huge pride in it and although we recognise the commercial value in teaching it to people at events such as this, we still want people to respect it and us. We hoped to raise people's awareness about the Maori tribes by bringing the Haka to the western world. In a way, we are hoping to educate and entertain. There, you now look like the brave warrior you are within.' He stood back to admire his handiwork.

His words filled her with confidence. They echoed Nanny Olive's message to her. 'Thank you.' There was a sense of wanting to perform the dance properly for him and for Tane, the way they would want it recreated, to do their efforts justice, a feeling that she expected the other singletons shared with her. Nico clapped his hands and folded his arms across his wide chest. Tane mirrored his stance with equal solemnity.

'You have done well today and we both have been impressed by your commitment. It's now time for the performance when both halves will come together. Please get into position at the front of the room.'

A sudden seriousness fell across the room. Even Fairfax who usually treated everything flippantly looked fierce and intense. Chloe resumed her spot between Jacqueline and Neats. Alex, Rob and Sean were in front of them. Opposite were Tim, William and Fairfax and behind them, Eleanor, Danielle and Michelle.

Both groups began the war dance with facial gestures – bulging eyes and tongues displayed from opened mouths – before beginning the stamping, swaying and chanting that was the war dance. Chloe was grateful Fairfax had been placed in her direct line of sight. He was completely immersed in the moment and as he rolled huge eyes and made gestures at them, none of it felt silly. They were clapping rhythmically and chanting in time. They were working as one – a tribe. A rush of elation swept over her. She'd never been part of anything like this before, and she became more vocal and went through the movements to the sound of the beat. It was rigorous and fun and when it was over, they cheered each other.

–

'Better than a gym workout,' said Neats as she removed the markings from her face with a wipe.

'I thought I might leave my makeup on. It'd go down well in the pub. I wonder if it'll last long enough so I can scare my kids,' Danielle said.

Jacqueline joined them in the toilets. 'Just spotted Fairfax performing a private Haka for Eleanor outside. Gave a whole new meaning to private dancer. Who's got the facial wipes? I need to take this off and reapply my usual war paint. I'm going back with Sean to discuss a suitable date. What a hoot that was.'

Chloe had finished cleaning her face and was debating whether she should confront William and find out why he'd joined the singleton club or go straight home and hope he'd never show up again.

'You spoken to the new guy, William?' Jacqueline asked as if reading her mind.

Chloe pretended to be checking her handbag for lipstick. She didn't want everyone to know about her history with William and yet it would be hard for them not to find out. She needed to talk to William and ask him to keep quiet about their relationship and more importantly about her identity as C J Knight.

Danielle interjected and saved her from having to answer. 'He's dead sexy. I kept hoping he'd strip to the waist like Nico and Tane. I bet he sports a six-pack.'

Kaisha agreed. 'He's drop-dead gorgeous. His last girl-friend was a Swedish model.'

'Shit! No kidding? A model? I don't think I'd stand a chance then,' said Danielle, staring at herself in the mirror and pulling a face.

Chloe sidled off before they could ask her opinion. Alex was waiting outside the toilets for her, face also wiped clean. 'You want to buzz off straight away?'

'I do but I also need to speak to William.'

'Sure. I'll hang outside by the car and wait for you.'

She thanked him and re-entered the room where William was talking to Tim and Rob about football versus rugby. She steeled herself and crossed over to them. 'Hi, sorry to interrupt but can I have a word with William?' She sounded more assertive than she felt. William blinked in surprise, then excused himself and followed her outside.

'Fancy seeing you here,' he began.

She shook her head. 'What's going on?'

He pulled a face. 'Don't know what you mean.'

'Stop playing games.'

'Honestly, I'm not,' he said. He sighed heavily and turned grey eyes full of remorse onto her. 'You're right to be pissed off with me but it's over between me and Lilly. I've messed up hugely and I know you won't have me back but maybe we could become friends at least. I don't want anyone else in my life but I do want a life. A friend suggested I join this club and it seemed like a good idea. I came along to see what sort of things they offered and that's when I saw you. Nobody could have been more surprised than I was to see you here. This is so unlike you, Chloe. What happened to shy, timid Chloe? I was so taken aback I didn't know how to respond. I wasn't going to sign up but Eleanor convinced me to come along to this session. I understand if it makes life difficult for you and I won't come to any more if you don't want me to.' He held her gaze, his face softening as he smiled at her. They'd shared many years together and he knew her inside out. She knew him too, or so she had believed until he had cheated on her.

'I won't tell a soul here about us, if that helps. I don't want to upset your chances of finding somebody else,' he added.

'No. That's bullshit.'

'Chloe, this isn't like you. Why would I lie to you?'

'I don't know, William, maybe because you lied to me so many times before.' She didn't know if it was due to the feeling she'd got from dancing or being painted in warrior makeup, or knowing she had a group of friends who liked her, but she wasn't going to back down. Before the break-up she'd have hung on his every word, but that was then and she'd changed. 'It would be better if you didn't come again. I don't want you to come. Stay away from me.'

His mouth dropped at the corners. 'Oh Chloe, you don't mean that. What harm can it do for me to enjoy a few events? It's hard for a single guy to meet new people and everybody in Appletree knows about Lilly and about you. I can't show my face in the pubs at the moment and there are precious few other options. You know how social I am. I can't sit around the house night after night, going over my mistakes. This seemed like a good opportunity to have a little amusement. Looks like you had the same idea.'

'I was coerced into this. And in fact it's none of your business how I came to be part of the club.'

'Well, you have no right to be annoyed with me for wanting the same thing you do: friendship. Eleanor is looking to increase membership and is rolling out a considerable programme of events the year, so we'll probably not bump into each other very often.'

She opened her mouth to speak again but a babble of noise alerted her to the other women's presence. Danielle and Neats had left the building and were headed in her direction. She whispered, 'Just stay away, William.'

'Ah, there you are, Chloe. You joining us at the pub? You could come too, if you like,' Danielle said to William.

'Another time. I have to get off. I made other arrangements,' he replied with a charming smile.

'Shame. You coming to the next event?'

'I'm not sure yet. I'll have to check my diary. Nice meeting you all.'

He sauntered away in the direction of his car.

'I have to go too,' said Chloe.

'I thought you were coming with us for a drink.' Danielle looked crestfallen.

'Love to but I have to drive Alex home,' she said, glad to have an excuse.

'Okay. Hopefully there'll be another opportunity.'

'Have a good time,' said Chloe, making a dash for her own car. Alex was leaning against the tailgate and moved to the passenger door when she arrived.

'Thanks for waiting for me.'

'He coming back?'

'No idea. He said he and Lilly have broken up and he felt like joining the singleton club. Part of me believes him and part doesn't, but for the life of me I can't see what else he'd hope to gain by joining up. He wants to try something that isn't connected to Appletree because everyone in the village knows about his broken relationships and he's finding it difficult to go to his usual haunts. He wants to meet people who don't know his past or judge him.'

'Well, maybe it's no more sinister than that,' Alex said with a shrug.

'I don't think he'll be coming to any more events,' she said and hoped she was right. She'd certainly stood up to him and made her feelings clear. They pulled out of the car park and away from the centre. Chloe didn't want to think about William any more. She was irked he'd appeared again and just being near him had wound her up. She cursed herself for believing she could live a life without him being in it at all. She'd naively assumed he'd remain with Lilly in Appletree and their paths wouldn't cross. Had it been an innocent belief? Or had part of her wanted to see him again? If she'd truly wanted him completely out of her life, she ought to have moved to a house hundreds of miles away from the village of Appletree and the county of Staffordshire. Had she been kidding herself all along and been hoping deep down for such an opportunity? She slowed down to overtake a cyclist and shoved all thoughts from her mind. She wasn't ready to consider those possibilities.

Chapter Nineteen

Faith was clear on the matter.

'Well, if he does turn up, there's no way you should stop going to the club events. It took courage to go to each different activity, and now you've reached a point where you feel comfortable with the other club members and are actually enjoying a proper life. There is no way you're going to drop out. I remember what it was like trying to cajole you to go out with me. You always made excuses. I understand how hard it is for you to even talk to one person, let alone a group of people, and anyone who can go from that to performing a Haka, well, it's nothing short of a bloody miracle.'

'I look at that video clip on the website and can't believe it.'

'But you did and you looked scarily ferocious too.'

'I don't know, Faith. I don't want William to worm his way back into my life.'

'There's a simple answer to that problem.'

'Which is?'

'Don't let him. You don't have to bother with him if he has the audacity to come along to another. They're group events so you can talk to any of the others instead. It's not like when you were married.'

Chloe glanced at Ronnie who'd laid his head on her lap. He hadn't missed William in the slightest.

'Anyway, you have the gorgeous Alex on your doorstep. He looked pretty darn good in the video too. Nice firm thighs. I paused it to check him out.'

Chloe released a snort. 'Trust you. He has got nice legs though.'

'You seen him this week?'

'No.'

'How can you live within a few hundred metres of each other and not see each other?'

'To start with, it's a few thousand metres and secondly, he's working on the building the furthest away. I don't want to pester him when he's working.'

'What about after work?'

'I don't like to disturb him. He goes to bed early because they start work early.'

'Oh, you know that, do you?'

Chloe blushed. 'I noticed the upstairs lights were on when I walked Ronnie a couple of times after dinner.'

'You need to do something about it, you know?'

'I don't know what you mean.'

'Honestly, Chloe. You're not stupid. You know exactly what I'm inferring. You definitely have a thing for Alex. Go and talk to him. Or invite him to race Ronnie around the reservoir or something, please. Every week for a month, I've watched your face transform when you talk about him. You have feelings for the man!'

'I haven't. He's leaving once the houses are up, and he's moving to Spain. And besides, if he'd liked me in that way, he'd have asked me out by now. We haven't been out just the two of us since we went for lunch on New Year's Day.'

'Didn't he invite you to the pub after work one night?'

'Oh yes. He was supposed to come here instead for Sunday lunch but got called away before we'd even started it.'

'Did you invite him over another time? No, of course you didn't because that's not in your nature. I bet if you had, he'd have come over in a shot. He was probably hoping you'd invite him again.'

Chloe chewed over her words. 'But what if you're wrong and he refused my invite? I don't know how I'd feel. And I wouldn't want to make things difficult between us. I nearly messed it up over Jack's motorbike. We're getting on well again. I don't want to spoil that.'

'You overthink everything, Chloe. Trust your instincts.' Faith spoke kindly.

Chloe stroked Ronnie's head. She knew in her heart that Faith was unlikely to succeed in persuading her to do anything about the Alex situation. It was true she really liked him and even wanted to spend more time with him, but there was little point given he'd be departing. It wasn't to be and that was that. Ronnie's ears suddenly pricked up and after some scrabbling to get out accompanied by low woofs, he rushed from the room.

'Don't need a doorbell when you have a Ronnie,' said Chloe.

'Somebody at the door?'

'It seems so. He's barking, so the answer is probably yes. Speak soon.'

'Bye, hun.'

The screen went blank and Chloe hastened to the back door. Eleanor waved at her through the small glass window. 'Co-ee!'

No sooner had Chloe let her in than she began speaking at speed, simultaneously patting Ronnie. 'So sorry we left you and Alex in the lurch. We're growing the business and had to talk to some people about franchising it. We're keeping the Staffordshire club under our control but gradually rolling out our business model to others who want to take on the events manager role. We can't be shooting off from one end of the country to the other on a daily basis, and it's best to organise local events for local people. So, what did you think of the Haka, yesterday?'

Chloe marvelled at the fact Eleanor had managed to say all that without appearing to take a breath.

'Huge fun. You want a coffee?'

'That'd be great. I'm not interrupting anything, am I?'

'No. I was chatting to a friend on Skype. We'd finished when you called around.'

'Ah, the internet! Where would we be without it?'

'Without food,' said Chloe, searching for two mugs in her cupboard.

Eleanor slid onto one of the stools. 'There are such things as supermarkets.'

'I don't like pushing trolleys with wonky wheels or navigating aisles and aisles of food,' said Chloe. She'd practised this answer before, ready for when she'd been challenged by acquaintances and hadn't wanted to explain the true reason for never going into shops. 'Quieter and simpler to do it all online.'

'You have a point, although I like to check out the produce to make sure it's in date and choose the best-looking fruit and veg. However, if we get much busier, I'll be shopping online too.' She gave a breezy smile that didn't quite reach her eyes. Chloe noticed the purplish hues – tell-tale signs Eleanor hadn't been sleeping well.

The kettle boiled and Chloe prepared the drinks, whilst Eleanor talked about the market she used to visit in Derby before they had moved. Chloe cringed. Markets were another no-no for her. She passed Eleanor her drink with a smile and sat opposite her at the breakfast bar. Eleanor continued, voice light.

'You're probably wondering why I came around. I wanted to pick your brains.'

'Me?'

'Yes, you're a member of the singleton club. I wanted to know what your thoughts were on the events you've attended so far and if you think we've got the right number of people going to them. You're my market research.' She blew on the coffee and took a sip. Chloe was honest with her answer.

'I've enjoyed all three events and in my opinion there were more than enough people at each. Having a low number of participants makes the gatherings more intimate, and I've got to know everyone in a short space of time.'

Eleanor didn't seem to be really taking in what she was saying, just nodding along. 'Fairfax thinks we need to increase the number of people attending each event. We've got quite a list of new subscribers and I'm trying to work out how best to handle them all. We advertised the website and club at the beginning of the year and I think half of Staffordshire decided they wanted new year challenges. I was considering advertising events and the first ten people to sign up for each will be able to go. That seem fair to you?'

'Yes but only if the same ten people don't keep signing up before the others,' Chloe offered.

'I hadn't thought of that. That's a possibility, isn't it?'

'You could offer the same event a few times the same week. That would enable more folk to sign up and have the chance to do it, or even offer it several times in the year.'

'That's a good idea. I like that. Thank you.' Once again, she sipped her coffee and studied Chloe's face. Chloe had the distinct impression she hadn't really come around to ask for advice. Eleanor was a businesswoman. She'd have ideas and thoughts that didn't require any input from Chloe. A familiar prickling began in her scalp and she was suddenly overcome with awkwardness. It could hit her at any time. Even with friends or people she felt comfortable with. She would suddenly think they were judging her.

'You've guessed, haven't you? The *true* reason I came around?' said Eleanor at last.

'No.'

'You look like you suspect me of something and you'd be right. I'll come clean: I spotted you and the new guy, William, talking outside the Arts Centre, and I wondered if there was a little spark between you. I know I shouldn't interfere and Fairfax told me to butt out, but I think William really likes you. I caught him staring at you at the wrestling before Neats knocked you out, really eyeing you up and down with a look on his face that I can only describe as hungry, and I watched him again yesterday. I couldn't help but notice the way he kept looking across at you, whilst everyone was learning the Haka. He's as keen as mustard. It was written all over his face. So, I had to find out your thoughts. He's very dishy.' She gave Chloe a wink.

Chloe swallowed hard. 'It isn't ever going to happen.'

'Why not? He's the best-looking guy there and totally charming. He's a regional sales director for a big stationery company and has a great set of teeth.'

She'd have to explain. 'I don't want it bandied around but William's is actually my almost ex-husband.'

Eleanor let out a gasp.

'He didn't have a clue I'd be at the Haka event and I didn't know he was coming. We had words afterwards, so it's unlikely he'll attend any future events. If he does turn up, then I'll drop out. You understand, don't you?'

'No, don't do that! Please don't leave.'

'But if you have lots of new members, you don't need me to come along.'

'You're one of the family. You can't drop out.'

'I've really enjoyed it but I don't want to keep meeting other people. That's not who I am. I don't feel comfortable around new people all the time. I like familiarity.'

'Chloe, you mustn't give up.'

Chloe wasn't going to argue. The fact was that if different people, other than those she was becoming accustomed to seeing, were going to be coming along to events, she'd leave. She only wanted to be with those she'd grown used to.

Eleanor released a sigh and cupped her mug with both hands. She lowered her head. When she next raised it, she had tears in her eyes.

'I'm in a bit of a pickle. I lied about the new members. That was bullshit. I'm full of shit. Sometimes I almost believe it myself. Fairfax does. I've not exactly been completely honest with him either. We only have the ten members in total if we include William.'

Chloe blinked several times. 'But you gave the impression...'

'I know. I talk that talk, don't I? It's the way I am – loud, gregarious and bold. I give the impression everything is super, even when it's going badly. I haven't told anyone

– not my folks, not Fairfax, nobody.' She paused to swipe at a tear.

'Fairfax and I gave up everything to establish this company. We gave up paid employment, put our hearts and souls into it. We've even put up our house here as collateral with the bank so if the business goes belly-up, we'll be homeless. Fairfax has worked like a demon to organise events with companies and come up with all the ideas and put the website together. I worked on the marketing and fronted the company.

'Last year we tried two patches: one in Derbyshire and one near Birmingham but we couldn't get the idea to take off. Numbers were so few that those who attended the initial events dropped out quickly. We figured we were doing something wrong or we were targeting the wrong areas. We relaunched the website and began again, this time in Staffordshire. In spite of all the publicity we generated, it hasn't been as easy to drum up interest. There was a promising spike at first. It appeared we'd have enough members to set up several centres but although we had lots of enquiries, they didn't convert into memberships. The few who actually signed up in August and September at a special reduced rate began dropping out once we increased the fees. We were almost out of money and hope but we tried one last desperate attempt before Christmas and carried out several street promotions with leaflets and banners and promises of exciting events in the new year. You've met everyone we cajoled into joining. We're fresh out of ideas of how to encourage people to join. We need it to grow organically and it isn't happening. The only card we had left to play was to try and sell franchises.

'We'd really pinned our hopes on the couple in Scotland to buy into it but they're unsure because we don't have a strong enough business model to show them. Advertising and marketing costs have drained our bank balance, and the monthly fees people pay just about cover the costs of putting on the actual events.' She wiped at another tear.

'The stupid thing is, I still believe we can make a go of it. The Haka video attracted more hits than anything else we put on the site. I'm trying to involve newspapers and magazines and I'm certain that if we can see it through the next six months, we'll make it. I'm sure we will, but it's hard. Much harder than I ever imagined and I keep putting on a face and talking it up, especially in front of Fairfax, when inside I'm terrified we'll lose everything: the business and our home. I don't want to give up. I'm not a quitter. Michelle who came along to try it out has decided she doesn't want to sign up. If you stop coming to events, it's almost certain Alex will too, and then there'll only be eight people, who'll tire of each other quickly, and our business will bomb.'

Eleanor looked up at Chloe. A tear that had broken free of her lashes trickled down her cheek. 'Not the high-flyer you thought I was, am I?'

'I had no idea. You are so energetic and positive and convincing. I thought the club was doing really well.'

'I wish that were the case. I let Danielle off paying this month's fees because she couldn't afford them, just to keep her coming along. I didn't tell Fairfax what I'd done. He'd have advised me against it and I can't keep letting her come for free. William signing up to the club was a relief. I needed his cheque for the month. I don't want to give up on this. It was my dream and Fairfax backed me on it. I'll be letting him down too. I can't let it fail.'

'I'm so sorry.'

'Don't be. When you and Alex signed up, it helped not just financially, but it gave the group a new dynamic. I was beginning to think they'd all quit too but as soon as you both came along, they paid up on time for another month, and I'm really grateful for that. There's no point in folk coming to events if there's only one or two people at them. I need to grow it and I can't give up.'

Chloe thought for a second. 'You need William to keep attending, don't you?'

Eleanor gave a helpless shrug.

'Okay. I'll speak to him and if he wants to come to the next event I won't stop him or make a fuss.'

'That's really kind of you. You're a good friend and neighbour.' Eleanor stood up and moving around to Chloe's side of the table gave her a hug.

Chloe felt for the woman. For all her supreme confidence and cheerful disposition, Eleanor was struggling to make a go of something that mattered hugely to her. She'd done a fantastic job of hiding that fact and Chloe admired her tenacity.

'Is there anything I can do to help?' Chloe crossed her fingers behind her back and hoped Eleanor didn't ask for her to drum up business. She'd be useless.

'Don't tell anyone, not even Alex.'

'Okay.'

'And I'll keep your relationship with William secret.'

'Alex and Sean know but they're not likely to say anything.'

'I shan't discuss it with anyone.'

'Thanks.'

'You'll still come to the event tomorrow?'

'Of course, I shall.' It appeared Chloe wasn't the only person hiding the truth from people. The least she could do was support Eleanor for the time being and hope her instincts were right and the business took off.

Eleanor got ready to leave. 'Thanks for the coffee and chat and for listening. You're a good listener.'

'Any time.'

—

She'd hated making the call to William but it had to be done.

> William, it's Chloe.
>
> Chloe, is everything okay?
>
> Of course. I wanted to say I'm sorry about being bitchy at the Arts Centre. I was shocked to see you, that's all.
>
> Naturally. You did behave a little out of character. I wasn't doing anything wrong.
>
> If you want to go to the events you should go.
>
> Are you still going along?
>
> Yes.
>
> And you're happy if I come too?
>
> Yes.
>
> Glad you saw reason. It isn't like you to be belligerent.
>
> No. I said sorry.
>
> Yes. You did. I was hurt by your temper tantrum. Still, that's water under the bridge. Thanks for ringing. See you tomorrow.

Chloe stared at herself in the mirror after making the call. With only a few words he'd made her feel she was completely in the wrong. She reminded herself she'd done this for Eleanor and Eleanor now knew about William.

She'd told herself she'd be fine tomorrow. She had friends at the club. She'd be fine. Her trembling hands told a different story.

Chapter Twenty

'Hold on tight!' Chloe couldn't have held on more tightly if she tried. Ed was driving the six-wheeled amphibious all-terrain vehicles flat out like a man possessed, his neat teeth clenched on display like the clay character, Wallace. His grey ponytail was flapping wildly and Chloe had to periodically lean to one side to avoid being whipped by it, as well as try to remain in her seat.

'Yay!' yelled Ed as the Argocat reached its top speed of 30mph and belted around the purpose-built course, earth flying as it drifted out of the woodland and around a muddy bend. It wasn't the speed that concerned Chloe as much as the fact the machine had no steering wheel and was being controlled by two levers which locked either set of four wheels at any time and Ed had been taking huge delight in doing just that and sending them spinning around their own axis until she felt dizzy.

He released a cry that sounded like a cowboy taming a bucking bronco and straightened out the vehicle before hurtling down a steep slope towards the lake at full tilt.

'Ed!' Chloe shouted but her words were carried away by the wind and they thundered into the water at speed, a tidal wave washing over the bonnet of the craft and soaking them both. The machine slowed to a tenth of the speed and puttered across the body of water.

'Awesome sauce!' he shouted.

Chloe couldn't work out at what point Ed had transformed from a mild-mannered man who could barely manage a full sentence without looking at the back of his hands, into a maniacal hipster driver who was determined to outmanoeuvre all the other amphibious crafts taking part in the race on the specially-designed course, but to say he'd become enthusiastic was an understatement. She attempted to unclench her balled fists. The Argocat could only manage three miles an hour in water. She had time to brace herself for the ascent the other side.

'Wicked, isn't it?' His face was shining with enthusiasm.

'Certainly exhilarating,' she said, not wishing to crush his excitement. She'd never seen him so animated. 'You ever driven one of these before?' she asked him.

Ed, who usually rode a bicycle to events and spent half an hour chaining it to the nearest lamppost, hadn't struck her as a car fanatic, let alone capable of driving one of these surprisingly agile vehicles. So far they'd navigated ditches, hills and mud slides and now the water. It was just as well they were dressed appropriately, in event-issued overalls. She was plastered in mud. Ed gave a wry smile.

'A long time ago I was a member of the Royal Armoured Corps. Used to drive FV430s. They're small armoured vehicles that could be converted to go into water. This reminds me of those happy days when I was part of a team – a group of like-minded fellow soldiers who had my back, even if they did call me Cilla.'

'Cilla?'

'On account of my surname – Edward Black. Military nicknames are funny like that. I didn't mind. We all had crazy names.'

'How long did you serve in the army?'

'Sadly only four years. I wanted to sign up for longer but my wife had other ideas. I came out at her insistence. Being a soldier can take its toll on a relationship. It was a choice of career or marriage and whilst I missed the military way of life and my comrades in arms, I wouldn't have chosen otherwise. I was lucky with Mary. Not everyone finds their soulmate but I did.' Now he'd started talking there was no stopping him. He lifted his eyes towards Chloe.

'We made it to our silver wedding anniversary before Mary became ill. She passed away a few weeks after our twenty-sixth. It's been horribly lonely without her. You get used to one person always being there for you and sharing your world. It's a darker place without them. Still, I don't want to sound maudlin: it's been six years since her tragic passing and I've met all you wonderful folk, so here I am today having fun. I thought I'd never be able to enjoy anything again. I couldn't have imagined I'd be in the driving seat of one of these vehicles. It's marvellous. It's a real tonic. I'm very glad to be here. I have Katy to thank for this. I'll send her an email later to tell her all about it.'

'Who's Katy?'

'My granddaughter. She dreamt this all up herself and bought me a subscription to the club out of money she earned herself. She's a bright girl. Studies Politics in Bristol.'

'I bet you're very proud of her.'

'Ridiculously so,' he replied and fell silent with a smile on his face.

Chloe looked over her shoulder. William and Jacqueline weren't far behind them, although at the moment, she and Ed were holding their lead. She could make out other vehicles further back still. Her partner was a man on a mission to succeed. Although he'd been chatting, he'd kept one eye on instruments and the other on the direction in which they were travelling. He was clearly comfortable with the vehicle's controls. William however, wasn't someone who gave up easily. He liked to win and he was a sore loser. He'd be doing everything within his power to catch up and Jacqueline was competitive. The water swooshed under the vehicle and Ed suddenly spoke up again. 'Better hang on. We're almost across and we've got that hill to climb followed by one more circuit through woods to victory. You ready?'

'Ready.'

The Argocat's engine picked up as they drove out of the lake and rumbled up the hill towards the finish line.

—

'Congratulations, Ed. You certainly pushed your vehicle to the limit.'

William may have been saying all the right things but his eyes glittered, a tell-tale sign to Chloe that he was irked at losing. He slapped Ed on the shoulder in a manly fashion. William had always been a people person – her polar opposite, yet watching him now, she wondered how much of what he said and did was merely an act. He'd climbed up the promotional ladder at speed to become one of the youngest regional sales directors in the company, and now she wondered how many people he'd trampled on to attain his lofty position. He wouldn't stop until he was manager or even director. William loved success, which was another reason their relationship had broken down – in his eyes, Chloe wasn't a winner.

William suddenly grinned widely at Jacqueline and pulled her into a friendly side hug. 'Sorry, team buddy. I let you down.' She airily brushed her hair away from her face.

'No, you didn't. We just couldn't beat the Argocat master here.'

Ed gave a small, nervous cough. 'I'm afraid I had the advantage. I've driven similar vehicles before in terrain not unlike that course, so it wasn't too great a challenge for me. And I had Chloe as my co-driver.'

William's smile grew ever wider. 'You're a worthy winner then. And you have something to remind you of that.' He pointed at the small trophy in Ed's hands, a pewter Argocat on a wooden base.

The group was in a jubilant mood after racing around the muddy track. It had been an adrenaline high for most of them. Chloe headed to the large box by the shed to drop off her dirty overalls that would be washed and ready for use at the next event. As she peeled them off, her own clothes clean underneath, William joined her.

'That was exhilarating, wasn't it?' he said.

'Definitely.' Suddenly aloof, she didn't want to be alone with William. She cast about hoping Jacqueline or one of the others would come across but they were still discussing the day's event.

'You did really well. It can't be easy for you, coming to these events. As I recall I couldn't convince you to come away for a quiet weekend in Rome, let alone to anything like this.'

'Crowds, William. I couldn't face huge numbers of people. You knew before you married me.'

'And we were together for almost five years and in all that time you'd never have agreed come to something like this. You wouldn't even go to the cinema with me. Now look at you – wrestling in a stupid suit and racing about in an Argocat.'

'What are you suggesting? That I was faking my disorder?'

'No, just commenting that you appear to have made a remarkable recovery.' He turned up the smile that in bygone days would have melted her and prevented her outburst. This time it didn't work. Her hackles were up. How dare he insinuate such a thing! He of all people should understand how hard it had been for her to cope on a daily basis. He knew her history. He'd comforted her when she'd broken down after Nanny Olive's death and he'd been there for her in his darkest hours, and to have this, a disorder that left her feeling fragile and incapable, that tormented her regularly, spoken about in this manner was too much. He should understand that for her to even be here was a mammoth step. More importantly, he should be pleased that she'd made any progress.

'You bastard.'

His mouth turned down instantly and shook his head repeatedly from side to side to reassure her.

'No. Chloe. You misunderstand me. I don't mean to upset you. Far from it. I'm hugely impressed by what you've achieved. It must have taken enormous courage. I kicked the stuffing out of you with what I did and yet, here you are fighting back and overcoming far more than just me treating you like shit.'

As if by magic, the anger disappeared. She was over sensitive. How could William still manage to press her buttons and make her so defensive with one complimentary sentence. She mumbled, 'That's okay then.'

'Chloe, don't think too badly of me. I *was* a bastard. I hurt you and I'm truly sorry for that. I can't tell you how much I regret my actions. I shouldn't have done that to you. It was cruel. Horribly cruel. You had enough to contend with and I ought to have been more understanding and supportive instead of throwing in the towel and searching for something I thought would be more satisfying. I should've respected our marriage vows and stuck it out with you. We were good together. Once upon a time we were really good.' He let his words hang and then, as he dropped his overalls into the bin he whispered. 'I'm so proud of you. Well done.'

His words sideswiped her. She balled her overall and dropped it into the bin on top of his and watched his retreating back. He bumped fists with Rob and moved away to talk to Sean and Danielle.

Eleanor scurried across. 'Is everything okay? He's not been annoying you, has he? I'd hate that, especially as you convinced him to remain part of the club. I'm sorry, Chloe. I don't want you to be miserable. I can always ask him to leave.'

Chloe assured her that wouldn't be necessary. 'He was quite… sweet,' she replied.

'Oh, thank goodness!' Eleanor rubbed at an angry spot that had formed on her forehead. Chloe noticed there were two of three others around her nose and she had a cold sore on her top lip.

'It's fine. Honestly, and the event was amazing.'

Eleanor's shoulders dropped. 'I'm so glad you enjoyed it. We were hoping a photographer from the *Staffordshire Newsletter* would turn up to take some pictures but he didn't. Fairfax has taken a few shots and a short video of the Argocats charging out of the lake and up the hill, and we're going to send our own article to various papers and put it on social media. I don't understand why more people aren't joining us. Don't people want to have fun?'

'They will. Once they see what's available.'

Eleanor gave a small nod. 'Positivity. That's what's needed. Glad you and William are okay.'

'We are.'

People were leaving. Ed was still in his overalls and headed towards her, passing Eleanor who was on her way to thank the event organiser. He halted in front of Chloe.

'I hope I didn't scare you too much. I don't know what got into me.'

'I enjoyed it.' She realised it was the truth.

'Tomorrow is another day and I'll be boring old Ed the gardener. It was great to… to feel alive.'

'I didn't know you were a gardener.'

'Been in the business since I left the army. I used to work with a major landscape gardening company but now I do my own thing. I prefer to work at my own pace.'

'I could do with some advice. I have a completely blank canvas of a garden and I don't have a clue how to set it out.'

'Would you like some ideas?'

'I really would. I can plant and look after things but I'm lacking inspiration regarding what to buy, what would grow well in certain soils, and how to look after it. Internet sites are useful but I'm getting bamboozled by all the information.'

'I'd be delighted to help you. Would you like my contact details?'

She copied his phone number into her contact list. 'When are you free to come and see it?'

'Midweek. First thing Wednesday morning. Would that suit you?'

'It would. Thank you so much. I'll text you the address now.'

Her fingers flew over the phone keypad and his screen lit up with a soft beep.

'Got it. See you Wednesday. I'd better get out of this overall now before it sticks to me.'

Her feet bounced across the tarmac as she walked across to the few remaining people. She wouldn't have to search for strangers to come and work in her garden. Ed would help her. The relief was palpable. Today she'd won a race, found somebody she didn't feel awkward with to sort out her garden and William had been sorry. He was getting into his car and she watched as he drew away. He stopped for a second, lifted his hand and smiled at her. The hurt was still there and she couldn't trust him, but he'd acknowledged he'd been in the wrong and he was proud of her. Today was a good day.

Chapter Twenty-One

'It's absolutely stunning up here, isn't it?' said Ed as he took in the views from Chloe's garden.

'Thank you. It's the main reason I bought the house.'

'Easy to see why, although the garden is somewhat on the large side.'

Chloe winced. 'It is. I don't know what I imagined. Probably a friendly farmer cutting the hay for me or some grandiose layout like one of Capability Brown's gardens. To be honest, I didn't think it through. It looked so different when I came up when the house was being converted. The garden seemed half the size with machines on it and piles of rubble from where they were digging for the septic tank. In hindsight, I ought to have considered the exterior as much as the interior.'

'I enjoy a challenge so let me have a walk about and see if I can come up with any ideas we can try to make it as user-friendly as possible. You had any thoughts yet?'

'I drew out a plan but it got messed up. Not that it was very good. I thought an avenue of cherry trees over there to wander through to a flower meadow.'

He nodded wisely, and Chloe thought that at one time he must have been a good-looking man. His eyes were the colour of honeycomb and his cheekbones fine. Although his hair was now grey, there was a hint of colour in one or two strands that suggested it had been a deep auburn. His hands were elegant and the nails neatly clipped, not at all the hands she'd expect of a gardener.

'You have any preference for plants or trees?'

'I want it to be as natural as possible so birds and insects can benefit from it and I'd like it to be as low-maintenance as possible.'

The corners of his mouth lifted and he chuckled. 'Bit of a tall order that. How much land do you own?'

'Five acres. It's hopeless isn't it? I've been an idiot to kid myself I can look after this amount of land.' She wrung her hands at the realisation. She'd been fooling herself ever since she bought the house. Somewhere in the recesses of her brain she'd known full well she couldn't possibly manage an estate like this, even if she spent every day at home. The garden at her house in Appletree had only been less than half an acre and both she and William had worked on it.

'I'm sorry. I'm wasting your time. You must think I'm as daft as a brush.'

He rubbed his whiskered chin. 'Not at all. If I bought this house, I'd convince myself it would be easy to sort out the garden. I wouldn't want to pass up on the opportunity to drink in that view on a daily basis. No, it's a problem that requires a solution. We can work it out. Let me have a walk around and a think about it and I'll come up with some ideas for you.' He tucked the clipboard he'd been carrying, under his arm and took off in the direction of the fence to the far side of her property.

'You idiot, Chloe. You're going to have to get a professional company to sort this out,' she muttered.

'First sign of madness,' came a voice she recognised. Alex was standing near Ed's car.

She scowled. 'I wasn't talking to myself. I was chastising myself. There's a difference.'

'Whatever,' he said with a grin. 'Came to warn you the electricity's going to be cut off for a while at ten. The electricity company are working on power lines down the lane and all the houses are going off for about two hours. Better get that cup of tea before that happens.'

'Thanks for letting me know.'

'No probs. What's Ed doing? Is he divining?'

Ed appeared to be pointing at the land with a stick. Chloe gave a short laugh. 'He's trying to come up with some ideas for a garden layout. He used to work for a landscaping company. Now he works for himself.'

'Okay. That's useful to know. Maybe he could help me out too. I've got mine laid to grass but it could do with some nice planting to make it more attractive. I might have a word with him too before he leaves here if that's okay. Don't want to poach him from you.' He clearly intended to make his place more attractive to potential buyers. She tried to ignore the reminder that Alex was planning on moving back to Spain. She gave him a bright smile instead.

'If you like, I'll tell him you're after some help too and send him in your direction.'

'Cool. I'm over at barn three. We're thinking of calling it The Granary.'

'Was it used to house grain?'

'No, it used to be a cow barn, but I prefer The Granary to Bovine Barn. How's the writing going?'

Chloe looked around to make sure no one had heard him ask the question. 'Slowly. I wrote a few chapters –

around ten thousand words, but I didn't like them when I read them back, so I deleted them.'

'Ouch. Harsh. Must have taken ages to write them. Can't you put them somewhere for another book?'

'I suppose so, but they didn't feel right A lot of the time it's about trusting your gut and writing what you feel. It wasn't pithy enough.'

'Pithy! I like that word. I'm already looking forward to reading it, if it's going to be pithy.'

'There's not a great deal to read of it in its present state. By changing my mind, I've put myself behind schedule and Faith is going to be exasperated. The book's due in by the beginning of March and I'm way off target.'

'Don't know how you have the patience to sit and write that amount. I get racked off composing long emails. Hope you find another ten thousand words easily.' His phone buzzed in his pocket and he withdrew it, read the message and rolled his eyes. 'It's from Dad. Even though he's on holiday, he keeps sending texts and checking up on me. I wish he'd let me get on with it. He's supposed to be relaxing. He wants to know if I've ordered the bathroom accessories for The Granary. He asked me the same thing three times yesterday.'

'And have you?' she gave him a grin. He chuckled in response to it.

'No. I'm waiting for a price from a supplier before I decide who to go with. Better chase them up again for the quote or the old man will only text me again. Maybe you do have the better job. At least you don't get hassled every day or have to make sure the crew is working on the right job and not sloped off for a crafty fag or an extra tea break. Talking of which, I'd better get back to them. Catch you later.'

He strode off, hands deep in his coat pockets, his breath forming tiny clouds that floated away as he walked into the distance. He exuded a confidence that Chloe could only dream of. It was nice he'd come over personally to tell her about the electricity. He could have just texted her.

Ed was making his way back over the bare clods of earth, a small figure in the vast expanse of terrain. He stopped and turned a full circle, made a note on his clipboard and then approached her. She tightened her scarf around her neck. The wind was getting up again and her long hair had begun to flick into her face. She tucked it behind her ears and headed over to Ed. 'What do you think?' she asked.

'I reckon we could work something out. I've realised the Marsh family farm is around here, just on the other side of that hill. They farm the land all around here and I know Keith Marsh quite well. We were in the same regiment. I'll have a word with him and ask if he'd be willing to take about four acres of grassland for silage. I'm sure he'd want it. He's got a decent herd of cows. I'll then plot out the remainder to give you a meadow and a wildlife-friendly garden. I've taken some photographs of the place to give me an idea of what I'm working with. Once I've got a rough layout, I'll come back and show it to you and then you can decide if you want to go ahead with that or not. I won't be offended if you don't like it.'

Chloe wasn't sure if it was his gentlemanly manner or the way he kept his gaze lowered as if slightly timid, or the fact she knew he was somebody who'd lost his one love, but she experienced a rush of affection for the man. 'I thought you were going to say you couldn't help me.'

'I can always help a lady in distress,' he said with a small stiff bow. 'Besides, I'd enjoy working here. That is, if you'd like me to. I'd be happy to come and give you a hand in it afterwards if it gets too much for you. I sold our home and I live in a flat these days. I miss not having a garden. It'd be a joy to work up here.'

'You've lifted a huge weight from my shoulders. I wasn't sure I'd be able to cope alone.'

His cheeks turned pale pink and he tidied a strand of hair behind his ear. 'I'll be in touch once I've drawn up some ideas.'

'Thank you. Oh, before you go, Alex asked if you could spare some time and see him too.'

'Definitely. Where is he?'

'He's over in the big barn at the far side of the development where all the noise is coming from.'

'Okay. I'll seek him out. I'll try and get the plan done this week. It would be best if we started planting early March and that'll be on us before we know it.'

He kicked off some mud from his boots and climbed into his car. Chloe waved him off with a hearty smile. A feeling of lightness had crept into her soul. The garden problem had been resolved thanks to the singleton club. Now she needed to tackle the more immediate problem of the new book.

—

No sooner had the electricity gone off than her mobile rang.

'Hi. Just seeing how you were.'

Chloe could hardly speak.

'Chloe?'

'Yes, William.'

'I hope I haven't caught you at a bad time.'

'No.'

'I wanted to make sure you'd forgiven me for the other day. I know it must have sounded bad. I wanted to express how happy I was for you but I phrased it all wrong and upset you.'

'You explained on Saturday.'

'I wanted to double check.'

'Okay. Thank you for ringing and checking but you apologised and I understood what you meant.'

There was a hiatus during which she heard him take a painfully long breath as if building up courage.

'Good. What are you doing?'

'Just been trying to sort out my garden.'

'In this weather?'

'I wasn't working in the garden. There is no garden yet. I'm getting it sorted out for springtime.'

'Ah, I see. Ours is looking miserable. I think it misses your magic green fingers. You kept it looking so nice. The cherry tree by our bedroom window is so beautiful in spring. Like cascading pink snow.' There was an unmistakable tinge of sadness to his tone. 'I need to tidy the leaves and the whole garden up before prospective buyers come around.'

'You had any interest in it?'

'Not much but with spring coming the estate agent's hopeful we'll move it quickly. Living here again is harder than I imagined it would be. The house… it's not the same without you.'

'I found it difficult too after you walked out.'

'I'm so sorry for that.' He left another short pause before saying, 'It feels wrong living here without you, and knowing I'm going to be moving out once it sells, it's like living in a vacuum.'

She shook her head even though he couldn't see it. He was feeling sorry for himself. Lilly and he had split up and he was trying to get good old Chloe back on side. She wasn't falling for his line. '*You* insisted we sold it and divide the proceeds, and given I put all my inheritance money into the house and now need it to pay the mortgage on this place, I don't see there's another option. It'll be easier once you find a new place to move to. Any idea where you'll go?'

The sigh turned into small shuddering noises. William was in tears. She listened acutely. He was releasing small sobs.

'William?' she asked cautiously.

There was another gap before he spoke nasally, congested by tears. 'Chloe, I'm in a state. Sorry. I shouldn't be ringing you. I don't know what I was thinking of. I'll go.'

'No, don't go, William. What's wrong?' She couldn't erase years of living with a man she loved. He needed her and no matter how badly he'd treated her, she couldn't turn her back on him. He sniffed and continued.

'I was wrong about Lilly. The day I walked back into this house – our house, that you and I shared all our married life – I knew I'd made a colossal mistake. You'd just moved out and the house was so… sad. I broke up with Lilly that same day. I moved here alone. I didn't join the singleton club because I wanted to meet people. I joined up because I knew you had and I needed an excuse to be near you.'

'How?' Chloe couldn't finish her sentence.

'I picked up a magazine at Appletree surgery and spotted an advert for the singleton club. Your photo was on it. You were wearing reindeer antlers and smiling, and I knew in an instant I had to see you again. Watching you at the events, I've seen you've moved on, but I can't, Chloe. Not yet. And I'm not sure I want to.'

Chloe stared ahead, mouth agape. She had no idea where that had come from. William had been adamant the day he walked out that their marriage was not only on the rocks but had been for some time...

'Chloe, infidelity isn't the fault of one person. Both parties are to blame. It happens because there's a problem within the relationship and you know there is one. Things have been wrong for some time.'

She pushes the carefully marinated steak to the edge of her plate. Her appetite has deserted her and to control the violent hammering against her ribcage she stacks the fried potatoes, one on top of the other until they topple over. William's not eating either. He's resting his elbows on the table and staring hard at her but she can't meet his eyes. She wishes she hadn't mentioned the stupid receipt she has uncovered in the breast pocket of his best jacket. She should never have looked through the sodding pockets in the first place. Why had she? If she hadn't removed all the clothes to give the wardrobes a proper clean, she'd never have felt the rustling of paper and she wouldn't have uncovered the receipt from a restaurant she's never been to, in a place she's not heard of, on a day when William was supposed to have been at a conference in Birmingham. The same day she'd been cleaning Nanny Olive's house and packing away her treasured belongings for the final time.

He was relieved when she brought up the subject of the receipt, like he'd deliberately left the clue for her to find and to draw the inevitable conclusion. He immediately admitted he'd been with Lilly. Yes, it had been a few days after Nanny Olive had passed away and while Chloe had been crying alone in her grandmother's house, he'd been eating oysters and drinking champagne with Lilly. There'd been many restaurants, hotels, liaisons, and even week-ends away since, and Chloe had been in the dark about them all. Or had she? Like many who'd been cheated on, she'd had an inkling, an instinct something was awry, and she'd known William was keeping something from her. She'd believed the fault lay with her and had chosen instead to ignore the obvious signs.

Now she's let slip about the find, William doesn't want to hold back about all his indiscretions, and she fights back the rising nausea and the pain in her chest as she listens to his excuses.

'You can't lay all the blame at my feet, Chloe. You've become increasingly withdrawn and reluctant to enjoy life. I understand why but I feel trapped in a prison of your making and I can't escape.'

'You go out,' she says in a small voice. 'I don't ever stop you.'

'You know what I'm talking about. We don't behave like normal couples do. When I get you to agree to come to a function or something, you are such hard work. I feel I have to make up for you all the time.'

'That's unfair,' she says, but he isn't listening.

'I'm unhappy and I think it's time we both stopped pretending,' he says.

'I've never pretended—' she begins, but he holds up a hand to stop her in mid-sentence.

'Don't say anything. I don't want this to turn into an argument. Fifteen years is a long time to be together. I think it's time for a change. We've had a decent past but we don't have a future together. We ought to end it before it becomes bitter and horrid. I still have feelings for you. I just can't live with you any longer. I've arranged to move in with Lilly.'

'You already made arrangements?' Her words are feeble, weak like her.

'I was going to talk to you about it tonight. You beat me to it.'

'I don't understand. Why didn't you talk to me about how you felt? I'd have tried harder.'

'There'd have been no point. You can't change who you are.'

His words grind her heart to dust. William has been her rock, the one person who comprehended the difficulties she faced in daily life, and who'd stood by her because he loved her. She still loves him. Why has everything suddenly changed? The answer is Lilly. Lilly has entered his life and shown him how it could be. He's been lured away.

'You can stay here, although we'll need to sell the house. Once we pay off the mortgage, we'll share the proceeds.'

'I can't...'

'Well, stay here until you find somewhere else and then I'll arrange the sale.'

She stares at the steak, cooked exactly as he likes it. She's wearing the black dress he likes so much, although now she sees it's so tight her stomach falls in rolls, even held by the tight Spanx underwear. She won't cry. She won't let him see how much he's hurt her. She nods. 'You'd better go then. Lilly will be waiting for you.'

The memories of what had happened rushed by in an instant and evaporated as she was brought back to the present by his concerned voice.

'Chloe?'

'Yes. I'm here. I don't know what you expect me to say.' William had calmly told her that they no longer had a future and had chosen Lilly over her. He'd even initiated divorce proceedings and now, only four months after he'd walked out of their home and out of her life, he was telling her he regretted his decision.

'Appletree doctors' surgery,' she said suddenly. William was rarely ill. 'Why were you at the surgery?'

He sighed again. 'I needed sleeping pills. I've been in such a bad way I haven't been able to sleep. I miss you, Chloe.'

'Oh.'

'Okay. I've said my piece. I wanted to make it clear that I was wrong. That's all I wanted to say. I won't ring you again. I only wanted you to know how I felt.'

'Right.' She was stumped for an appropriate response. She couldn't suddenly switch the love she had for William back on. It had slipped away, little by little, along with tears and sorrow. Before she could say another word, he whispered a goodbye and ended the call.

Faith was aghast when she heard the news. 'Has he had a personality transplant or something? The William I know was pig-headed and rarely said sorry about anything.'

'I know. He seemed so… forlorn. It was weird.'

'How do you feel about it?'

'I don't know. Confused. Taken aback. Sad that we went through all that heartache for what?'

'You're surely not thinking about getting back together with him again, are you?'

Chloe chewed on her bottom lip. It was the question she'd been asking herself before she rang Faith. 'I have no idea. My feelings are all jumbled up. I've only just managed to shut him out of my life. I buried all the hurt and anguish and have been getting on with being me. I feel differently about life and about myself now. How do I know making up with William won't send me spiralling back to where I was before?'

'For what it's worth, my advice is to not encourage anything. Leopards don't change their spots. He was controlling and put you down at every opportunity. I wouldn't trust him. At least, not until he's given you very good reason to. I don't mean to sound negative but I love the new you. You're beginning to sparkle. I've known you for a long time, Chloe, and I've never seen you so independent and decisive. You're a different person. Don't let him turn you back into the old one.'

Chloe took on board her friend's concerns. It was true she'd begun to feel more confident but five years of marriage was a significant time to throw away and she said so.

'Hun, you didn't throw them away. He did. And Lilly wasn't the only woman he slept with. Tread carefully.'

Faith was right. After he'd moved out, she learned he'd slept with a work colleague too. He might be full of regret at the moment, but he'd been the one to break her trust and hurt her. He'd left their marriage, not her. She'd heed Faith's advice.

She ended her phone call and collected Ronnie's lead from a hook by the back door. He bounded to her feet. 'You don't miss William, do you?'

Ronnie looked at her with his tongue out, oblivious to her words.

'No, I didn't think you did.'

Chapter Twenty-Two

Chloe studied the innocuous legal document again. Such an unexceptional piece of paper that would alter the direction of her life. Stamped with a red seal, the decree nisi sent from the local court was the first step to no longer being married to William Blakeney. She was almost single.

She wasn't as upset as she'd expected to be. She'd reverted to her maiden name soon after he left, and the exhausting three months she'd spent alone in their home in Appletree had drained any emotion she had felt about her marriage break-up out of her. William might be experiencing something similar now, but it would be nothing compared to the all-consuming heartbreak she'd endured from the beginning of October, when Faith had feared for her friend's sanity and stayed over with her for several nights while Chloe cried and cried until she'd ran out of tears.

For a brief moment she considered ringing William to see how he felt about the decree nisi arriving, but she stopped herself: not only had William cheated on her with Lilly and others, he'd admitted he felt imprisoned by her behaviour and condition. This was what was right for both of them. There could be no going back.

She slid the piece of paper back into the envelope and put it into the kitchen drawer and made herself some toast. Nothing had changed. William was feeling remorseful and Chloe was Chloe. She couldn't change enough for William and even if she did, she couldn't trust him again.

'You never liked being called Ronnie Blakeney anyway, did you? You've always been a Piper.'

Ronnie barked for a piece of toast and was rewarded.

—

'How did it go?' Chloe asked Sean whose wide grin stretched across his face.

'Fantastic!' came the reply. Sean had been out with Jacqueline for the first time the night before. Chloe was thrilled for him. They'd been to an open mic comedy night in Derby. 'The comedians were really funny. I mean belly-laughingly funny. We saw four of them and they were all as good as each other. What a great way to get to know somebody. We were so relaxed after the acts we just chatted over drinks like two old friends.'

'Is there a second date on the cards?' she asked.

He nodded. 'Sure is. She pulled out the chocolate-making date out of the jar so we're going to try that next.'

'I'm so happy for you.' Chloe meant it. Sean looked different — more confident. He'd changed his hairstyle slightly and was wearing new chinos. She wondered if Suzy had advised him on his new image.

'Thank you. I feel great. First date in years and it couldn't have gone better.' The familiar rumble of the Ducati's engine became evident. Sean craned his neck towards the car park entrance to welcome her then thought better of it. 'She'll think I'm over keen.'

'That's right. Play it cool,' said Alex, who'd been party to the conversation.

Sean rubbed his palms against the tops of his thighs. 'Don't want to scare her off. Suzy said much the same. Told me to be chill. Can't believe my teenage daughter is giving me advice on how to handle women.'

They were gathered outside a farm offering bed and breakfast and afternoon tea, and no one could guess the activity. Although William had arrived ahead of them, he was deep in conversation with Tim and had only acknowledged Chloe with a wave.

Jacqueline was swiftly followed by Danielle and Neats arriving together in Danielle's car. Ed brought up the rear in cycling garb with a backpack over his shoulders containing shoes and suitable outfit for the event. Chloe was thrilled with the plan Ed had shown her for the garden, and he'd also arranged for the farmer at Marsh Farm to cut her fields for silage, so she no longer had to worry about looking after so many acres. Ed was going to order all the plants and shrubs and together they were going to plant her entire garden in early March. Another weight had been lifted from her shoulders.

Although she was chatting to Kaisha, Eleanor kept glancing across the car park as if expecting someone. Chloe wondered if it was a new member or a journalist. She knew Eleanor had tried again to garner interest in the club by sending press releases to the local papers. Chloe looked for signs of any arriving vehicles but there was nothing. The road was silent. Although she'd spoken to Eleanor on a couple of occasions, neither had mentioned the failing singleton club and Chloe hoped she and Fairfax had come up with some new ideas to keep the business afloat. They'd certainly been out a great deal over the last couple of weeks.

Rob arrived, dressed in a collarless jacket and shirt that sent Jacqueline into paroxysms of giggles. She sidled up to Chloe and whispered, 'He looks like Donald Pleasance as Ernst Blofeld in *James Bond*. He only needs a monocle and a scar and he'd be the spitting image.'

Chloe bit back a laugh. It was true. How Rob managed to carry off being a pantomime dame was beyond her. Jacqueline whispered again. 'I think Neats is keen on our Bond villain. She's only going to take her grandchildren to the panto to watch him again. Said he was fab. Love is in the air.'

'Really?'

'Too early to say. I have hopes. Fancy a bet on it? I reckon they'll be in a formal couple before March.'

'I'm no good at spotting the signs,' Chloe replied.

'Well, you certainly have a few good ideas for dates. Sean confessed you'd helped to get me interested in him.'

Chloe cringed. She didn't want Jacqueline to assume she'd played any great part in Sean's plan. 'Whatever he told you, it was all his idea and plan. He came up with the jar idea. I merely gave him some suggestions for interesting dates. I imagined you want to do more than go out for a drink.'

'You were right. I might not have been so swayed if he'd come up with the usual ideas. You know me pretty well. Thanks for whatever part you played.' She gave Chloe a warm smile.

'Merely an advisor.' The fact was, she didn't know Jacqueline at all, but having heard about her adventures in Mexico and from what little she knew about her, she'd drawn her own conclusions. Also, she begun to model her character Laila more on her new friend, Jacqueline, who was the same age as Laila and just as feisty. Jacqueline's quick wit and devil–may–care attitude was evident in the character. Chloe had been reworking her novel and the unattainable but desirable ambassador bore more than a familiar resemblance to Alex and, if truth be told, every one of the singletons featured in the script one way or another, from nervous, cardigan button-twisting Danielle, to Ed 'Cilla' Black, everyone, that was, with the exception of William.

By now, all the members had arrived and were awaiting instructions. Fairfax said something to his wife who gave a quick shake of her head, checked her watch then clapped her hands together for attention.

'You might be wondering what we're all doing in this car park. This is Happy Valley Farm which not only serves excellent cream teas and has some top-rate accommodation but offers two very entertaining activities. Today, ladies and gentlemen, we're going to be duck herding. Medals will be awarded for the best duck herder. Enjoy yourselves!'

They trundled across the car park and to the rear of the farmhouse which opened onto a field. There they met the farmer, Bob, who was ready to show them how to instruct a sheep dog. To one side stood a pen inside which a group of lively white ducks flapped their wings and called out loudly at the arrival of the unwitting herders. A black and tan border collie, with alert eyes that never left his master's face, waited beside the pen, oblivious to the quacking beside him. The farmer held a shepherd's crook in his hand and in a quiet voice with a Welsh lilt explained the commands they'd need to get the dog called Koby Jones to round up the twelve ducks.

'These ducks are a breed known as Indian Runners. In a short while you'll find out why that name is appropriate. You need the following commands to help round them up. "By" means clockwise so the dog will go to the right on that command. The opposite direction is "Away" and he'll go anti–clockwise if he hears you say that. To stop the dog, you say "Stand". "Walk", means walk forwards and "Steady" means slow down. When you finish you tell him "That'll do", and he'll return to you.'

'I'll never remember all of that,' said Danielle, gnawing her bottom lip. 'I barely can tell my left from my right under pressure, let alone remember a whole new word for it.'

'Work with the dog. Koby Jones is your best friend and will do whatever you tell him so it's important you give him clear commands. What you have to watch out for is the duck that always tries to break free from the group. You need to keep your eyes open and your wits about you. I'll demonstrate how it's done,' said the farmer. He released the ducks who, pursued by the border collie, set off at a fair pace, waddling at speed, beaks open as they sensed freedom. They didn't get far before Koby Jones was instructed to guide them through a small polythene tunnel. Whilst the others eagerly headed towards the mini tunnel, the largest of the gang lifted his head at the sight of the dog, turned back and attempted to make a run for it.

'By.' Koby Jones circled from the left, halting the bird's progress and turning it around to join the flock. A few more commands and the birds were fenced inside the far pen.

'See? Easy,' Farmer Bob said, rubbing his hands. 'This is my son.' He motioned towards a young man in his late teens sitting on the ground with his arms around another border collie. 'He's brought his dog, Poppy, to help out if things go awry. Right! Who's going first?'

He wielded his stick in the direction of Rob who took a step backwards.

'Probably allergic to dogs. Can only handle white cats.' Jacqueline hissed in Chloe's ear with a stifled snort.

Sean was about to put up his hand when William volunteered with a cheerful, 'I'll have a go', and as the ducks were sent waddling back to the starting point, he tried a few practice commands with Koby Jones and swung his shepherd's crook in preparation.

'You ready?' Bob asked, lifting a stopwatch.

'As I'll ever be. Release the ducks.'

'Ready, steady, go!'

The pen was opened but by the time William managed to shout 'Away!' and swung his crook at the gang of ducks heading rapidly in his direction, three had broken free and with heads held high were racing across the field. 'Get them!' he shouted to Koby Jones, sending everyone into hysterics. Koby Jones, with tongue out, waited for instructions he could comprehend, and was first sent spiralling left then right and left again until he managed to round up the escapees. William ran around in front of the birds, waving his arms and his stick, yelling every command he'd been taught. Ten ducks ran in a huddle of white feathers towards the tunnel, but two new breakaways scarpered across the field, quacking in triumph much to everyone's delight. Their joy was short-lived when Poppy was sent in. She smoothly rounded up the runaways and drove them back to their group. Once the fence was shut and the ducks imprisoned, Bob looked at his stopwatch and read out the time quietly to Eleanor who marked it down on a sheet.

'It's much tougher than I imagined,' said William, scowling at some mud on his shoes.

Jacqueline laughed. 'Never mind. You gave a good performance. I swear those ducks were laughing as they ran off. You were brave to go first. Now we all know what we're up against. Ducking and diving ducks.' William smiled at her comment and shot a glance at Chloe who said nothing. It was best if she kept conversations with him to a minimum. She turned her attention to Sean who was stroking Koby Jones's head.

'Ah, good tactics. Going for the dog whisperer approach,' Jacqueline called out, earning a grin from Sean. The ducks, having almost tasted freedom, seemed even feistier and flapped wings as they waited to be released once more. She lifted a thumb for Sean, to wish him luck. The ducks quacked in unison. Heaven help her when it was her turn.

–

Danielle lifted the china cup to her lips, sipped the tea and made an appreciative noise before saying, 'That poor dog! He must be wondering which way to walk home now. We all drove him bonkers. He was so patient with everyone and so gentle. Where is he?'

'Probably had to go to a canine therapist for treatment.' Jacqueline popped a piece of scone into her mouth and chewed thoughtfully.

Sean spoke up. 'I think I'll strike off shepherding from my list of jobs I might like to take up. I blame my accent. Koby Jones couldn't understand a single word I was saying.'

'That's an excuse and you know it.' Jacqueline replied, winking at him.

Ed raised a china cup of tea in Chloe's direction. 'Well done. You were by far the best.'

She blushed fiercely. She hadn't expected to win the medal. 'It was probably because I'm used to shouting instructions at Ronnie, although he's nowhere near as well behaved as Koby Jones. I wonder if I could train him up.'

William snorted. She threw him a hurt look. His eyebrows lifted in apology. Alex shook his head. 'No. Ronnie has his own talents. He's an excellent sniffer dog for one.'

Chloe acknowledged the comment with a small smile and fondled the medal, fingers sliding over its shiny surface and the tiny raised lettering which read 'Winner'. Despite her literary success, she'd never won a trophy or medal before and the feeling of achievement was a new experience. She'd not only herded all the ducks into the pen in the fastest time but Koby Jones had taken to her and remained fast by her side while she received her medal. Alex had told her it was because the dog trusted her and that felt good to know.

The whole singleton experience was proving hugely beneficial to her and when Eleanor asked if she could take photos of her with the border collie and the ducks, she readily agreed, even knowing Eleanor would send it to the local papers. The wave of euphoria had numbed her usual reluctance to oblige and she reasoned it was the least she could do for her friend.

'Any good news?' she whispered after Eleanor had snapped the picture.

'I'm still hopeful,' was all Eleanor said. 'Thanks for this. Can I ask you for a quote about why you like coming to the club events?'

'Erm, how about: *I'd never have met so many interesting and fun people and had such a laugh if I hadn't joined the club.* Does that sound okay? Not too lame?'

'It sounds good to me and honest. I'll send it in with the photograph. By the way, what job shall I put for occupation? I don't want to put Chloe Piper, unemployed. Journalists always want your name, age and occupation.'

Chloe couldn't think quickly enough. What should she say? She certainly didn't want to divulge her actual occupation. She couldn't let many people know her identity. Her heartbeat increased sending a thudding beat to her temples that drowned out reason. The damn panic was rising again as it always did when she suddenly felt out of control. She spotted Sean talking to Jacqueline, her head back, white teeth on display. 'Bookshop assistant.'

Spotting the look in his direction, Eleanor gave an approving nod. 'That's great. The club not only brings together new friends, it creates opportunities. I might have to use that in my next press release or on the site.' She scribbled it down. Chloe studied the ducks, now pecking at some bread. She'd have to explain the lie to Sean. He'd understand. For a moment she considered buying her own ducks and putting them in a pen on her land. She could use their eggs and they'd be great company. She could even train Ronnie to help her herd them. He was clever. Far cleverer than William had ever given him credit for. Nanny Olive knew he was a bright dog too. He'd demonstrated his intelligence on many an occasion and the day her grandmother had had her stroke, he'd remained by her side the entire time she was unconscious until the paramedics took her away, and then he'd sat in his basket waiting until Chloe collected him, as if his canine brain had understood Nanny Olive would never be coming home. She turned back to join the others and froze. Eleanor was talking to Sean and Jacqueline and pointing in her direction. She quickened her pace.

Jacqueline was quick to congratulate her. 'You kept that quiet. You're going to be helping out Sean, I hear.'

'He asked me a while ago. I only just made up my mind. I needed to get settled into my new home first.' Chloe tried not to cringe at yet another lie.

Ed joined the conversation. 'It's too easy to procrastinate at home. Bad for the mind and bad for the health. Glad you've found a job, Chloe.'

'What job?' said William.

Sean spoke up. 'She's going to manage the bookshop on Wednesday afternoons.'

'You are?'

She nodded, wishing the ground would open and swallow her. How had she managed to back herself into this corner?

William gave her a warm smile. 'Good for you. I'm very pleased for you.'

The group began to break up and leave. William walked towards her nonchalantly. His voice was low and he spoke close to her ear. 'Really proud of you, Chloe. You've shown me, haven't you?'

'Shown? I don't understand.'

'What a bloody idiot I've been. Look at you: a winner, a popular member of this club and you're going back to work. I ought to have remembered your qualities. They were always there waiting to shine again. You only needed time and space. You're amazing.'

He walked away again, leaving her discombobulated. He was being incredibly nice to her. Had Faith been wrong when she talked about leopards and spots. Could William actually have changed?

Chapter Twenty-Three

'Come on hold them up so I can see,' said Faith.

Chloe giggled and lifted the Valentine Day cards. The first was simple and had a picture of a dog holding a rose in his mouth. It had been signed *Ronnie*.

'I know this one's from you.'

'What makes you say that?'

'It's got a London postmark and I recognised your writing.'

'I confess I helped him out. Ronnie has many talents but writing isn't one of them. If I'd known you were going to get so many other cards, I wouldn't have made him walk all the way to the post office to send it to you.'

Chloe blew her friend a kiss. 'Love you.'

'Love you too, babe. Where are the others?'

Chloe held up a card with a pink heart and the words 'Happy Valentine's Day'.

'Five out of ten points; this one is lacking imagination. Surely the person who sent this could have come up with something more romantic or amusing? There are a gazillion cards with romantic, even suggestive verses. I reckon that's from somebody who's not serious about you being their love; probably a friend, someone who wants you feel loved and wants you to know they're thinking about you. Message?'

'Just a kiss.'

'It's definitely from a friend.'

'Thank you, Doctor Faith, the card analyst. You mean someone like Sean?'

'I mean exactly like Sean or maybe even your new gardening buddy – Ed.'

'He wouldn't!' said Chloe.

'You can never tell. Just because he's older than you and lost his wife to cancer doesn't mean he can't fancy you and besides, didn't you say he's offered to help you in the garden after he's landscaped it? Could be him. Could be either of them. Next card.'

Chloe lifted the large object so Faith could see it clearly. She winced at the glittery letters, 'Be My Valentine'.

'Bit too sparkly but I quite like the earnest little bear holding a heart-shaped balloon. What's inside?'

'If only…'

'Cryptic. I like that. He's redeemed himself. Okay, ten points for the message and five for the card.'

'Who do you think might have sent it?'

'Tricky question. Of all those people you know up there and have spoken about, I'd say it might have come from Alex. It's the message, "If only", more than the front of the card that makes me suspect it's him. *If only* he had more time to spend with you… *if only* he had the guts to ask you out… *if only* you weren't such a hermit… could be him.'

'I disagree. If anything, he'd be more likely to send the first card. In fact, I don't think he'd send me a card at all. He doesn't strike me as all that romantic.'

'Chloe, you've no idea how romantic he might or might not be. You haven't given him much of a chance.' Chloe gave a small shrug. It was true. She was hugely attracted to him but wasn't prepared to invest in their relationship knowing he was going to leave soon after the last house was built. That would be crazy. Maybe *If only* referred to the possibilities that might have taken place between them if he hadn't been leaving for Spain.

'Okay. Perhaps it's from Alex then, and what about this one?'

Faith squinted and read out the words on the front of the card, 'For you my heart is full of love, floating to the clouds above.'

'Well?'

'Flash and clichéd.'

'Valentine's Day is all about hearts. How can this be clichéd?'

'To start with it is overly large and how many hearts do you need on one card? That's a snowstorm of hearts over a heart-shaped box topped with a red rose. I'm surprised the rose hasn't got a heart-shaped head. And the rhyme – yuck! It's a romantic overload. Did he write a message inside?'

'No, he drew a heart. Come on, Doctor, who do you think it's from?'

Faith shook her head. 'I'm beaten. It's either a starry-eyed stalker or a really nice bloke. Or, it might be from William. He's been pretty nice to you recently and regrets his actions.'

'William never bought me cards. He said Valentine's Day was nothing more than a commercial event fabricated by card companies and flower shops and that you didn't need a special day to tell somebody you loved them.'

'Yep, I forgot about that. He really was a keeper, wasn't he?'

'To be fair to him, he had a point. It can be a waste of money, especially when you're married. Besides, he made other romantic gestures.' Chloe scowled. Why was she sticking up for him? Was it because she thought the card could actually be from him?

'You're only saying that because he brainwashed you into believing he was right. Look how happy you are that you received cards this year. It's nice to feel wanted and have mysterious admirers.' She offered a cheeky grin. 'Want to see mine?'

Chloe moved closer to the screen to study the plain pink card Faith was showing her and guffawed loudly. '"Annoyingly I like you way more than I planned",' she read. 'That it? No hearts, no flowers, no cute bears?'

'No. Simple and to the point. Who said romance was dead?' Faith replied and sat back, eyes twinkling. 'Tell me about the person who sent me this.'

Chloe screwed up her face. 'It's quite good in that it's different and stands out. It's a guy with a sense of humour. Any message inside?' Chloe asked.

Faith opened it up and revealed the phone number written at the top.

'Oh, he's not shy, is he? Have you rung the number to see who sent it?'

'I already know this number. It's a bloke I met on Barbados. We've been out for drinks a couple of times. He's called Greg and he's an audiobook producer. We've been in negotiations to record some of my authors' books.'

'Is he nice?' Chloe could tell by the way Faith twiddled with the strand of beads she was wearing that she thought so.

'I like him,' she said eventually.

'I'm very pleased for you. I'll want updates on this budding relationship.'

'Not a lot to say at the moment. We get on very well. He's divorced and lives about twenty minutes from me by Tube. It's very early days but he makes me laugh. A lot. Which is good, isn't it? I rang him to thank him for the card and he told me he's got us tickets for *Wicked* and booked a table at some swanky restaurant but which one we're going to is a surprise.'

'That's great!' Chloe was genuinely happy for her friend. Faith had been alone for a long time and deserved some love and happiness again.

–

Humming as she prepared a sandwich for lunch, Chloe got a shock to see an enormous bunch of roses bobbing past her kitchen window. She scurried to the back door in time to greet the person holding them. It was Eleanor.

'They're not from me. They'd been dropped off by your front door and I thought I'd bring them around for you. Didn't want them to wilt. You have an admirer.' Eleanor handed them over. Chloe searched for a card to see who had sent them but found none.

'It would seem they're an anonymous admirer.'

Eleanor gave her a small smile. 'Well, I'm no detective but I spotted Alex leaving here earlier.'

Chloe's heartbeat increased at this news. Surely he wouldn't? 'You don't think he'd have left them, do you?'

'If I were to put two and two together, that's what I'd come up with. Ask him.'

'What if they're not from him.'

'Then he'll say so.'

'Or, if he doesn't want to be confronted.'

'Chloe, a man willing to spend a serious amount of money on a dozen beautiful red roses for Valentine's Day is definitely going to want you to guess who sent them.'

Chloe lifted them up to her nose and breathed in their scent. 'They smell wonderful. Such a delicate fragrance.'

'You lucky girl.'

'Did Fairfax treat you to flowers?'

'Fairfax is well-trained. He brought me breakfast in bed complete with a single red rose, a lovely card and this.' She held up her wrist on which she wore a bracelet bearing a single pink heart charm.

'That's beautiful.'

'I know.' Eleanor gazed at the bracelet and without warning her face crumpled and she wailed, 'Oh Chloe, I don't deserve this present, or any present. I'm a horrible wife. Only last night I told him the business was improving and we'd had enquiries from potential clients and it's not true. I can't face telling him we're getting nowhere.'

'Sit down. I'll make us a pot of tea.'

Eleanor blew her nose. 'I'm making matters worse. By the time I get around to telling him the truth, the business will be on its knees and he'll lose confidence in me.'

Chloe turned serious blue-grey eyes on her friend. 'It isn't my place to say this but in my experience you shouldn't keep back anything from somebody you love. Lies, no matter if there are good intentions behind them, have a habit of getting out of control and from what I know of Fairfax, he'd rather be in the mess with you than kept in the dark. He's a wonderful support and he loves you. I'd tell him the truth now before it gets out of your control.'

Eleanor's eyes filled. 'He had such conviction in me and this business model. He sank everything in it for my sake. I don't want him to think I've let him down.'

'He won't think that, but he might lose trust in you if you keep this from him for much longer.'

She left Eleanor digesting her words and made the tea, bringing it and two cups to the table before joining her guest. 'Have you had any enquiries at all?'

'Two but nothing came of them.'

'Then you weren't horrendously deceitful. You actually had enquiries. I'd come clean if I were you. You're partners, not just business partners. You won't be able to maintain this pretence. He'll see the accounts or the number of members or something and work it out for himself.'

'He usually deals with the organisation of the events so I've managed so far.'

'That doesn't mean you'll be able to keep it up. He's not a fool. He can count and see only the same ten people are attending events no matter what you tell him.'

The sobs came faster. 'I kept hoping it would improve. I spent a fortune advertising for new members this month. I put ads in the magazines for a Valentine Special and still, I only had two enquiries. I keep emailing press releases and getting no response and have no success in getting the articles into papers. I was sure they'd love the Sumo wrestling article or the Argocat photographs. What am I doing wrong, Chloe?'

Chloe didn't know how to help. Faith always handled publicity for book launches and her authors. She had a huge list of contacts, and maintaining it was about networking rather than advertising. Whenever there was a book launch, she'd invite all the journalists she knew to a free drinks event and give away signed copies of the book together with a goody bag. It always worked. The reviews would come thick and fast and positive articles in all the press. 'I really don't know what to suggest. You need a lucky break or somebody important to participate in the events. Have you thought of inviting journalists and local dignitaries like the Lord Mayor, or council officials to participate for free? Give them all a day to remember. If the journalists enjoy it, they'll surely write about it. Who doesn't love freebies?'

Eleanor sat bolt upright. 'Why didn't I think of that? That's an incredibly good idea.' Her eyelids fluttered as she considered the possibilities and finally she smiled at Chloe. 'Thank you. I'll do that as soon as I get back. Fairfax is out today. I'll phone the local newspapers and invite the editors to a really good event. In fact, if you don't mind, I'll nip back home and get onto it immediately. Chloe, you could be a life-saver. You ought to be a consultant.' She leapt to her feet, hugged Chloe in a tight embrace and dashed off.

Chloe poured herself a cup of tea and collected her hastily abandoned sandwich. Who'd have thought it? People coming to her for advice. She laughed at the thought. Her eyes alighted on the roses, now in water in the sink. They were beautiful. She couldn't believe Alex might have sent them. He hadn't given any indication he was interested in her romantically. Or had he, and she'd missed the signals because she was so wrapped up in her own world? She might wait to see if he mentioned the flowers rather than her bring up the subject. She didn't want to make a fool of herself, in spite of what Eleanor said.

She finished her sandwich and went in search of a vase for her flowers. So far, this was the best Valentine's Day she'd had in years.

–

The online forum for sufferers of social anxiety disorder offered all sorts of advice and help for those who required it. Since moving to the new development and joining the singleton club, Chloe had found herself dispensing advice almost as often as requesting it. Hitherto, she'd have skulked in the online shadows hoping for answers to soothe her insecurities rather than asking questions, but she'd become bolder of late and chalked her progress up to recent events. She was following a thread with some interest. One member of the group was anxious about giving a speech to fellow work colleagues and asking what he could do. At the moment he was plan was to throw a sickie rather than face a room full of people.

Chloe visited the forum regularly. If nothing else it helped her to know there were others like her who suffered to a lesser or greater extent and at least understood how she felt. The person giving the speech was advised to try calming techniques with which she was familiar. Another person was trying out a new therapy treatment that involved imaging the worst scenario possible, so in this case, people jeering at the speech, laughing or sneering, and then when the speech was given and the result nothing as bad as expected, it would be an advancement.

It was an interesting approach and she decided to research it further. She had good reason to, now that she'd agreed to take up Sean's offer to work in the bookshop on Wednesdays. She'd taken to the place and if it were as sleepy as he suggested, she would manage. There wouldn't be crowds of strangers, only a few children and fellow book lovers and she would cope. At least, she hoped she could. *You're stronger than you think.* 'I'm trying, Nanny. I so want to get back to at least where I was before I met William and maybe even beyond that,' she said out loud. Reading the threads in the online forum was her way of building up to her first day at the bookshop. Sean had taken her to one side after the revelation she'd made to Eleanor after the duck herding...

> *'You don't have to do it. I understand you were put on the spot,' says Sean.*
>
> *'It just came out. I didn't want to confess I was a writer and I saw you and...'*
>
> *'It's not a problem. You don't have to take up my offer. I'll tell people I decided to keep the shop closed on Wednesdays. Some excuse about not enough customers.'*
>
> *'But there would be customers if you kept it open.'*
>
> *'There would. Especially if I let the toddler group use it. I've already had a few minor complaints from some who have come by on a Wednesday, only to find the shop shut and I miss out on passing trade, but you don't have to step up to the job. I know how tough it is for you.'*
>
> *Chloe thinks of William and the pride on his face. She's come a long way in a few months and she might be able to take yet another step – an important one. It isn't as if she's never worked in a bookshop before and if the toddler group comes*

in it will be super. She'd love to see the little ones'
faces as they read through the picture books. It could
work out for them both. 'If you're willing to take
me on a trial basis, I'd like to do it.'

    Sean holds out his hand and shakes hers.
'Then, I'd be delighted to employ you, Miss
Piper.'

Chapter Twenty-Four

Saturday, 3rd March

'Is Eleanor not here yet?' Jacqueline said before tugging off her gloves with her teeth.

'She's on her way,' Chloe replied.

Jacqueline shoved the thick leather gloves into her helmet and looked about. 'Where's Alex? He is coming, isn't he?'

Chloe thought back to earlier that day when Alex had knocked on the door...

> 'Morning, I came to check you are going to the event today. I haven't seen you for so long I'd almost forgotten what you look like.'
>
> 'I look like this,' she says, pointing at her face.
>
> 'Ah yes! Now I remember. I keep meaning to come around to visit and then something else goes wrong and I have to buzz off. I haven't had a minute to myself. Dad's left me to it again.'
>
> 'Where's he gone now?'
>
> 'Rome. It's their ruby wedding anniversary and the old romantic whisked Mum away for a few days. I couldn't complain about him going though: forty years is worth celebrating.'

'Definitely. I think that's a lovely way to spend an anniversary. He is a romantic.'

'Like father, like son,' he says with a grin.

'Are you a romantic too?'

'Oh yes, totally, candlelit meals for two, snuggling under one blanket in front of log fires, roses.' he replies.

She suddenly starts. The roses she received on Valentine's Day have come from Alex and she hasn't thanked him. Eleanor told her she'd seen him near her house. She speaks again, 'I never thanked you.'

'For what?'

'The flowers. The beautiful roses you left for me. I should have thanked you straight away and I didn't. They meant a lot.'

He gives a nonchalant shrug. 'You're welcome. Just wanted you to have something pretty in your new home.' He glances at his watch. 'Must dash. I told my folks I'd pick them up from the airport, so provided there are no flight delays I'll get to the event on time. I wanted to let you know in case you thought I was avoiding you or bailing on you. See you there.' Chloe's veins fizz at the revelation that the flowers have come from Alex after all, and yet she is puzzled by his ambivalence about such a romantic gesture. She has no time to pursue it further. He is striding away, leaving her staring at his retreating form and wondering what might happen next between them.

'He had to fetch his parents from the airport.'

'I thought they went away over New Year. One of the Balearic Islands.'

'They came back from that trip. They've been in Rome this week. It was their wedding anniversary.'

'That's sweet. Never been to Rome.'

'Me neither. I've never been abroad.'

'You're kidding.'

'I have a dog,' said Chloe quickly, hoping Jacqueline would make the assumption she didn't travel on account of Ronnie. She did.

'I guess you don't fancy putting him in kennels.'

'He'd tunnel out on day one and escape.'

Jacqueline didn't quite meet her smile. She kept looking about, searching for others to arrive. Chloe assumed she was waiting for Sean.

'How did the chocolate-making date go?'

'It was good,' Jacqueline replied.

'You chosen your next date?'

'Yes… at the Wedgewood factory in Stoke. It's a tour followed by a lesson, learning how to throw a pot.'

'Sounds brilliant.'

Jacqueline nodded. 'Yes, can't wait. How are you enjoying the bookshop?'

Chloe had only worked a few afternoons since she'd agreed to help out and had enjoyed the experience far more than she expected. In spite of her concerns, the shop had remained quiet and the few customers who'd visited were elderly individuals who'd been delighted to find the place open on a Wednesday afternoon. The small group of three and four-year olds who'd trailed in in brightly coloured coats and wellingtons had been another matter. Chloe's heart had melted at the sight of their looks of pure joy at opening various books with pictures of animals or pop-up fire engines. She'd cooed after them, making sure they were settled in the more private of the reading rooms, and observed them as they enjoyed story time, legs crossed, bright faces lifted to the woman reading from one of the books. It had been another hurdle surmounted. She felt comfortable there and happy to watch people walking by, cocooned inside the charming shop. She'd bought four books and read them while working. Sean had joked she'd end up spending all her wages on books if she didn't get more customers in. She didn't mind. Little by little she was changing and the bookshop was another milestone in her journey to combat her ever-present anxiety.

'It's a super place to work. I'm loving it. Especially when the little kids come in for story time. They're adorable.'

'That's good.'

Chloe couldn't put her finger on it but Jacqueline was aloof and not her usual self. As soon as Jacqueline spied Danielle's car, she excused herself and scuttled off, leaving Chloe puzzled about what might have caused the change in attitude. They'd become good friends but today there was something different. William who'd also pulled into the car park, strode towards her, raising his hand in Jacqueline and Danielle's direction as he passed them.

'Hi!' He stood so closely she could smell his cologne, fresh and light. She breathed in the citrus scent and recalled how on nights when he'd been away, she'd spray it on her pillow to feel as if he was in bed with her. She flushed at the memory.

'Hi.'

'How's it going?'

'Good.'

'You working at Sean's bookshop?'

'Only for one afternoon a week.'

He nodded approvingly. She noticed he hadn't asked about the writing.

'Not seen you for a while. Not spoken since...' he left the rest of the sentence hanging. She knew what he was referring to: the phone call.

'I've been busy. Ed's started work on the garden and I've had stuff to do.'

'I understand. I just hoped you might've picked up the phone and called me.'

She lowered her eyes and looked at her shoelaces. Maybe she ought to have rung to see how he was. He'd bared his soul and she hadn't rung him since.

Others arrived, and their conversation was interrupted as Fairfax began to usher them towards the entrance to the sports centre.

'Come on folks. We have to get you trained up before the others arrive.'

'Have you any idea what he's talking about?' asked Tim who'd appeared by Chloe's left shoulder.

'Not a clue.'

Tim continued animatedly. 'That's one of the best things about this club, you never know what we'll be doing.'

Kaisha had sidled up to him quietly and offered her suggestion. 'Might be goggle football. My brother played it at a stag party. You wear weird goggles that make everything look too near or too far away and then play a 5-a-side football match. You try to kick the ball but it isn't where you think it is, nor are your opponents. My brother said it was like being drunk. The video they shot of their match was hilarious. They kept missing the ball and falling over.'

Ed shook his head and said, 'I'm not much of a foot-baller. I can miss a ball and fall over without goggles.'

'Maybe you can claim you already have a handicap and not wear them,' Kaisha said. Tim chuckled at the comment.

'What's this about being drunk? We making and drinking cocktails? That'll be a good afternoon.'

'Danielle! I was talking about goggle football,' Kaisha said with a laugh.

'Oh, Lord, I hate footie. My old man used to watch every sodding football match. Hope it isn't that,' Danielle grumbled.

Chloe expected Jacqueline to join in the banter as she always did but she kept her head down and trailed beside them in silence. Something was definitely up with the woman. Ordinarily, she'd be the first with a wise crack. She glanced at her friend. Sean must have picked up on it too because he bent and said something to her. Jacqueline shook her head.

They grouped around Fairfax and waited for instruc-tions. 'Great to see you all. We're very excited about today's event. Ah, here's Alex.' He stopped as the front door clattered open and Alex rushed inside full of apolo-gies. 'You're just in time. I'm about to take you through and hand you over to Neil, who'll explain everything. This way please.'

The doors to the gym opened and they entered. The room had been set up on a court. On both ends stood five huge black and white inflatable stones, in front of which stood black boxes marked with five spots resembling a face of a large dice. Masks, bows and foam-tipped arrows were laid out on a trestle table close to round archery targets on stands.

Fairfax introduced them to their two instructors, and Neil, a broad-chested young man in a tracksuit began the briefing. 'Welcome to archery tag. It's a sort of mix between dodgeball and paintball but using bows and arrows. I hasten to add the arrows are foam-tipped so it's almost painless if you get struck by one. Notice I said, almost painless.' He got a titter from Danielle and Neats. 'In a while we'll be holding a game, so for all of you *Hunger Games* fans, it'll give you a chance to perform like Katniss Everdeen. But first, I'll demonstrate how to use the bows and you can have a quick practice run.'

Set up with appropriate equipment, five of them faced the targets, each drawing back bows and aiming for the centre. Chloe watched and waited for her turn and didn't hear William as he sidled up to her again until he whispered, 'I didn't get a chance to ask earlier. Did you like the roses I sent you for Valentine's day?'

She swallowed hard. The flowers hadn't been from Alex after all. William didn't wait for a response, instead he whispered, 'For you my heart is full of love, floating to the clouds above.' That was the verse in one of the Valentine's cards. He moved away before she could respond. Her heart sank. All morning she'd assumed the roses were from Alex, and worse than the disappointment they weren't was the thought she'd thanked him for them. Why had he let her believe they were from him? It made no sense.

'Can we have the next five contenders, please?' Neil's voice brought her back to the moment. She moved towards the table and took her bow, staring assiduously at her target and avoiding William's smug gaze as he lined up next to her.

Chloe was drawing back her bow for the second time when she heard a knock at the door and a soft 'Hello!'

The sound of footsteps and shuffling indicated a group of people had trooped in. Chloe's pulse accelerated and her hands turned clammy. Strength seemed to drain from her shoulders and the arrow slipped out of position and flopped onto the floor. William caught her eye and gave a small shake of his head along with a sympathetic smile. It was his way of reassuring her. He understood the arrival of the strangers would have triggered an anxiety attack. It was what he used to do when they went out together – an unspoken command. She would look to him and be reassured. No sooner had she acknowledged his smile than she was angry with herself. She'd managed for weeks without William and here she was, turning to him the first time she encountered a difficulty. If he hadn't been there, she'd have coped. That coupled with the fact he'd sent the roses and was trying desperately to get back into her good books irritated her further. He should leave her alone to get on with her life. He had no right to wriggle his way back and confuse her again. She rubbed her palms with her fingers to remove any moisture, drew back the bow once more and fired directly at the target scoring a bullseye.

'Nice shot!' Neil removed the arrow from the target. 'Right, now you've had a chance to practise, I'll go through the game with you while our newbies have a quick practise with Tyron.'

Chloe turned around. At least ten people were gathered beside Eleanor, a sea of smiling faces. She was introducing them as their team rivals. Rooted to the spot, Chloe could do no more than stare at the floor. A warm arm on her shoulder alerted her to Sean, who'd moved immediately behind her. He whispered, 'It's cool. I'm here with you. We can go take a walk if you want.'

She shook her head. Eleanor was still talking, hands waving and face expressive. She'd missed what had been said.

'And so, please don't kill them all off too soon. Be gentle with them,' said Eleanor. The new group moved away as one to collect bows and take their spot in front of the practice targets.

Chloe took several deep breaths. *You're stronger than you think.* 'It's okay. I'll be fine,' she mumbled.

'Well done. We're a team. We're all here together.' Sean's voice was soft and melodic, his words a balm to her panicked soul. She knew her teammates. She could do this. Sean's hand continued to rest lightly on her shoulder, warmth seeping through her jumper and skin to her very bones. She drew another breath. William broke off from the group and joined them.

'You okay? Don't let that bunch of hacks put you off.'

Her knees almost buckled. They weren't just new singletons, Eleanor had gathered together a group of journalists and was going to show them a good time. Her livelihood depended on what happened at the event. Chloe couldn't let her down and bolt.

'It doesn't matter who they are,' Sean growled.

William ran a hand through his hair. 'I'm only trying to help. Be supportive, mate.'

'Well, you're not succeeding, so back off.'

'There's no need…' William began then checked himself and showed white teeth. 'Sure. I don't want to make it worse. I'm here if you need me, Chloe.'

The group, oblivious to the exchange, had huddled around Neil who was explaining the game rules to them. Chloe now over the initial panic and with Sean by her side was able to concentrate on the instructions.

'In summary, both teams hide behind the inflatable bunkers and try to be the first team to knock out the centres of the five-spot target on the opponents' side of the field or eliminate all the members of the opposing team,' Neil explained, pointing at the dice-shaped target. 'It's a game of skill and fun. You'll have to duck and dive to retrieve your spare ammunition from that point over there and you know what to do to get a player back into the game.'

Once clear, they collected protective masks and bows for the game. Chloe was back on course, her initial wobble over. The journalists were clustered around Tyron receiving the same information they'd just had in preparation for the game. Eleanor glanced across at her and lifted crossed fingers in her direction. Judging by the intense expression on her face, this was her big chance to show off what the singleton club could offer.

Chloe shut her eyes for a brief moment and imagined her sister, Georgia, who would have been the heroine of the hour, dodging arrows and throwing herself whole-heartedly into the game. It would take a powerful imag-ination to pretend she was Georgia but Chloe had that in her favour. She gritted her teeth as she slid behind a bunker and waited to kill off the enemy team.

–

Danielle ran a comb through her hair and with a shake of her head to let her hair settle back into its natural hairstyle said, 'What an absolutely brilliant game! We showed them what we were made of, didn't we?'

'Certainly did. When Alex caught that arrow and brought you back onto the team, I wanted to hug him,' Ed replied.

'Didn't we all,' Danielle said, elbowing Chloe and giggling.

Chloe chugged the water from her bottle. The mood was infectious. The team had not only killed off all the opposition but taken out every one of their targets, and Chloe had proved to be a decent markswoman.

Alex was pink-faced after all the exertion. He'd thrown himself wholeheartedly into the event and had saved three of the team. 'It was a team effort.'

'I wonder if we'll be in the newspapers,' Tim said.

Kaisha nodded. 'Pretty sure that'll happen. That skinny bloke with the orange-framed glasses asked me how to spell my name and how old I was.'

'Nah. He fancied you. It was a chat-up line, wasn't it, Jacqueline?' Danielle guffawed.

Jacqueline smiled wanly. 'Definitely a chat-up line. Look, I have to get off,' Jacqueline said as she stood up. 'See you all next time. Bye, Dan. Bye, everyone.' Jacqueline gave a small wave to Sean who returned it with a broad smile.

They started talking again about the event but Chloe was concerned about Jacqueline. She slipped out after her and caught up with her outside. 'Hey, wait up. I wanted to check if everything was okay. You seemed a bit down today.'

Jacqueline stopped in her tracks and hesitated before speaking. 'To be honest, I feel a bit shitty.'

'You sick?'

Jacqueline shook her head. 'No. Just some crap I have to deal with. I'll be fine. Need to go home, that's all.'

'If you want to talk about it...'

Jacqueline studied her nails briefly. 'Thanks, but I'm really okay. Nothing you can help me with. See you soon.'

Chloe sneaked back inside to retrieve her things before slipping back out again unnoticed. She couldn't face William, or Alex for that matter. Alex must have wondered what she was talking about, rabbiting on about roses and it was still a puzzle as to why he'd said he had sent flowers when he hadn't, and Sean… well, Sean was lovely and had helped her but she didn't want there to be any confrontations between him and William. She was relieved she'd driven alone to the event. No one would miss her if she left now. She needed some time to think. Chloe walked briskly to her car and got in. The interior was cool and quiet, a sanctuary. She slotted in the key and was about to drive off when she spotted William running across to Jacqueline's bike. She paused for a second and observed the pair. An argument or discussion seemed to be taking place, during which William shook his head several times and held his hands up. She'd seen that gesture on many an occasion. He always did it when he was trying to say sorry. Why was he apologising to Jacqueline? Chloe had no time to dwell on the question because William glanced around and quick as a flash pulled Jacqueline into an embrace. Chloe sunk down into her seat to avoid being seen. What the hell was William playing at? And Jacqueline for that matter? She was supposed to be seeing Sean. Chloe remained in position, hoping neither had noticed her. The door to the entrance opened and William pulled away from Jacqueline, assuming a casual stance as if simply talking to her. Sean, Danielle and Alex came out of the building. Chloe couldn't watch any longer. She put her car into gear and pulled off, away from them all. She looked up in her rear-view mirror as she pulled out of the car park to see William waving goodbye.

Chapter Twenty-Five

Chloe was climbing over the rickety fence at the bottom of the field when Alex's father, Thomas, slowed his car and wound down the window.

'Morning, Chloe. Morning, Ronnie. It's been a while. How are you getting on?'

'Good, thanks. It's lovely up there,' she said, nodding back at the hill.

'Glad to hear it. Sorry I haven't been around to see how you've been getting along. I tend to go away during the colder months. Old age and arthritis – terrible combination. I need sunshine at this time of my life,' he said with a cheery smile that crinkled his deeply-tanned face. 'And Alex is better off without my interference. I promised Patricia I'd take a back seat this year and let the lad take charge. I'm headed up there to see how much progress is being made. Haven't been on site in ages. I might have a buyer for the Granary.'

'Already?'

'They're hot properties,' he replied. 'Not many like them available – individual properties in a perfect rural location with land – they're gold dust. I've had a lot of interest in Number 5 too and we've not even begun work on it yet. Mind you, with summer around the corner, we'll be able to get it sorted in no time. You sit tight there for a few years and you should see Sunny Meadow Barn soar in value. We had Alex's house valued last week, and it's shot up in price.'

It was another reminder that Alex wouldn't be staying for much longer. Thomas continued, 'He told me you thanked him for the roses. He was pleased you worked out who'd they'd come from.'

Chloe cocked her head slightly. Why would Alex tell his father about Valentine flowers?

'He was worried you'd read too much into receiving them. I told him pink roses were fine. It's not like it was a bunch of red ones. I said you'd appreciate the gesture.'

The penny dropped. Alex had left her the house-warming pink roses. They'd been at cross-purposes. When she'd thanked him, he'd thought it was for those flowers.

'I'm glad you get on together. He was telling me about all the things you've been up to at this club he's signed up to. Good to see him get out again. He's had a rough time over the last couple of years – the break-up with his fiancée, Jayne – and although he hasn't said much about it to me or his mother, his sister knows the whole story and he took it badly. He buzzed off to Spain and we wondered if he'd ever come back. Good to know he's getting out and about and hopefully moving on at last. Anyway, he's pleased you worked out he sent the roses. He thought I'd spilled the beans about them but I assured him I hadn't. I did well to keep quiet about them, didn't I? Not normally very good with secrets. Oh, unless they're about writers who wish to remain anonymous. How are you getting on with the writing?'

'Slowly. I'm getting there.'

'Good. Patricia's chomping at the bit for your next book.'

A car appeared in the road and finding its path blocked, slowed down, waiting for them to finish their conversation. Thomas acknowledged the driver and began to wind up his window. 'It's doing him good going to those events. You know what they say about all work and no play... Certainly was the case for Alex. Well done on convincing him to get out and about.' He beeped his car horn and set off, moving closer to the hedgerow to allow the oncoming vehicle to pass.

Once both cars had gone, she and Ronnie crossed the road, where she let him off his lead and he raced off, nose to the ground. It was a relief to know she hadn't made a fool of herself over the flowers, although she had to admit to feeling disappointed the Valentine roses hadn't been from him. 'Why would he send me Valentine roses? I'm not his girlfriend,' she said to Ronnie who ignored her and scurried off, nose to the ground. She wondered how well she knew him after all. Alex hadn't mentioned a fiancée. It would certainly explain why he was still single and living alone on a hill in Staffordshire, and why he'd probably wish to head back to Spain. The thought of him leaving depressed her. She'd been sure there was some spark between them but now it seemed he was just a really nice guy who didn't want to get heavily involved. She whistled for Ronnie's attention and hurled a stick after him, watching him bound after it. Stuffing her hands in her pockets, she reflected things weren't too bad after all: at least she and Alex were friends and she hadn't given him further reason to think she was off-the-wall with her crazy talk about roses.

'Hi.' Alex held out a box.

'What's this?'

'Open it and see.'

She lifted the lid. Inside were a dozen doughnuts with various iced toppings. 'I don't understand.'

'I figured if I bought the breakfast, you'd make the coffee.'

'That was somewhat presumptuous of you. What if I told you I don't like doughnuts?' She tried to keep a straight face but failed.

'Then I'd have to give you these,' he replied, pulling out a paper bag from behind his back. 'French pastries. Who doesn't love French pastries for breakfast?'

'Come in.' She shook her head in mock dismay. Ronnie bounced about at his feet.

'You like pastries, Ronnie?' Alex asked.

'You bet he does. He's a great big, greedy hound.'

She put the box on the kitchen top and pulled out a cafetière complete with plunger. 'I assume you'd like proper ground coffee with this gourmet breakfast?'

'That'd be wonderful.' He pulled off a piece of pastry and balanced it on Ronnie's nose. 'Stay.' Ronnie waited obediently until allowed to eat it.

She smiled at the pair of them. 'Why the breakfast?'

'You disappeared yesterday and didn't come with the rest of us for afternoon tea. I thought you deserved to celebrate too. After all, you were our champion shot.'

'I had to come home to Ronnie.'

'It wasn't anything to do with William earlier, was it? I saw him hanging around you.'

'It was nothing. A misunderstanding.'

'Didn't look like nothing to me. You were pretty upset.'

Chloe fussed about with the coffee rather than meet Alex's eye. She'd still never broached the subject of her disorder with him. It was probably time to do so, and yet she really didn't want to have to go through it all. Not everyone understood. She'd been lucky Sean had experience of it. 'It was something and nothing.'

Alex fell quiet for a moment then said, 'I don't like to see you upset.'

Chloe's hand trembled as she added the coffee to the cafetière. She didn't dare look at him but she was certain his eyes were on her and would be full of sympathy and kindness and maybe something more, but the thought he was leaving the development held her emotions in check and prevented her from responding appropriately. She fought to speak but shyness took over. 'You want any orange juice with this?'

He didn't falter. 'Brilliant! A proper continental breakfast. Apart from the doughnuts. Probably more American. I enjoyed yesterday's event.'

'It was really good. I don't know how Eleanor and Fairfax keep coming up with all these ideas.'

'Me neither. I must admit, I really didn't want to join their club. When Eleanor first asked me, I wasn't at all keen.'

'I didn't want to either. I still don't quite know how they managed to hoodwink me into signing up. Alcohol was to blame. You, however, had no excuse. You weren't drunk when you agreed.'

'I joined because you were a member.'

She pushed the plunger on the cafetière gently and tried to calm her quickening heartbeat. 'Really?'

'You must know I like you by now. A lot.'

'You do?' She spun around.

His face broke into a smile. 'Why else do you think I attend these events. I have a million other things I ought to be doing, but I go along because you go and I get to spend time with you. You're so busy writing the rest of the time, I don't like to disturb you.'

She blinked a few times. Her life was getting strangely complicated. First William professed to want her back her and now Alex was bringing her breakfast and claiming he liked her. 'I like you too.'

'Good. We like each other. That's a start, isn't it?' The lines around his eyes crinkled slightly.

'I don't know…'

He stopped her. 'I'm not making a very good job of this, am I? I've wanted to be more than a friend for a while. I was intrigued about you even before we met. I'd seen you up here talking to Dad. The first time we actually met, when Ronnie ran away, I knew I wanted to get to know you better but you were fresh from a break-up from your husband. I figured you'd need space and time to heal, so I've been keeping my distance, not because I wanted to, but because it seemed the right thing to do. I was in a similar situation myself a few years ago after my fiancée and I parted, and she, well, she fell straight into someone else's arms. A few months later she rung me in tears. It had been a rebound relationship and she needed a shoulder to cry on. It was messy. Complicated and messy. I didn't want to be that rebound person in your life. And there's been William. He keeps staring at you at the events. I can't shake off the feeling he's still in love with you and I don't want to get in the way of that.'

Chloe gathered cups and saucers, all the while trying to make sense of what she was hearing.

'When you thanked me for the flowers yesterday, I took that as a sign of encouragement. It's the first time you've acknowledged any of my pathetic attempts.'

She stood stock still. He continued.

'I hoped you'd work it out – the flowers, my first footing on New Year's Day, tagging along with you to the events and the Valentine's card.'

She blinked again and asked, 'Which card did you send?'

'How many cards did you get?'

'Four. Three if you discount Ronnie's.'

He fought back a grin. 'Ronnie! Oh, okay. I see. There are rivals for your affection.' He cast about, his regard falling on the large bunch of red roses, still in bloom. He didn't mention them. 'Which one did you think was from me?'

It was a test. She hoped Faith had been right with her deductions. 'The card with the message that read, "If only..."'

He nodded. 'Sorry if it wasn't what you expected. I struggled to find something that didn't have some uber-romantic message on it. I didn't want to scare you off.'

'It was really lovely. Thank you.'

He coughed – a brief, nervous cough. 'So now you know how I feel, and I've even wooed you with dough-nuts, is there any chance you'll come out with me? Nothing heavy. Just a good night out. I've got tickets for a charity ball – a black tie event – at Shugborough Hall, and I can't think of anyone I'd rather invite.'

'I... I can't.'

The smile disappeared in an instant.

'It's not that I don't want to go... I do... but I can't.'

'You don't need to make any excuses. I'm sorry. I misread the situation. It's my fault.' He rose abruptly.

'Don't go.'

He gave her a gentle smile. 'Not much point in staying. I've made enough of a prat of myself.'

'No, you haven't. Let me explain.'

'It's okay. I won't tread on William's toes.'

'William hasn't anything to do with this.'

'The guy's still got feelings for you. You've got feelings for him. I'm guessing he even sent the roses over there?'

'He did but I didn't find out until yesterday.'

'And he bought you a card with a loving message?'

She nodded, yet all the while fighting to find the words to explain how she felt. She didn't love William and she would like to get to know Alex but not at a major event stuffed full of people.

He strode towards the door. Her head screamed at her to tell him about her condition but he moved away quickly and was out of the door before she could stop him. She slammed the coffee canister back onto the shelf and poured the contents of the cafetière down the sink. She'd had the chance to explain why she couldn't go to the ball and she'd messed up, and now he'd got some ridiculous idea she had feelings for William. Shit! The only consolation was that he didn't intend staying around for a long time. It would have been a short-lived relationship even if it had got off the ground. She threw a doughnut for Ronnie to catch and went in search of her mobile. She needed to talk to Faith.

–

'What a mess. Look, why don't you go around to his house and explain?'

'What's the point? I tell him I can't face crowds; he says, "Oh what a pity!" and pisses off with someone else to the ball. I have to face it, Faith, I'm no great catch. William at least tried to understand me. No one before him grasped how difficult it was for me to mix. Until I met him I was lost, really lost and he anchored me. For a few years I was a little better and now...'

'Now, you're making huge strides by yourself. You can't trust William. From what you said, he's definitely making a play for Jacqueline as well as chancing his arm again with you. You going to tell Sean about what you saw?'

'Jacqueline should speak to him about it, not me. Besides, he's been so kind to me, I don't want to be the person to shatter his hopes. He really likes her.'

'Probably wise. Sometimes it's best not to meddle. What now?'

'Buggered if I know. Alex will probably stop going to the events and I'll carry on being me. William will be the two-faced arse that he's come to be, Jacqueline and Sean will stop going out together and Ronnie will get ginormous on all the sodding doughnuts I keep feeding him.'

'I meant about Alex. Don't you want to get to know him better?' Faith persisted.

'What's the point? The fourth house is coming along quickly now and he'll be off in a few months.'

'I give up. There's a lovely man who's keen to start up a relationship with you and you aren't even prepared to give it a chance. What have you got to lose by telling him why you turned down his offer?'

'I'll think about it.'

'Which probably means you'll do nothing about it.'

Chloe's shoulders dropped. Faith knew her too well.

–

Sean's phone call couldn't have come at a worse time. Chloe was feeling incredibly low. Her writing had come to a halt again and she'd spent the last hour hating herself. All the weeks of confidence-boosting seemed to have been pointless.

'Hey!' Sean sounded like she felt, his voice flat.

'Hi.'

'You got half an hour to spare?'

'Sure.'

'I've got a family size tub of salted caramel ice cream and I need a buddy to help me out with it.'

'I'll be there in twenty minutes.'

'Good, cos if you aren't they'll find me on the floor tomorrow morning – death by ice cream. I've already demolished one tub.'

'Jeez. I ought to bring back-up.'

'If you mean Ronnie, yes. It's a pretty huge tub.'

–

Sean hadn't shaved and with his dark stubble and blue marks under his eyes, looked worn out. He greeted the pair warmly and showed them straight upstairs to his flat.

'You weren't joking, were you?' The ice cream pot was the largest Chloe had seen.

'Comfort eating.'

'I do that too. That's one of the reasons I put on so much weight last year,' she replied.

'Looks like it's all fallen away.'

The compliment cheered her up although the sight of Sean was a concern. He seemed almost lifeless, head hanging, shoulders drooping. He'd no doubt been dumped by Jacqueline. She wasn't going to say anything about what she'd seen in the car park. If Jacqueline had chosen William over Sean she was crazy. Sean was far more honest and dependable.

'So, why the comfort food?'

'Got some bad news.'

He piled a few scoops of the velvety creamy brown dessert into a plain blue bowl and passed it to her, then set about filling his own bowl. Carrying spoons and bowls they went into his sitting room consisting of arty furniture and large photographs of him and Suzy on the walls. He dropped onto one of two fat round leather chairs. Ronnie joined Chloe and sat at the foot of hers.

Sean stared at his bowl, spoon hovering above the creamy mound. 'Rachel's moving to France taking Suzy with her.'

'Oh, Sean!' Chloe was lost for words.

'I know. It's shit, isn't it? The new man in her life has got a work promotion but it means moving there. They've already found a place to live.'

'What does Suzy think about it?'

'She doesn't want to leave her friends or school but she's not got much say in the matter. Rachel thinks it's a great idea and that it'll do Suzy good to be educated in France. There's another reason they're leaving: Rachel's expecting again. She wants the child to be brought up in France and be bilingual. Her boyfriend's keen too. He's half French and his parents live in the south west of France.'

'Rachel can't deny you access to Suzy. It's not right.'

'She's Suzy's mom. She can pretty much do what she wants. She said I can see Suzy whenever I want, but I can't exactly nip across to France every five minutes, can I?'

He prodded the melting ice in his bowl, and with chin down released a sound that came from deep within – a moan of distress. 'It's taken so long for me to gain her trust and become close to her, and now this. I don't know what to do – maybe I should uproot too and head after them to be closer to Suzy.'

'But your business… your life?'

'Suzy's my life,' he replied and placing the bowl on the floor, beckoned Ronnie over.

'I'd be careful about making a major decision like that. How would you support yourself? If you found no job or couldn't work for yourself, you could well find yourself sinking into depression or becoming a person Suzy wouldn't like as much. I know what unemployment and loneliness can do to someone. I've been that person; it can send you slowly mad. Suzy idolises you. She won't want you to give up on what makes you the person you are and change into one she doesn't like as much. Can you even speak French? Who would you mix with? It's taken a lot to join the singleton club here, how would you manage in a foreign country?'

'I don't know, Chloe. I don't want her to be shoe-horned into this new move without letting her have some sort of say. It's a massive change to her life – a different culture, language, schooling and a sibling on the way. It's a hell of a lot for a teenage girl to cope with. I should be around for her.'

'I know very little about children but I know teenagers are more resilient than you imagine. Ask her what she thinks about it all. She might have clear ideas.'

'You think she'd want to stay with me if I ask her?'

'I'm not suggesting you try to persuade her to stay with you because I think she should get to know her new baby brother or sister. She needs to feel included and if she's here with you, she won't. At least let her know you want her to be part of your life.' Looking at his despondent face her heart went out to him, but she knew that you didn't have to physically see or be with somebody to maintain a healthy relationship going. Thanks to the internet, she and Faith had kept in touch long after Faith had moved from Appletree and were as close today as when they lived next door to each other, if not more so.

'You can Skype her or use WhatsApp to stay in touch regularly. I do that with my friend and from what little I know of the French education system, pupils have extraordinary long holidays – about two months solid in summer, during which time she could come and stay with you if she wants. The main thing is to let her know you are here for her and whatever her decision, you'll support it. It'll be difficult enough for her to move away from her life and her friends and familiarity, without feeling she'd be losing you on top of that.' Chloe had drawn on her own experience of losing her family to give the advice. Whether it was right or not was another matter but it seemed to give Sean some comfort. He stroked one of Ronnie's silky ears.

'It's crappy, Chloe, that's what it is. You don't get much time with a child before they grow up and move away, and I've lost enough precious time with Suzy already. I'm frightened of losing the rest.'

'I know. But some time is better than no time.' She fought back the sudden sorrow: her time with William had been short lived and she had nothing positive, like a child, to show for the relationship.

'True. Jacqueline will be gutted too. She and Suzy really hit it off. I rang her earlier but she didn't pick up. I expect she's at one of her motorbike rallies or something. She's so dynamic. I feel really lucky she's interested in a guy like me.'

Chloe swallowed hard. She couldn't tell him what she'd seen. He'd had a bitter enough blow today already. 'And she's lucky too. You're an empathetic, understanding, caring man.'

'Don't forget book crazy,' he added, a tiny smile creeping across his features.

'And book crazy,' she repeated, lifting her spoon as a toast and licking off the ice cream.

Chapter Twenty-Six

Chloe had remained indoors since Sunday. Apart from scurrying out over the fields with Ronnie, she'd stayed in her office working on *Oh, Ambassador!* New ideas kept popping into her mind and as her fingers flew over the keys she was aware of how authentic her characters were. She envisaged Alex in his mansion, inviting friends to a raunchy Play-Doh themed party where multi-coloured sculptures of favourite sex positions had everyone rolling about with laughter. The ambassador and Alex had morphed into one sexy and thoroughly desirable figure.

Her phone thrilled, and when she pressed the button without checking who was calling she heard a hesitant, 'Chloe, it's Jacqueline.'

Chloe looked at the paragraph in which Laila was attempting to make the overly large appendage on her pink plasticine sculpture stay upright to a background of whoops, and pressed the save button.

'Hi.'

'Chloe, can I ask your advice?'

Why was everyone coming to her for advice? She hadn't much to offer and to suddenly be the person everyone entrusted with their secrets was a novel experience for Chloe. It could only be about Sean. Jacqueline knew she and Sean got along well. She braced herself for Jacqueline's revelation that she was now seeing William and said, 'Sure. Do you want to come over to my house?'

'I'd rather speak on the phone. I'm still in my PJs. I can't face the world at the moment.'

'Okay.'

'I know I can trust you with this secret. I went out with somebody else.' Jacqueline's heavy sigh was audible at Chloe's end. 'I don't know why I agreed to accompany him to a business event; probably because I was in a good mood and he is a nice guy. We'd shared a laugh together, and he had one of those irresistible puppy-dog looks on his face when he said it would mean a lot if I went with him. He's been really struggling since the break-up from his girlfriend. She was seeing a photographer behind his back and it hit him for six when she told him she wanted to end their relationship and for him to move out. I felt sorry for him. It's horrible going to those work things alone, so I went along as his escort and it was a really great night – good food, friendly company. There was live music and dancing and fireworks and I had too much to drink and to cut a long story short, at the end of the evening he kissed me and I stupidly responded. The whole thing had been so romantic that I'd got carried away, but as soon as it was over I knew it wasn't what I wanted. I explained I was seeing Sean and I didn't want to ruin that. He put an arm around me and said it was a shame but he understood and if it didn't work out with Sean, he'd be waiting. God, Chloe, he was so… masterful and sexy. He actually made me go weak at the knees.'

Jacqueline paused for breath and Chloe didn't dare interject. Jacqueline hadn't mentioned the anonymous man and Chloe wasn't going to encourage her to. She didn't want to explain her relationship with William – it would alter the dynamic of her relationship with Jacqueline, who trusted her enough with this information.

'I want to give Sean and me a chance. He feels comfortable. He's so considerate and I don't want sexy and wild in my life. I've had my mad time. Sean is a safer, surer bet at the moment, so after some soul-searching, I decided that although I'm attracted to this other man, I want to give Sean a chance and see what develops. I really like him and his daughter. They've just accepted me as part of their unit, and it feels like I've known him far longer than I actually have. The problem is this man is persuasive. He won't let it lie. He's sent suggestive text messages, and the other day he caught me unawares and kissed me again and I have to admit it was thrilling in a way. He said he wanted me to know he's serious about me and if he wants something, he usually gets it. Chloe, I actually am in a quandary. You know Sean, probably better than I do. I'm so confused. I'm like some hormonal teenager. I want to see Sean but this new man is exciting and a little bit dangerous. I can't help but be attracted to him. What would you do?'

The answer was simple: she'd run a mile from William. She had a niggling suspicion William was after Jacqueline purely to get at Sean who had supported Chloe so much. Was he capable of such vindictiveness? She imagined he was; yet that wasn't something she could run past Jacqueline, not without revealing she'd seen them together, and her own involvement with William.

'I was married to somebody who I thought was exciting and very sexy. He made me feel I was the only woman alive and pursued me when I rejected him.' She recollected the first time she'd met William…

Chloe has finished displaying all the copies of the latest E L James on the front table. She's read it and although she's marvelled at the writer's imagination, she's been thinking that she could write something similar, maybe something with more humour in it. She's always been good at English and has a powerful imagination. She's needed it to survive. She checks the display and takes a photograph of it for the bookshop's social media pages. That's her forte. She's the go-to social media guru. Not that many go to her. There are only a few employees and most of them are over forty so it's fallen to Chloe to drag the bookshop into the twenty-first century with an online presence.

She enjoys it. She spends most of her life online, much to Nanny Olive's dismay. However, Nanny understands why Chloe would rather stay at home night after night than go out with people her own age. Her social anxiety disorder holds her back from forming new relationships and she is happy enough at home. Nanny is thinking of getting a new dog. Paddy has been gone for a year and both of them miss him. Chloe's been browsing dog homes and breeders to find the perfect canine pet and thinks she's stumbled on the one. He's only a pup, one of a litter of mongrels, with large brown eyes and has the cheekiest face. He hasn't been given a name but she thinks Ronnie would suit him. She and Nanny are going to look at him tomorrow on her day off to decide if he'll be suitable.

The ancient doorbell rings, its melodic sound reaching the back office where she is now checking to see if an order has arrived. The bookshop is her sanctuary. Whilst she can't face crowds of people, the shop, with its ancient wooden staircase and tall bookshelves provides enough calm for her to deal with the customers who come through its doors. Her colleague has nipped out to buy some cough medicine, so it falls to Chloe to see who has entered, and serve them.

She scurries to the desk, head lowered, to wait for the customer to appear with a book. Chloe likes to see the books people choose. You can tell a lot by what a person reads. Only the day before, a woman in her early sixties had bought The Wonderful World of Pooh Bear. Chloe imagined she bought the book as a present maybe for a grandchild. As Chloe passed the purchase to the customer, the woman wiped away a small tear and whispered it was a gift for her ailing husband who'd requested she read the stories aloud to him as he could no longer see. 'He read it as a child and loves Winnie the Pooh's positivity,' she said, obviously keen to offload her sorrow.

'He is a very wise bear,' said Chloe, earning a smile.

Lost in thoughts of the woman reading to her blind husband, Chloe doesn't hear the customer until he coughs lightly and she starts.

'Oh, sorry,' she mumbles and looks up into amused grey eyes.

'You were miles away.'

The man is in his thirties with film star looks and dark thick hair cut in a fashionable style. He makes Chloe immediately think of Grey from the books she's been arranging. Her throat dries and her face feels like it's been blasted by a furnace.

'Have you read this? I wondered if it was any good.'

He lifts a copy of Stella Rimmington's first novel. She coughs to clear her throat.

'If you like fast-paced crime, you'll enjoy it.'

'I'll give it a go. And this please.' He passes her a self-help business book about succeeding and adds, 'I need all the help I can get in my business.' He waits, expecting her to pick up on the conversation and she does, albeit reluctantly as she rings through the purchases.

'What business are you in?'

'Stationery sales. You need a top-of-the-range pen, I can get you one — best pen you'll ever own. Or an exquisite new notebook, envelopes, paper, special notepads... I'm your man!' He reveals white teeth.

'I don't need a pen.'

'Of course you do. We all need pens. They're like pieces of jewellery but practical, and you can't beat the feel of one of our fabulous Cross pens. Here, try it out!' He produces a stylish silver pen and slides it across to her. It's metallic cool between her fingers and sits nicely balanced. She scribbles on a pad by the till and the tip glides smoothly across the paper leaving an inky black trail. She admires her tidy handwriting. She's always enjoyed writing and the pen feels like an extension of her own hand. 'See, I can tell you like it. You have lovely handwriting. Mine's such a scrawl I ought to have been a doctor.'

She offers a shy smile. 'It's very nice.'

'It's yours. A gift.'

'No, thank you. I can't.' She suddenly becomes flustered, waving her hands in anxiety.

'Yes, you can. I have literally thousands of them outside in the car. I'd like you to have it. It matches the silver light in your eyes.'

She lowers her eyes immediately.

'You can repay me by having dinner with me.'

She stammers she can't accept and he keeps his eyes on her. 'I don't give up easily. I'll return tomorrow and the day after that and each time I'll give you a pen until you say you will go out with me.'

William had been true to his word. He'd come into the bookshop every day for three weeks, each time with a new pen for her until finally she'd agreed to having dinner with him but only if they could be alone. She'd expected him to duck out of the date but to her surprise he'd taken her to an expensive Italian restaurant which was completely empty. It transpired he'd hired the whole restaurant to ensure there'd be no other customers, and only then did she explain why she couldn't go out with him again. He'd been fascinated rather than repulsed by her disorder and made it his mission to help her through it.

But William had given up on her in the end. Chloe no longer represented a challenge for him and he had turned his attention elsewhere. She feared Jacqueline would be yet another casualty of his need to seek out what seemed unattainable.

'Only you can decide what you want to do. I can offer advice but ultimately we all have to take the risks or make choices ourselves and live with the consequences. You and Sean might make a go of things. It's early days, but you'll never know what could have been if you bail at this stage. Sean's a caring man who likes you hugely and the effect you're having on him is evident to me. He's happier. Much happier. I'd give him the chance he deserves if I were you, and if this new man is as keen on you as you think he is, let him wait. If he's as crazy about you as he professes, he'll wait for you.'

Jacqueline had gone quiet at the other end of the phone. Chloe strained to hear a response. It came after a few seconds. 'I knew you'd be the person to ask. You have such a calm way of looking at everything whereas I'm hyper and it's got me into sticky situations in the past.'

'You make me sound way wiser than I am.'

'Don't put yourself down. You're definitely much more sensible than me. You always seem aloof, like you're weighing up everything and Sean thinks the sun shines out of your… oops!' She gave a brief giggle. 'I could do with calming down. I'm getting too old to behave like a child. It's just that I'm not used to such flattery or attention. I'm usually the one doing all the running after blokes and suddenly, not only do I have Sean keen to impress me, I get the full attention of a gorgeous guy. I joined the club to have a laugh and maybe meet somebody and bingo! I get two hot men chasing after me.'

'That's because you're huge fun and stunning.'

Jacqueline snorted. 'Stunning? Not me. You should see the photos of me a few years ago. I used to be a right old frump – thick glasses, mousy hair, crooked nose. That was until I had an epiphany and made the big decision to leave my husband. You see, I didn't have to be that woman. I had laser surgery, ditched my glasses, had my teeth whitened and got some rhinoplasty and a facial lift. After that, I had my hair cut and remodelled into the latest fashion, bought my motorbike and left on my epic journey where I reinvented myself, and you know what I discovered?'

'Go on.'

'You can be whoever you want to be if you face up to your fears. You can reinvent yourself, so to speak. I also discovered I am actually both of those women – the quiet, frumpy one and the fun-loving one. I enjoy a good time but I also crave some semblance of normality *and* a quiet life. I can only be crazy for so long before I need to relax back into my other identity.'

Chloe's mouth dropped open slightly. The Jacqueline she thought she knew had only been in existence a short time. Was it that easy to change? Jacqueline's voice was back, less confident again.

'What do you think I ought to do, Chloe?'

'You've answered your own question. If you need to be grounded and want normality, you should continue seeing Sean. He'll offer you the chance to be whichever one of those two women you feel like being on any given day.'

'I'm so glad I spoke to you. I was sure you'd understand. I didn't want the other women at the singleton club knowing about it. You won't say anything to Sean, will you?'

'I promise I won't.'

'You're looking after the shop later, aren't you?'

'That's right. He's picking up Suzy from school and then taking her to McDonald's in Lichfield.'

'Do you think he'd mind if I pitched up?'

'I think they'd both be very pleased to see you.'

'Then, I think I'll surprise them both. I've got some outrageous pink nail varnish for Suzy. She admired mine the last time we met, so I bought her a bottle the same colour.'

After thanking her, Jacqueline hung up. Chloe thought of Nanny Olive who would have applauded Jacqueline's words and commented on how far Chloe had come. She'd have got along well with Jacqueline, and Faith too, and been very happy that her granddaughter had made such good friends. She reread the paragraph she'd been writing. Laila was chuckling with her partner about the rude sculpture they'd created and he was flirting with her, their knees touching underneath the table. She was fully aware that the person sat next to Laila was a Canadian popstar who was based on Sean, and that she'd been gradually working their relationship into the script. She hoped Jacqueline took her advice. William had a record of letting down women he professed to care about.

Chapter Twenty-Seven

Saturday, 10th March

Eleanor shook her head. 'What a bloody shame! It won't be the same without Alex. Fairfax is going to stand in for him so we keep the numbers balanced.'

'Is he ill?' Chloe asked the question, knowing full well she was the reason Alex wasn't coming along to the event today. She hadn't seen him all week and it was only when she clambered into Fairfax's truck that she'd found out he'd texted Eleanor to say he wasn't coming.

'Said he has some important business to attend to.'

'Oh.' Chloe hoped Eleanor didn't spot the tell-tale reddening of her cheeks. She felt guilty for her part in it. Alex would probably never attend another event and it was all her fault. She hoped the journalists who attended the archery day had worked their magic and Eleanor would soon get lots of interest in the club. She didn't dare broach the subject in front of Fairfax in case he was still unaware how poor interest had been.

'Still, we can't expect everyone to make every event, can we? We try to put them on at convenient times – weekends, evenings and so on – but not everyone can be available. There are always other commitments.' Her breezy confident tone led Chloe to suspect she hadn't come clean to Fairfax who pulled a face and, adopting

316

the voice of the late Sir Bruce Forsyth, claimed anyone who didn't come along today would be missing, 'a good game… good game.'

Their destination was a clay pigeon shooting ground, and before long all the singletons were being kitted out with guns, earplugs and ear defenders.

Kaisha edged closer to Chloe. She'd not spent a great deal of time with Kaisha who was always a little vague and distant. They'd chatted briefly but neither was terribly talkative so it came as surprise when Kaisha asked her, 'Do you think I'm too geeky?'

'No.'

'Good. I've tried hard not to be. My mum always says I'm too serious and geeky and that's why men shy away from me. I've never had a boyfriend. She thinks it's unnatural. She'd had a few boyfriends at my age and was already married. That was before my dad left her. She wanted me to apply for that show, *Love Island*, and try to snare a guy that way, but I don't look like a supermodel and the thought of sharing a bed with a stranger and being filmed doing it doesn't appeal at all. What happens for example if you fart in the night or sleep with your mouth open and snore loudly and that gets broadcast, or if you talk in your sleep? Nightmare.' Her dark curls shook gently as her head moved side to side.

'I think they cut that sort of stuff out. It wouldn't do to embarrass the contestants,' said Chloe who had a penchant for the show and admired anyone willing to strut around in a micro bikini for several weeks on national television.

'I only watched one episode. It's not my thing.'

'What do you enjoy watching?'

'Not much. I'd rather play a game than watch television. I prefer the virtual world to the real one we're

destroying bit by bit. You know we're completely anni-
hilating our oceans? Not satisfied with cocking up the
surface of the planet with our polluting ways, we've
dumped our poisonous junk into the oceans and are
killing of all the inhabitants there, yet we still send rockets
into space and talk about building settlements on Mars!
It's bonkers.'

Chloe was beginning to understand why she had difficulty finding a boyfriend: she really was quite serious.

'Mum insisted I join this club. She says I need to get
out more and she thinks that sitting around in virtual
chatrooms is unhealthy for me.'

'You enjoying it so far?'

Kaisha shrugged. 'It's okay I s'pose.'

Chloe remembered skating around in almost silence
with Kaisha at the first event she'd attended until the girl
had apologised and said she wasn't too good at conversations and Chloe had replied similarly. They'd laughed
and in the last few minutes of the skate date she'd learned
Kaisha was still living at home with her mother. She
worked in technology but what she did was a mystery.

'What do you do for a job, Kaisha?'

'I'm chief designer for a leading car manufacturer. I
help develop the software that goes inside cars. It's all a bit
hush-hush. Can't let our competitors know what we're
up to. I spend most of my days behind a computer. We're
all a bit secretive there about what we're doing so it's not
exactly a hot spot for chatting with work colleagues.'

Chloe shut her mouth quickly. Kaisha was some sort of
genius! She ought to try and wangle something into her
book to that end.

'You ever been shooting before?'

The curls jiggled again. 'I'm not into hunting, shooting or fishing. I'm a conservationist. Although I shoot people virtually. I level up pretty quickly on shooter games. That's different though, isn't it?'

'You'll probably still be a good shot here and at least there are no animals to kill.'

Kaisha gave a grave nod. Chloe was called over for her equipment and left Kaisha staring into space. She was such a pretty girl, yet seemed lost in her own world and too blinkered to see that Tim had been looking hopefully in her direction.

–

Divided into two teams, Chloe was pleased to find Sean on her side and William on the other, although Jacqueline looked uncomfortable to find herself on William's team. Each team had to hit as many flying clay ducks thrown into the air and running rabbit clays hurled at ground level as possible.

Chloe found herself cheering at each splattered clay, especially when Kaisha hit every single one of hers, blowing them into tiny fragments. She didn't fare so well and only chipped one of her clays. William rolled his eyes dramatically as she returned from her position, and made a sad face similar to an unhappy clown's. She shrugged. She wasn't the worst there and she was angry he'd made a play for Jacqueline so soon after declaring he still had feelings for her. William was definitely a leopard who couldn't change.

William's team won and having taken it upon himself to be team leader he took the victory as his own and congratulated all his teammates with hearty handshakes and hugs, holding Jacqueline in an embrace longer than the others.

Back in the hut, Jacqueline drew Chloe to one side.

'He had the bare-faced cheek to try it on again. He offered me an emerald green pen and said it reminded him of my eyes! I told him where to poke it! I'm glad I made my choice. Sean was so pleased to see me at McDonald's the other day and we went bowling afterwards – all three of us. I have a feeling this is going somewhere. Thanks for letting me dump on you.'

Chloe couldn't help but offer a small smile. She ought to be thanking Jacqueline for making her feel wanted. 'I have everything crossed for you both.'

'We're going out again tomorrow on our chocolate-making date and I can't wait.'

'Jacqueline, can I have a quick word about your bike?' Fairfax said, appearing from behind her.

Chloe moved off to let them talk and, passing Tim who was chatting to Kaisha, went outside for some air. It was a crisp day and the range was surrounded by trees, dark twisted shapes with curled wooden arms and skeletal fingers stretched to the sky waiting for their foliage to appear and unfurl and cover them in green glory. She wandered across to a track leading into a wood and inhaled the musty scent as she kicked up dried leaves and moss. There was a hint of spring in the air bringing its message of hope. She loved the season when snowdrops, crocus and tiny daffodils would push through the damp grass announcing the beginning of a new cycle of life. She searched for any but saw nothing yet. It wouldn't be long. She'd plant spring bulbs in her garden. Ed had already suggested the perfect location – in full view of her kitchen window so she could look out onto them every morning.

'Hey!'

The voice made her start. William, hands thrust deep in his pockets, breathed in deeply. 'Love the smell of the woods. Reminds me of all our walks.'

A tidal wave of memories threatened to drown her — walks hand-in-hand through wooded glades, passionate kisses under a canopy of leaves, her heart overflowing with love for the man beside her. They'd taken many walks in areas frequented only by the odd dog-walker. She held her breath and waited for the images to evaporate.

'I can't do this, Chloe.' Getting no response, he continued. 'I can't live without you.'

A knot twisted in her stomach.

'Leaving you was the biggest mistake of my life. One I regret enormously. You *are* the only woman for me. I still love you, Chloe.'

How she wanted to believe those words. She shot a look at his face, full of sincerity. William understood her personality and knew every intimate detail. They'd shared memories and secrets, and loved each other with passion. He'd helped her when she had bad days due to her disorder, but did she really need him? Jacqueline's words flooded back to her: she didn't have to be the person who struggled to socialise. In truth, she'd already transformed from that person. Like Jacqueline, she'd reinvented herself. Yes, she still found some situations too difficult to handle but she'd changed nevertheless.

'Think about it. Maybe you could give us another chance. You know I don't give up easily. I'll bring you a pen and ask you again and again until you answer yes.' He held up an emerald green pen. The corners of his mouth turned upwards and his eyes widened, an earnest look that would once have melted her but this time she found herself unimpressed. He'd tried with Jacqueline and failed, and had decided to give poor old Chloe another shot. The knot inside her burst and inflamed her stomach with heat. How dare he think she'd be so weak as to fall back into his arms with gratitude, especially after chasing after Jacqueline. And who would come next? There'd always be somebody to attract his eye: another Lilly, another adventurous Jacqueline, any woman who was exciting and different would appeal to William.

She faced him and was rewarded with a wide triumphant smile. He cocked his head and raised arms to draw her to him. She moved closer to him, lifted her hand and smacked him hard across his face. 'How bloody dare you? Fuck off, William. Fuck off out of my life.'

She turned on her heel and marched back to the hut where Eleanor and Sean now standing outside had observed the entire scene.

'Don't ask,' said Chloe. 'He had it coming.'

'Want me to drive you home?' Sean asked.

'If you wouldn't mind. That alright with you, Eleanor? You probably have to wait until everyone leaves.'

Eleanor's brow furrowed. 'Sure. You are okay, aren't you?'

'Never been better.'

'I'll just tell Jacqueline I'm off.' Sean disappeared quickly. William had vanished from sight, presumably back to the car park or into the woods to nurture his bruised ego. Chloe couldn't have cared less. Eleanor shuffled a type of square dance, mouth opening and then closing. Chloe spared her discomfort.

'Don't worry. I'm not upset.'

'Good. Good.'

'Pissed off at him but not upset.'

The door opened and Sean emerged. 'Thanks again for organising it, Eleanor. It was huge fun.'

'It really was,' said Chloe.

Eleanor's head bounced up and down as if on a spring. 'Good. I'm so glad.'

–

'Want to talk about it?' Sean's calm voice drifted towards her as she strapped herself into his passenger seat. Somebody had hung an air freshener smiley face from the rearview mirror. It swung side to side, hypnotising her with its ridiculously happy grin. She felt like returning it.

'He came onto me. Gave me some bullshit about wanting me back but I didn't fall for it. I've heard he's been asking out other women.' She wasn't going to offer up Jacqueline's name. Jacqueline might not have told Sean about William.

'I heard too. I didn't want to say anything to you about it.'

Her forehead wrinkled. 'Who told you?'

'Tim. He spotted William with his arm around a striking blonde in the Bullring Shopping Centre last week. Tim waved at them but William didn't notice. Tim was complaining earlier. Said it was a bit of a cheek coming these events if he wasn't single. He was going to mention it to Eleanor. Don't know if he has.'

The woman might have been anyone but Chloe suspected it was Lilly. She pressed her lips tightly together to prevent comment. What was William's game? The answer evaded her. Maybe he simply enjoyed the thrill of the chase. Some men did. Whatever he was doing, she had little interest in it. She had a book to write, and she wasn't going to stop going to the singleton events even if it meant seeing him there.

'Suzy talked about Jacqueline all the way to school. I reckon she's taken to her.'

'You spoken to her about moving?'

'We had a heart-to-heart. You were right to get me to talk to her. Poor kid's been in a bit of a state about leaving everyone she knows, but she's up for it and still definitely wants to be with her mom and new brother or sister. She's pretty excited about the baby. Funny, you never know what children are thinking. I figured she'd be feeling left out with the arrival of this new addition but instead she's looking forward to meeting it and helping out with it and being a big sister.'

'What about you?'

'She doesn't want to desert her old dad. That was one of the main issues. She was worried I'd slip back into my old ways and be lonely and lost with her gone. I think that's one of the reasons she likes Jacqueline so much. She sees Jacqueline as somebody who'll look after me when she's in France. We're talking about her coming over for a month in the summer and a couple of weeks at Easter and a week at Christmas. Schools get a couple of weeks off the end of February too, so I could go over there and take her skiing. Not been skiing since I left Canada. I always fancied teaching her. There are some ace ski resorts over there. It'll be tough without her but I've worked out I'll be seeing her pretty much the same amount of time, more if I go over for my holidays or a long weekend. I might buy a little pied-à-terre near where they'll be living, so Suzy can stay with me when I'm there.'

'That'd be great.'

'It was Jacqueline's idea. She reminded me I don't have to be glued to Uttoxeter and that the world's a big place and property can be picked up fairly cheaply over there. Seemed a neat idea. I'll probably rent one of those bed and breakfast places in the area to start with and look around to see what I can afford. So it's not the end of the world I thought it might be.' He patted the steering wheel with the flat of his hands in a drumroll.

'You'll be able to be in the shop on Wednesday afternoons again,' said Chloe.

'You want to quit on me?'

She shook her head. 'No, but you won't need me.'

'I thought I might still take the afternoon off, put the time to good use. If things continue with Jacqueline, we'll have to leave the singleton club and start looking for activities of our own to enjoy. She wants to try out golf and says I'd make an ideal caddy for her.' The deep chuckle that followed the statement only served to confirm Chloe's suspicions that Jacqueline and Sean would make a good couple.

'I'm thinking of leaving the club.'

'William?'

'If you and Jacqueline go it won't be the same. Neats and Rob seem to be getting close too and I wouldn't be surprised if Tim and Kaisha started dating soon. That'll only leave Ed, Danielle and me.'

'And Alex.'

'He won't be coming back. We had a misunderstanding,' she said.

'I see.'

'He asked me out and I refused because it was to a ball and he took it the wrong way, thinking I was rejecting him.'

'You obviously didn't explain why you couldn't go to the ball.'

'I can't bear being judged. I've been wondering if William didn't initially get together with me because he saw my disorder as some sort of nut he could crack – a challenge. When he couldn't, he gave up on me. It makes sense when you consider he tried to schmooze me today. He's seen a glimmer of light. I've changed in the last few months and somehow become appealing to him once again.'

'You know him best, Chloe. However, I think you ought to tell Alex. He's an easy-going bloke. He's quite different from William.'

'I know and I would if he wasn't leaving after the development is finished, but with things as they are it doesn't seem worth the effort. It's a big deal to explain about it and even if he understood and asked me out again – what would be the point?'

Sean shrugged. They were about to pull into the driveway when a Land Rover joined them from the other direction, Alex at the wheel. He lifted a hand in greeting and let Sean turn first. 'Talk of the devil.'

Chloe couldn't reply. A stone sat heavy in her chest as she realised how much she'd missed sharing the event with Alex.

Sean dropped Chloe off by her door and having refused the offer of a drink because he had a meeting with his ex-wife to discuss Suzy and various other arrangements, he beetled off. Chloe clumped back home to an exuberant dog and after rubbing his stomach for a few minutes decided she'd open a bottle of wine. She deserved a glass. Today she'd made a stand and tomorrow – well, who knew what tomorrow would now bring?

Chapter Twenty-Eight

'It's cracking off at last!' Eleanor's lips were pulled back so widely Chloe feared her mouth would split open. She waved the local newspaper in her hand as explanation. Chloe twigged quickly.

'One of the journalists who was at the archery day has written about it.'

Eleanor bounced lightly from one foot to the other. 'And we're being featured in the *Staffordshire Life Magazine* next month *and* I've been invited to BBC Stoke Radio for an interview based on this article.'

Chloe scanned the positive piece of journalism. It appeared the free event had worked. They'd enjoyed the originality of the activity and the effusiveness of the hosts. She passed the paper back to Eleanor. 'I'm really pleased for you.'

Eleanor's eyes sparkled back. 'But there's even more. An ITV news programme want to come along to our next activity and broadcast it. This is going to swing it for us, Chloe. It's the luck we needed. Imagine being able to say "as featured on ITV"? We're going to get out of this hole we've been in and make the business succeed. Fairfax is over the moon. He's going to add all our media items to the website and... oh, thank you. Your idea was pure genius!' She threw her arms around her neighbour, dousing her in the lemony scent of her perfume.

'I can't tell you how grateful I am. Danielle has said she can't pay any more subscriptions and it's on the cards Sean and Jacqueline will leave. It's only a matter of time, and William...'

'I'm sorry if he doesn't come again on account of me.'

'Don't worry. If everything goes to plan, we really will have new members queueing up to join our club. Now, you will come on Saturday, won't you? It's going to be the best event yet and I need you there. I don't want it to be a flop with four or five people there and Fairfax can't stand in because he and I will be interviewed.' She tugged at the shawl wrapped around her shoulders. 'And, it was your idea so you deserve to be on camera.'

Chloe flinched at the thought. A camera filming her every reaction and then beaming it into everyone's sitting room was one step she couldn't make.

'I don't think so.'

'Don't be silly. I already checked with Alex and told him you were coming and he definitely is going to be there so there's no pulling out.' Chloe's eyes widened at the news. Was Alex going to give her a second chance? He'd said he'd only attended the events to spend time with her. Eleanor was still talking. 'Everyone's a little camera shy, Chloe, you'll get over it.'

'No, it's worse than that...' Chloe began. Eleanor's mobile played its familiar tune and she looked at the screen.

'Number withheld. Maybe it's another journalist,' she squeaked. She tapped the accept button. Her eyes grew wide and she mouthed 'New member', before scampering off towards the back door, mobile tucked under her chin as she put on her boots and raced off to her own house.

'What am I going to do, Ronnie? I can't face television. I'll make an idiot of myself.' Ronnie stared mournfully at the shut door. Eleanor hadn't had time to pat him goodbye.

—

Faith was out of the office and not answering her mobile so Chloe rang the only other person able to offer her advice.

'I can't do it, Sean. I've just actually thrown up at the thought.'

'Tell me why you can't do it.'

'Because I'll make a fool of myself.'

'How will you do that?'

'Any number of ways: I'll clam up if anyone asks me a question; I'll blush and forget what I'm supposed to be doing; I'll suddenly begin shaking like crazy, or be sick over a cameraman. I have literally no control over my body.'

'I'm going to come over tonight with Suzy and we're going to make an Instagram video of you. I'll give you a simple task to perform in front of the camera and you'll do it.'

'What?'

'Yes. And we're going to post whatever you do and say online and millions of people will have access to it.'

'Have you gone mad?'

'Some may disagree but no, I'm not mad. I've been looking at some of the new treatments that are available for people with your disorder and making the subjects face their fear is one of them. As far as I can tell, you've been doing that consciously or unconsciously. Each event you've attended has made you a little stronger. You may not be aware of it but you've been giving yourself therapy. You've been videoed before. We were all on the Haka video.'

'That was different. It wasn't national television.'

'Poppycock. Television, videos – it's all the same. We're going to give my way a go.'

She began to protest then stopped; Sean had a point. Since being forced into the club she had faced some huge challenges and passed them. She hadn't let herself down in any way. 'Ok-ay,' she said stretching the response to two syllables. 'We'll try it.'

'Good girl. I'll send you a link to the therapy I've been reading about. I wish my mom had tried it.'

–

The treatment seemed to be similar to one she'd seen mentioned in the forum, and bringing up the original thread, she asked about its effectiveness and was instantly bombarded with praise for it. It could be worth a go. If she could face a camera crew and appear on television she'd be able to conquer many of her fears.

It was true she'd already worn a giant Sumo suit and wrestled with the others, performed a Haka and got an unruly flock of ducks into a pen without much fuss and not frozen or been sick or had a wobbly. There was hope for her. She might just be able to face the prospect of having her round face shown on national television. Her stomach flipped at the thought and she bolted for the bathroom. As she knelt over the toilet pan she hoped Sean was right.

'Hi Chloe! Ooh, isn't your dog lovely?' Suzy's pale face beamed as she bent to stroke an over-excited Ronnie.

'Good to see you again. That's Ronnie. How come you're at your dad's today?'

'I've got extra time with him until we leave for France. We're going at the end of this term, sometime in April, so I'll start the summer term at my new school in France which will help me get settled. It means I get an extra night with Dad as well as the usual Wednesday, and every other Saturday night and Sunday.'

Sean put a hand on his daughter's shoulder. 'And Suzy's looking forward to helping you with your project.'

Suzy's face broke into a smile. 'I think it's hilarious.'

'Do you?' Chloe kept the smile on her face as she led them into the kitchen.

'What project?' she hissed.

Sean winked.

'Okay. Where do you want to do it? Here in the kitchen?'

'Yes,' Chloe replied.

'Dad said you wouldn't know what to twerk to. I've got some great music on Spotify.' She held out her phone.

'You have got a speaker, haven't you?' Sean asked.

Chloe pointed at the black Bose system dumbly. Suzy was too busy connecting her phone to the system to notice Chloe's discomfort. When she was ready, she put the mobile down on the kitchen top then taking up a position, hands on hips said, 'It's dead easy, look, I'll show you.'

Wiggling her hips and backside like a professional dancer she twerked up and down. When she stood up again, Sean applauded.

'Come on, Chloe. Copy me.'

Suzy's enthusiasm took the edge off her nerves and she had a go. It took some practice but eventually she could manage to twerk in time to the music. Sean joined them and soon they were all guffawing loudly.

Sean picked up his mobile and waved it in their direction. 'Okay, ladies, that's enough making fun of the old guy. Let's do this.' Suzy adjusted her top, pushed away a strand of hair and faced Chloe who remained glued to the spot.

'Imagine I'm not here,' said Sean.

'As if,' said Suzy with a snigger. 'You're six foot one. Nobody can miss you.'

'Pretend. Come on, Chloe, if this is no good I won't upload it.'

'Come on, Chloe. It's only like taking a selfie. I do this all the time. You pretend you're dancing in front of a mirror.'

Chloe tried hard to imagine herself in front of a mirror but that made matters worse so she imagined Laila instead. *You're braver than you think.* Suzy skipped across to her own phone, set up the track again and returned quickly. The music began and Suzy started her off. She shut her eyes briefly. Laila is twerking at a nightclub, her skin-tight jeans revealing her muscled thighs and well-rounded backside. All eyes are on her as she throws back her head and gives it her all. Chloe shook her booty for all she was worth, imagining the hot steamy nightclub and the man who only had eyes for Laila – a dark-haired man with shining brown eyes, who oozes masculinity: Alex.

–

'I don't look as frightful as I imagined.'

'I'd say you look hot,' said Sean.

'Dad!'

'Well, she does. Look at that pout, and I like the dramatic tossing of the hair like a supermodel. I think we have a winning video right here. This is going straight up on Instagram with lots of hashtags.'

'No, don't. People will see it.'

'Surely that's the point? Why else do it? You want people to watch you. *Especially* if you look hot,' said Suzy.

'Spot on, baby girl,' said Sean. He fist-bumped his daughter who giggled.

He fiddled with his phone and waited for a while then held the screen up. The video was being processed. It was too late. The clip would soon appear and everyone could watch Chloe twerking. It was strange but she didn't feel too ill. Suzy's bright face made the whole experience easier even though she didn't actually appear in the video. Sean had ensured his daughter was out of shot. 'Right, with the filming in the can I think we all deserve fish and chips. Chloe, do you fancy some? There's a van in the village. I'll get them from that.'

Chloe realised she was hungry. 'I'll get the plates ready.'

Suzy offered to help set the table and play with Ronnie.

'Okay. I'll leave you two starlets here and get the grub. Ronnie, would you like cod or a sausage?' Sean called on his way out.

–

Some of the comments were good and a few a little hurtful. One person had criticised Chloe's backside and another claimed she looked like she was trying out for a porn movie. Sean scoffed at those more critical comments.

'There are always people willing to put you down. It happens. You have to grow a thick skin. The main thing is most people thought it was good. Look at all the likes the video got. More importantly still, you did it. You performed a ridiculous dance online and you're still here in one piece, the same old Chloe. Nobody has thought badly of you. And everything, online, on television, or in newspapers gets forgotten so quickly, it doesn't matter anyway. I'm going to delete the video now. It's served its purpose.'

Chloe ended the phone call with thanks for his help. She had to admit she felt marginally better about the event that coming Saturday. Now she just had to hang onto that confidence.

Faith's Skype icon flashed on the screen. She couldn't wait to speak.

'I've just seen a video of somebody who looks remarkably like you, twerking in a kitchen. Please tell me it was you.'

'It was.'

'Oh-my-gosh! That is incredible and you weren't half bad. Who filmed it?'

'Sean, and his daughter, Suzy, taught me how to twerk.'

'A-ha, the marvellous Canadian is behind the video.'

'We're being filmed on Saturday and he's trying to prepare me for it.'

Faith's features rearranged themselves into something resembling Edvard Munch's painting, *The Scream*, with hands clasped either side of her face and mouth agape. 'Filmed?'

'ITV news.'

'Is that really Chloe Piper I'm talking to or has an alien taken over her body? First you slap that tosser of an ex-husband across the face and now you tell me you're going to appear on telly. Come out, Chloe! I know you're buried in there somewhere. Come out!'

Chloe beamed happily. 'Bonkers, isn't it?'

'Bonkers certainly describes it. Well, how's this all come about?'

Chloe explained.

'I agree with Sean. You're only going to an event like you usually do. There'll be a cameraman and a presenter but they'll be filming everyone. The camera won't be focusing on you so just enjoy whatever you're all up to as usual, as you always do.'

'How come you saw the video? It wasn't up for long.'

'I have Google alerts set for all my authors, with real and pen names, so if anything comes up I check it out. It was a surprise to see your name crop up. Usually it's book reviews for C J Knight not Chloe Piper that come through. You're doing so well, Chloe.'

Chloe fiddled with a pen and said pensively. 'You know, I think I am too.'

'Then go to the event, enjoy being with everyone and don't dwell on it any longer. How's that book going?'

'Good. I've only a few chapters left to write then the first draft will be complete.'

Faith applauded. 'See, writing mojo is restored and a brave new Chloe is facing her demons. I'm proud of you, hun. I'm looking forward to reading it.'

'How's Greg?'

'Pretty damn amazing. He booked a private pod on the London Eye and had it set up with canapés and champagne. We watched the sun setting and talked. We talked a lot.'

'It's getting serious then?'

Faith blushed. A rare occurrence. 'I think we can say it is.'

'Then you'll have to come up with him when you're both free. I'll make sure the honeymoon suite is available,' Chloe joked.

'We'll do that. He'll love it there. He keeps saying we need to escape the grimy city for a weekend and ingest some fresh air.'

'The offer is there for whenever you want to take it up.'

'It's a date.'

Faith had to get back to work and as soon as she disappeared from view, Chloe settled down to finish her novel. The last few chapters were always the ones she found the hardest. Not because they were difficult to write, but because she was coming to the end and would have to part from all the characters in her head. She'd grown fond of them all, especially the daring Laila. She had two endings for this character in mind – one predictably happy, the other traumatic and thought-provoking. Which one should she go for? If it were real life it would be the latter because, although there were moments of happiness and joy in life, things didn't always go as expected or hoped. She thought of Alex and what might have been and began typing.

Chapter Twenty-Nine

Saturday, 17th March

The rising sun brought to mind a fried egg yolk, its radiance breaking over the landscape like uncooked white. Chloe stood in a nightshirt and slippers by the window and tearing her gaze from the sky, marvelled at the faint green patches forming on ochre soil that would eventually turn into grassy fields.

She drained the glass of water, the third she'd drunk since she'd risen in the early hours, and rinsed it out. In spite of the video and her friends' assurances, she'd been violently sick in the night and afterwards spent an hour shaking under her bed covers, body slick with sweat as if suffering from flu, until she'd abandoned all hope of sleep and padded downstairs to her office where her computer had offered her comfort.

Daylight had lessened the anxiety. Either that or she was too tired with no energy left to feel ill at ease. She would have to tell Eleanor she couldn't attend the event today. Ronnie's wet nose on the back of her bare calf made her start. He gave a beseeching look.

'You want to go out? Come on then. A walk will do us both good.'

Dressed in a brand-new sports vest, zip-up jacket, leggings and trainers and with an eager dog by her side she paused outside. A distant hammering indicated work had started on the fifth and final barn – a reminder that soon she'd have to get used to new neighbours and say goodbye to one she'd grown used to in a short space of time. She set up the Fitbit she'd also purchased online. She'd been surprised to discover she'd lost almost two stone since her arrival at Meadow Farm. Not only had she bought fitness gear to go running with Ronnie, she'd bought other clothing online to wear to events, and now her wardrobe was looking quite up-to-date. Even if she didn't attend the singles group any more, she could wear them to work at the bookshop.

She began at a steady pace with Ronnie bounding like an excited kangaroo beside her, delighted at the new regime. She decided to stick to paths and roads rather than fields where she might turn an ankle, and ran lightly down the driveway, hoping that the exercise would help quell the nausea she was still experiencing. She'd have the run, follow it with a shower and then go and tell Eleanor she wasn't going to the event. She'd miss the people from the events but hopefully she'd still see Sean and Jacqueline regularly, and Ed of course. It wasn't the end of the world if she didn't go again, although a small voice inside told her she was letting herself down.

'Chloe!'

She kept running but looked around at the sound of her name. The momentary turn of the head caused her to stumble over Ronnie who'd nipped in front of her, and she clattered to the ground. Ronnie danced about her as she lay dazed, then ran off to greet the man racing towards them.

'Shit! I'm sorry. Are you alright?'

Alex's face swam in front of her.

'I think so.'

'It was completely my fault. I shouldn't have shouted out.'

His muscular hand was under her armpit lifting her and he gently placed the other under her other arm to ensure she was stable on her feet.

She checked herself over. There were no rips or any evident damage to either her new outfit or her body.

'I feel so bad about it. You sure you're okay?' His eyes were filled with concern.

'I seem to have made a habit of falling at your feet.' The comment eased the tension and his lips pulled into a small smile.

'If you're sure.'

'I'm sure.'

'I wanted to have a quick word with you. I saw Sean on Saturday and he told me what happened with William.' His lids lowered briefly and he fought for words. 'Look, I was wrong about you having feelings for William. I wanted to say sorry for jumping to conclusions and for behaving pettily. It wasn't very mature of me.'

'You weren't petty.'

'I stormed off. Same thing. It was childish. I wanted to clear the air before this afternoon. Eleanor's persuaded me to come to today's event.'

'I'm not going.'

'Why not?'

'Don't feel too good. Think I'm getting flu.'

One eyebrow lifted. 'Really? Why are you running then? You ought to be in bed or taking it easy.'

Her shoulders drooped. Tiredness flooded every muscle in her body and she had a longing to relieve herself of the burden she carried. Alex could judge her accordingly. He was off in a couple of months, so what did it matter if he knew? She explained her disorder in a few brief sentences.

'So that's why I couldn't take up your invite to the ball. I can't face crowds. It wasn't because I didn't want to go out with you.'

Alex nodded gravely. James the carpenter yelled Alex's name but he didn't acknowledge the man. Chloe searched his face for a sign of disapproval. There was bound to be one. Ronnie suddenly began scratching an itch and rolling on his back, wriggling side to side growling playfully. Alex laughed at his antics then spoke.

'Don't pull out of the event today.'

James shouted again and Alex yelled he was on his way before looking deep into Chloe's eyes. 'Please don't.'

She found herself reeling in confusion as he jogged towards the barn where he was needed. Had he comprehended after all? She checked her Fitbit was working and set off again at a gentle pace. Maybe she could manage this afternoon after all.

–

Eleanor was dressed in a yellow jumper with huge yellow earrings and blue trousers that matched her hair colour. Fairfax had opted for a jazzy waistcoat teamed with jeans and a white shirt. Both were like excited toddlers and by the time they'd arrived at the venue, Chloe was a bundle of nerves. Alex had kept quiet the whole journey, but given that Eleanor hadn't stopped talking, it would have been difficult for anyone to interject. They'd found out that the event was based on the games from a popular television show called *The Taskmaster*, but since neither Chloe nor Alex watched the programme they were none the wiser.

'They're here!' Eleanor's voice had risen several octaves.

Chloe spotted the van with 'ITV OUTSIDE BROADCASTING' written across it.

'It'll be fine,' said Alex his voice fur-soft. 'If you can face twerking on Instagram, this will be a walk in the park.'

'How did you know about that?'

'Sean told me. I didn't see the video but I wished I had.'

'What video?' demanded Eleanor.

'Nothing. It was taken down.'

Eleanor lost interest in the subject and, spotting a figure she recognised as a presenter, beetled off to introduce herself.

Alex dismounted and joined Chloe while Fairfax and Eleanor chatted animatedly to the camera woman and presenter. 'Doesn't appear to be onerous, does it? One camera, one presenter.'

Chloe clenched her jaw to prevent her teeth from chattering. It would be swiftly followed by a full body shake if she didn't do something to distract it.

'Chloe, about social anxiety disorder. I don't know much about it. I did a quick internet search and it can be quite debilitating, can't it? I had no idea.'

She somehow managed to coax her lips apart. 'I've been trying to beat it.'

'And done a bloody good job so far.' Alex's smile lit his eyes and made the edges of them crinkle. 'I was over-sensitive when you turned me down. It's taken me some time to get over somebody and I think I half-expected rejection, but when you said no it was like a body blow. It had taken a bit of courage to ask you.'

A cloud scudded across the sun scattering beams of light. Chloe got the impression he wanted to say more but two cars arrived simultaneously and Neats, Kaisha, Tim and Rob all poured out of one and Sean and Jacqueline out of the other.

'Is this my best side? Or this?' asked Rob loudly, turning his head left and then right. Neats punched him lightly on the arm – a friendly gesture that made him smile.

'Never been on telly before. It's pretty exciting. My mum is tuning in to watch. She's invited half the estate to our house to watch it. Hope I'm actually on film at some stage or she'll be bitterly disappointed,' said Tim who was wearing a Superman sweatshirt and jeans.

They gravitated towards Alex and Chloe and hung about like a group of teenagers, surreptitiously glancing at the camera woman as she hoisted the apparatus onto her slim shoulder and aimed it in the direction of the bald-headed man, Nick Hanson, well known for his half-hour news broadcasts that looked at interesting regional stories and one-off specials that usually hooked the nation.

Ed arrived, not on his bicycle as usual, but in William's BMW. William with hair slicked back and in a stylish shirt and dark chinos swept everyone with a wide smile. 'Looking good. Anyone would think we had a film crew here. Oh, we have! Is that *the* Nick Hanson? He's the presenter? Crikey, I feel like a celebrity already.'

His comment received some chortles and he greeted each member with a peck on the cheek or a handshake as if he were hosting the event. He stopped before greeting Alex and Chloe and asked, 'They started filming already?'

'Looks like he's doing an introduction,' Rob replied. They watched as the presenter, holding a fat, black-topped microphone, shook himself, stared directly at the camera lens and spoke as if addressing a small audience in front of him.

Eleanor and Fairfax approached the group and in hushed whispers directed them down a path away from the filming.

The path led through some trees and opened out onto a wide space. The group burst into laughter at the sight of giant yellow rubber ducks lined up against a wall.

'This is a Taskmaster event based on the hit show. If you've seen the show, you'll have a good idea what's expected of you. There are several rounds based on Taskmaster games. Obviously, you've seen the ducks we're using for one round but we have other games set up too, some inside the hut.' Fairfax pointed at the wooden structure. Eleanor took over from him smoothly.

'And Fairfax will be the taskmaster. You don't think he brought out his best waistcoat just for the cameras, did you?'

Fairfax stuck his thumbs in the pockets on the coat and spoke again. 'You'll be divided into two teams and for each round you will nominate somebody from your side to go against a contestant in the opposing team. At the end of all the games, we'll add up the scores and the overall winners will get these wonderful little rubber ducks as prizes.' Eleanor held up a colourful duck bearing a cheeky grin.

'What about the filming? Is the presenter going to talk to us?' asked Kaisha.

'Nick said to try and ignore the camera. Concentrate on the games and he'll just be observing. He'll only interview people at the end of the day. Danielle isn't here today but there are still ten members so we can have five a side. All your names are in here.' She held up a plastic tub.

343

'Ah, Nick, just in time, could you pull out the first name please? These will be team captains.'

The pleasant faced man approached with a smile and said hello to the group. He dipped his hand into the tub. 'William.'

'William, you can captain team A.'

'Neats.'

'Neats, you captain team B. Okay, William, here's your first teammate.'

Nick again fumbled for a piece of paper and read the name on it aloud. 'Kaisha.'

Chloe rubbed her hands against the legs of her trousers. She didn't want to be on William's team. She'd had enough of him. As if reading her mind, he cast a cold look in her direction. Her knees threatened to buckle.

'On team B we have Sean.'

Her heartbeat quickened. Alex nudged the back of her hand with his own. He was making sure she was okay without drawing attention to her anxiety. Gratitude flowed through her veins and she almost didn't hear her name. In spite of her prayers, she was on William's team. Thankfully, so were Alex and Jacqueline, as well as Tim.

The first game was inside the hut and Fairfax prepared them. 'This game requires somebody dexterous and who isn't colour-blind.'

'What does dexterous mean?' asked Tim.

'Nimble-minded,' William replied confidently.

'Or nimble-fingered,' said Chloe absent-mindedly, and immediately wished she hadn't spoken.

William sneered. 'We don't all eat dictionaries for breakfast. Why did Fairfax say choose someone who isn't colour-blind? Has anyone here watched the show?'

Tim nodded. 'I saw a couple of episodes. The taskmaster sets a fun challenge and the team who completes it successfully wins. It's really funny but I don't recall anything to do with colour.'

'Since you know what dexterous means, why don't you go first, Chloe?' said William.

'I don't think I can,' she stammered.

'Why not?' William gave a wide-eyed innocent stare.

'I might mess up.'

'That doesn't matter, does it? We've got other rounds. None of us know what the task is and the others might be better suited to different tasks. We don't want to play the wrong player.' His logic had resonated with the others who nodded with the exception of Alex who narrowed his eyes.

'I… the camera…' Chloe began to shake her head side to side.

Alex spoke up. 'I'll go first. It's a bit daunting with the filming taking place. It's understandable you're a bit nervous but once you get into the games, you'll forget the camera. They won't show all the footage they shoot anyway, so there's every chance you won't even be on it.'

William maintained his smile, even though his eyes had turned flinty. 'Alex will do this game then.'

With contestants chosen, they headed inside the hut where large bowls heaped with coloured Smarties were waiting for them. Beside each bowl was a pair of boxing gloves. Alex stood behind one bowl and Ed behind the other.

Fairfax tugged at his waistcoat. 'Wearing the boxing gloves, each contestant must separate all the blue sweets from the sweets in the bowl in front of them.'

Ed's lips twitched in amusement and as he tried to put on his gloves, he began to snigger and finally burst out laughing, proper belly laughs that set off the rest of his team. The woman with the camera appeared out of the shadows and seemed to zoom in on his face. Chloe shivered and moved closer to Jacqueline.

–

The game had been a terrific icebreaker, a close match with Ed losing by only one sweet, and most of the singletons had forgotten about the filming, keen to choose a player for the next round.

'We need somebody with a good eye and a steady hand. Chloe, I reckon that's you. You performed well at the archery game so, as captain of this team, I nominate Chloe.' William might have appeared earnest but she recognised the glitter in his eye. Alex couldn't step up again to take her place. She had to do it and William's face was the catalyst to make her rise to the challenge. He'd thrown glares in her direction at every opportunity during Alex's challenge, but instead of reducing her to a trembling mess as he might have done in the past, she had concentrated her attention on Alex as he dived about searching for blue sweets with his gloves and triumphantly managed to balance one between the heels of his hands and drop it into the smaller bowl. He'd winked in her direction as the sweet clattered lightly into the porcelain bowl and the singletons roared their approval. These were silly, fun-filled games, played by people she knew and liked. William could get screwed.

'Okay,' she replied.

She made her way to the rear of the hut as instructed to discover two basketball hoops attached to the building.

She was up against Rob. Fairfax coughed solemnly and then began his spiel.

'The object of this game to is shoot an egg through the hoop. Eleanor, you have the eggs?'

Eleanor came forward with two boxes of eggs.

'Oh dear, I neglected to say these are not hard-boiled eggs, so watch out for the splatter! If you break an egg, you must get a replacement. The winner is the person who succeeds with the least number of eggs.'

William decided to give Chloe a pep talk. 'You can do this, Chloe. Don't think about the filming, it's not important that the ITV crew are here broadcasting to national TV. Just concentrate on the hoop.'

His words had the desired effect. The confidence was immediately replaced by shaking, her hands trembling as she took the egg from Eleanor. She was mindful of the woman in dark clothing trained on her every movement. Tonight, viewers would watch Chloe's hands shake uncontrollably dropping egg after egg unable to throw one through the hoop, and they would laugh at her and comment on how utterly useless she was. As she cast about, her eyes alighted on William obviously expecting her to do a runner or break down. He knew her too well. Somebody shouted, 'You can crack this, Chloe!' and a titter rang out.

The shaking worsened and then Sean shouted, 'Substitution!'

'I don't think that's in the rules,' William replied.

'Fairfax?'

'Nothing to say you can't substitute,' he replied graciously.

'Rob, do you mind if I take over?'

Rob passed his egg to Sean. 'Go ahead. I didn't fancy getting yolk all over me.'

'Okay, Chloe. Fancy making scrambled eggs with me?' Sean said.

Tears of gratitude rose and she blinked them back. 'Let's do it.'

They waited for Fairfax to give them the go-ahead then began launching eggs towards the net.

'Come on, team, egg me on,' shouted Sean, rousing everyone into a shouting frenzy that alternated between both sides. 'I can't hear you. You need to egg-cite me!'

Chloe raced over to Eleanor and grabbed her fifth egg and launched it high, missing the hoop by a mere centimetre. The camerawoman was invisible again, lost somewhere behind the cheering onlookers who yelled encouragingly. The sixth egg hit its mark and went through the hoop. At about the same time, Sean succeeded too but Chloe had won.

Sean pulled her into a hug and whispered. 'Well done.'

'Thank you. Did you deliberately let me win?' With Sean's height he ought to have been able to shoot the egg through the hoop far more easily than she.

'I certainly did not. You were an egg-cellent player.'

William applauded politely but didn't congratulate her verbally. She no longer minded. She'd faced up to her biggest fear and won. She had friends – Sean and Alex and all the others who liked her exactly as she was. William had no power over her. She had control. She spared a thought for Nanny Olive who would have been so proud of her.

–

The games came to a glorious end with Sean's team winning. Having performed her challenge, Chloe had no longer bothered about the camera woman circling the contestants, and instead had enjoyed each round, yelling as loudly as the others when William and Neats, both wearing blindfolds, attempted to blow up the biggest balloon and on several occasions burst it.

Nick appeared as the team was collecting their rubber ducks from Eleanor. Up until that point, Chloe had forgotten he was there. 'Is it okay if I interview one or two of the singletons? We'll do it behind the hut where the light is better,' he asked.

'Anyone in particular?'

'I'll start with the team captains, if I might.'

William and Neats wondered outside with him, trailed by the camerawoman. The others chatted cheerfully about the day.

Chloe spoke to Alex. 'Thank you so much. I couldn't have done it without you... and Sean.'

'Seems like we both had your back but ultimately, *you* did it. That's the main thing. You conquered your fears.' He kept his voice low so others couldn't eavesdrop.

'I never imagined I'd be in this situation. It's surreal.'

'Chloe, would you go out with me if I suggested somewhere different to the ball, somewhere where there are no crowds?'

'Probably.'

He nodded earnestly. 'I have a friend who owns a canal boat moored towards Fradeley. Maybe we could take it out for a day... find a quiet pub. If it's a decent day we could even get a drink outside in the pub garden...'

'I'd enjoy that.'

'Great.'

'But you have to understand, I'm not an easy person to get along with. William thought he could magically cure me. Every time he wanted to go out, I wasn't able to.'

'That was then.'

'I have relapses.'

'That might be the case but at least you now know what you're capable of. Maybe you didn't when you lived with William. Nobody here has any idea about your condition – apart from Sean. Nobody could ever guess. You act like the rest of us – well, maybe slightly mad at times. We all have secrets and pasts and fears we hide. Some of us are just better than others at hiding it. I haven't wanted to be sociable since I split up from Jayne, my fiancée. I believed it was my fault she left me – that I was too boring, and afterwards I wanted nothing more than to hide from everyone. I didn't much care for the world or the individuals in it.'

'But you're so confident and always in control.'

'Say that to my sister and watch her laugh. She knows what a complete basket case I was before I went to Spain. She was the one to encourage me to come back here and work on the development. If it hadn't been for her, I'd still be working abroad.'

Chloe chewed on her lip. It was all very well him unburdening himself and showing interest in her, but he'd be returning to Spain, and where would that leave her? Where would that leave them if they got close? She opened her mouth to speak and was stopped by a scurrying towards her.

'Is it true?' Eleanor's eyes burned brightly. 'William just told the presenter you are *the* C J Knight, author of *Spank Me Harder, Vicar*. Nick almost swallowed his microphone. He wants to talk to you. This is mega.' She bounced up and down in front of them both. Behind her, Nick and the camera woman were approaching at speed. Further back, William leant against the wall of the hut, a smug smile spread across his face.

'The bastard,' Alex began, darkly.

'Chloe, I wondered if you'd like to comment on the revelation that you are actually the mysterious writer behind the best-seller, *Spank Me harder, Vicar*?' Nick's face was shining with enthusiasm at having discovered such an unexpected scoop.

William knew she'd crumble. The only question was why had he told Nick? If she'd meant anything to him, he wouldn't have said anything. Did part of him want her to revert to the frightened Chloe who put all her faith and trust in him? No, the answer was written on his face, it was nothing more than meanness. He'd not liked the fact she'd moved on without him, that she had friends and others she could place her trust in and he was being vindictive. It saddened her and angered her that he'd be so cruel. They'd shared an intimacy – an understanding and been partners – and now, he'd done this to watch her squirm and be dismayed and maybe to even horrify her new friends. She looked at him and he opened his palms to suggest he'd accidentally let it slip, but nothing he could do would convince her he was an innocent party in this.

She felt a solid presence by her side – Alex. His hand brushed against hers, sought her fingers and squeezed her hand gently. A flurry of thoughts scurried through her mind like clouds racing across a sky on a windy day: Faith's solid belief in her as both a friend and a good writer; Jacqueline's reminder that anyone can change if they want to and Sean starting out on a new relationship, leaving behind the old messed up Sean. Nanny Olive's voice was in her head, quietly urging her on. Chloe pictured Laila who would never have let anyone do this to her and spoke quietly to Nick.

'That's right. I am the infamous C J Knight. No doubt that comes as a surprise. I don't do interviews but if you'd like, I'll do a one-off with you for your show. I've just finished the follow-up to *Spank Me Harder, Vicar* and I'd be happy to tell you a little about it.'

Chapter Thirty

Faith's squeal of elation almost deafened Chloe. 'The interview will be broadcast on Monday evening on the *Nick Hanson Special*. That gives me enough time to send out press releases and so on. We must capitalise on this. Chloe, I am so proud of you, hun. Honestly, and I can't wait to see you again. You sure next weekend is okay?'

'It'll be great to see you and Greg.'

'Yeah, he's a diamond. You'll love him. Lord above, I can't believe you gave an interview, let alone to *the* Nick Hanson. He's a legend. I know he sticks mostly to regional stuff nowadays but in his time, he's interviewed the great and mighty.'

'He was charming and easy to talk to. He didn't probe into my personal life too much, kept it mostly about books, and asked what else I have planned. Now it's out it in the open, it doesn't seem such a big deal except almost all the singletons have asked me to sign their copies. Sean's going to order extra copies for his bookshop and I'll pre-sign them. I'd still rather not do full-on book signings yet.'

'You said *yet*.' There was no disguising the keen look on Faith's face, like a child anticipating the arrival of Father Christmas and a sackful of toys.

'Maybe. We'll have to see. I might do one at Sean's shop.'

'We'll talk about it all when I come up there.'

'I have to go now. I've got a visitor.'

Faith blew her a kiss. 'Can't tell you how happy I am for you and I know this next book will outsell the first.'

'You read it already? I only emailed it yesterday.'

'I wasn't going to wait, was I? It's got best-seller scrawled across it. The publishers will be very happy with it. You better start thinking up ideas for your next one.'

Faith waved merrily, her bracelets catching the light and sparkling like stars, and then disappeared from view. Chloe stared at the screen long after her friend had gone. There was no visitor but she was mentally exhausted and needed some time alone. This morning she'd been a frightened, sick individual who'd planned on skipping the singleton event and here she was at the end of the day, a brand-new person. She was still somebody who would balk at the idea of mixing with crowds of people and have bad moments, but she'd found a strategy that worked for her and a group of supportive friends to help her when she wobbled. The memory of everyone congratulating her and telling her how much they'd enjoyed the book filled her with warmth greater than the fleece blanket she snuggled under to watch television. These people had genuinely enjoyed her work and were eager to bring their copies for signing – even Rob, who admitted he'd read it three times. William had been nowhere to be seen. She still didn't know what had made him tell Nick and as far as she was concerned she didn't want to know.

After the Taskmaster event, she hadn't returned with her neighbours, instead, once everyone had departed, she'd conducted the interview in private inside the hut where Alex had tried to sort out blue sweets whilst wearing boxing gloves, and afterwards, Nick had ordered a taxi to drive her home.

She pushed her chair away from the desk and threw back her head in a lengthy yawn. Tiredness seeped into every fibre of her body. Probably a reaction to the stress of the day – a day that had changed her life.

The next morning, Chloe was eating a bacon sandwich when Alex tapped on her window. Ronnie hurled himself against the glass door tail wagging. She tempted him away with the remains of her breakfast and wiping crumbs from the corners of her mouth, opened the door.

'Horse trekking,' he said.

'Sorry?'

'We could go horse trekking after our canal boat experience. There's a riding school nearby that offers quiet horses for pedestrian-type rambles away from the madding crowds.'

'You better come in. I've been doing some thinking.'

'That sounds ominous. Morning, Ronnie. Is that ketchup on your chin?' Ronnie tore across for a tummy rub.

'Why are you asking me out?'

'Because I really like you and I think we'd enjoy each other's company,' he replied. His words were cagey and creases appeared on his forehead. 'I thought you felt the same way.'

'I do, but there doesn't seem much point in getting too heavily involved when you're leaving soon.'

'I am?'

'Your dad told Eleanor you were only remaining until the development was finished and then you'd be returning to Spain, and he told me you've had your house valued for sale.'

He ran a hand through his thick hair. 'Ah, yes...'

'So you see, I don't want to get involved with some-body who's going to be leaving so soon.'

'That was the original plan. When I first came back, I didn't want to be here. I only returned because Dad needed me to project manage and because Ashleigh asked me to help him out. Age is against him now. He's got health issues and this will be his last development. I'd planned to return to Spain as soon as it was finished, that's absolutely true, and I also figured I'd make some money by buying one of the houses on site which was guaranteed to rise in value once the development was complete, and then sell it on for a profit to fund a new life in Spain. But I don't want to do that now. The reason I had for leaving doesn't matter anymore. This place – this area – it harboured happy and bitter memories of Jayne. I haven't shared a lot with you, but she was more than a fiancée. She dumped me on the actual morning of our wedding. I was devastated and embarrassed and confused and a million other things I can't even begin to express. At the time, running away seemed the easiest option – out of sight and all that. Coming back was bloody hard for me, really hard, but I'm not the same man. What happened happened and I'm not hurting any more. I've exorcised those demons and I'm okay living here, in fact, I love living here.'

'But the valuation you've had done on the house? Surely that was for selling purposes?'

'No. It was Dad who organised it. He wanted to get an idea of what to ask for the houses we haven't yet sold.'

'And you have no plans to leave?'

He shook his head. 'None. In fact, I have a very good reason to stay here – I met you.'

'You know what you're getting into if you go out with me?'

'I think so. If you tell me all about it, I'll be wiser. It doesn't put me off, if that's what you're worried about.' He cocked his head to one side. 'So, do you fancy coming horse-trekking? We can find loads of other stuff to do if you don't want to try that.'

She looked at Ronnie, sitting peacefully at Alex's feet. 'Horse-trekking sounds perfect,' she said.

Epilogue

Saturday, 15th December

'Ronnie, drop that!'

'What's he snaffled now?' asked Alex, trying hard not to laugh at the dog with mushroom paste down his chin.

'One of Eleanor's *special* vol-au-vents that have a splash of brandy in the mixture. Evidently, I didn't put them out of the greedy mutt's reach.'

He kept his gaze on her, looking her up and down. 'You look dazzling. A very sexy author. A very sexy and successful author.'

She ran her hand down the front of the black dress, across her slightly swelling stomach and gave a warm smile. No one would be able to tell but she and Alex knew the reason she'd requested his assistance to zip up the dress. Tonight's gathering wasn't merely a celebration of their recent engagement, it was to make an announcement – a special announcement.

'Everything under control?' She gave Ronnie a crisp and sent him to his bed.

'Apart from Ronnie, yes. Don't fret. Everyone's coming. Faith rang to say she's about half an hour away and… there are our first guests now. Want to bet who it is?'

'Got to be Eleanor and Fairfax,' she replied.

'I'm guessing Sean and Jacqueline. They're always early to everything.'

'You're on. Loser does the washing up.'

'The dishwasher does the washing up. The loser gets to load it.' He strode away and hearing Eleanor's voice, she gave a wry smile. A whirlwind of orange pursued by an overjoyed dog rushed in.

'You look divine!' Eleanor gushed. The cobalt blue hair had been replaced by a vibrant orange, the same colour as the swirls on the red evening dress she wore. She drew Chloe into an embrace.

'I hear you've sold another three franchises,' said Chloe once she'd been released from the cloud of Chanel N° 5 perfume.

'I know. Who'd have imagined it? A year ago I was tearing my hair out, convinced I'd made a complete bollocks of everything and now I'm one of the premier singles event organisers in the UK... although I miss the ambiance of the early days. I get much less time with the singletons these days so I don't have that affinity I had with everyone when we started out. Oh yes, I meant to tell you: Fairfax ran into your ex-husband the other day. He's back with that Swedish model, Lilly. That's the fourth time they've split up and got back together. Apparently, she's been giving him a right runaround and those rumours about her with the Manchester United footballer were true. Anyway, Fairfax said William's looking much older – his hair's beginning to recede. Must be the stress of keeping up with his young girlfriend.' She threw back her head and barked a laugh. Fairfax arrived into the kitchen holding a bottle of vintage champagne.

'Come up for air, Eleanor. Sorry, Chloe, she's been absolutely dying to tell you the news for a while. This is for you. Congratulations on being the number one best-selling author for the second month in a row. Over three million copies sold! That's pretty damn good going. How many countries are your books out in now?'

'Twenty-two but we've more interest coming in.'

Ronnie began barking at the arrival of more guests. 'All the singletons coming?' asked Eleanor.

'Yes, except none of them can be called single now: Rob and Neats, Jacqueline and Sean, and Tim and Kaisha. Fairfax, would you open the wine please? Alex has taken his eye off his hosting duties.'

Fairfax lifted the corkscrew and waved it at her. 'You could have knocked me down with a feather when Ed announced he was moving in with Danielle. How he'll cope living with teenagers is a mystery.'

'I'm sure he'll manage. He's such a calming influence.'

'He'll need to be. Her bunch are wild. Still, it seems to have given him a new lease of life.'

As the kitchen gradually filled with the people who'd helped transform her life, Chloe caught Alex's eye. He winked at her and her veins fizzed with love. Ronnie suddenly sat up and with a whimper raced for the door.

'I'll get it,' said Chloe, following the dog. Faith was on the doorstep, standing next to a slim, handsome man who held a huge teddy bear in his arms. Faith flung her arms around her friend and after hugging her tightly, pulled away to dab at a tear.

'I'm not one to blub, but I've been an emotional wreck ever since you told me you were expecting. I've been nagging Greg to drive faster all the way here so we wouldn't be late.'

Greg kissed Chloe on both cheeks and passed her the bear with quiet congratulations. He helped Faith out of her coat and hung it on the peg by the door. Faith gave him a blissful look then asked Chloe. 'How are you getting on with the next book?'

Chloe gave a cheeky grin. 'Let's just say I'm really enjoying the research.'

Faith laughed loudly. 'I'm sure you have *plenty* of fodder for it. Okay, where's this party? You know, I never thought I'd ever say that to you. Fancy *you* holding a party. I take my hat off to you, hun. It's been quite a year, Chloe Piper.'

'Chloe Piper soon to be Mrs Chloe Collins.'

'I still favour C J Knight. It has a magical, lucrative ring to it,' said Faith, following Chloe into the kitchen.

Chloe caught the look in Alex's eye as she walked into the kitchen, the bear in her arms, and relished the bubbling of warmth that rose from deep inside. She caressed the bear's silky soft fur and sent silent thanks to the universe that she had everything she could wish for and her world was complete. She may struggle from time to time but the year had taught her one valuable lesson. If you wanted to change – really wanted to change – you could.

She glanced across at the Christmas tree decorated with baubles and the little reindeer called Piper she'd bought the year before when she'd visited the Christmas Farm with Eleanor and Fairfax. On the mantelpiece was a photograph of a fine-looking woman with olive-green eyes and a small smile on her face. Chloe's eyes alighted on the picture and she blew it a kiss and whispered. 'You were right Nanny Olive: I am stronger than I thought.'